BLOOD BURNING MOON

BLOOD BURNING MOON

Gilbert Cooper II

IGNITED THOUGHT
PRESS

2008

ISBN 978-0-557-36601-9

Cover Art by Brandon Reese

THE WARNING

Henry Wadsworth Longfellow

Beware! The Israelite of old, who tore
The lion in his path,—when, poor and blind,
He saw the blessed light of heaven no more,
Shorn of his noble strength and forced to grind
In prison, and at last led forth to be
A pander to Philistine revelry,—

Upon the pillars of the temple laid
His desperate hands, and in its overthrow
Destroyed himself, and with him those who made
A cruel mockery of his sightless woe;
The poor, blind Slave, the scoff and jest of all,
Expired, and thousands perished in the fall!

There is a poor, blind Samson in this land,
Shorn of his strength and bound in bonds of steel,
Who may, in some grim revel, raise his hand,
And shake the pillars of this Commonweal,
Till the vast Temple of our liberties.
A shapeless mass of wreck and rubbish lies.

"The evil that men do lives after them;
the good is oft' interred with their bones."
Shakespeare, *Julius Caesar*

TABLE OF CONTENTS

PROLOGUE

There was only silence to announce the ominous evil that words cannot convey on this morning after the moon shone red like blood, proclaiming that today was not to be as other days. No, today death was ebbing his way closer to the plantation, slowly inspecting shelters, cabins, and ragged soiled garments with icy fingers, quietly making his approach to the whipping tree where the slave Jakeel was to be scourged. The tree was no stranger to death, its gnarled branches barren, stretching out with pointed stems as if in a frozen lover's embrace. Her relationship to death was nothing short of intimate, never washing death's stains from her deeply creased bark. After many mornings such as this, the effect of this relationship began to alter the tree's appearance, so much so that even in death's absence his presence was still felt, seen, even smelled by those whose paths compromised the close perimeter of this tree.

No one stirred this morning, even though waking hours were long past. Everyone stood as if stillness would stay death's impending arrival. They knew better, but their instincts urged them to be still. They closed their eyes and squeezed their hands over their ears, hoping to shut out the screaming silence, but the hands cupped over their ears only served as conduits of silence, making it all the more horrible, as they heard death's lofty footsteps approach the tree, give it a creaky kiss, and lean into her branches.

Jared Tolby heard the silence, too, and sneered, revealing a row of jagged and blackened teeth, the result of years of neglect. Stretching out his arms and toes and inhaling deeply, he thought of Zelia—her supple lips, her brown skin, and her coarse hair. He had spent the previous night in her bed—a slave like Jakeel but one who provided Jared with the pleasure no white woman could. Jared recalled how he had sat up that morning in the bed he made for his passions, yanked the covers off Zelia, and kicked her in her shins. She woke up, giving him a puzzled look, her brown body recoiling from the blow. Zelia had been warned by other slaves not to give Jared willingly what he wanted from all beautiful slave women, but she thought that her generous spirit would lessen the cruelty that every slave on the plantation was to bear. She'd given Jared her body, transferring her labor from the fields to the feathered cushions of his bed, hoping vainly that by giving herself freely she would establish a life of leisure. However, no matter what comforts she had acquired, she remained his servant and under his control.

Jared rose from bed, revealing his excitement, glaring at Zelia but not speaking. Hastily putting on his clean trousers and white linen shirt, he grunted to Zelia, and she immediately rushed to strap on his boots and make his morning water for shaving, warming the oil over the dying embers still glowing under the hearth, helping him prepare for this morning's deadly activity. She hated every moment but made sure not to make eye contact with Jared; acts like that would acquaint her with the tree. And Jared did not even ponder the irony of sleeping with a member of that very same race he now took such care to denigrate and destroy.

Going down to the slave quarters the night before a hanging or a scourging had become Jared's habit. "Put 'em in the frame of mind to learn whose boss 'round heah," Jared would proclaim. As the master of his deceased father's cotton plantation, the largest in South Carolina, Jared yoked the service and toil of more than six hundred slaves. Every white man, including Jared, knew Jared was not the man his father was, but every slave knew his reputation for cruelty, vileness, and corruption, and they feared him. All slaves hated him, but the hate only seemed to fuel his wicked temperament.

All the other slaves were brought out of their quarters to witness the carnage, trembling as they looked at the tree. The Carolina earth around the tree's base had turned Georgia red from death's stains, and vegetation refused to encroach upon her base lest it fall prey to that same fate to which so many slaves had succumbed during the forty-eight year reign of the Tolby masters. Metal braces screwed into the tree's sides in four points held four linked chains, each ending in wrist and ankle cuffs. The contraption gave just enough room for someone to flinch under the bullwhip. Depending on the mood, a slave would be chained facing the tree or facing the whip; either way, if more than eight lashes were received from the cat-o-nine tails, the slave's survival would be nothing short of a miracle. The cat-o-nine, a whip made of leather, had nine metal-hooked prongs woven into it. The hooks dipped outward, giving the whip the appearance of a cat's outstretched claw. From the first lash it drew blood and chunks of flesh from the body of its victim.

The silence was broken by the curdling screams of Jakeel's children and wife as they watched him brought from "hell," the name given to the holding house where a slave was kept before his execution or punishment. "Youse gointer go to de hell if ya keep talkin' lak dat," slaves would advise those who had yet to feel the wrath of injustice. The sound of moaning and undecipherable incantations came from the wetted lips of grieving slaves who had witnessed this process all too often. They rocked back and forth like swaying cane stalks before an approaching storm, bowing before her unforgiving blasts. But no one seemed to notice the calm on Jakeel's face—no one but Ivan, the head taskmaster, and he found it unnerving. Even more, he felt it irritating. Not only was Jakeel calm, but there was the slightest hint of a grin upon his face. *"Crazy nigger don't realize what's about to happen to 'im,"* Ivan thought.

Jakeel surprised everyone when he was released by the men who escorted him from "hell." He simply approached the tree steadily, placing his back against the trunk and stretching his own arms and legs to be shackled to her cold, splintery embrace, his head cocked back, resting against her callous bosom. All paused; Jakeel's compliance caused Jared's mouth to fall open, but he quickly recovered. In fact, Jakeel's calm only increased Jared's hatred. Everyone but death was still for a pause, but death unsheathed his sickle and readied his stance in eagerness, for he also knew what only Jakeel recognized at this moment. He had been privy to Jakeel's prayer just hours before dawn and had been pleased with the response. Death cared not from where he got his orders just as long as he had work. Jared finally got enough gumption to speak.

"Naw, naw nigger. Ya think ya worthy to look me in the eye while I beat ya? Naw sir, turn 'im round and fix 'im to dat tree." Four men eagerly obeyed the master's wishes, turning Jakeel around and cuffing him face-to-face with the tree. His body was now tight against the bark, his nose bent against the unyielding trunk. "Youse' gointer have to wonder when my lash is gointer fall on ya back. Ain't no such thing as a courageous nigger! Youse just scared tuh death and want to know when the next blow gointer come! Naw, naw nigger. Taint gointer happen! Turn 'im round!" But Jakeel's actions had an effect on the slaves witnessing this scene that Jared's hoarse words could not undo—they brought to life a feeling within them that had long been dead, and Jared, Ivan, and the four men could see that feeling in their eyes. Knowing that if he did not act quickly his reputation would be damaged, Jared pointed toward Ivan and barked the order to begin the scourge.

The sun was just cresting the horizon, poking rays of piercing light into the watchers' eyes. Its radiance oozed an uncanny glow over the crops and fields, casting eerie shadows on the tree. Ivan walked toward the tree, deftly uncoiling the whip before taking a preparatory snap. All the while Jakeel remained still and calm, pressed against the tree, while Jared, the men, and the slaves looked on, a myriad of emotions filling each.

No one could see Jakeel's lips start to move rapidly as he closed his eyes and cradled his head into the tree's crease. He knew his faith would be tested; he knew his deliverance would come. "Damn boy think he gointer sho' some courage! Gimme dat whip, Ivan. Time for some severe teachin'!" Jared snatched the whip from Ivan and spat. He stood, poised with the whip, smirking, but his expression was not enough to disguise the fear and puzzlement that Jakeel's stalwartness invoked.

CRACK!   CRACK!   CRACK!   CRACK!

Jared struck four neat blows, causing blood and flesh to immediately fly from Jakeel's muscular back. Jakeel tensed stolidly and bit his lip. A small trickle of red ran down his chin, but he emitted no sound.

CRRAAACK!!

Pieces of skin and tissue spewed from Jakeel's back, putting a fresh coat of blood on the barren ground surrounding the tree. Jared curled the whip and hitched one hip to the right. Chuckling, he casually inspected the whip and fingered a tangle of flesh caught on the metal spur before flicking the piece to the ground. Rubbing his thumb and forefinger together, he smeared the blood into a thin paste. "You gointer scream, son, so might as well open ya damn mouf now and let it out." He continued to rub his thumb and forefinger together, eyeing the wet whip. Beads of perspiration slowly popped onto the tip of his nose as he let the rope uncoil and slither to the ground.

SSWWATTCCHH!!!

Marks, first white, then slowly running red, continued to appear on Jakeel's back. A spray of spit flew from his mouth in an exhale as his head snapped forward and ricocheted off the tree.

CRACK!

Jared swung the whip faster, this time creating an arch of blood that struck the earth with a plop. Jakeel's lips, though quivering, still moved rapidly. A stifled yelp escaped his mouth. His legs shook as his naked calf muscles balled up into formidable lumps, striated with blood-engorged veins. Tears rolled uncontrollably from the sides of his eyes as his fingers gripped the tree, digging for root. He gripped so intensely, trying to bear the pain of the lash, that he did not comprehend the pop of his thumbnail separating itself from the flesh. He was trying hard to maintain consciousness, dignity, and faith.

His master reached into his pocket and retrieved a small leather pouch. Ivan looked at Jared and slightly frowned. Ivan was an evil man and enjoyed a good scourging just as much as the next taskmaster, but what separated Ivan from most was that he knew where to draw the line. He also knew what was in the leather pouch and what purpose it served. He didn't think its use was necessary. He felt an eerie presence paw his spine and noticed the Braille-like goose bumps on his forearms, attempting to tell him now was the time to stop, that something was not right—a premonition.

"You sure you want to do that, sir?" Ivan spoke. He was careful to temper his tone as not to appear rude or discourteous to Jared, but Jared's only response was a grunt as he poured a handful of salt into his sweaty palms, quickly sidestepping the approaching Ivan to sling the pain-inducing granules into Jakeel's open wounds. With the salt still clinging to his palms, he rubbed those spots that he felt had not been filled enough with the stinging substance. As he did Jakeel jumped back as if avoiding the strike of a deadly snake, finally emitting an ear-piercing scream. His master smiled again and laughed, mounting the whip in his belt and licking his palms, tasting the fruit of his labor. Cackling, he pawed his hands together and hopped around like a child on Christmas morning who has just opened a box of his favorite treats.

"I tole ya he was gointer scream! Hot damn!"

Jakeel saw a flash of white, then red, then her—her face. His body alternated between stiff and soft involuntarily. He did not know when the next blow would come, but he knew his sacrifice was now accepted. He continued to mumble words between his howls of pain and pants for air. Usually a man was nearly dead after the eighth lash of the cat-o-nine, whereas regular whips often took hours to produce the same effect. Jared regained his position and let loose another powerful lash. It was the eighth strike. This time the whip did not return because a spur had become hooked deep within Jakeel's back. Jared swore and yanked on the whip, but it only dug deeper, so he tugged with both hands, creating an ominous sound as a slab of flesh tore from Jakeel's back before it loosely slapped back.

As Jakeel pressed into the tree, his whole body trembling, his mouth slowly yawned open and he—miraculously—issued a sound more triumphant than defeated, though his blood, skin, and flesh cluttered the stained earth. It was when Jared raised the whip for the last time that Jakeel's shout was answered.

What happened next had never before been recorded in history since the time the Hebrews commanded the sun to stand still. The sun, which had just begun to settle into morning, slowly began to recede. Those present began to panic, and murmurs filled the air as slaves tried to grasp this phenomenon. The moon, a lesser light, had drifted back to its place in the night's sky, only this time its reflection was red, deep red—a blood burning moon.

For the first time, Jakeel spoke. *"Akoko ominira ti de."* My time of liberation has come. No form of brutality or sordid discipline could keep the unshackled slaves from scurrying away to their quarters, a hushed commotion falling among them. They remembered stories about the gods and their wrath, and memory informed them of signs told of the gods' displeasure. This was one of them. Few realized what Jakeel had been mumbling just minutes before.

During his last trip to a southern plantation the previous spring, Jakeel had returned talking about the Jukas and their mysterious ways. Everybody but Bella laughed at him, calling him naïve. Every slave wanted to convert to Christianity as it seemed to make the masters more comfortable. Slaves like Bella were constantly verbally abused, for she refused to give up her spiritual practices, passed down to her from two generations of Obeah worshippers. She kept a cup full of acorns, parsley leaves, and various other spiritual ornaments, and an old round, wooden board that was smooth as polished marble in the center, covered with carvings of scorpions, beetles, and snakes around the perimeter. That spring, when Jakeel had come back talking his voodoo nonsense, Bella had asked him to come to her quarters. He obliged. At that meeting she brought out the board and chanted in a language he could not understand. She then cast the contents of her mysterious cup onto the board and stared at the results. After a spell of silence, she looked up from the board, tears slowly collecting in her eyes, and gracefully reached out and touched Jakeel's lips with her fingers. It was then she had whispered of this day.

Now four men were standing, staring, at Jared for instruction, but all he could muster was a nervous laugh.

"By the gods! The slave beast has managed to reverse nature!" Ivan exclaimed. Jakeel began coughing and cackling violently, constantly repeating, *"Akoko ominira ti de!"* louder and louder while yanking at his chains, blood drooling from his swollen lips, his legs now twitching rapidly like a swamp toad that had been stabbed with an arrow. One of the local farmers who had assisted in chaining Jakeel ran over to him, not quite knowing what to do.

At that moment the wind started abruptly, causing dust and debris to fly through the air. Tiny dust tornadoes danced and flirted with each other on the earthen floor. Quietly, Jakeel slipped one hand loose of the chain, revealing a white ring of exposed flesh that became filled with blood on the fresh wound.

"Get his hand back up dere! And get deese niggers under control! I want every one of dem dragged back out here to see dis. I'll be damned if I let myself be tricked by voodoo. It taint real! Taint nothin' real for these coons neither but dis here whip! Now get da situashion in orda!" Jared screamed wildly over the wind. Were it not for what they were witnessing, the four men would have laughed at Jared's slurred command and the disheveled mess that had once been his slicked-down hair. His eyes darted left-to-right like a frightened squirrel's.

Just then a bolt of lightening blazed the dark morning, projecting an eerie silhouette around the tree. A white hot jolt shot through Jakeel's body, causing smoke to rise from his back and sparks to fly from the tree as ghastly shadows danced an orgy on the barren ground. Tom Theedle, one of the four escorts, ran to put Jakeel's free arm back into the cuffs, but the smell of burnt flesh made him gag, filling his mouth so that he felt he was going to be sick. He had to get closer to Jakeel, who against all odds was still alive. Tom was shaking; the odor was sickening. His nostrils detected evidence that Jakeel's bowels had about just as much strength as his limp forearm, releasing their contents into the stained garments that barely covered his buttocks. Tom stumbled and tripped on an exposed root, falling into Jakeel's back, his face meshing into the bloody flesh. It was all he could take, and Tom growled up his breakfast, adding yellows and browns to the monotone red that colored the earthen canvas surrounding that part of the tree. He looked stupidly at Jared. "Sorry, Mr. Tolby."

"Just finish tha job, dammit!" Jared retorted. Tom just sat there, sweating profusely. He spat and burped, his abdomen heaving violently, jerking his body in a forward motion.

"I don't much feel too well, sir. I think I need to go." A stream of half-digested food once again fell from his mouth to the ground. When he reached out a hand to steady himself and inadvertently touched Jakeel's flesh, Tom's hair stood on end.

"You taint goin' nowheah, ya yella belly, 'til ya get that got-damn arm up in dat cuff!" Tom gulped as he hastily grabbed Jakeel's slippery arm to put it in the cuff. His dizziness and concentration were so intense he didn't hear the *whoop, whoop* of the approaching hatchet, but Jared saw it. So did Ivan, but neither had the benefit of time to warn Tom, who died instantly as the hatchet's bloody blade embedded itself firmly into the back of his head. As blood sprayed from his skull, Tom dropped to his knees, his body slumping forward, his head finally resting against Jakeel's squirming body. All stood silent, filled with shock.

The impossibility of what was happening stymied Ivan, but he now retrieved the horn from his belt to blow the warning. Somehow, he knew that the hesitation would cost dearly. Immediately, a hail of arrows flew by him, striking three of the four men who had brought Jakeel from "hell." The visiting plantation owners, who were always invited to entertain themselves with a slave's death, now were scurrying to avoid their own deaths, but many had been struck down.

Ivan was amazed at the accuracy of the arrows. Who were these people, these invaders? Ivan was a seasoned soldier who had spent many years as a pirate on the seas, robbing and looting merchant vessels before becoming head taskmaster at the Tolby plantation. Next to the carnage he himself inflicted, he thought that he'd seen the last of war. But now Ivan reached for his gun, a revolver that he kept holstered, loaded, and strapped on the side of his left thigh, flicked open the leather clasp, withdrew his weapon, and fired three shots in the direction of the arrows. He always kept six bullets neatly stacked in loops in his belt, not for use but merely out of habit. He called it his lucky six—Ivan needed luck today.

As Ivan watched, helpless, another flurry of arrows whizzed past his ear toward Jared, and one wedged itself into Jared's left shoulder blade, sending him to the ground. Another arrow pierced the horn, tearing it away from Ivan's mouth, while yet another ripped into his now-empty hand like a blurred insect. Ivan could only stare at the arrow before falling to the ground and rolling toward the tree, both arms shielding his head. He desperately wanted shelter, but he instead used all his might to remove the arrow.

Jared was hugging the earth, screaming, too scared to remove the arrow from his own shoulder. At last one of his men crawled toward him, grasped the arrow, and yanked it painfully from his flesh, taking tissue and drawing blood, much as Jared had done to Jakeel just moments before.

Ivan was trying to reload but could not quite steady his fingers to put the bullets in their place. The sky was so completely dark now that he felt certain a tornado would soon tear a deadly path across the plantation. The bullets slopped from his fingers and rolled onto the ground. Looking up, he saw Tom slumped against Jakeel, whose mouth was open, a stream of spit running from it; he looked dead or unconscious. Water and blood formed a mangled nest in Tom's hair. Ivan moved away in disgust, swearing that if he made it out of this day alive, he would carry two revolvers instead of one. He tried to reach for another bullet, but the pain from his hand wound had grown too intense, so he stayed flat on the ground, his hand stretching out slowly toward the bullet, careful not to arouse the attention of his predators. He was almost there. He thought of his daughter, newly born, and the woman who bore his child, a woman to whom he always had difficulty expressing what she always wanted to hear, "I love you." He didn't realize until this moment the reality of that emotion, and he prayed to God that he would have the chance to speak those precious words face-to-face.

As his fingers crept closer and closer, inching their way across the floor of the earth, Ivan began to feel confident of his survival. He was a sure shot if the target caught his eye. But just when his fingers caught the bullet, they were crushed flat by a large, calloused foot. He looked up to see a fist rushing toward his face; turning his head to avoid the oncoming blow, he glimpsed the red moon, then darkness.

Chapter 1

Bella

Isiki rose from the body he'd just rendered unconscious and kicked the bullets away from the gun. He despised the white man's weapons, although he did acknowledge their power. They lacked the honor, creativity, and spirit that the Indians had taught him while he learned the art of hunting after his escape from the plantation. How could the spirits work through these artifacts of man that bore them no respect, no symbols of godly recognition? He went to Jakeel and swiftly unlocked the cuffs, but Jakeel collapsed, Tom's body forming a crude cushion for his fall. Isiki moved cautiously and steadily; knowing his men, he had to be quick if there were to be no casualties for the Maroon tribe. The farmers had managed to arm themselves, and bullets and arrows rained across the plantation between the shouts and howls of the wounded. Isiki was undaunted by the apparent danger. Blessed with the shield of lightening, he believed it would shelter him from harm. He would take care of the immediate task—the rescue—and then the latter task—death to the Tolby plantation.

Isiki had yet to lose a man from one of these attacks, and that fact had earned him the reputation of a fearless leader. His mission was simple: kill and retrieve. Stooping his muscular frame, he hoisted Jakeel onto his shoulders and moved quickly to the densely populated forest on the plantation's perimeter where ten of his men were hiding. They removed bits of shrubbery to reveal a makeshift cot on which Isiki gently laid Jakeel before ordering the men away.

The plantation stretched more than five hundred acres, including the big house where the master and his family lived with their indentured servants. Surrounding the main house were three large storehouses where corn, wheat, hay, and tobacco were kept. Another housed the cattle and horses, and the last barn stored the carriages. These buildings were placed strategically side-by-side in front of the big house so the master could easily step on his front porch and view any activity surrounding the barn. A long dirt road connected the plantation to the main road, winding up past the barns on the right, facing the house on the left, tapered by green grass and the rosewood trees that looked splendid during the spring. Past the house and barns stood the whipping tree, and past the tree were the slave quarters, miserable shacks that barely resembled anything more than piles of rotten wood. Were it not for their orderly positioning, one would even question if they had been assembled by design. There were thirty of these abominations, and past them lay the fields of labor and then a thick forest. It was in this forest that Isiki was waiting for and thinking of his revenge.

Isiki crept from the forest through the cornfield with lightening speed, not even stirring a cornstalk. He had learned well from the Phoenix chief who trained him in the art of silence. Remaining calm, he released his breath in controlled increments, his body now slick with sweat and Jakeel's blood. Once he reached the perimeter of the cornfield, he surveyed the slave quarters for any sign of the enemy. The slaves were all inside, despite Jared's orders, and five white indentured servants were milling about, shouting for the slaves to come out but not quite sure what to do next. Some of the farmers had fled home, whereas others lay dead on the ground, arrows protruding from their bodies. Isiki wiped the sweat from his eyes and then slowly removed another hatchet from his thick ankle bracelet. He waited breathlessly for the men to turn away from the field. One of them pointed in the direction of the woods behind the cornfield and then turned back toward the tree and the big house. Isiki crept twenty paces to the side of the closest quarter, hatchet in hand. He invoked the patawa spirit of the silent owl and calmed his bloodthirsty excitement. Although he intended to spill as much blood as possible, his ultimate target was Jared. This insolent man had caused much pain, much suffering. How could the gods allow Jared to live? No, it was Isiki's duty to balance the forces of evil and exact blood from Jared's miserable gut. The time was right.

The farmers had become distracted by a woman who was chanting in a foreign tongue. She had run out of her slave quarters naked and shiny with sweat, her breasts slapping off her skin, her buttocks rumbling against the weight of her flesh. She was beautiful yet powerful and heavy, her muscular arms bearing insignias of what Isiki thought to be tribal distinction. They held a familiar pattern. Telling her to shut up, the men were trying to pull her inside the cabin, but she fended them off with strong blows. Isiki was distracted by the deftness of her punches, as if she had received formal training from the chiefs. He noticed the men were getting aroused as they began laughing and pawing at her breasts, feigning as if their lustful touches were only an accident. Isiki knew of their true intent—they wished to take her inside her own cabin and rape her. He'd seen it all too often. He was amazed at how quickly men could forget danger in the face of lust. Death was all around them, yet here they were persisting with their base behaviors. This realization only intensified Isiki's purpose.

A bow would have been too cumbersome for such an intimate mission as bows were indifferent and impersonal killers. He'd brought with him only those weapons that required close range attacks so that he could feel the warm blood of his enemy, so he could bathe in it. Kneeling down, he surveyed the scene while neatly drawing out two cleverly concealed blades. One he clenched in his teeth, the other in his right fist. One of the men had managed to grab the woman about the waist and was grinding his pelvis on her from behind. Isiki swiftly stood and, away from his shelter, slung the hatchet with deft accuracy, hitting the man squarely between the shoulder blades, severing the spinal cord, causing instant paralysis. The man didn't even scream but just fell backward, dead. Isiki rushed the three remaining men. The woman spun and punched the nearest offender to her right, sending him staggering backward two steps where he met Isiki's oncoming blade, a gust of wind escaping from his punctured lung. Isiki slashed left while opening his mouth to drop his second blade into his hand, then slashed right, cutting the throat of one farmer and the chin of the other. By this time the naked woman had kicked over the dead body of the first man killed, removed the hatchet, and tossed it to Isiki, who promptly plunged it into the chest of the man whose chin he had sliced. He eyed the woman and, with his head, motioned for her to go back to her cabin.

The riot was silent now; the surviving farmers had returned home to guard their plantations from possible attack. The woman turned and squared herself confidently before Isiki.

"Isiki." The woman spoke, and Isiki stood startled. Had he met this woman before? He didn't believe so.

"You speak my name with familiarity, but I know you not. Speak your name, woman."

"I am Bella. The winds foretold of your coming. The man you seek is up by the big house. But I must warn you—your time of revenge is yet to come. Go and tend to your men and the wounded one you rescued from this place; I will take care of the bodies and calm the slaves. Understand that your presence here is felt, along with that of the one who sent you." Isiki stood motionless for a moment, staring Bella in the eyes, faintly detecting recognition. He was impressed by this woman's absolute calmness as she fought off her oppressors and now stood before him, fearless in her nakedness.

"You speak well for a slave. Perhaps we may talk at another time on how you accomplished the white man's tongue. As for the time and place of my vengeance, I alone am the determiner of that. Go inside and find shelter, woman, lest death catch you unaware." With that Isiki turned to go find Jared.

"I have a shelter that you have yet to understand, warrior. I shall do as you ask, but you shall regret not heeding my advice." Bella immediately turned and went inside her shack, closing the shabby door behind her.

The sun was again cresting the horizon for its usual morning rise, and the dew that had regained its cloak about the earth was melting away. Isiki ran up the path that stretched fifty yards between the slave quarters and the big house, concentrating on making his body as light as possible until he felt he was almost floating on the air above the ground. His feet made tiny patters against the earth, barely leaving a print of his path. He had one blade left. Running to the last slave house, he hid behind the still-remaining shadows. It was then that Isiki saw Jared, who was cussing and kicking his boots against unforgiving dirt. Isiki counted his breaths and measured them against his heartbeat. It would take about ten beats if he crept up on Jared unsuspectingly, five if he rushed him. But just as Isiki was about to make his decision, events unfolded that would alter his plans.

CHAPTER 2
THE PRICE OF COMPROMISE

Zelia never left her quarters for the morning exercises of death. She knew all too well the plot, the climax, and the sordid resolution before they even took place, and she didn't care to witness it any more than any other slave. Jared would allow her to stay in bed after she laid out his clothes and did any other task he asked of her before he went out to work. It was one of the habits he had that caused Zelia to believe he actually cared for her. She'd heard the noise and commotion and felt true fear when she saw the sun go back down. The events of that day had caused her to remember talking to Bella one night about matters she really didn't understand but knew to be true. That day had been an eerie one, and Zelia shuddered as she realized how it related to this very moment. She had not believed that what Bella had said could possibly be true, but after what Zelia witnessed this morning, anything was possible.

She remembered it being a Sunday evening when she met with Bella. Slaves usually were allowed to relax on Sunday in observance of the Sabbath. Jared would have two slaves bring out a large, heavy wooden keg of beer, which he kept safely stocked within the basement of the big house. The slaves were encouraged to wet their palates with the mind-altering brew as a suggested act of kindness. What Jared intended, and what most slaveholders engineered, was a coy plan of keeping the slaves content and always two steps away from realizing the truly fetid nature of their lives. Zelia, having a little too much ale, sauntered toward Bella's quarters. Strangely, she felt no fear that day, and she did not care about what the others might say or think of her. She was going to find out just what all this voodoo mumbo jumbo was about that everybody, including the white people, feared so greatly.

Zelia didn't bother to knock on the door but rudely pushed it open. She found Bella wrapped loosely in a blanket and enshrouded in a fume of sweet-smelling smoke that was wafting from glowing embers piled in the middle of the hut's dirt floor. It had been the middle of July, far too hot to be wearing a blanket.

"What cha doing, ole witch?" Zelia slurred. Bella did not respond; her eyes were closed, and she was rocking gently back and forth as she whispered a mantra repeatedly. "You look slike you had too murch ta drank!" Zelia said as she laughed and loudly burped before collapsing on the floor, knocking over a basket woven out of cherry tree branches, spilling its contents of bones, nuts, and several feathers neatly tied together out on the floor. Bella opened her eyes and glared but kept her pace in rocking gently.

"So, the whore of the new world has darkened my humble home this blessed Sunday evening. To what do I owe the pleasure of entertaining Jared's bed dog?" The juxtaposition of Bella's calming smile and contemptuous words was cutting, and Zelia felt their bite even through the fog of her drunkenness.

"I taint no bed whore, voodoo witch! I do whats I haftta in orda ta survive! Ya just mad cause I fount luv, and taint nobody likes yourn fat back no way!" Bella smiled at this, revealing a row of pearly white teeth. She used to get extremely angry when people made fun of her build; she was pretty, but her labor made her solid and muscular. She was often teased and hurt by Zelia types, women who possessed all that men wanted and who used their sex to upgrade their lives from unbearable to tolerable. It bothered her until she discovered the secret rites of her family, her roots.

"And so, the beautiful whore sells her soul and her body to the white man and now thinks she is someone to be regarded, to be respected, for her accomplishments. Zelia, you're a fool living on a short chain. The yolk of bondage is no less heavy on you than on me, and sadly you have lost what little dignity you had by freely giving yourself to your bastard master. Yes, I may have to sleep on a dirt floor, but what little hours I have of sleep I sleep well knowing that I'm not the master's willing whore. I sleep well knowing that any white man who dares approach me to take my body better come prepared to yield up his life as I am prepared to yield up mine in order to maintain my pride. But you didn't stagger all the way down here to discover just how worthless a piece of dung you are now, did you? Tell me child, what is it that I can do for you? And speak quickly, for my patience grows thin with your presence."

Still smiling, Bella reached behind her and produced a sharp blade that she placed gently beside her lap. Zelia's mouth opened with astonishment as

Bella's words struck through her drunken state, and soberness began to settle in. She didn't know whether to be angry or appreciative of Bella's words. Bella's smile seemed unrealistically genuine, but her words pierced like mortal wounds.

Zelia opened her mouth and stuttered out a slurred question. "Wha, why dey call you da devil's chile?"

"Because I am, ain't I? Don't I belong to masta' Jared suh?" Bella's slave dialect struck Zelia as amusing but convincing. Zelia always considered Bella to have "talked white."

"Ya know what I intend," she said like a child, "Why dey call you da voodoo woman? Why people so scairt of youse? Just cause ya always talkin' to yaself don't make ya no devil's chile. Just means ya crazy, dat's all." Zelia really wanted to know. She never did understand why so many people kept their distance from Bella. Ivan, the taskmaster who used intimidation to maintain order, and crazy Ben, a man who appeared to be extremely tough, also avoided Bella. It was true—Bella didn't sell her body or her principles for comfort or respect, but Bella managed to get more than the other slaves, including Zelia. Maybe she did not gain the comforts Zelia did, but all men seemed to give Bella a certain degree of respect that Zelia wanted and thought she would receive once she let a man touch her "sweets." Bella sighed, a languorous smile now leaving her lips as she looked directly into Zelia's eyes.

"Child, there is so much your little ignorant mind has yet to understand and I fear will never comprehend. You have forsaken the wondrous faith that once made us a great people. You have given yourself, your precious self, to the very ones who hate you and oppress you and will not hesitate to kill you if you so much as look at them wrong. The source of pleasure is continuous and can always be found in many different places, persons, or things. Once your body wears out, you will be replaced like a piece of furniture in Master Jared's house."

"But why dey—?"

"Here is why, Zelia. Look at these coals here, these burning embers, red like blood. Look carefully, Zelia, closely." By now the sun had set, and the evening stars had popped out into the night's sky. The hot embers cast a red glow on Zelia's face, creating a shadow that made Zelia finally start to rethink her purpose for coming here. "Are you paying attention, whore?"

"Stop calling me tha—" The embers at which Zelia had been looking began to stir and jiggle together, making a little clanking noise. Zelia let out a little "wooo" that was between a gasp and a shout. "What's happening?" The embers were now rattling loudly against each other when one suddenly, smoothly, rose out of the ember pile and floated twenty inches above the rest, slowly rotating and spinning like a lantern on a string. In her amazement, Zelia reached out to grab it, but Bella gave her a warning glance that made her think better of it. Smoke was now wafting heavily through the room, a slight haze covering the floating ember. Zelia at first thought her eyes were playing tricks on her, but the smoke started to congeal into shapes that seemed familiar to her. She saw the shape of a face, which would dissipate and then reappear again. After about the third attempt, Zelia recognized the face—it was the face of her mother, and her mother was crying.

Zelia's mother had died not long after being purchased by Jared. It remained a mystery because her mother had been strong and healthy. But after a day with the mistress of the house, Zelia's mother had taken home her supper and gotten violently ill. She left the world in agony. Life had been nice for Zelia when her mother was there with her on the plantation. Her mother had always told her to keep herself from the hands of her master, to never give in to his desires. But Zelia had instead built a life for herself by betraying her mother's advice, and her choice filled her with guilt.

"Make it go away," she said. A sudden gush of wind flitted past the shabby doorway and disfigured the face of her mother, then obliterated it completely. Only the glowing ember remained, its form slowly turning, undulating red color and heat amid little black dots swimming in its midst. "What is that Bella? How did you do dat? Dat ain't natural, ya know. What does it all mean? And how did you get my mother in dat smoke?" Just then the ember's red color began to fade as it slowly settled down onto the earth beside the little fire pit from where it came, two more embers rising from the pile and settling in the earth adjacent to the first. The first ember shook briefly and then split its top open, causing tiny little red coals to leap out and glow ferociously. Then the split ember rolled across the earth toward the two other glowing embers, spitting out a fiery blue haze that caused the ember to ignite and burn out of existence. The third ember quickly rolled back into the fire pit. Bella sat still for quite a moment, shaking her head sadly as she looked at Zelia.

"It's called the blood burning moon, child. The ember spinning around in the air like that tells me how long before the event happens—three months. The ember could have been black, ashen white, or red. Every so often, the moon reflects the color of the sun. Some call it the devil's eye; I call it the blood burning moon. It's a bad omen, and somebody or something will die under its watchful glimpse. You, my dear, will be extinguished, burnt out, just as you saw the ember die out just now. One who controls an army will come here. I don't know if it's providence because you sold your body to another man willingly. I know your mother's tears indicate the sign of your total loss from this miserable planet. Perhaps, if you return to your mother's upbringing, you can stay the oncoming evil that has been revealed here today."

Zelia sat absolutely still for a moment. This woman just said she was going to die in three months unless she gave up doing the only thing that brought her the small privileges that made her life bearable. Who did she think she was? Predicting life or death was up to God, and this ugly hag was far from him. Zelia, now fully sobered and shaken from what her mind relentlessly fought to establish as trickery but her eyes reported to be reality, leaped up from her squatted position and backed on wobbly legs toward the door. Her nostrils flared to suck in much-needed breath. "Ya voodoo witch! I sees why dey call ya da devil's chile. Ya don't know nothin' 'bout me! Ya just as ignorant as da rest of dem dum womens here on dis plantation. Youse just stay out of my way, and I'll stay out of yourn. Whats I do in my bed is my business. I rather be da whore of Jared den da whore of Satan!"

"Be it as you say, Zelia; your days are numbered. Now get out, before I put your eyes out with one of these burning coals!" With that Zelia staggered out of the shack and ran clumsily back to the one Jared had set up especially for her. Flinging herself on her comfortable bed, she wept in the pillow. Her mother! She had just seen her mother crying, looking at her as if she were a total disgrace, and it broke her heart because she knew if her mother were still around, there would be no way she would allow Zelia to carry on as she did. Bella was right—she had sold herself to Jared. It was one thing to be sold against one's will, but she had given herself willingly, and that was the real disgrace. When Jared's buddies came over from Calvert's big house plantation, Jared would call for her to come up to his own home after his wife and children were asleep, and the men would all go to the cellar where Jared would have her remove her clothes for his guests. They would pay him handsomely for the favor and would comment on how he was one hell of a master. She never saw one cent of that money, and, if she had, would that have made it better?

Zelia was jolted from her thoughts by a quiet rustle outside her window. With all that had transpired this morning, she couldn't help but remember Bella's words. She had not stopped her ways, and now death had come right to Master Jared's plantation. "I don't wanna die," she mumbled. But what if she could change the prophecy, stop the destruction? She must warn Jared. Then she would save herself and show him her true dedication; that would have to have meaning.

Zelia came out of her quarters to run toward the big tree where she suspected she'd find Jared. As she left her door she saw out of the corner of her eye a form twitch in the bushes beside her shack. Glancing back, she saw a man on his way out. She looked at him, puzzled, but kept moving toward Jared. All the other slaves were inside their cabins, and the plantation now felt quiet and desolate. The white women and children who had come to watch the whipping had been rushed into the big house where they were trained to protect themselves in case unexpected events took place, as it had today. From the windows were barely visible the eyes that were waiting to see what would occur next. All that could be heard was the sound of a wailing baby in a shanty adjacent to Zelia's.

By this time, Jared had regained his composure and was furious. His body ached, but what hurt more was his ego. How the hell did all this just happen? Words could not explain, but he was determined to have his vengeance. In all the commotion, five of his slaves had been shot—three men, one woman, and a boy of twelve—a total value of two thousand one hundred dollars.The boy had been a bargain at the last auction he attended, only one hundred dollars, but the three adults had bid high at five hundred dollars a piece. He had had the money to spend, but damn if he was going to just throw it away. The fact that he wouldn't be able to replace his investment angered him intensely. He walked over to the woman's crumpled body and kicked her, praying for a sign of life. But when her head rolled over it exposed a gaping bullet hole in her right check. He could see her gums and a partially destroyed row of shattered teeth, and he watched as blood and saliva ran freely from the new orifice in her face. Although the men could do more work, the women were especially precious because of their reproductive capabilities. Hell, this woman could have potentially given him eight new slaves after breeding with that queer Crazy Ben.

Jared searched for a weapon, but every weapon he picked up was empty. He tried prying one from the hands of one of his indentured servants, but the grip on it was like iron, and Jared was tired and still shocked from seeing his day literally turned backward. In his house he kept a rifle above the fireplace where it rested on two elk antlers his father had hung after a hunting expedition. He decided to go there and secure the plantation and make sure any of these bad-blooded niggers who dared step on his property would receive its fury.

Jared was so focused on his thoughts of revenge that he didn't notice the shadow emerging from the slave quarters, taking the form of a man who was methodically making great strides toward him. Finally, he sensed he should look up, and he was startled to see Zelia running in his direction.

Perspiration immediately leaped from his pores, and his heart felt as if it were going to explode out of his chest. He was so unprepared! So scared! So unlike his father, who always was on guard. Zelia looked as if she'd seen a ghost, and with this morning's events, he wouldn't even be surprised if she had. She rushed up to him, out of breath. "Jared, ya must get to da big house! Something evil is coming for ya!"

"Evil been here already, honey. And I'm a still standing. Look at ya. You shivering like you got a fevah. Go on back to your house; I'll be there shortly after I take care of some business."

"No, Jared, ya life is in danger. Bella tole me about dis day three months ago. Ya must get ta—" Her sentence was abruptly cut off by a harsh smack to her mouth. It stung intensely, but the hurt to her heart was earth-shattering.

"You knew about this and didn't tell me? Since when you be talkin' to Bella? Zelia, if I find out you was involved in this, so help me I'll see to it that you spend a week in the "hell" and then an hour on that tree!"

Zelia and Jared argued back and forth, Zelia denying and Jared implying. This gave Isiki the opportunity for which he had been waiting. He would have his revenge. Slowly he crept out from the shadows and began trotting, hunched over like a feline, ready to pounce on his prey. He held his blade in tightly gripped hands in front of him. Five more heart beats to go and then he would use his blade to pull out Jared's heart. Isiki was mentally envisioning himself invisible, but Zelia's beauty broke his concentration, and Jared looked up and caught him in a haughty glare. Quickly, Jared grabbed Zelia by the hair and whipped her in front of his body for protection against Isiki's oncoming rage. Reaching into his back pocket he extracted a blade of his own in a leather sheath, popped open the sheath with his thumb and forefinger, and with one quick motion of his wrist flung the sheath onto the ground.

Through all this Isiki's approach slowed but never stopped as he encroached closer to Jared. He was tossing his blade from his left hand to right without even glancing down to see if he were on target. Zelia screamed, "Go away ya devil! Can't ya see ya ain't hurtin' nobody but us slaves!" She was breathing hard; Bella's words kept pounding in her ears. She could not believe the predicament she was in. Why wasn't this crazy nigger stopping? Didn't he care that Jared had a blade to her throat? A lazy drop of blood slowly began to trickle down her pretty neck.

"All right, nigga, one more step closer and the wench dies!" Jared said through clenched teeth. Isiki didn't even pause; his steps were sure and always forward. "I mean it! Your cause is ovah! Drop your blade and I might let you live, but I swear if you take another step closer I will rip my blade through this nigga woman's neck!" Jared strained to hide his fear. Why the hell wasn't this man stopping? Didn't he care about his own people? Jared's hands were shaking violently, producing striations on Zelia's neck where the blade was digging deeper and deeper into her flesh.

"Jared! Ya hurting me! Stt—stop—it!" Zelia's feet were kicking out instinctively against Jared's firm grip as she was beginning to have difficulty breathing.

"Kill her, Jared. She won't be the first, but she will be your last. I don't have remorse or feelings for those who sell themselves to you for personal gain." Isiki had finally stopped, crouched, his knife pointing straight at Jared and Zelia. He was calm, his breathing controlled and intense. "Where the hell is everybody?" Jared thought. He couldn't believe this morning! Neither could Zelia. Jared's breathing became more and more staggered. Zelia looked into Isiki's eyes and knew that her time had come; she wanted to relax, but her body's desire for life kept her fighting. Through this clamor, no one noticed that Ivan had regained consciousness and was preparing to end this madness.

CHAPTER 3

ZELIA'S DEMISE

Ivan regained his equilibrium and was putting the bullets that had earlier cascaded to the ground into the chambers of his weapon. He went over to one indentured servant who died gripping a gun and tried to pry it from his atrophied hands. When that proved impossible, Ivan quickly removed a blade from his belt and sliced through the man's fingers as he would have a banana and removed the weapon. He cocked both pistols and ran about fifty yards around to the slave quarters, deliberately moving with quickness and purpose to the place where Isiki had been hiding only moments before. He was going to savor the moment when he blew this bastard's head off. *"Should have kilt me, lad."*

As Ivan was preparing to shoot, Jared looked up and caught sight of him. This was all he needed to calm his nerves and he relaxed, a mistake Jared would regret. Isiki, trained to observe his opponent's every move, facial expression, even the rise and fall of his chest to indicate strained breathing patterns, took immediate notice of Jared's distraction; it was the moment for which he had been waiting. In an instant, he sprang to life and ran at Jared and Zelia full stride. His senses told him to invoke the buffalo's mantle, a shield all warriors had the benefit of using for a limited time in battle, just as the chief elder had taught him many years ago.

Out of pure reflex, Jared pulled the knife forcefully across Zelia's throat before he even had a chance to realize his actions, pushing her toward Isiki in self-defense. She spun, a torrent of blood spraying from her open throat, which she tried desperately to clasp closed with one hand. For a moment that seemed an eternity, Jared saw the look of betrayal and hurt in her eyes, and his belly froze. But Isiki sidestepped her and rushed into Jared before he had a chance to raise his arms in defense.

Just then a loud boom startled them both as Ivan placed a carefully aimed shot right at Isiki's head. He was off slightly, so the bullet plunged only into Isiki's shoulder blade. As he was falling, Isiki stuck out his hand, gliding his blade haphazardly across Jared's left nipple and down the left side of his stomach, creating a vertical jagged cut, opening a large wound. Isiki thudded to the ground and rolled over three times, as he'd been trained to do to avoid any oncoming attacks, while mentally viewing the battlefield in order to estimate the location of the shot and his enemy, Jared. He didn't have much time, so he relied strongly on reflex and training. The third roll put him only slightly out of Jared's reach, but it was enough room to accomplish his task. He stopped to check his shoulder and found half the bullet sticking out, but there was no blood. Thank the gods! The mantle had worked. He would have his revenge yet. Tightly, he grasped the part of the bullet that projected from his flesh and tugged, dislodging the metal. He experienced only minute discomfort as he readied himself for his next attack.

Jared's brow furled, indicating his pain. His shirt was torn, revealing a deep white flesh wound dotted with tiny beads of blood. His fury now raging, he turned and kicked at Isiki, who looked up just in time to catch Jared's boot with his right arm and quickly pivot his waist, swinging his right leg hard and directly at Jared's. Jared's left leg slipped out from under him, and he fell hard to the ground. Isiki rolled over once and was on top of Jared. He placed his hands firmly around Jared's neck, digging both thumbs deeply into Jared's voice box. Isiki's calloused hands were like two cold bricks. Jared felt his throat giving way just like Zelia's; tiny black dots danced within his vision as he glared up at Isiki, hatred pouring out of his eyes along with his tears. But another shot hit Isiki in the back, throwing him off of Jared. This time a warm wetness dampened Isiki's back as the bullet penetrated flesh and now bone. The mantle was wearing off. He didn't know if he could take another shot. The naked woman's words echoed in his ears; perhaps his vengeance would be delayed. Ivan fired again, the bullet tearing past Isiki's ear, whistling, causing bark to split from a tree twenty yards ahead. Feeling vulnerable, Isiki rolled on his back and tilted his head forward to see the man he knocked out running toward him.

"Another time, Jared," he said. He caught a quick glance of the beautiful mulatto girl lying in a widening pool of blood and thought her death had been a waste. He turned to stare into Jared's frightened eyes, which looked like two little shiny beads gyrating in a dark hole. Sweat rolled down Isiki's nose, poised at its tip, and flung itself down towards Jared's face, landing directly on Jared's quivering lip.

"Get off me you damn—" Jared's words were cut off with a forceful grip from Isiki's hands. He knew no breath was entering or leaving his body until Isiki allowed it or Ivan finally made a good shot. For a moment, Isiki thought about cracking the little coward's neck, but then he rolled over again and hastily crawled on all fours as Ivan fired shots in his direction. Isiki leapt forward, and his powerful legs caught his momentum and aided him running into the woods.

Ivan approached Jared, whose wound was now bleeding profusely, unabated. "Master Jared, let me get you to the house!" Jared just stayed where he fell, his head rolling impotently on the ground, picking up dirt and leaves like a dust mop. Ivan fought back feelings of reproach. He absolutely hated any blatant sign of weakness in a man. Jared clawed the earth in bitter frustration and embarrassment. Never before had his world been turned so completely upside down. He would look like a weakling in front of all the other slave owners in the region, once again defaming the name of his father, who had been well respected. He'd lost money, his slave concubine, and almost his life! And the predator who was responsible got away with barely a scratch. It looked as if Jared would never break the pattern of failure that seemed to litter his life. Ivan hovered over him, like his father would have done, glaring, reaching out his hand to help up the poor baby. Jared squeezed his eyes shut to close out that image of contempt he had so long endured. Hot tears slowly streaked down his face, and he swung his hand to his mouth and bit it hard to stifle a whimper. *"Get a hold of yourself, dammit!"* He hollered in his mind. *"You cry and Ivan will never respect you again in your miserable life! Now get hold and get up!!"*

"Master Jared."

"Back up, damn you!" Jared sat up with his own strength. The world spun, and then he settled his vision right on Zelia's corpse. "Who tha hell taught ya to shoot? Ya should have nailed that bastard on the first shot!" Jared's attempt at command was feeble, his voice coming out as a high-pitched yelp, which was not his intention.

"I did."

"What?"

"I nailed him with the first shot. The bullet struck his shoulder and threw his body to the ground. We're not dealing with ordinary slaves here, Master Jared." Ivan was speaking calmly while looking down at the man he now saw as weak. He admittedly acknowledged the morning's events as extraordinary, but this was not the time to cry about it. They needed to think about the next plan of action in order to prevent the hazard from happening again.

"I don't believe it! If you'd of shot 'im in da shoulder with that pistol ya got there, it would have blown it clear off! Every nigga is ordinary, Ivan! Hell, deys less than ordinary."

"Master Jared, we should really get to the big house. We don't know if there are more in the woods planning another attack." Ivan didn't even regard Jared's words of disbelief. He had heard rumors of strange events concerning certain African tribes when he was aboard the sea vessels. Sailors talked of what they'd witnessed on the middle passage while importing slaves to the islands and to America, disturbing tales that made a man's skin crawl, but he had only believed it to be sailor lore, until today.

Ivan turned from Jared and walked toward the big house, but Jared just sat on his haunches like a child who'd been knocked down, with dust streaks on his face cleared by the tears that escaped his eyes. He was looking at Zelia now. She had been so sweet, so warm, and so very good in bed, much better than his old bore of a wife could ever hope to be. Now, she was gone forever. He would have to find a replacement for her. And that meant more money, but worse than that, he knew that no amount of money, however large a sum, would ever reclaim the memories and feelings he had for her. She had honestly loved him, even when he was wicked toward her and used her for his sexual pleasure and that of his friends. And she had made him lots of money.

Jared's wife was pretty, a northern girl, the daughter of an aristocrat who was friends with his father. Their parents had basically arranged the marriage, and he was much obliged because she was better than any girl he could get without force. She agreed because Jared's father was a well-respected landowner, but after the honeymoon, their marriage had rapidly fallen into a state of boredom and misery. She was always comparing Jared to his father and making unrealistic demands on him as to how he should run the plantation. She wanted to control his life—the money, the management of slaves, the way he dressed. Hell, she even wanted to control the way he ate. She said she would not feel sorry at his funeral if he died because he did not listen to her about changing his improper diet. Sex came less and less often until it virtually ceased, and when it happened it had to be her way, and if it wasn't, her wrath was kindled. And now Zelia, the woman who had provided him physical and mental escape, lay dead, killed by his own hand. Guilt began to flood his heart as he remembered their past.

He had purchased Zelia and her mother, two very beautiful women, at the peak of his marital misery. He saw the two of them on the auction block, striped to their waists, revealing beautiful mulatto skin. Jared was told they were mother and daughter, and he marveled at the way the mother had maintained such a womanly shape. Her breasts stood brazen against the noon's glare, her shoulders firm, her stance straight. He moved in for a closer inspection. Her daughter was absolutely the most beautiful creature he had ever seen, a purer vision of what he imagined her mother used to be. Were she white, he would have left his wife without hesitation and proudly displayed her as his love for life.

Other men also had huddled in a crude line waiting to inspect the two. When Jared's turn came, he went to the mother first, savoring every moment. He grabbed the mother's pretty face and commanded her to open her mouth so he could inspect her teeth, but the look of hate in her eyes squelched his lust. She opened her mouth slowly without ever taking her eyes off him. She had hateful yet fearful eyes. Jared inspected the teeth with little interest—it was just a formality—he was more interested in her body. He cupped her left breast with his left hand, lifted it up, and let it fall. His heart quickened as he watched. Then he spun her around, primarily to get away from her stare but also to check her back for whip stripes. There were two, which meant that she was well trained or that she used her beauty wisely; either way, he saw potential.

Next, he stepped over to Zelia, her hair thick and fair, a rich brown color. As he pondered how miscegenation had produced such tremendous beauty, he roped her hair around his hand gently, then he tugged it roughly just to keep his wonder from being too apparent. He grabbed both her breasts and pushed them together and released them quickly as if he were trying to see something important. It made him look foolish, and a few of the white women in the crowd whispered among themselves with distaste and jealously. He was thankful that his wife had remained at home that day. She had instructed him to go to the auction to purchase two breeders, a male and a female, in order to increase the Tolby wealth without paying for it. It was a good idea, one his father used rather successfully. His wife had given him one thousand dollars. But at this point, Jared would have sold his soul to the devil for one night of pleasure with this young woman, and he expected to get more than that from her with far less a sacrifice.

The daughter started at one hundred dollars and the mother at three hundred, because she was a skilled seamstress and could thus generate more money by hiring out her craft. She would not bid much higher because of her age, maybe a couple hundred. When the bidding began, many men bid on Zelia. Jared at first put in a bid of three hundred, hoping that would fend off the other bidders. But she was beautiful, and the men were all prepared to pay for years of sexual satisfaction. Before he knew it, he had bid one thousand dollars; unlike the other bidders, Jared didn't know when to quit. There would be other auctions with other pretty slave women who would sell for less; one just had to exercise a little patience. But Jared could not be patient, and he bought her that day, even though he knew it would draw his wife's wrath.

He remembered how Zelia began to cry as she was ripped from her mother by two burly men, who chained her in preparation for transit to Jared's plantation. Her mother was weeping silently as well but was trying her best to exhibit what little dignity she could with her shirt pulled down around her waist for inspection at the auction block. She held onto Zelia's hand until their grip was forced apart. Jared's heart had filled with compassion, and he hated himself for it. *"Compassion for the slave is a sign of weakness, Jared!"* His father scolded him the day he cried when his black childhood friend, Lot, had been forbidden from coming over to visit him any more. "It's time you learn how to 'sociate with coloreds, boy. Ya rule over them, not wid them. You and Lot gettin' too close. One day you'll own Lot for yourself, and you don't want no feelings gettin' in the way of you handling your business." His father had smacked him hard across his face, rudely smearing wet spit dribbling from his mouth across his fat jowls.

"I'll take the wench for four hundred and not a penny more!" Jared stood back on his heels and punched his hands into his pockets, feigning authority. The other slave owners at the auction stifled grins as they observed Mr. Tolby's little boy. How he ever turned out so different from his father was anybody's guess. It wasn't the fact that they could not afford to purchase Zelia's mother; one of them, Mr. Brunnells, thought to purchase her out of pure spite, but he was budgeting for a pretty mulatto girl, and they seemed to be getting more expensive by the day. Everyone wanted Zelia, but no one was particularly interested in her mother; Jared could have bid two hundred and fifty dollars and gotten her. But he was ignorant to this and spent four hundred dollars over his budget. But Zelia was pretty, and he intended to make good use of his purchase.

On the way home his stomach gurgled at the thought of the scolding he would receive from his wife for spending so much money. Why couldn't she just leave him alone, let him make the decisions, be the man? He thought of killing her once, shutting her mouth once and for all, but his fear of being caught quickly perished the thought. When he looked over at Zelia, her beauty washed away all his doubts and fears. She smiled at him, acknowledging her thankfulness for him not separating her from her mother. He glanced over at the mother, an attractive woman but a little too old for his taste, but she turned from him, scowling and looking the other way.

The carriage bouncing along the sodden road made Zelia's cheeks shake in a way Jared considered utterly delightful. Her head bobbed and swayed, rooted firmly to her shapely figure, which also danced with the currents of the lively carriage. Jared felt himself getting aroused. He'd never felt that warm inside, not even on the first night with his wife. This girl was special—she was worth one thousand dollars. He guessed that was why she was regarding him with such awe. Nobody ever looked at him that way, not even his own children. Perhaps if he had spent such a pretty penny on them they would have looked upon him with favor. But they reminded him of their mother, and he treated them that way.

The three pulled up to the big house to find Jared's wife waiting on the front porch, drying off dishes with one of the slave women. She was smiling and speaking to the slave when she looked up to see Jared approaching. Immediately, he could see the disgust and surprise in her eyes as he drove the carriage around the driveway and gave Henry, the slave in charge of horses, the reigns. She stood up, threw the towel into her chair, and pranced over to the railing of the front porch, eyeing Jared all the way.

"I'm curious to hear how you going to have these two women breed us some slaves, honey," she said with sarcasm.

"I'm going to hump them myself, you ole' woman," Jared thought.

"These heah some strong women; the negras we got already will do dem plenty action and give us plenty mo' slaves. You nevah mind the breedin; I'll see to it that we gets our money's worth." *"While I'm in the bed with this pretty gal heah."* Jared couldn't help but smile at the thought.

"So how much did you spend on these slaves? Five, six hundred dollars?"

"One thousand four hundred dollars." Jared hopped off the carriage and ran about to the stairs to go inside and get a drink. He turned to Henry, who was preparing to take the horses and carriage to the stable.

"Henry, you take these gals to their quarters down front. They'll be in old Walker's place. Tell them how things work 'round heah, then tend to the horses and my carriage."

"Yassuh, Massa Jared." Henry hastily tied the horses' reigns to a post a few feet forward and helped Zelia and her mother off the carriage. As Jared turned to go up the steps, his wife put a stiff hand on his chest and said, "Did I hear you correctly?"

"One thousand fo—"

"That's what I thought you said! Just what were you thinking? I gave you one thousand dollars to buy two breeders, one male, one female, and you buy two damn women! Then, you go four hundred dollars over what I gave you! And don't think I didn't notice you ogling that light-skinned slave girl either, Jared!" His blood boiled. He'd asked her kindly to refer to him as "Sir" when in public, and she blatantly refused. His anger was kindled by her loud arrogance and public display of disrespect. He'd never raised a hand to hit her, but the grin in the new slave girl's eyes almost made him smack that defiant look right off his wife's face. Just then Zelia, who was being herded away by Henry, turned and said, "Thank you." And all Jared's anger melted.

He looked at his wife and said, "Damn if I tell you how I do my business around here, woman. Not git dinner ready! I'll soon be ready to eat." Mrs. Tolby's mouth flopped open, her eyes glazed with disbelief. The slave's grin further widened, but Jared walked into his house without another word.

Now all that was gone, spilt carelessly at his own hands. His memories were flooded with uncontrollable grief as he glanced at Zelia's corpse. Finally, he rose and followed Ivan toward the house. He would have Henry take care of the burial and say kind words over Zelia. Henry always had a way with words that Jared could never master. He could imagine the sneer that would grace his wife's face when she discovered that the other woman was dead. He tried to keep it a secret from her, but he knew that his efforts were in vain. Her eyes were so often accusatory, or was that just his own guilt? Anyway, Zelia was dead; he hated his marriage and his wife, and he hoped to find a quick replacement for Zelia before the grief dug in too deeply.

CHAPTER 4

THE GATHERING

Isiki's energy was running low. He had been hurrying back to the Great Swamp where his village was snugly hidden from the militia and bounty hunters who kept him so very busy for the past several years. He couldn't understand why a country would continue to invest so much in an evil cause that he felt sure was bound to come to an end. His thoughts raced and eventually paused on the latest development in his recent mission—his men and their newly rescued member, Jakeel. There was a reason that the priestess felt that Jakeel was significant to the cause of war and peace between slave and free man, and he wanted to be sure that his part was conducted correctly so Gausje would be pleased with him. He smiled at the word *member* because it really did not live up to his true meaning. If Jakeel refused membership, he would be put to death so as not to risk the secrecy and sanctity of the Maroon tribe. Gausje, chief priestess of the tribe, was unnervingly accurate in her pronounced suggestions for the tribe, which was why she was their leader. But then she could also be excruciatingly deadly when angered, threatened, or challenged. Gausje would not tolerate any attack on the tribe, however mild, and consequently her stable leadership role was maintained more out of fear than love, even though she was loved by many for their rescue.

Isiki's generations stretched back more than one hundred years, meaning that there were decades of miscegenation of blood, culture, and knowledge between American Indian and African. As early as the 1650s, his enslaved African ancestors had escaped into the American wilderness to form their own separate communities, a New World adaptation of an African form of resistance. These Outliers, as they were often called in North America, had set up small communities in swamps and other areas where they were not likely to be discovered, and this had been the home into which he'd been born. Although most members focused on their own survival—building homes, raising crops and livestock, fortifying the community against attack—others engaged in guerilla warfare against neighboring plantations and provided a refuge for other fugitives.

Isiki had taken pride in being born into a family of warriors who took the knowledge amassed from Africa and that learned from the Native Indians and formulated a fighting style unparalleled in North America. They had mastered the art of the shaman, building on an extensive pool of magic, natural herbs for healing, and exquisite fighting styles and weaponry. They did not yet have the fire sticks that their enemy possessed, but that was inconsequential against their spiritual power. Under the right circumstances, it had even been rumored the top shamans could stop bullets.

Isiki had been given his own army of soldiers after his father's death, and he led them well. Thus far, he had been on three missions. During the first his men killed ten of the enemy without suffering any losses. On his second mission they had managed to kill seven, but he had lost two, with one seriously injured. On both occasions they had attacked without the use of magic, as Gausje had directed. Isiki felt affection for her as he would his own mother, and he longed to see her. His wound was bleeding profusely now due to his exertion while trying to kill Jared and his long journey home. The mantle had fully worn off, and pain was pulsing throughout his entire nervous system. He'd stopped in the Kalehari Forest and chewed Golden Seal leaves, which, though extremely bitter, had an equally powerful healing ability. With his saliva he had made them into a paste that he had placed into the wound on his shoulder blade.

It was nearing dusk before he could see the traces of his home. Woven tapestries of feathers, wool, and carved bark marked the territory of the Maroon camp, which to the outsider said, "Stay away," but to Isiki said, "Welcome home." These manipulations of feather, thread, and tree were believed to invoke the protective presence of the spirits. Isiki had studied the markings since he was a child and knew them all by heart. He only had to be able to "manifest," and he then could qualify as a chief elder himself. Of course, there were other elements that he needed to master, such as war chants. These provided protection and direction for warriors, but war was not an elder's priority, and thus it was not necessary for acceptance into the council of elders. His teacher, Tsonoma, had mastered all the elements of the phoenix sun, a complicated mastery of herbs, spiritual channeling, and fighting styles, and as his pupil Isiki wanted to honor him by doing the same, if not better.

The forest floor began to turn to wet mulch, but Isiki trudged on until his waist was fully immersed in muddy water. The place for their city was perfect due to the thick fog that crept in as the sun set and rose. Isiki would eventually have to use his instincts and knowledge of tribal signs to find his way to the city gates. Underneath the murky waters, the early leaders of the city had set thick logs four feet in diameter. One had to walk barefoot to first find the logs and then follow them to the city. The path was treacherous because there were traps set that could be triggered by touch or by the watchman who saw all but yet remained unseen. He lived in the trees, moving about with uncanny ability and ease, and he would not hesitate to extinguish unwanted guests.

Isiki's feet deftly traced the underwater paths. He soon approached the entrance to the city and walked out of the swamp and up the steps to the huge city doors. The city walls were made of formidable trees hewn down during its earliest development. The wall reached thirty feet into the air, and a deep moss carpeted its frame in variegated spots. Men who excelled in carpentry and masonry forged metal bands to reinforce the logs' connection to each other, making the doors lofty shields, bolted shut from the inside by twenty foot ropes that would pull the doors open once a cabled lever was triggered by the gateman. Isiki carried a wooden key made to fit a secret lock that was hard to discern with the untrained eye. He fitted it into its place, starting a chain reaction of cogs and coils turning, causing the great doors of the city to open, creaking under the strain of their own weight. Once the doors cleared enough room, Isiki ran inside the gates and turned immediately to the opposite side of the wall and retrieved the inner key. This action initiated a recoiling mechanism that would suck the key placed on the outside wall to the inside, once again leaving a place to be filled for another warrior who may still be outside the protection of the walls.

Inside, the city was alive with activity. Negro and Indian children ran about playing innocent games under the watchful eyes of the learned mothers who earnestly took on the role of teachers—enlightening the young on the ways of the elders. Africans and Indians alike had a rich oral tradition, passing along their wisdom by word of mouth. Isiki was happy that these children would receive the same learning as he had as a child.

The city was built on an elevation about one foot above the marshy ground. The floor, though manmade, was as tough as real earth. The inhabitants had planted gardens for food and beauty, and there were stolen cattle, along with fertile soil. A mixture of African and Indian tribal markings that told of rank, craft, and family history decorated the homes of nearly everyone in the city. Although the homes were not situated by rows, there was a neatness to them that made every resident proud to be a dweller.

In the city's center was a large circle made of tall spears driven deeply into the manmade floor. This was where the council of elders met. As Isiki walked down the central path, the children spread out of his way. It was a sign of respect, and every child in this place had that, as lack of respect could mean expulsion. Past the council was Gausje's tent, the largest in the city. Isiki approached her door reverently and prepared to make the customary signal when she called to him. "Come, Isiki, I wait for you."

In addition to her appearance, her foreknowledge had a way of disconcerting Isiki's strong spirit every time. He loved Gausje because of the strength and fortitude that she represented, and that made her looks bearable, even admirable, to him. She was sitting to the back wall of the tent behind a low fire, clothed in only a small loincloth. No one knew her age, but she was alive and priest of this community while Isiki's grandfather was still living; that had to make her close to a hundred years old. Her skin was wrinkled and bumpy, like rotted leather, tough to the touch and extremely dry. It hung loosely and rolled in thick folds along her belly and sides. Her breasts looked like deflated gourds, and her head no longer bore the rich, thick tuft of hair that it had in her youth. In place of youthful verdure now were tiny, tight beads of hair follicles that managed to stay black after all these years.

"Gausje, I thank you for your invitation. I have not let you down; the mission was successful."

"Look at me, Isiki." She rose like a mist, her loin cloth falling to the floor, revealing nothing Isiki cared to see. But Isiki soon realized that what he thought was a loincloth was instead a leather scroll that Gausje had been reading. He wondered why a woman of her age would choose nakedness over clothing.

"Embrace me, my son." Isiki obeyed and walked timidly around the circle of fire at the center of the room to give Gausje a soft embrace. She was pleased with him, and that was all that mattered. That was his ticket to the council of elders, for which he'd work so hard.

"Now, tell me of your failure to kill Jared." Gausje looked into Isiki's eyes with a knowing gaze that made Isiki involuntarily shudder. Slowly, she resumed her seat and placed the scroll back into its proper location. Isiki began to perspire, this time out of sheer anger and frustration, yet he remained controlled.

"Your perception is impervious to my weak disguises, Gausje. I imagine that today was not the day for Jared's death. Fate controls matters beyond my will."

"That depends on your relationship with fate and your knowledge and respect of her charted course, Isiki. Were you warned of this fate today?"

"Yes, Gausje."

"And why did you not heed the warning?" She was still smiling. Isiki could detect no anger or disappointment in her voice, and that worried him. Her head tilted to one side as she waited for his response. She picked up an ancient pipe and began to smoke a fragrant herb poultice, slowly and deliberately.

"I—I felt that it was time. Tsonoma taught me to take control of my destiny."

"Tsonoma." Gausje said incredulously and sighed. "Isiki, I care for you as I would my own son. You are brave, strong, and intelligent. You have made much history in your short life, yet I fear that Tsonoma's teachings will eventually be the end of your noble leadership." Isiki could not believe his ears. Tsonoma was the most honored and respected elder in the community. He was one elder who was young enough and strong enough to still practice what he preached. How could Gausje disrespect him to this degree? He strained not to show his emotion.

"Gausje, I do not understand your words this moment. Tsonoma is a recognized and respected voice in the community."

"That he is; however, he has yet to fully embrace the kindred spirit of the elders. He prefers the spirit of war, and while for now that may have its place, it is not a balanced perspective, or does it seek for the balance and peace of the future. You are young enough to still balance out your nature and become whole with the earth, sun, moon, and stars. That will make you the greatest warrior of the new world. You could be a true legacy. But it means you must listen, Isiki. You must learn to listen to the spirit, which speaks through chosen vessels and often goes against what you imagined to be the course of action to take." Isiki resisted the urge to look away from Gausje and at the ground. He was shamed. "Bella was chosen by me, and I was directed to choose her to communicate that message to you. By not listening, you risked your life unnecessarily and have brought death's attention to your doorstep. You see, death and fate often work together; that is why it is so important to respect them both as if your life depended on it."

Gausje spoke her last sentence in a harsh hush. By this time, Isiki was not surprised that Gausje knew Bella; his training had showed him mysteries that would stupefy the ordinary man as the events of today had. He realized that Gausje was right. He had acted irresponsibly, and once again his efforts to be accepted on the council would be denied, but he could only be angry with himself.

"I appreciate your words of instruction, Gausje. May they serve me well as I obey and heed them."

"Well done, Isiki. That is the right attitude to have. May the gods continue to serve you well. We will soon go to the council; it's time for you to meet our new guest. But before we go, turn around and sit."

Isiki did as he was told. He knew all too well the benefit of obedience to Gausje, and the price of disobedience as well. Gausje walked over to him and placed her hard, leathery hands over his shoulder blades. As she let her fingertips move over his wound she closed her eyes. There was a brief pause of silence, and then the air moved with a hush. Isiki could see a small ripple in the air, like that of a heat wave, and he felt a warm, burning sensation in his wounded shoulder. His face grimaced in pain but then eased in pleasure as the sensation of healing quickly ebbed over his body. His shoulder wound had begun to weep, a sign of healing brought about by the herbal potion that he had put there. As Gausje moved her hands, the weeping began to work in reverse, flowing inward into the wound. The flesh around the wound reddened and pursed like one's lips after tasting something bitter, then the skin relaxed and fell into place. His wound was healed.

"There, go now. The council waits."

Without hesitation, Isiki thanked Gausje, turned, and walked out of her tent. The tribal council had already assembled within the circle of spears.

CHAPTER 5

SARAI

J ared stumbled clumsily into his bedroom and slumped in the chair located in the corner opposite the bed. He sat slouched, letting his hindquarters hang off the seat in such a precarious position that one wrong move would have left him sitting on the floor. He often sat like this, brooding, when events didn't quite go right, and today marked the epitome of such an occasion. It was only now that he had time to fully consider the events of this early morning and realize he was in serious jeopardy of losing his life. He'd heard of occurrences like this before from his nanny as a child, but he'd thought of them only as horror stories, even though she'd always sworn they were true. She told him that if he were to grow up to be a good master he'd not have to worry about such events. As a child, these stories frightened him, and he could barely sleep without seeing the glowing red eyes of the "bad-blooded niggers" who had gone mad due to the torment that they had experienced, finally taking out their crazed vengeance on innocent whites.

He remembered one story in particular about Sarai, and although it scared the hell out of him, he'd often ask Nanny to tell him the story again, even though he knew the outcome.

Nanny had told him about Sarai, a beautiful fourteen year-old slave girl who had been sold by her once-wealthy master to a Georgia plantation to pay off a gambling debt. Her new master, Detterick Newsom, began to rape her from the beginning. Newsom regarded her as his property and his concubine. Jared remembered he liked the story so much because the idea of a woman with whom he could have sex at will intrigued him. He remembered looking at Nanny's weighty breasts as she told the story when he thought she wasn't looking and becoming overwhelmed with excitement. Even now, the thoughts of his past encouraged his perversions as he sat slumped in his chair, making him want a woman—he wanted Zelia—but he forced his mind to continue to race back in time.

Sarai hated Detterick. He was sloppy fat, foul-mouthed, and had an ugly, red penis that pricked rather than stimulated her. He'd make her hold it, and Nanny described it as feeling like the warm small intestine of a pig that she made Jared clean when he was just nine. The intestine was lumpy, still full of feces, and stank to high heaven. Steam roared out of the poor pig's gut because it had fought and run so wildly before its life was violently sucked away. Just the touch of it made Jared's skin crawl, and he fought back the tears produced by the gag that rose in his throat. Nanny made him hold it while she prepared the cleaning utensils. She told him she would tell him no more sex slave stories if he told anyone about what they did. She had him. He was weak, even as a boy, to his nanny's whims, because she had that which he desperately wanted—forbidden information.

Nanny told him how Detterick would make Sarai hold his cock and spit on it while she rubbed it until the lumps hardened out a bit, but they would never fully solidify. Then he would make her stick it in her. Detterick would sweat profusely, and Sarai would cry every single time she had to go through this terrible ordeal.

For five years, Detterick forced his sex on Sarai. She gave birth to two children, both fathered by him. When a slave named George became her lover, she tried to stop Detterick's sexual advances by first asking the white daughters of her slaveholder for help, but it came to no avail.

Sarai was desperate for an end to the life she had been living for what seemed like an eternity. Her misery felt like an everlasting reality. She had even tried defecating and urinating once in the midst of the sexual act, hoping to disgust Detterick to a point where he would stop. She had eaten the most atrocious of food combinations, and the steaming feces were extremely foul-smelling. At first, the warmth of the urine stimulated Detterick, and his lumpy member stiffened a little. But the smell soon became overbearing, and Detterick uttered, "What the devil is that smell?" He leaped off Sarai and stared in absolute bewilderment at the mess that was in the bed. He inspected his own body for any excrement before punching Sarai in a fit of rage. She took the punch, hoping that she had finally brought to an end the feel of his sickening body on top of hers. She felt a tinge of victory for just a moment, but then it all came to a crushing end when Detterick decided to add to the foray himself. "So you like it rough, huh? Well, why don't I add my own concoction to the pot?" He turned to her and pissed a foul, yellow stream right on to her face. She started to scream, but his hands caught her by the throat as he straddled her body, pushed her back down in her own excrement, and raped her, further stimulated by the loathsome act they had both committed.

Afterward, Sarai, unable to believe the degree of filth to which she had sunken, became depressed and considered killing herself. The other slaves could see her morbid state and feared she would take her life at any moment, but that's when life became better for Sarai. One of the slave women, the oldest on the plantation, took Sarai aside one day while working in the cotton fields and began whispering to her of ancient tribal rites of passage and protection. She told her that she had not been raped or whipped for the last seven years since she had committed an act of attrition and sacrifice to the gods of the old land. At first, Sarai listened with only moderate interest, but as the days passed, and her depression increased, along with the incessant sexual abuse, the stories and rituals became all the more appealing. Soon, she became an ardent pupil rather than a passive listener. She began to memorize chants and rituals of sacrifice that she would practice on the sick chickens that the master would allow the slaves to kill and eat. The old woman relished knowing that she finally had someone to whom she could transfer the knowledge of the homeland. At night, Sarai would sneak into her cabin where she would copy patterns of spirit incantations in the earth. The woman told her that if she mastered these, she could then put a curse on the person she hated the most, and the spirits would honor her loyalty and dedication to them with protection.

The event that let Sarai know she was ready was when she put a minor death spell on one of the sick chickens that Detterick gave her. First, she drew a circle in the barren earth of her cabin floor and placed seven stones in the center of it. She then took a twig and drew out seven lines from the stones to the perimeter of the circle and placed a frog leg, a portion of the chicken's feces, her spit, and a drop of her own blood on top of the stones; this she allowed to dry for two days. On the evening of the second day, she lit a small fire that would only burn for a short time, using feces as fuel. The frog leg cooked to a crisp, and Sarai recited her incantation with practiced perfection. She then fed the frog leg to the sick chicken on the morning of the third day, and by the evening she noticed a strange change had come over the chicken. It began to cluck incessantly, run around in vicious circles, and its eyes began to bleed. It eventually fell over, coughed up a clump of blood, and died. She now had confirmation of her powers; after a year-and-a-half of practice, Sarai felt it was time for her final act of attrition and sacrifice.

She pleaded with Detterick to stop raping her and warned that she'd hurt him if he continued. She directly confronted him sometime before the summer, and Detterick brushed her aside and, as if to emphasize his right to have sex with her, informed Sarai that he was coming to her cabin that night.

Jared remembered all this with acute clarity. He could see Sarai, a brown Negro woman in a long white blouse, a white bonnet on her head, full around the hips, and he would get fully aroused. He saw her get a stick, a big fat one, with broken off stems on it that would cut deeply if wielded by a powerful person. His mind traced Sarai's steps into her rickety, beaten down cabin as she concealed the weapon behind the door. He thought about Detterick's daughters, who may have been jealous this whore was hurting their mother's heart year after year. Even Jared felt it rudely ironic that the white daughters' hate would be directed not toward their father, who perpetrated these physical encounters, but instead toward the victim—Sarai. This, of course, was why he didn't hesitate to sleep with the first female slave he purchased. He believed no one, not even his own wife and daughter, would ever blame him for the improprieties were they to catch him.

Jared would look at Nanny and observe the eagerness with which she'd watch him while she relayed the story. He thought that maybe it was Nanny who was the old woman, as her white eyes and teeth glowed in the bright moonlight pouring in through his bedroom window. Nanny watched him with an eerie eagerness and placed her large, work-worn hands on his privates as she continued to tell the story. His belly would always utter a gurgle of nervous approval, and he'd want to pass gas but strain to hold it lest he would offend Nanny and she'd not finish.

That night, Detterick walked the sixty or so paces to Sarai's shack. When he entered her cabin he saw her sitting on the bed, a glaze of anger warping her face. By this time they had come to a tolerable sexual relationship that existed purely because Sarai was forced to endure it. She had grown tired of fighting and simply let her mind escape her body while the abuse took place. Detterick did not care; conversely, he absolutely relished in her abdication. As he walked over to the bed, he unfastened his pants and proceeded to remove his member from his undergarments. Sarai retreated to the corner of the room where she had hidden the stick. He followed her and, when he came within range, she brought the club down viciously on his head, sending him, stunned, to the floor. She had drawn blood, which could mean death for a slave. Detterick sat on the floor, dazed, muttering, and cursing while touching his head and examining the blood that returned with his hand. Fearing Detterick's wrath, Sarai raised the club higher this time and brought it down again on his head with full force, cracking his cranium, killing him instantly. Detterick fell to the floor, a puddle of blood oozing from his open skull.

When they found Detterick, every bone in his body had been broken. With delicate accuracy, his liver had been cut out of his abdominal cavity and was cleanly stuck into a slit in his throat, burgeoning like a weird bloom in spring. He was spread out in a star, his head, feet, and hands making up the five points. His eyes had been gouged, the sockets empty, revealing holes that led to his brain. Within the holes were tucked his testicles. Chiseled into his chest, over his heart, was a stick figure with hands pointing east and west. The figure was within a circle, and seven small pebbles were placed on its perimeter. Sarai had considered putting Detterick's body in the fireplace, but Nanny said that would defeat the purpose. She had to leave a message. Because no one knew that Detterick was at Sarai's home, it was two days before his body was found, giving Sarai time to escape with her lover George.

Nanny told him that a slave, being abused long enough, would have the aid of the spirits and would stop at nothing to exact revenge on his or her oppressors. The spirits gave Sarai the courage to kill Detterick and rewarded her with escape and protection, and if Jared himself became evil like his father, the spirits would kill him, too. With that she would scoot up on his bed, hike up her dress, and stuff his tiny ten year-old hand between her legs and let instinct do the rest. The wet hair and the smell of sex would excite him so intensely he would ejaculate within minutes, and Nanny would say, "Sleep well, little master," and walk out of his room. He remembered there was no expression in her eyes when she said those words. No love, no hate, not anything—just hollow eyes that he would take with him into his dream world, with his fingers, still bearing her scent, placed under his nose, keeping her memory bright. As his eyes closed, he could see Sarai running after him with a huge club, swinging violently, her eyes blood red, leaving red traces as she moved with the quickness of a stalking cat. She would gain on him and, just as the club was about to make contact with his head, he'd wake in a cold sweat.

Jared jumped now, perspiration glistening on his forehead. He'd brought upon his head the anger of the spirits, and they were going to make him pay dearly. He should have listened to Nanny; now his negligence could cost him all he possessed if he didn't act quickly. Placing his hands on his aching eyeballs, he stumbled his way to bed.

CHAPTER 6

TANJEE

White and black, light and dark, two bodies undulating with the rhythms of passion, of intimacy, of lust. One powerful and crafty, a leader of two hundred soldiers, fighting for capital, for a way of life; the other, an escaped slave come back to her master—her lover—her savior? Tanjee's blood boiled with excitement. The fact that she had outsmarted Gausje and the Maroon tribe to make it back to Colonel Hearns's plantation made the act of sex that much more pleasurable. What if she were caught by the tribe? What if the friction of their bodies sparked the flame of passion too high and the crackles of their lust were heard by Colonel Hearns's wife? His men? They could both be destroyed, yet her nipples stiffened and she moistened at the thought. She could feel Hearns was thinking the same as he squeezed her body closer to his, making them one. She bit down softly on his ear lobe, knowing he always liked that, causing a quiet gasp to escape his lips.

This was her eighth time making it down to his plantation, which was but a few miles away from camp, dangerously close. She knew the Maroons had strange ways about them that dated back to her ancestors in Africa. She still couldn't explain how they managed to sneak into Hearns's compound, find her, and make their escape without a soldier stirring. They were as silent and stealthy as cats. At one point they seemed to be walking on air; the leaves didn't even crunch beneath their feet. Or was it just her imagination? She had wished to be free, to be her own person, to make her own decisions, to be in charge of her own body, but it was her body that kept her coming back for more. Hearns had showed her an interest, had given of himself, had risked all to be with her, and when he was with her, he made her know satisfaction. But more than that, it was what he risked that created her excitement.

Hearns rolled over, never separating himself from her, positioning her on top. A beam from the moon commanded sparks of light to glisten from their sweat like tiny circling crystals. From afar they looked as if they were one living organism passionately separating and rejoining to form its own unique creation. From afar, Gausje was watching. Tanjee swiveled her hips faster, creating stiff friction made tight by her muscles yet easy by her moisture. Hearns responded, his member stiffening to its full extent. His back arched involuntarily, pushing him deeper inside his possession, and that act tilted her cup, and she spilled over and over, shaking, lightly convulsing. She fell forward onto him, her full lips enveloping his warmly. Hearns wanted this moment to last forever, but it was against his will. His body responded to the slippery warmness that now billowed over his crotch, and he soon felt the fullness of climax. They relaxed from the intensity, gratified.

Gausje continued to watch, intensely, angrily—jealously. She watched because she didn't want to miss anything that might help her save Tanjee from herself. She felt betrayed by this young girl who disregarded the tribal pact by returning to that which had controlled, humiliated, and stifled her, angry at the way Tanjee gave herself completely to the enemy instead of to the tribe, and jealous because it had been many moons since she had experienced such passion herself, so long she had almost forgotten.

Suddenly, Tanjee felt cold, exposed, scared. She shivered and pulled the wool covers up over their naked bodies. It was seventy-five degrees outside at night, and Hearns kicked the covers off of his body to keep from boiling. He turned to look at Tanjee, and, for the first time, he realized that he actually might be in love with her. But how could that be? She was not human; she was property, chattel, incapable of reciprocating emotion. He was just as bad as those shepherds he'd heard about having sex with their flock. But he could not deny the voice of his heart. There was more to this woman than any woman he'd ever known. Her beauty was breath-taking. Her skin still proclaimed splendor amid the myriad of stripes that lined her flesh from visitations to the whipping post. Her body was defined, artistically sculpted. She even had a smell that was slightly stifling but pleasurable. He found most slave women had that smell.

His mind played various scenarios in quick flashes that proclaimed the truth—that this woman sacrificed far more for him than any one person had ever done. She risked death for him; not even his wife would have done that. That had to be of value. At this very moment, he could care less if Tanjee was a Negro woman or a slave. Hearns was getting tired of all the killing, the fighting, the politics, and the brutality of this slave business anyway. For years he had fought in various battles; during that time, he'd lost many close to him and suffered from nightmares as his subconscious resurrected buried reminders of the horrors of war, holding him prisoner to the battlefields while sleeping in the comfort of his own bed. His life was being destroyed by war, pain, and guilt, and for what? He was wealthy. His family had enough money to last three generations if they never made another cent, and he would make sure he would teach his children how to invest the dollar to continue to make it prosper.

His wife used to tolerate his nightly spasms, but she began to get agitated when he'd wake up in a sweat or accidentally push her away in a feverish panic, thinking she was the enemy. Resting now in Tanjee's cloaked embrace, his brain flashed before him the day his wife curtly asked him to please sleep in the guest room so he would not disturb her or the children with his nightly tremors and screams. He was angry with her and appalled that his own wife couldn't understand the price of war. Yet, he swallowed his self-pity and obliged her and slept in the guestroom, still plagued by the nightmares. He then migrated to the study in front of the fireplace, which only warmed his reality with an agitated heat, and finally to the slave quarters to Tanjee.

He and Tanjee had been enjoying each other for a while, but that night had been different. It was the first night that the dreams had stopped, and ever since he had returned to her bed as often as possible. He'd never experienced such happiness, such peace, as while in her arms. Even now, weeks after her escape, he'd had one night a week with her, and each had been total bliss. His heart told him no, commanded him to cease dealing with the futility of slavery. Tanjee made him realize the humanity in Negroes, and the truth was that he was never happier than those nights spent with her, not only for the sex but also for the sacrifice. Tanjee made him feel like sacrificing for her, and that made his life worth living.

Tanjee shuddered against his embrace. He lifted his head from her homemade pillow and gazed at the back of her neck. He removed a portion of the blanket from her body to see her skin was a maze of goose bumps. *"Poor child must be sick to be so cold in this weather,"* he thought.

"Tanjee, are you feeling sick? You have chills all over your body, and it's hotter than the devil's piss down here," Hearns said.

"I feel fine, soldier. I don't know why I'm so cold. You just gave me the greatest, warmest feeling in the world."

"Then why don't you come back here, back to my plantation. I promise I won't do you wrong as I did before, Tanjee. I was acting out of my poor upbringing. I wish I'd never made you do those things with me and General

Ford. If you come back, I promise that I will never do anything like that again." Tanjee turned over and faced Hearns. When she looked directly into his eyes, he felt her gaze pierce past his eyeballs, through the sockets, and into the machinations of his brain, but he realized he had nothing to hide, so he returned her gaze willingly.

"Are you truthful? Do you promise?"

"I am. I promise. We could be together. I would personally set you free. You would be free to be with me. No more sneaking around."

"But what about your wife?"

"I'm leaving her. She will be gone by the time you return from the tribe." Tanjee shuddered again. "What's wrong? You're shivering again. Tell me." Hearns tightened his embrace. Her fear was making him aroused, but he wanted to ease her apprehension and make her comfortable.

"I don't know how long I can do this."

"Then don't!" His voice broke above a whisper. Tanjee put a calming finger to his mouth.

"I don't know if I'll even be alive to see you again. I feel like someone's watching me. Don't you feel it? It doesn't feel right. Not right at all." Hearns sat up in bed. He looked again into Tanjee's eyes, evaluating the words she was saying for validity. He felt absolutely calm, but her nervousness was making him uncomfortable.

"What are you talking about? Of course you will be back here alive. I told you my men will not harm you. They know just enough to be helpful, but not enough to get in the way."

"It's not your men who I am worried about."

"Then who, child? Who is it? I can take care of him. Is it one of the Negro slaves here? They wouldn't dare lay a finger on you with the right instruction. Just say the word, girl." Tanjee knew Colonel Hearns could back up his promise. He commanded armies and ran an efficient plantation. He didn't tolerate disrespect from slaves or his fellow countrymen. He had been wounded in battle and had lost many in his family. Colonel Hearns, a man acquainted with death, pain, and loss, could relate to her and, perhaps, protect her. He possibly was her only hope. She decided to trust him fully.

"The tribe I told you about. I think they know something. Gausje took me to the woods two weeks ago, and she told me about us; she said she'd seen us."

"What do you mean, she has seen us?" Hearns was looking more pensive.

"Hearns, this woman is not normal like us. She can do things."

"Like what? I can do things, too! I once peeled back the skull cap of a man with my bare hands. And I can shoot the whiskers off a cat with this pistol. Just point me in the right direction."

"I hope you're right. She showed me what she saw in a mud puddle. She took me to the forest, to a place where we worship at times. There are little puddles there. It's sort of swampy. Gausje told me to look in the puddle. I lied to her and told her I didn't know what she was talkin' about. She got angry. She made me look at the puddle real closely. I expected to see my reflection because it was noonday, but I saw us! You and me, making love in this shack! It was like I was someone else peeking in on you and me. I felt naked and low!" Hearns's eyes looked bewildered. He believed her even though what she was telling him was impossible.

"I wouldn't lie to you! But I'm telling you, this woman is a witch! People say she can stop bullets with her eyes, and they say she knows the future; others say she can stop time! These are the people who are part of my tribe. They believe in Gausje because she's rescued them. Many of them claim to have seen these wonders." Tanjee paused for a moment to let her point settle in. She rubbed her hands on her cold skin, making a sound like paper. Hearns was staring out the window, considering her words.

"Sugar, just think about me. Gausje got me out of here without you knowing. Even got me past your soldiers. If I hadn't come back and told you, you still wouldn't know where I was."

Hearns nodded thoughtfully.

"Last week at the camp, I saw some of the warriors staring at me mean-like. I think they aim to kill me 'cause they are scared I might be a threat to the tribe. They really have peace there and don't want to sacrifice that peace for anything or anybody. I thought I'd be happy there, but without you, my life has been just miserable."

Hearns thought for a moment. The infamous Maroon tribe lived not far from where he lived, and he had access to a member of their camp. That could be the way to improve his life, to get what he truly wanted. The Maroons had suffered little for all the pain, death, and money they'd caused owners to lose. The Maroons were powerful, organized, and crafty. Hearns remembered the generals talking about the Maroon's mischief, and he had attended meetings plotting the tribe's demise. What if he eliminated the Maroons? The army would give him an honorary discharge and money, and he would be a hero. He could then travel northwest or southeast, perhaps to Florida, with Tanjee and his children and start his miserable life anew. It would mean a few more deaths, but he believed this woman was worth it.

"Tanjee, go back to the tribe at dawn. Take this with you; it's my pocketknife. My uncle gave it to me when I was twelve. It's sharp as hell, so be careful. If any man tries to bother you, or woman for that matter, cut 'em! I will track you and find my way to your tribe with my men, and I will truly set you free. You will be free to go, even if you don't come back to me." Those were the words Tanjee needed to hear.

"Thank you, soldier."

"My men and I will follow the trail and destroy the village. And don't worry about that magic horseshit! No man can stop a bullet, especially when it's placed between the eyes!"

Tanjee felt reprieve from her fear. She lifted the blanket high, and the moonlight danced a ballet on her skin. She reached for that for which she had come back; it was ready, and they quickly resumed their turbulent choreography.

*****

Gausje sat up from her pallet abruptly, letting out a gargled moan. The dream she just had was upsetting and sad because she had address it. Three months ago she was asked by a tribe member for permission to rescue Tanjee from the hands of a slave owner, and she had granted the request. Two weeks ago she discovered that this slave, Tanjee, could not refrain from returning to the dark places of her past like a dog that returns to his own vomit. Gausje couldn't fathom this. She had rescued this woman, given her a plot of land on which to build, to till her own soil, to find a suitable mate, to share food within the community, and still she ran off to sleep with the enemy! Gausje was infuriated, but she had rationalized that perhaps this child would take more nurturing than the rest. At least she had thought so, until the dreams.

Tanjee probably would have gotten away with her acts were it not for the strange dreams Gausje was having. They were lucid, detailed, and real, unlike normal dreams that mixed reality with the supernatural. Gausje recognized that the dreams were from the spirits, as regular dreams were not this accurate. She did not share her dreams with any of the elders; instead, she watched intently and wrote them down. Her dreams were visions of Tanjee's escapades.

Gausje saw the path Tanjee took, every week diversifying her route so as to not alert the tree guardians. She saw the plantation and the man, although his features were not quite distinct. She could not see his face as she had seen Jared's, but she sensed he was not typical. He was a person of power and prestige. He had wealth from sources other than slaves and seemed to be acquainted with war. But no matter how hard she tried, she could not make out his face, just a brimmed hat, a rifle over the mantle, and a sword holstered at his waist.

Sometimes Gausje felt guilty about having dreams of seeing Tanjee pleasure this man, but she ignored her feelings until a recent vision revealed that Tanjee was sharing secrets of the Maroons with her lover. Gausje could not believe one of her own could do such a treacherous act. The dream revealed that Tanjee was not being a traitor, just careless, over a man whose body she could not resist. Finally, Gausje decided to approach Tanjee on the matter, arranging a private meeting with her in the forest where they could evade the speculation of the tribe. Tanjee was a beautiful person, one who could bring much to the tribe, and Gausje didn't want to weaken such a bright flame.

But Tanjee denied all she was told, only infuriating Gausje more. She felt it was time to let Tanjee have a glimpse of the power to which she had access. In the forest of Kalehari, she revealed to Tanjee in a mud puddle what she had seen. Every detail, from every gasp to every stifled, nervous burp, Gausje had seen it all, and she used her magic to replay it for Tanjee in the watery reflection of the mud puddle. Tanjee watched herself with amazed embarrassment; her skin crawled when she saw her own nakedness. She was so unashamed with Hearns, but she had blazed with shame. Was that how she looked when making love? Gausje had thought that sharing this vision would be enough to make Tanjee recognize the delicate line she was teetering between life and death. Against her better judgment, she decided to allow Tanjee another chance, and now the whole tribe, and their peaceful life, was at risk. Her most recent dream revealed that Tanjee had not only returned to her lover but also had confided in him more about the tribe. Tanjee had betrayed the tribe, and now this man was coming to destroy them.

A thick, white mist hung low over the ground that morning. Tanjee and Hearns were up before dawn, having never really gone to sleep. They'd loved, talked of the future, and then just lay, touching. Tanjee was planning her way back inside the camp, and Hearns was calculating his method of attack. Their plans were full-proof, at least by human standards. Tanjee would get inside the fortress and, after two days, would send Hearns a smoke signal of their own design. His men would already be in the Kalehari, so when the signal went up, they would storm the city. Tanjee would be captured and visibly taken prisoner by Hearns's best men to eliminate all suspicion that they had together planned this attack. Next, Hearns would personally capture Gausje, alive, and hold her prisoner as ransom for the total surrender of the Maroon tribe. With Gausje as bait, the loyal tribe would easily retreat and leave, the village would be burned, and the slaves would be resold to a new set of masters. The money from this sale would be split between Hearns and his soldiers. Then he would start life anew with Tanjee. But Tanjee did not know that Hearns intended to kill most of the Maroons while in the village, especially Gausje. He'd promised Tanjee no bloodshed, but he knew the soldiers would not settle for that. There had been too many whites slain at the hands of the Maroons. No, he was going to end this battle once and for all, and Tanjee would learn to cope with her role in her new home.

Tanjee used the cover of the fog to hide her movements as she returned to the Maroon village. She would race a hundred yards and then rest her lungs by walking fifty yards or so. She continued this process so that, by dawn, she was in the swamp. No one in the community got up at dawn anymore, probably out of rebellion from decades of early morning labor when they were slaves. Now that they were free, they would get up when they liked. She knew she would be safe from most, except Gausje. As Tanjee crept through the swamp, she reached for the knife that Hearns had given her. Hidden in her loincloth, it brought her comfort.

Her feet traced the underwater logs that led to the Maroon village. She followed the path all the way to the door and then eased into the swamp, which was roughly twelve feet deep. She paddled her way to a place in the swamp where the foliage was the thickest, then craftily climbed the wall using the vines that had grown fat from moisture from the swamp. Tanjee had given her secret key to Hearns so that he and his men could walk in the city without a brutal attack and thus spare many lives. This had eased Tanjee's conscience, as she trusted that the confrontation would be bloodless.

A smattering of hay for the cattle was stored in the corner wall of the village, so she aimed her jump at it and landed safely, barely making a sound. She stripped off her clothes, balled them in a bundle, put on a wool garment that wrapped around her body like a cloak, and then made her way to her hut. So far, she had done well. She walked upright as if she had been starting her morning activities, and then she proceeded inside her hut. Tanjee threw her clothes by the fire to dry and lay down on her floor mat to sleep. It was not uncommon for many people to sleep until noon, and she would be one of those people today. She searched for the proper position, placed her hand between her legs, and fell into a deep slumber.

But while Tanjee was sneaking into the city, Gausje was awake and meeting with Isiki, Phoenix, and Lunden. Gausje was unusually grave that morning. Up to this point she had told no one of Tanjee's betrayal, but she hated what she must do.

"Isiki, prepare the ceremonial fate catalyst." Although Isiki displayed a momentary expression of astonishment, he nonetheless went forthright to his task.

"Phoenix, prepare the spears of sacrifice. Lunden, go with Phoenix and set up the scaffold."

"Yes, Gausje," they said in unison as they backed out of the hut, always facing their leader. It was a sign of respect, a respect heightened because they knew what was about to happen, and they wanted to make sure they themselves would not be on the receiving end. Gausje was visibly upset, but no one knew why. They just wanted to make sure they were not the recipients of her wrath.

The elders' council was little more than a thatched hut of dried reeds from the swamp, dried mud, and leather tarp made from deerskins. Inside there were two extremely well-organized partitions that held the knowledge amassed for decades in neatly stacked leather scrolls. The first contained books of war, medicine, and magic written by African and Indian ancestry. The other partition held medicine, herbs, potions, gunpowder, and scrolls upon scrolls of information that Isiki had yet to learn. He located the ingredients for the catalyst: three stems from the Venus Fly Trap and rattlesnake venom. The potion made a mild acid that was to be used in the event that anyone deserted the tribe and was caught. The traitor would be placed in the center of the spears, and his or her tribal markings would be melted off with the concoction. Delicate precision had to be used to measure the portions of ingredients to make the mixture just right so that it burned the flesh efficiently.

Isiki mixed the potion in a molten lead bowl and carried it carefully to the circle of spears. In the middle of the area were three blue holes and one large red hole that was shallower than the others, each colored by dyed sand. Phoenix was already completing the task of placing the spears in the blue holes, and Isiki positioned the lead bowl in the sunken red spot. He hurried over to Lunden to pull the scaffold out of the barracks located on the eastern wall of spears. The scaffold had four large wooden wheels; its body was the trunk of an extremely huge oak tree. Drilled into the top of the trunk were two stockades from which hung leather thongs to hold a person's wrists and feet. The executioner would fasten the prisoner's hands and feet into the stockades and tie them with the thongs, readying the individual for execution.

When they had finished their duties, they returned to Gausje's tent.

"We are done, Gausje. All is in order." They found Gausje staring into the fire that stayed lit in her room. She remained poised before the flame before she looked up into each of their eyes.

"Sound the horn to announce the execution. Wait for the people to gather at the circle of spears. Then go to Tanjee's quarters and wake her. The four of you will meet me in the center of the circle of spears." They all hesitated. Tanjee? What had she done? They liked her, had hoped to have her one day. In the village, there was no need to rush love or relationships—no need to rush sex; time was a luxury they could now afford. Isiki dared to speak.

"All wise one, you are our leader, and we respect you."

"Then do not hesitate another moment and carry out my request." Gausje spoke harshly and turned her back to the three men. Knowing the conversation was over, they quickly backed out of the tent. Isiki went to his quarters, retrieved his horn, and sounded the announcement to gather. He then ran up and down the rows of homes, alerting the inhabitants to come to the circle of spears at Gausje's request. Although many were still sleeping, they quickly arose when they heard Isiki's voice.

A mixture of groggy and excited people crowded the pathway to the circle of spears. Women nervously donned their cloaks and picked up their children to carry them to the place. The warriors looked about questioningly, wondering who was to be put to death. No one had been executed who was their own. Could it be one of them? Many were tempted to stay at home, but their fear of Gausje made them come to the circle of spears anyway. Everyone came but Tanjee. She didn't hear the horn or the commotion of feet and chatter as people made their way to the place of execution. She was far too deep in slumber from her night's escapade, dreaming about Colonel Hearns and their future together.

The village settled; everyone had his or her place. Isiki, Phoenix, and Lunden stood by the entrance, waiting for Gausje. The scaffold was positioned in the center a foot in front of the three spears. Gausje walked slowly from her tent to the entrance and then to the center of the circle. Wearing a red robe that flowed down to her feet, her head draped with a white cloth, she held in her right hand a white cloth as well. The black leathery texture of her skin and the tight wrinkles in her fading hairline made the red robe and white headdress luminescent. She took her time, gazing at the audience, her eyes glossy. They returned nervous glances. Her spirit was sorrowful. Finally, she spoke.

"Members of the Maroon tribe, we are here to execute a traitor, someone who does not hold our sanctity, our preservation, at heart—a member who has broken a vow of trust and has put your lives and the lives of your children in mortal danger. A member who has slept with the enemy and shared our secrets." The crowd searched their memories, trying to remember a moment where they may have slipped, by accident, and given away a precious secret. The atmosphere tensed.

"It pains me to have to carry out this necessary act, but I value the peace that we have. Isiki, bring Tanjee to the circle." A small commotion broke out in the crowd as many expressed their disbelief. No one would have suspected that Tanjee would commit such an act of treachery. She was so nice, so inconspicuous. But they relaxed a little knowing that it was not going to be their lives that ended that day. Isiki turned quickly and headed for Tanjee's quarters.

Tanjee slept the sleep of peace. She and her lover had made plans, and he was going to carry them through flawlessly. He was an experienced soldier, and his acquaintance with death, strategy, and planning were second nature to him. Her body rose and fell with a rhythmic pace that almost hypnotized Isiki as he stood staring at her perfect form. She was beautiful. Her cloak had slipped upward as she rested, revealing smooth, buttermilk legs—the prize of being a master's mistress. Because Tanjee had not had to endure the arduous labor of the fields, she retained a feminine beauty many other slave women had long lost. He had hoped that maybe one day he could have a taste of what the white masters had sampled for so long. He thought the difference would be that he would taste with a willing subject, but now he knew that Tanjee had been willing, and that was why he was at her doorstep. She had given herself to the enemy when she could have had her pick of all the men in the Maroon village. A flush of anger moved across his heart. She probably would have denied him because he was too dark and had what the masters called kinky hair. She had sold her body and soul to a white man, and that was unforgivable, considering all that these Americans had done to his people.

Isiki shook his head, shaking off the lustful delusions he had when he first stepped through her door. He walked over to her bed, ripped off her cloak, and grabbed her roughly by the neck. She reached for the blade she had strapped to her thigh, but Isiki dropped his weight on one knee, placing it on her inner thigh. The pain shot a paralyzing jolt straight to Tanjee's back. He reached his left hand out quickly and grabbed her right wrist just as she clasped the blade. Isiki took her wrist and applied strong pressure to the left and right sides of it, making her fingers involuntarily release the blade. It fell to the floor, and Isiki swept it away with his left hand. All this happened in a moment, the excitement causing him to perspire.

"Get up, traitor!" Isiki growled. Tanjee's eyes rolled about in bewilderment. She opened her mouth to speak, but she only choked on her own saliva. Her skin pimpled with goose bumps as she frantically attempted to fight off Isiki's powerful grip.

"Isiki! What's the meaning of this?" She managed to squeeze out between gasps.

"You have been found out, and Gausje demands your presence at the circle of spears!" Isiki tried to remain calm but found that his jealously of her choice was beginning to cloud his discipline. Her naked body was also causing him to become unnecessarily jittery. Finally breaking his grasp, she attempted to cover her nakedness with her hands. Her eyes, at first glazed with sleep, finally illuminated with realization.

"No! No, Isiki! It was going to be peaceful—"

"Silence!" Isiki grabbed both her wrists and led her briskly to the circle. Tanjee screamed in protest, her feet dragging and kicking at Isiki's shins. When they reached the circle, Phoenix joined Isiki and brought Tanjee to the center of the arena.

"Bind her hand and foot," Gausje commanded. Phoenix held Tanjee down while Isiki ran to the shed to get the rope. He returned quickly. Tanjee did not resist Phoenix as much because she couldn't; he had pinched a pressure nerve in her neck that had a mild, paralyzing effect. Phoenix looked as if he were going to rape her because he was practically on top of her, her hands bent behind her back. The crowd watched in astonishment as Isiki tied her hands and feet with thorough agility. He was sweating profusely now, as was Phoenix. The sun was up, its heat blazing the atmosphere. Gausje's face remained stone, emotionless. Tanjee was sobbing, spit forming a wet crust around her mouth. All pretense had left her. She was naked and humiliated and angry that her plan did not work. Hearns wasn't scheduled to attack until the day after tomorrow, and there was no way she could contact him; she would be dead before the ceremony was over.

Gausje turned to pick up the bowl of acid, cradling it as if it were an infant. She then gave Isiki and Phoenix a knowing look. They reached down and lifted Tanjee from the ground. The sweat of her body had attracted a blanket of dust, lightly powdering it. Her flesh moved and jiggled as they carried her to the scaffold and tied her to its trunk. They placed her hands above her head and fastened her feet to the base of the trunk. Gausje first held the bowl of acid over Tanjee's heaving stomach while her head was ripping back and forth from side to side. Tears of frustration streamed down her face, and veins ridged her forehead in strained attempts to feed blood and oxygen to a frantic brain. Gausje spoke to Tanjee.

"You have chosen this path my child. I have no cho—"

"Go to hell, witch!!" Tanjee screamed hoarsely as she spit onto Gausje's red robe, only to see it bead up like water in a hot frying pan and roll to the ground.

"I've been there already, my child. Now it's your turn." Again, she spoke without malice. Gausje's voice remained even and controlled. Tanjee's tribal tattoos were on her right shoulder and above her belly button, and Gausje poured the contents of the bowl first on Tanjee's shoulder and then on her stomach. Instantly, steam began to rise and the mixture began to bubble. It poured into Tanjee's navel and down the sides of her stomach, charring tiny channels of burned flesh in its path. Tanjee's body arched against the pain, her body struggling against the ropes that would not yield. Nothing was left of the tattoos, only a shadow of an emblem. Although the skin was melting mildly, there was no blood. The acid pooled in her navel and was beginning to burn through the layers of her flesh. Gausje commanded Phoenix to pin Tanjee's body to the trunk of the tree so the acid would not spill. Gausje bent over to Tanjee's ear and whispered, "Tell me how your lover plans to get here."

"Go to hell!" Gausje took the bowl of acid and poured a portion of the contents into Tanjee's hair. Smoke slowly rose from her head as it began to melt the skin off her skull. She banged her head hard against the tree.

"Soon, the acid in your navel will work its way through your flesh, burning your insides like a slaughtered hog. I've been told the pain is enough to nearly kill a man—nearly. Do you want to suffer, child? Oh look, your hair—it's melting." Gausje sounded mournful, but her voice rose to a loud hush. "Tell me the plans, or I'll burn your eyes out with this acid!" Tanjee screamed. Maybe if she told Gausje, if she confessed, maybe Gausje would let her live. Maybe Gausje would make the pain stop! Tanjee's beautiful skin was now disfigured. Her hair was melting. No white man would want her now. She could stay with the tribe as a loner. She had learned her lesson.

"Okay! Okay! I will tell you! Hearns has my key. In two days I am to light a fire in my tent and send up puffs of smoke when everyone has gone to sleep. Hearns will already be in the swamp. He will open the door and take everyone prisoner. He promised there will be no bloodshed!!" She issued her words like an auctioneer. "Gausje, I've learned my lesson. I have been unfaithful to the tribe and to you. I want a second chance! Please, please forgive me. My belly! It's hurting!" Gausje commanded Phoenix to get up. Tanjee twisted her body awkwardly and spilled the last of the acid out of her navel. Her skin was now even more marked, her eyes even sadder. A red wound gaped where her navel once was.

"Release her from the trunk of the tree, but keep her hands and feet bound." The three men did as they were told. A light stench of burnt flesh wafted through the air, and those who smelled it involuntarily brought their hands to shield their noses.

"But I thought you were going to let me go!" Tanjee said.

"Oh I am, traitor. I am going to let you go to a place we just aren't quite ready to see yet—the afterworld." Tanjee writhed angrily, shouting curses and spitting. She banged her head on the trunk of the scaffold repeatedly, and it was difficult to free her body without releasing her hands and feet. When the three managed the process, Tanjee rolled her body off the trunk and fell to the ground. Lunden started to grab her but was stopped in his place by a raised hand from Gausje.

"You three, return to your post at the door. See to it that no one gets out." They went to the doorway. The crowd had begun to get restless, and there was commotion all about the circle of spears. No one present wanted to die or feel Gausje's wrath, and no one but Isiki had noticed the man who they had rescued, Jakeel, slowly stumble out of his quarters and begin making his way toward the circle. Jakeel had been unconscious as he healed from his deep wounds, but Isiki guessed the screaming and cursing had finally broken him from his sleeping spell. Jakeel still looked bad, and Isiki thought it would be best for him to return to his quarters for his health but, more importantly, to avoid Gausje's attention. Jakeel alone had permission to remain in the infirmary because everyone thought he was incapacitated. Subtly, Isiki motioned for Jakeel to go back, returning his attention to the scene before Gausje noticed he was there.

Jakeel caught the signal and at once began to return to the infirmary, but just as he had taken three steps he again heard shouts of pain and terror emanating from Tanjee's throat. Curiosity held him prisoner, and he turned back toward the circle of spears, painfully trudging forward. Isiki, Phoenix, and Lunden faced the execution, unaware that Jakeel had returned. In his weakened state, he stood inconspicuously against the outside wall of spears and peered through tiny slits between the weapons. Tanjee was hopping up and down, making her way toward the entrance. She was nude, and her breasts bounced violently in round swirls with the motion of her jumps.

Jakeel noticed Tanjee's beauty, albeit markedly diminished in her anguish and what appeared to be torture, and wondered for what crime she was being punished. Thoughts of his most recent scourging made his skin crawl. Jakeel believed in discipline but not brutal murder or painful torture just to make a point. Somehow, what he was seeing bore resemblance to the type of cruelty he had experienced when he was a slave. But that did not fit within the scheme of life here in the camp. He had been rescued from his oppressive situation. Surely his rescuers would not indulge in the same evil practices as did the slave masters. He had to see for himself.

Tanjee had nearly made it to the guards at the door, her body now dripping wet with her own perspiration. She had stumbled and fallen twice, and the fact she was able to get up was a pure miracle. Gausje was chanting quietly; Jakeel recognized that she was invoking the spirits. Whatever this girl had done, he knew it was bad by the prayer Gausje was saying. He'd begun learning it from Bella while still a slave. It was the chant of Ifa—the god of fate. Ifa brought about curses and blessings, deciding the outcome for a person. Ifa could be bought with gifts like small animal sacrifices, fire worship, and bloodletting and then would turn fate into the hands of the giver.

With much effort, Tanjee was just getting to her feet. The dust of the ground clung to her flesh and became striated as tiny streams of sweat ran down her body, her belly heaving in and out with exhaustion. The crowd remained silent as they watched these events unfold. Isiki and Phoenix moved to grab Tanjee, but they were held still by a raised hand from Gausje. Isiki tried to look firm and emotionless, but inside he was a tumult of fear, excitement, and power. His eyes were fixated on Tanjee's physique, dripping, heaving, and frantically searching for release.

Then the air moved. Isiki's throat went dry, and he felt as if the hair follicles around his ears were alive with invisible static. Tanjee's eye's jerked wide with newfound bewilderment. Her arms, bound and set below her navel to maintain balance, suddenly whistled in the air above her head. Isiki thought he heard bones snap. The air looked like a sweltering mirage; one could almost detect ripples in the waves, but it was no longer hot. A cool springtime breeze wafted over the Maroon village as Tanjee's body slowly levitated off the ground. A child's shriek was quickly stifled by a mother's hand clasped tightly across the child's mouth. Never before had anyone, not even the warriors, witnessed a feat of this nature. The audience gasped in disbelief, minute whispers and quiet bellows escaping from their frightened lips. Tanjee's body continued to rise steadily until every head was tilted upward, watching her float toward the three spears set in the middle of the circle. All was now silent.

Tanjee felt her throat close and dry up. Her mind was a mélange of frantic thoughts, and she wished she had never met the Maroons. She was now thirty feet above the spears. Gausje remained calm, quietly calling upon the spirits. And then she hushed. Tanjee's body twirled slowly about like a pig on a stick being slow-roasted over a fire. Tears crystallized on her eyes and began to fall freely, the land and sky exchanging places within her field of vision. The air was cool. She looked down and saw the spears and slowly came to recognize her method of execution. She felt the ropes around her legs fall free as if they were melted wax, her body tilting upright and her legs pushing apart as her body formed an upside down "T." She wondered if the spears would pierce her in the same place Hearns had once occupied to bring her deep pleasure. How long would she recognize pain? She dropped, yet the fall seemed to go forever. Her life flashed before her in milliseconds—all she had ever known, wondered about, seen, and lived, moved by her in a flash. She felt a quick burst of pain, then warm wetness, as her insides slid out of her body, then total, unyielding darkness. The sound was enough to make Jakeel vomit and fall over, unconscious.

Tanjee's body was now impaled on the three spears that had managed to penetrate straight through her diaphragm, upward alongside her spine, and through her heart, throat, and skull, forming a bloody mass outside her cranium. Her body jolted involuntarily as if an invisible god were manipulating a tiny frog on a toothpick. Blood and a dark substance ran down the spears, forming a huge puddle at the base of the three instruments of death. Other witnesses began to get sick, many turning their heads away from the disturbing scene. Gausje walked over to the pool of blood, placed the white napkin in it, and then folded the cloth into a neat square. Phoenix and Lunden were at the entrance to keep the crowd in the circle. Gausje lifted her hand to quiet the melee of noise.

"My people. This is what we will look like if Tanjee's plans are carried out. As we sit here today, an army of white men are making plans to take our little village, and this child is the cause of their plan. They have a key to the city. Tanjee has given them the secrets of the forest, and if we are not ready, our fate will be as hers. Let this serve as a lesson. We are our own people in a foreign land. Look not to the enemy for your deliverance but to each other. Stay together; let me lead you to the life our ancestors planned for our generation while yet in Africa. Let us band together and make these white men wish they had never met Tanjee or heard of the Maroon tribe! I want peace as much as any of you, and I am willing to suffer dearly for it. Are you?"

The audience was stunned by what they heard. An army? Coming to kill them? Their sickness turned to anger at the traitorous ways of their former member. They focused on Gausje. She could see their commitment. She knew the time was now.

"If you are with me, sip of the blood of this lost one to please the spirits. They will be with us in battle." Gausje took the blood-soaked square of cloth, stuck it in her mouth, sucked, and then swallowed. When she removed it, it was completely drained of fluid, only a stain of red remaining.

The crowd formed a line, taking a swath of their own clothes, and they joined in drinking the blood of Tanjee.

CHAPTER 7
THE MIND OF JARED

The mind is uncanny in its way of making attempts to save those too unaware to use it to save themselves. Though Jared had been caught off guard, he immediately made the connection to the bedtime stories of Nanny. Jared shuddered to think that his own version of Detterick was about to happen. Forces were at play here that could not be explained by sciences known to man. No, this was more than natural. He decided to take a walk around the property, hoping to clear his mind and search for clues to piece together the events that had occurred on his plantation. He was mindful to arm himself with more than a whip this time as he moseyed out to the grounds. Looking around his compound, he felt the urge to visit the slave quarters. He realized he heard the sounds of nature because the sound of tools, slaves working the land, and Negro songs had ceased.

He still puzzled at how such a devastating takeover could have been accomplished. He remembered rumors of a slave named Nat Turner, a self-proclaimed minister of God who attempted the largest slave revolt in American history, killing seventy whites, but his tenure as leader and revolutionary was short lived when one of his own members turned on him and told bounty hunters of his whereabouts. They found Nat Turner and killed him. Jared had never before believed the rumors, but now he accepted them as absolute fact. His mind searched for a link as he continued to walk farther into the plantation, not realizing where he had stopped to rest.

Standing in front of Nanny's house, his heart palpitated like it did when he was little. Why did this woman have such an effect on him? Jared nervously looked about; his nanny's quarters were situated a bit apart from the other slave quarters, on slightly elevated ground. Her shack was better than the others in that it had a door that could be closed and locked and windows constructed in the same manner.

As he walked by the shanty houses, he felt subtle shame at their dismal level of disrepair. But why was he feeling this way? These beasts were niggers and thus didn't deserve treatment considered fair to a dog! The battle had left deposits of splintered wood, broken vessels, and other carnage that made these shacks look worse; however, even that shouldn't have made him feel sympathy for niggers. Jared chided himself at the thought. Maybe it was Nanny and his relationship with her that was making him so emotionally unstable, or the fact that he spent too much time with Nanny as a little boy, giving her time to tell him stories that were now coming back to haunt him. "If you grow up to be a good master, then these ills will not affect you." Jared remembered her saying these haunting words to him. Had he been a good master? His father would certainly say no, and he couldn't even blame him. Would Nanny think of him as a good master? Jared's mind raced back to the whipping tree and other actions he had taken that would have made her blood boil. Jared felt the eyes of the other slaves on the back of his neck. It was unnerving just how quiet they were in the face of what happened. It was so quiet one could hear a rat piss on cotton, as his father used to say.

His nanny had died when he turned twenty. She had raised him and many of those people whose eyes were peering at him from their shacks, and they all loved her and missed her. Nanny had shown them what no one else could, and that was how to live. For Jared, when he was little, she introduced him to the nuances of forbidden passion, and thus, in his mind, increased the quality of his life. And now, in death, he felt she had one more gift for him— one more message. He knew there would be a price to pay, but he hoped their arrangement of exchanging pleasure would count in his hour of need.

Jared trembled as he sat down on Nanny's porch. His father forbade anyone to go near the cabin, let alone go in it, and he had refused to allow anyone else to be housed there. Instead, Nanny's quarters served as a shrine to her memory, and slaves would plant flowers and leave makeshift charms by the deserted porch in reverence of her memory and in deference to Master Tolby's wishes. But that was not the reason why Jared shook so violently. No, Jared's mind raced back to his twentieth birthday, the day that Nanny died "before her time," as his father would always say. Again, his mind opened to clearly present to him the events of that horrible night he had worked so hard to suppress.

For the Tolby generations, the twentieth birthday was a celebration of tremendous significance. It was when the father officially signed on his son as partner and heir to the wealth the family had accumulated over the years, a time when patriarchal traditions were passed on—some of which were of a malevolent nature. Jared had never had much success in keeping friends, let alone peers, of the female persuasion. He was clumsy, mean-spirited, and spoiled by his father's legacy. He did a poor job of reading social cues and often embarrassed himself and his family with more than a few social improprieties, like saying the word "breast" instead of "best" when giving a speech about his mother on Mother's Day for his fourteenth birthday, or by wetting his pants after over-exerting himself in a wrestling match with the oldest son from the neighboring plantation. He knew he would lose the match twenty minutes before it ended because he was exhausted. He had kept going until he knew defeat was imminent, but he unexpectedly became incontinent, urinating on himself to the amusement of his so-called friends, who continued to laugh about that incident to this day.

It was well known among the entire population that Jared's father had an ongoing sexual relationship with Nanny, who had raised most of the Tolby family from birth, with the exception, at that time, of Jared. Jared's brothers and sisters often joked about him being different and less loved because he never received the extra attention they did from being attended to by a slave. Jared practically begged his dad to allow Nanny to serve him as well, and he did not understand why he was excluded. The truth was that he did suspect that his father didn't look kindly upon him because he was so socially inept, so his father left him to the charge of his biological mother, a woman Mr. Tolby despised. He couldn't tolerate the minutest of moments with her, and his son Jared wasn't particularly fond of her either, despite her doting on him, trying to take solace in the fact that they had both been excluded from the central figure of the Tolby plantation. But when Mr. Tolby's eldest son mysteriously disappeared, Mr. Tolby decided to allow Jared to be under Nanny's supervision to learn the various trades around the house; it was then the illicit affair and subtle teachings of Nanny began. It got to the point that Jared hated a day that went by that he did not get to work with this slave because of the pleasure he experienced when she finished telling him her stories. They shared jokes, knowledge, and physical pleasure, all of which they both kept secret. Nanny was the only one who treated Jared with any similitude of respect, allowing him to experience himself and his own self-awareness in ways he never could have had he not met her. Ironically, Jared now realized that it was Nanny who taught him how to manage the plantation through her open conversation and her patient ear and responses to his many questions. His father never allowed him that, and had Nanny gotten to him sooner, he imagined he would have been more efficient at the matter—but, alas, that was his father's fault.

On the twentieth birthday of the son, the father would clandestinely take the men to one of his barns where hay would have already been placed in a series of sacks, and a frightened young slave girl would be held for what would either be consensual or coerced sexual activity. Jared heard his brother speak of this night with much lewdness, and it developed a deep-seated anticipation within Jared's mind. He had wanted a woman to desire him for him, and the only one who seemed to fit that description was his nanny. No one knew of his intimate experiences, but Jared maintained the charade so as to keep the tradition going. He didn't want anyone taking away this privilege thinking he did not deserve it because he had become an experienced lover. Never mind it was with an older woman who was his nanny, who had also borne four bi-racial Tolby children by his own father. He liked feeling her warm, calloused hands on his privates; he enjoyed the inviting wetness and fullness of her womb; and she showed him secret sexual acts his brother never mentioned, even when he was being ribald.

The day was going as planned—a big breakfast feast in the morning, a special song sung for him by the slaves, dancing and various other entertainment put on by the slaves from his father's and the neighboring plantation, to be following by an evening boxing match fought by the biggest and toughest slave either plantation could find.

Everyone was invited to stay for the fight, and everyone would always oblige. A huge fire would be built in the center of the plantation, and women would bring food and blankets to sit on and watch while the men stood and drank beer or whiskey. The ring was a giant circle of barren earth around which was dug a one-foot trench. The rules of the ring were simple: fighters were to stay in the circle or forfeit a point to the opponent; fighters weren't allowed to quit; and the fights were always determined with a knockout. Even if fighters were knocked out of the ring, the frenzied crowd would often kick them back inside for more brutal punishment. There were times when the fights ended in death, much to the relished enjoyment of the crowd. Slaves, having pent-up aggression, never quit, and the fights were always vicious and bloody. An overseer usually kept watch in case the two brutes decided to turn their attention to beating up one of the unsuspecting masters and flee, but the tradition had continued for so long that no slave attempted escape; instead, the slaves actually prided themselves on being the best fighter for their masters. The depravity was so deep even Jared himself was awed when he witnessed, during a Thanksgiving dinner, two slaves fighting over which one had the best master.

Tonight, everyone was excited because Mr. Tolby had brought out one of his toughest slaves, a slave they simply called Buck. Buck had huge shoulder muscles and heavy pectorals that inspired the female slaves to lord over how handsome his body was, despite his mean-looking face. Buck was nearly seven feet tall and weighed close to two hundred ninety pounds, every inch of him pure muscle. His abdominal muscles flexed involuntarily when he breathed, and his back rippled over its heavy muscular frame when he made even the slightest movement. His thighs were the size of barrels, and his huge feet were up to the task of carrying this giant without difficulty. Known for his mean temper against other slaves, Buck had beaten a man down more than once for violating rules by which only he lived. He was gentle with the women, however, and never got into a spat with Mr. Tolby, because he and Mr. Tolby had made a lot of money traveling from town to town, staging fights against other slaves and betting on who would be the victor.

Buck had remained undefeated, and his body didn't have any wear or tear other than the protruding eyebrows of a fighter and a mashed nose that was made even more prominent as it was already wide. Mr. Tolby treated Buck well and allowed him even occasionally to eat in the big house, but whether it was in the big house or in the field house, Buck always ate well. His chore was keeping fit, and as long as he was winning fights and cooperating with Mr. Tolby, the whip never touched his flesh.

Buck was readying himself in one of the barns with one of the slave hands, getting oiled down to prevent skin cuts and lifting and tossing away large bails of hay in order to get ready for the fight. Mr. Tolby and the owner of the neighboring plantation, Mr. Coltan, had both been drinking profusely when Mr. Coltan raised his glass to settle everyone down before the match began. No one knew who he'd brought to the match this evening, and none of the foreign slaves attending Jared's birthday celebration looked like a match for Buck. Mr. Coltan waited until everyone was silent, his eyes ablaze and still sharp even while intoxicated, his cheeks slightly flushed.

"Ladies and gentlemen, on this auspicious occasion, Jared's twentieth birthday, I thought it would be a fine time to give Jared an opportunity to win money to add to the great wealth Mr. Tolby has already established." Coltan paused for effect, and the crowd "oohed" their approval.

Coltan continued. "I have recently purchased a fighter I strongly believe can and will destroy your Mr. Buck, and I have ten thousand dollars in my possession as a sign of my good faith." Mr. Tolby continued to sit quietly, and from the look on his face, no one could tell that he was completely intrigued. "I'll wager that my slave will beat yours, and if I win, you owe me not a single dime. If my fighter loses, then you will have become ten thousand dollars richer."

Coltan paused again and, barely holding back a sneer, looked, with raised eyebrow, at Jared and Mr. Tolby for approval. Jared stood ready to take the bet, but a glance from Nanny prompted him to stay put and remain silent. No one but Jared caught the exchange, because no one but he looked to Nanny for direction. Jared's upbringing and environment influenced him to believe that no good could come from a slave except labor, but experience and respect had informed him otherwise. Never before had Nanny led him wrong. But, he now looked to his father, who took his cue and spoke.

"Well now, I 'spect a little wager on my son's birthday is in order. And I jus' love takin' people's money, even friends'." The audience chuckled at this, and Coltan smiled. Mr. Tolby had a genial way about him when he wasn't dealing with slaves. "Cept I'll heighten ya' wager. Let the fight go to the death. If my Buck loses, then you take any one of my prized negras, plus ten of my best horses." With that, Mr. Tolby swallowed the rest of his whisky and put his glass on the tip of his armrest, indicating he needed a refill, which was promptly brought by one of the house servants.

The crowd became a mixture of buzzing excitement and dismay. Fights to the death were never looked upon kindly by slaves, and no one wanted to be traded to another plantation because life could always get worse, rarely better. Jared glanced at Nanny, who wore a look of absolute consternation mingled with anger. He remembered her stories of the "bad- blooded" niggers, and he felt a bristle briefly flitter down the back of his spine. He sensed that this wasn't right; still, he had every confidence Buck would win, as no one could match this slave's brute force and intensity.

By now the sun had set, the large fire casting shadows against the trees and the faces of those who surrounded it. The sky was cloudy, and there was an illuminating presence above the clouds that made them look like bright pillows slowly wafting across the atmosphere. Yet, instead of a bright white appearance, the clouds had a reddish dull hue. No one paid them any particular attention, but Jared kept noticing Nanny glancing at the sky and clasping her hands together nervously. Such behavior was unusual for Nanny because she was never nervous no matter what. What was it about those clouds that made her uncomfortable? Jared assumed that it was the fire that was casting its fiery presence into the sky and thought nothing of it. He was anxious to see the fight but more anxious to see what girl his father had selected for him to have sex with. It wasn't until a strong breeze caused the fire to toss sparks carelessly into the conglomeration of anticipating faces that Jared realized what was bothering Nanny. It was the moon. The breeze caused the clouds to ease out of the moon's glare, and Jared saw what looked to be the angry eye of God staring right through his soul. The moon was blood red. Never before had Jared witnessed this, but his mind recalled the stories that Nanny had told him. But those tales, although extremely believable, couldn't possibly be true. Always in the back of his mind his faith wavered, and he only accepted the stories as fantasy. But now he knew he was witnessing a phenomenon. The hammering of his heart told him so. He was so enraptured by the moon that he didn't see the prize Coltan had brought with him, or how smoothly Nanny slipped away from the events. The chattering of the crowd caught his attention. The young children of the white plantation owners were running about in a frenzy, and the women were nervously clutching each other's arms and covering their mouths as Coltan's slave stepped into the circle. Jared glanced back at the moon before reality riveted him to his seat as he looked back in the direction of the slave.

In the middle of the ring stood a monster with only a vague resemblance to a man. The darkness silhouetted a body that was equal to Buck's, if not bigger. The flicker of the flames shimmered off the monster's black, oily skin. The beast wore just a loincloth, which barely sheltered his privates. The man's hair was coarse and wild and, upon closer inspection, had what looked to be roots, or leaves in it, as if a bird had made attempts to nest inside its atrocious mass. His face was in a constant contortion of blank pain, and drool haphazardly oozed from his parted lips. He looked at no one and made no other move but to stand, bow-legged, in the middle of the ring, breathing heavily. He wore around his neck a large metal collar to which was attached a heavy chain held by an equally ominous-looking overseer. Another man stood nearby with a rifle and a whip coiled about his belt. The caution Coltan and his overseers took alerted everyone that this slave was a dangerous man, and the crowd responded with heightened excitement.

Even Mr. Tolby looked astonished by the sight, his mask of emotion completely ripped away in the face of such manhood, such brute power. Mr. Tolby's mind was signaling that he might be making a mistake. Why would Coltan make such a generous bet to benefit Mr. Tolby's clumsy son unless Coltan knew that there was no way the beast could lose? Jared looked at the slave's body again and noticed that his flesh was striated with scars from head to toe, wounds bearing testimony that this slave had probably never known a moment's peace in his miserable life. Even his face had scars on it. Jared rose from his seat for a closer inspection. Although the fire was bright, the flames could only illuminate so much. Jared bravely walked closer to the ring. The slave turned his head to look at Jared but made no move with his body. Mr. Tolby uncharacteristically spoke a warning to his son.

"Don't ya' get too close, Jared. This boy taint right in the head." As Jared turned to acknowledge his father's words he heard the chains jerk to life and the slave utter a guttural sound from deep within his throat. It was taking two taskmasters to pull on the chains attached to his neck. They were practically choking the slave, but he made no move to relent his attack. His naked feet dug hard into the earth as he lurched for Jared, spit frothing from his mouth. Jared noticed that one of the slave's eyes was milky white and that his two front middle teeth were missing, which made him look canine. Jared stumbled back, perspiration instantly coating his back. The crowd was now operating in another mode entirely. Gone were the genteel mannerisms so lauded in the south, and in their place were raucous laughter and shrill screams.

The scene seemed to move in slow motion as servants continued to serve beer and whiskey. Jared wondered where Nanny had gone, and again his eyes, although he tried hard to resist, involuntarily moved toward the moon—dazzled by its brilliant redness. At that moment, Jared sought to have his father stop the fight. He sensed that this just wasn't right. The slave's other eyeball had rolled up in his head as he strained with all his might to get to Jared, who still sat dumbly near the ring line. When one of the taskmasters shouted for Jared to get away from the ring, he quickly obeyed. The taskmaster with the rifle shouted to the beast, and he returned to the middle of the ring and resumed his dumb stare at nothingness, the slobber continuing its deluge down his wet and heaving chest. This slave was an animal. Jared made his way back to his father.

"Pap, dis don't feel right. Don't take this bet. Buck cain't take this nigger!" Mr. Tolby pulled a cigar from his front vest pocket and slowly struck a match, careful not to let the night's wind extinguish his flame. He cupped his hands over his cigar, took care in igniting it, then tossed the flaming match to the wind were it was caught in the breeze and blown out. As he inhaled the rich smoke, he eyed his son with contempt.

"Boy, this here life is a gamble. And if ya don't learn to take risks, ya never realize the po'tential of what ya life could be." Mr. Tolby took another deep inhalation of the cigar smoke, then chased it with a sip of whiskey. He addressed his son. "Buck is a beast of burden, yes, but he ain't no ordinary animal. He's learned, in his own niggardly way, ta outwit every opponent, and he'll do it 'gain tonight. Buck has never let me down, and if he was not a nigger, I would almost believe him capable of minor thought. Trust me son, the beast who damn near took ya head off in the ring on your twentieth birthday is gointer ta suffer his death tonight. So try to relax and not ruin a good evening. We gonna make an easy ten thousand dollars." With that, Mr. Tolby clapped his son on the knee and ordered Buck to be brought to the ring.

When Buck stepped into the lighted circle the crowd cheered. His bald pate shone, and his muscles bulged, his intimidating size making him a full two heads taller than his opponent. The crowd went wild when the shackled slave started to pace back and forth and occasionally leap at Buck, who just stared at the poor fellow with animosity. One of the taskmasters stepped into the ring and used the butt of his rifle to hit his slave in the back of the knee, while the other pulled the chain attached to the collar around his neck. The slave knelt down and relaxed while the taskmaster with the gun pulled out a key and released the slave from the chain. The slave remained in the kneeling position until all were cleared from the ring. Then all hell broke loose.

Buck's muscles were primed and ready. He tipped from toe to toe, keeping his body lithe and limber while moving his arms in a circular pattern and tucking his chin close to his neck as he eyed his opponent. The beast hurled itself at Buck with lightening speed, but Buck quickly sidestepped the attack and heaved a fantastic punch at the creature's jaw that broke it, immediately drawing blood. The crowd screamed its approval; Mr. Tolby slapped Jared's knee again and gave him a whimsical look that said, "What I tell ya?" The creature, apparently stunned, shook his head, drizzling the earth with blood and saliva, while Buck danced away as fluid as a leaf blowing in the wind. Mr. Tolby never tired of seeing how this heavy beast of burden named Buck could move so effortlessly without growing tired.

Buck saw the slave stoop over and quickly enclose the space between them for another punch, dealing a series of punishing blows to Buck's unguarded abdomen. Buck let out a grunt and backed up, attempting to evade any further damage to his torso when the slave again hurled himself full throttle at Buck, pushing him with both hands so hard that Buck lost his balance and fell to the ground. The beast leaped on top of Buck and began clawing viscously at his face and chest. The crowd, now screaming for Buck to get up, was on its feet.

Jared and his father rose from their elevated seats on the porch and hurried down to the crowd, where they had to push their way to the front. Mr. Tolby hollered at Buck to get up. Buck cast two fierce blows to the slave's face, and when that did little to thwart the beast, Buck went for the privates and gave them a powerful squeeze until he felt them burst and give way in his hand. The slave let out another grunt and leaped up from Buck, holding his privates. Those close enough to the front could see a viscous fluid leaking down the sides of the slave's muscular thighs, and the men in the crowd instinctively bent over involuntarily in imagined pain and sympathy. The women just stood open-mouthed at the monstrosity of manhood that bulged out from between the slave's fingers.

Buck got to his feet, blood shining on his black face and visible wounds weeping on his chest. He had never been downed before, but he had never fought an opponent like this before. Rage took over momentarily, and Buck ran over to the hunched-over slave and delivered a well-aimed elbow to the creature's exposed back. Both went down in a deluge of flesh, and the beast writhed violently on the ground while Buck pummeled fierce and punishing blows to the creature's head, neck, and back. Buck leaped up and tried to come down on the creature's neck with a foot stomp, but his giant foot only slammed into bare earth. The slave was quick and seemed impervious to pain. The vicious blows that Buck already delivered would have sent most men either to their deaths or caused them to pass out, yet this beast rolled away, its guttural voice still grunting, and executed a well-timed kick to the Buck's shin. Buck howled in pain and jumped up and down on his other foot. Just as the beast was getting ready to attack again, the gun sounded, signaling the end of the round, and Buck instinctively hopped outside the ring while the slave creature, still slightly stooped holding his privates, simply stood in the middle of the ring, staring into blank space, allowing drool and blood to flow from his now slack jaw.

Mr. Tolby hurried to Buck. A slave had run over with a metal cup of water, which Buck hastily drank. "Buck, are ya gointer to be able to take this beast? Ya hurt?" Mr. Tolby questioned.

"I don't know, sah. Ain't never fought nobody like dis befo'. He a tough one." Buck exclaimed the last line with a certain pride, although Mr. Tolby was certain the correct response should have been fear.

"Want me ta stop the fight, son?"

"No! No sah, Mr. Tolby, sah! I'se gointer take dis one down, sah. Jus gointer take me a little time, sah," Buck confidently retorted.

"Well, I hope ya right. I hate to lose ya to this here animal. But if you say ya all right, go on and beat this animal!"

With that the signal was given to begin the next round, and Buck hurried back into the ring. Many noble attributes could be given to Buck, the most prominent his bravery, which he exhibited this night. Buck regained his legs and was once again bobbing and weaving, avoiding relentless attacks and issuing punishment unwaveringly to the slave, whose face was now becoming a massive heap of swollen flesh. The sound of Buck's powerful fist slamming into the beast was unsettling, like a hammer being brought down on a swollen stomach. Each blow was delivered with accuracy and determination, and the slave was starting to breathe harshly between gasps while Buck seemed to only grow in strength. However, Buck was in reality beginning to tire, and by the fourth round, the knuckles on his fists were raw. The people marveled at how his opponent kept getting up and fighting, not once going ringside to break or drink water or get instruction from his master. He simply stood, hunched over, in the middle of the ring.

Jared noticed that both of Coltan's slave's eyes were nearly swollen shut, and it was only then that he had confidence that Buck would finally be able to end this brutal match so the men could get on with the night. The fifth round signaled, and Buck was back at the beast when the slave hurled a huge upper left-hand blow to Buck's exposed neck, followed by a strong kick to Buck's gut and a body charge that sent him tumbling to the ground. The slave then leapt on top of Buck and took a savage bite at his cheek. His teeth ground in Buck's soft flesh and dug themselves in until they could go no further. Then, with a mighty wrench, the slave twisted his head and body with full might, coming away from Buck, leaving a visible trail of blood on the ground. People in the crowd screamed in the horror while Buck desperately clawed at the side of his face, which now looked as if he was wearing a permanent smile. His teeth glistened in the gaping hole the beast left in the side of his face as intermittent spurts of blood gushed out. Buck's eyes were wild with paranoia, and he clawed at the earth, screaming for someone to help him.

Jared instinctively moved toward the ring, but his father's strong grip held him back. Jared eyed his dad in hatred as his father shook his head "No," although Jared could detect sorrow in his father's face. Buck kept screaming, "My face, my face!" But it sounded more like, "My fashe! My fashe!" The audience gasped in disgust as the beast chewed Buck's cheek and then swallowed it.

The beast then sniffed the air, his eyes nearly swollen shut now, until he turned in Buck's direction. Buck was still lying on his back, twisting in pain, when the next attack came. The slave leapt into the air to land on Buck, but Buck kicked his foot into the slave's exposed stomach. Fluid sprayed out of the slave's mouth as he was repelled from his attack, but he ran back for more. Buck started kicking fiercely until the slave caught his leg, hugging it tightly while falling to the ground with a twist. Jared winced as he heard the leg snap with a loud crack. Again, Buck's screams filled the night.

More wood was thrown on the fire, and the flames lit a gory pit of blood about the two wounded men. Buck was now on his side, trying to move away with his remaining good leg, pushing against the earth, but the beast was all over him, slapping Buck's face and punching him in the head, neck, and stomach. The slave's sinewy muscles rippled with each movement, delivering pain and violence. Coltan, who had all the while been silent, let out a raucous yelp and shouted, "Finish him nigger! Finish him!" Several of the female slaves screamed out, "No!" but this only incited the men and Coltan, who continued to hoot and holler, "Kill that nigger, nigger!"

Buck looked helplessly at his master, Buck's powerful body sprawled on the ground, his teeth peeking out between torn flesh. He groaned in soft words, but no one could understand him. The beast fell on Buck in what seemed a full embrace, but soon Jared and his father realized what he was doing. The beast of a man had wrapped one powerful arm around Buck's neck and with the other pawed at Buck's eyes and nose until his calloused fingers found their mark. One of Buck's eyes gave an audible pop as it flopped out onto the place where he once had a cheek. The glob of jelly wriggled violently, and a black substance oozed down his sweaty face. As a scream escaped his lips, his body tensed. Every muscle bulged while Buck fought to hold his neck in place, but the slave fought incessantly, consistently against him. With one hand he continued to punch at his opponent, miraculously landing solid punches against an already scarred, swollen face, but to no avail. Buck's strength was waning. The beast exerted more pressure, his bulbous eyes straining against the tight constraint of his swollen eyelids.

Buck's throat became constricted as he experienced the raw burning sensation of air trying to get in and out of a valve that is nearly closed. Only he could see the motes of tiny bright lights that popped into his vision, and only he could appreciate how pretty the lights looked juxtaposed against the black night. Buck's remaining eye found Mr. Tolby, pleaded with him and, for a moment, its gaze was beyond sorrowful, encapsulating all that they had shared together in one long, tenuous moment. Finally, Mr. Tolby turned away from the sight. All sound began to slowly fade from Buck's hearing, and in one final attempt at strength he cried out, "Massa!!!!" as his neck broke, the sound like a ripe melon being struck by a wooden spade.

A lady at the front of the crowd spewed vomit into the trench around the ring, fell on all fours and collapsed, her head and arm inside the arena of violence. A man beside her tried to keep her from falling, but the frenzied crowd, in their bloodthirsty exhilaration, pushed him down. People were shouting and slapping each other on the back, aroused by the brutal nature of the fight. Children were crying for their parents; a man nearly fell into the massive bon fire, and loose sparks caught his hair and started smoldering as he frantically beat himself about the head.

Mr. Tolby had fought his way back to his chair on the porch, and, while no one was looking, quickly dabbed his handkerchief against his moist eyes.

Oddly, he felt a terrible loss with Buck, whose crumpled form lay still. In the commotion, no one noticed the inhuman slave crawl over to the woman who had fainted. Drool bubbled from his mouth each time he made that guttural sound. Every two feet or so he would sniff the air and pat the ground until he found himself touching the woman's soft hair, drooling in it. A man who tried to save her was immediately rendered unconscious as the slave delivered a quick punch to the man's face. The slave started to pull the woman toward him, slowly awakening her from her stupor, and dragged her fully into the ring. Shadows pranced along the fringes of the scene, shedding light onto what was happening in well-timed glimpses. The dragging of the woman's body against the ground created a friction that slowly ripped the shirt from her torso, causing one breast to flail about, carelessly exposed. The beast sniffed and found it with one hand while the other tore violently at the rest of her clothes. Coltan was laughing loudly on his way back to his chair when someone shouted and a gunshot went off, but the crowd, captivated by what had just happened, paid no attention. When Coltan turned around to see the beast pawing at a white woman, he quickly sobered up.

"Get your damn hands off of her, nigger! Get off of her! Get your damn hands off!"

Coltan reached into the lining of his coat jacket, opposite where he had the ten thousand dollars, and pulled out a pistol that he repeatedly fired into the air until the crowd gasped at what they saw in the middle of the ring. The woman was now completely topless, and her bottom garments had been ripped off enough to partially expose her privates as the slave began to shed his loincloth. Men intuitively grasped for weapons of any sort, horrified at what they were seeing. The woman, still dizzy and semi-conscious, weakly but ineffectively pushed against the slave's powerful approach. Coltan rushed to the front of the crowd, placing his body between his slave and the angry mob, and cocked the pistol against the slave's gruesome temple. He had to protect his investment but at the same time stop this travesty.

"I'm goin' blow your damn brains out!" He shouted. "Control yourself, nigger! And come away from her!" Spit flew from his mouth as he spoke, and his lips shuttered violently. "I said come away!"

The slave looked at his master and began to retract from the woman. Coltan swung a mighty blow with the butt of the gun against the slave's head, but he merely huddled on the ground and continued to make the guttural sound. The two taskmasters, now alert, ran into the ring with the chains and locked them to the shackle this beast's neck. Then, upon Coltan's nod, they began whipping the slave unremittingly until he was a bloody heap. But he let out no scream of pain, and still he lived.

"Take the nigger to my coach, and get the hell out of here. Someone attend to this woman!" Coltan ordered. The nervous crowd had started to disperse. Jared walked over to his father, a queasy feeling overtaking his stomach. Just as he was about to sit down, his father got up and mumbled, "Happy Birthday. I am going to bed." He began to walk toward the house, but Coltan hurried up out of the ring to catch him. Before Coltan could remind Mr. Tolby of his debt, Mr. Tolby said, "My son will show ya our best horses and take ya to the slave quarters ta have ya pick." He held out a hand to Coltan, but he barely had time to shake it or look into Coltan's eyes before Coltan responded.

"I thank you, sir. But I won't be taking any of your horses. The debt was mine to bear if I lost. But seeing that I didn't, I don't want to entirely spoil the day. Besides, the crowd loved the fight, and your Buck fought valiantly. It is a shame to lose such a beast. However, I will take you up on your offer for a slave. I already know who I want." Mr. Tolby looked surprised.

"Who?" He said.

"Nanny." Coltan replied. At that, Mr. Tolby could take no more. The tide of his emotion at losing his prize fighter had already brought him to the brink of despair, but the thought of losing his mistress, the mother of his mixed children, and one of the best hands on the property, was too much. His anger got the best of him.

"Not on ya life, Mr. Coltan! Ya know how much Nanny means to this family! She practically raised all mah children. She's a mighty fine woman."

"You don't have to sell me on her worth, Mr. Tolby; I realize it and desire it. And it was you who made the generous counter offer, remember? I know you to be a man of your word, Mr. Tolby. Have I misjudged you?" Coltan was collected and in control. He knew how to play this situation. It was a pity that men let pride get in the way of their judgment, because the price was always high.

"I am a man of mah word, Mr. Coltan. But won't ya please consida and pick anotha slave? There are plenty of young, beautiful mixed servants, even virgins, that I am certain will meet ya fancy in many ways. As a matter of fact, why not take two of mah young mulatto girls? Togetha they will fetch a high price on the auction block, should you decide to sell them. That is a reasonable offer, Mr. Coltan."

"Your offer was for any slave of my choice, and I select Nanny. Now, if you are going back on your offer, Mr. Tolby, then simply say so." Mr. Tolby's reputation for being a fair man when it came to his betting was renown throughout the South. He knew that Coltan would spread word of this loss, and that it would be verified by his taskmasters and the few people who were still loitering around waiting for the next part of the evening. If he was to spare his reputation, Mr. Tolby was going to have to sacrifice his best servant. But his mind was working on a way to save face and keep Nanny.

"She'll be sent ovah tomorrow, Mr. Coltan. You have yourself one hell of a beast. I've nevah seen anything like him before, and now you'll have a great servant gal. Treat her well."

"Thank you, Mr. Tolby. I am reassured. Your honest reputation is stalwart, to say the least. Trust me, Nanny will be in good hands. I look forward to her delivery tomorrow. Well now, on to the next activity?" The smug look on Coltan's face was enough to incite Mr. Tolby's own version of violence, but he kept his voice calm and even.

"I'm old and need to rest. You and your men may continue in the activities. Jared, I am sure, is anxious. Speaking of Jared, wasn't he just right here?" Mr. Tolby and Coltan both were looking for Jared, but all they saw was the torn-up corpse of the mighty Buck.

On his journey home, Coltan relished in his victory. His slave, who'd he never bothered to name, sat quietly in his cage, situated in the rear of Coltan's luxurious coach. Coltan prided himself on his well-crafted carriages shored up by metal that was still pliable enough to provide shock resistance against bumps in the road, the lanterns on the side providing class and illumination in the pitch-black darkness that overtook the south after sunset, and the retractable steps that flung themselves out and downward after the carriage door was opened.

Yes, Coltan lived a life of luxury, and he was about to increase his pleasure and wealth with the death of Buck and the newly acquired Nanny. Coltan despised the fact that Mr. Tolby had been so careless with his affair with a nigger woman that he had actually allowed her to give birth to several of his children, even caring for the damn animals. Tolby was an embarrassment to the South, and he had to be dealt with. When Coltan had seen this nigger on the auction block more than a year ago, he knew he had the key to fixing the problem. He didn't want to destroy Mr. Tolby; he just wanted to save him from his own destructive behavior. Nanny would meet with a swift execution, and one member of the inferior race would no longer contribute to the unnatural lust and fornication between slave and master. With a rapid flick, Coltan urged his horses forward home.

Jared had raced to the slave quarters where he hoped to find Nanny. The moon's red eye traced his rapid steps as he weaved around the farm tools to head down to Nanny's shack. A deep mist had risen and made the way perilous, causing Jared to trip over an object in his path, sending a resonating pain from his left foot up his shin. He decided he had better slow down. A low buzz of talk floated toward him from slave huts, no doubt of the destruction of their hero that night. Jared still had difficulty accepting what his own eyes established as truth—Buck was dead, and now Nanny was to be traded. This could not happen. Who would he talk to and make love to? Who would guide him and tell him the truth about life? Certainly not his father.

Jared was now moving at a slow pace. The chirping of crickets made a rhythmic harmony that only they could achieve, and the rustling of leaves had been stilled in the absence of breeze. Whereas the sky had been dotted with clouds, it was now just naked atmosphere, allowing the red of the moon to burn even brighter.

The door to Nanny's shack was open, and the steps creaked as he tentatively placed his foot on them. "Nanny?" He whispered inquisitively, timidly. But there was no response. "Nanny!" His inquiry was more urgent this time. "You have got to git out of here. Are you there? It's me, Jared!"

The only answer was silence. Jared quickened his movements, went across the small porch and in through the front door, quietly closing it. He reached in his pockets for matches, found one, and went for a lamp when he heard a splash, as if he'd stepped in a puddle. He paused and opened his eyes as wide as possible, hoping to let what little light that might exist in this quiet place to filter in through his widening pupils. He fumbled around briefly, looking for a rough surface on which to scratch the match, finally striking it on a plank of wood on one of the walls. He lit the match, and it momentarily cast a reddish halo around his now trembling hand. Jared instinctively sought the lamp and lit it, creating a moderately stronger nimbus of light to cast away the darkness. Though the beam shone in all directions, he caught no sign of Nanny. Perhaps she went to the big house, but he doubted she'd go there because Mrs. Tolby did not care for Nanny at all.

As Jared pivoted with the lamp, the light fell to where he had once stood, and he saw a dark puddle that was thickening on the floor. Bending down to investigate, he touched the substance with his forefinger—it was sticky. He held the forefinger to his nose to catch a scent, but the liquid was not foul smelling or urine or feces or mud. He then held the forefinger to his tongue and tasted it, and he found it to be salty. As Jared did so he heard a burping, gagging sound come from Nanny's bed. Jared froze; the hair on the nape of his neck stood ready for attack, but Jared was paralyzed with fear.

Jared rose from his stoop too hastily, and his foot slipped in the substance on the floor, which he now knew was blood. The lamp radiated eerie shadows on the walls of Nanny's shack. In an instant, Jared breathed a prayer to God to keep the light from going out, and in that same instant he received confirmation. The flame, although flickering, remained lit.

Jared tried to regain his composure, but his breathing was ragged and hurried. He walked over to the bed and saw a white sheet covering it, but a large dark spot was emanating from the place where Nanny's head usually lay. Jared slowly realized that a person was lying under the sheet. He thought for a moment he saw the area where the stomach normally would be move with breath. He had to satisfy his mind so, with shaking hands, he reached for the tip of the white sheet that he horribly surmised would be covering the head of the person lying there, and ripped it off the body.

He screamed as he realized it was Nanny, staring straight up into the roof, her eyes wide open, her throat slit, a trail of blood leading from her throat to her hand that dangled off the side of the bed, still holding the weapon. Air bubbled from her compromised esophagus, and Jared realized that what had taken place in the confines of Nanny's shack had happened very recently. His eyes watered as grief began to rack his body with turmoil. No matter how hard he tried to resist his sorrow it only intensified. Jared held his head in his now blood-soaked hands. He rose on his knees and brought up the lamp to look in Nanny's face and was frightened by the look of peace upon it. The cut on her throat was smooth. Only then did Jared's mind begin to recognize the image before him.

The sheet was pure white, except where there was blood. The covers had been pulled over Nanny's head, which meant somebody else did this to make it look like suicide. But who had committed this murder, and why? Jared was so immersed in his thoughts that he didn't notice the figure easing down from between two ceiling beams, headed right for his back. Jared just stood gazing at his friend, his mentor, as a thick hand reached out for his shoulder and seized him. Jared dropped the lamp and, this time, no prayer was incanted; the flame went out as a sharp pain erupted in the back of Jared's skull. He slumped over, face-first, in the pool of blood, unconscious.

When Jared awoke, he was still in Nanny's hut, but the blood was gone, as was Nanny's body. There was a black man sitting with his legs beneath him, simply staring into Jared's face. Wrath flared in Jared's soul as he looked at this man; he tried to rise up to strike him when he realized his hands and feet were bound tight.

"Please, Massa! Don' try ta resist. Nanny made me!" The servant exclaimed. "I know ya luv'd her, even tho she jus' a lowly servant gal, but we both know that Massa Coltan would have hurt po' Nanny to no end. She beg me to relieve her, Massa! She beg me send her home to her 'cesters, whar dere be no mo pain. I had ta give her what she wanted, Massa."

"You killed Nanny?" Jared's voice quivered with the question.

"I he'p her home. She beg me for it, sah! It's a heavy burden to be'ah. She asked me for passage to da place of da dead. I 'bliged her. She safe now, Massa, free from rape, torture, free from dis horrible life. A life she neber was sposed to live. Her work here is done, sah"

Jared's mouth trembled with hatred. The tears flowed hotly down his cheeks, and he fell on his side, his hands and feet still bound. He began kicking and beating his head on the floor, screaming. He allowed hate to burn in his throat, in his thoughts, in his muscles. How could this ignorant, pompous nigger take away the only person to whom he connected? He hated this nigger—and that hate extended itself to all niggers. He would make sure they paid for this impropriety against him. The Tolby name would be feared among slaves, and he would gain his father's respect. Nigger. Nigger. Nigger! Before long his thoughts evolved into words and he was screaming them when his father and friends rushed to find him, bound and bruised, in Nanny's cabin. The man to whom he talked that night was never seen again.

CHAPTER 8
THE COLONEL'S DISCOVERY

The low sun was already starting to nestle to its base in the west, its rays setting off sparks of light that glimmered slowly then dissipated from Hearns's line of vision. As he rode he thought about his plan. When the sun was at high noon, Tanjee would set off a smoke signal from within her tent. Two puffs of smoke would mean the village was ready for killing. Three puffs of smoke would mean wait an hour, the plans weren't quite ready yet. One puff of smoke would mean he had better retreat. And she had given him the key to unlock the doors to the Maroon's fort-like city, making the attack all the easier.

The heat was making him sleepy, and Hearns wanted to get home fast. It would be nightfall before he reached the outskirts of his property. Just the thought of it made him even more tired. He dug his spurs into the lower belly of the horse and picked up his speed to a slow gallop. As he rode he thought of the last night he had with Tanjee, and suddenly he felt alive as blood began to flow to his groin. The plan was going to work. He had every confidence in Tanjee's ability to carry out her plot. She was a clever girl—after all, she'd made it to his plantation many times without being caught by her people or his. He'd doubt if his men would have the agility or heart to dare attempt such a feat.

A smile crept across his face as he thought about the brilliant children they would have. His kids were spoiled by their overly protective mother and had her dull wit. He'd wanted so much more from his kids and desired to give them more, but his poor relationship with his wife constantly clogged up the resources of his goodwill until only disdain remained. But he and Tanjee, well, that would be a different story. She had not argued with his plans; she understood his plan and even added direction of her own. It was her idea to split his soldiers into two groups. She said that if the guardians of the forest caught wind of the attack, they would collapse on his men from behind and trap them in the city. With part of his troops outside, that attack could be countered. His wife could have never thought of that, not in a million years. His new life would be one of contentment.

An owl hooted softly. Dusk was fast approaching, and the embers of daylight were growing dim. Hearns's horse had slowed down to a trot, so he spurred him back to a deliberate gallop. His mind turned to Gausje and the weird tales Tanjee had told him—stopping bullets, being able to run over leaves without making a sound, Tanjee's own escape, Gausje showing Tanjee their love-making in a puddle of water. These thoughts made him shudder involuntary. Hocus pocus bull, that's all it was. Hearns crammed his mind with reassurance. These were the stories of Africa—just old African wives' tale!

"Can't nobody stop a bullet!" he said to himself, once again imitating the dialect of the slaves. He chuckled to himself at the way he sounded alone on his horse. After all the carnage he'd seen, it was good to laugh at something. But he still felt stupid despite his vain attempts to sober up. "Ya don't know da haf of it, shuga! Des got strange ways!" As he mocked the superstitious slaves again, he started laughing hilariously. Tears welled up in the corners of his eyes. "Strange ways, my eye! We'll see strange—how strange a face looks after it has been shot!" He removed a flask of whiskey from his saddle pouch and took a long swig. He just couldn't stop chuckling. He guessed his silliness was because he was sleepy. What the hell; no one was around to see it.

Hearns had been riding on an open dirt road, but now the way turned through a cane field, with stalks at least twelve-feet tall. Hearns was thankful for the shade that the tall cane provided from the weakening yet still powerful stare of the sun. The scent of cane pleased him, and he "whoa'd" his horse to a stop. Perhaps chewing on a piece of cane would wake him up. His eyelids were beginning to grow heavy with the coming darkness. Hearns stopped his horse in the middle of the road. A slow breeze picked up, and the cane began to sway. Hearns hopped off the horse and walked to the right side of the road to the cane. He fastened his hands around the cane at a joint in the stalk and broke it. When the cane gave way with a loud crack, he saw he had more than enough. He would save the rest for his children. Even though they were dumb and dull-witted, they were still his.

Hearns broke off a piece and began to peel back the green skin that protected the nectar of sweetness hidden beneath. As he bit into it he relished in the sugary splinters that filled his mouth. He drained every bit of sweetness he could out of his first chew and spit the useless dregs on the ground. His horse snorted and neighed. "Hey there, boy, what's got you all turned up?" He took another bite of the cane and chewed it and spit the plug into his hand; then he held his hand under the horse's flared nostrils and fed him the cane. The horse eyed him suspiciously before slowly chewing the cane, but then he stopped. Had the horse heard a sound? Hearns broke the stalk and put it in his saddlebag, then casually walked around behind his horse; he noticed its leg muscles twitching. His horse only did that when there was someone around he didn't know. Was there someone there? Hearns's hand involuntarily moved to his pistol. He thought he heard coughing coming from within the cane field.

"Stay, boy." Hearns commanded the horse. As he walked cautiously into the cane field, he withdrew his pistol. The cane continued to sway back and forth, and Hearns found himself moving with its fluid motion, his body ducked down in a predatory position. The coughing grew louder, and the cane grew thicker. Hearns could barely see what was ahead of him save a barrage of green. It was then he heard a faint "Help me!" coming from up ahead. Someone was in trouble. Hearns increased his pace. He didn't know how far he had gone, but he knew he could get back by simply following his trail.

Suddenly, the thick green of cane field broke open into a wide barren patch where all the cane had been uprooted or broken. Hearns heard a gag and more coughing and nearly fired his pistol from unexpected shock. There, lying in the middle of the cane brake, was a young man bound hand-and-foot with a black cloth tied tightly around his eyes and nose. His chest heaved as he took in frantic gulps of air. A mucus membrane was billowing in and out of one nostril, and blood drizzled from his wrists and ankles. His mouth was clapping open and shut like a fish out of water, and he coughed as if he were drowning on oxygen. Hearns took a step closer.

"Auugghh! Get back! Get away from me—cackk! cacckk!!"

"Ho there, son! Calm yourself." Hearns retreated back into the cane field for cover and knelt down on one knee. He cocked his pistol and surveyed the cane as he attempted to detect the presence of another, the person who put this poor boy down. Hearns couldn't tell. The swaying of the cane prevented it. Well, at least whoever else may be out there would have a hard time seeing him as well. "Who put you here, son?" Hearns harshly whispered.

"Who are you? How—how did you find me?"

"I was traveling home and heard you cough."

"Get back, 'for they get you! Get outta here!" The young man wailed as he was caught in another fit of raging coughs. "They got strange ways, mister. You best make your way back to the road before they get inside you!"

"Just who and what in the hell you talking about?" Hearns was getting angry. He was just worrying about dey strange ways in the privacy of his mind, and now he was here in the middle of a cane field hearing this stranger talking about the same thing. "Just point the way. Where are they?"

"They are inside me." More coughs.

"Okay, enough of this foolishness. I'm going to cut you loose. You're bleeding pretty bad. Just hang in there." Hearns believed the poor man was hallucinating. He decided he would take the man back home and see to him, nurse him back to health. Then he would get to the bottom of what had occurred.

The suffering man's face bore prodigious fear. He was salivating like a rabid dog, and the blood running from his wrists had quickened from a drizzle to a moderate stream. Hearns crouched closer to the cane break and then rolled out into the open. He looked around cautiously, then re-holstered his pistol and retrieved a blade from his pocket to start cutting the black ropes from around the man's hands and wrist. The man's chest was still heaving, and Hearns stepped back in case the man got sick.

"Let's get you out of here." Hearns reached to grab the man's wrist when a stream of blood and mucus bubbled up out of his mouth like a fountain and spilled down the sides of his cheeks onto the ground. The man's eyes rolled up into his skull, and the whites almost seemed to glow. His mouth arched open into a hollow, and Hearns could see the man's tongue stretch backward toward his tonsils. He was having a seizure. Dropping his weapons to the ground, Hearns ripped off his leather belt and folded it into a thick strap. He pounced onto the man's chest and pinned his arms down to the ground. The thick, foaming saliva and blood had stopped, and Hearns could see a strange object in the back of the man's mouth as he again coughed violently. Oddly, Hearns's mind registered the man's frantic belly heaving up and down under his haunches. He took a closer look, and could not believe what he saw.

It looked verdant inside the man's mouth, like a blooming leaf unfurling its wings at the presence of dawn. Hearns was stunned with disbelief. Suddenly, a bramble of vines, leaves, and roots spewed from the man's gaping mouth, ripping the corners of his lips. The vegetation poured out viciously and dug into the ground around the man's face. The raspy sound of leaves and gorged vines made Hearns's skin crawl. He blurted out "Oh my God!" as he scrambled to his feet. The man's face was barely visible underneath the mass of living greenery, and his hands and feet were thrashing violently against the ground, his head tightly pinioned to the earth.

Hearns now scrambled around in near darkness. The sun had set, and its red residual light was all that was left to illuminate night's approaching darkness. All Hearns could hear from the man were muffled gags. Hearns fumbled in the near dark for his weapons' belt, finally locating his pistol. Without even thinking, he fired three shots into the branches that were hideously emerging from the man's face. The loud pops of the pistol made the goose bumps on Hearns's flesh stand high, and the retort of his weapon forced him to stumble backward. Now, he was the one breathing hard, so hard his lungs burned.

Hearns stared at the man again in utter bewilderment. The up-and-down heaving of the man's chest had finally abated, and he lay on the ground, motionless, his hands sprawled out from his sides as if God had flung him to earth. Hearns stared, hoping to see the heaving resume. Praying, he took a step forward but stopped abruptly.

"Oh my God!" To his amazement, Hearns witnessed the leaves, vines, and tiny twigs retracing their steps out of the ground back into the man's mouth. The man's head wobbled back and forth on his neck as they retreated, making thick, raspy noises. Hearns fumbled for his matches, drew one harshly across his coarse pant leg, and watched a flame burst forth. He held the match to the man's face and cursed.

"Who the devil are these people?" The vines, leaves, and twigs retreated until they were no longer visible. Three wet, gaping holes shown in the man's face; from his eyes issued a calloused stare. Hearns blinked, but the cold stare remained. He holstered his gun and frantically ran back through the field as the cane slapped his face rudely, leaving tiny, thin cuts across his cheeks and his hands. He was frantic and lost. He tripped and fell over a thick clump of dirt. His brimmed hat tumbled from his head. He groped for it briefly, then resumed running wildly, leaving it behind, trampling cane under foot, falling, yelling, and praying. Hearns stopped when he felt his lungs would melt with fervent heat. He was angry and scared. When this man was discovered they would believe him to be murdered and would seek justice. Hearns could not afford to lose the liberties he'd experienced or the novelties that came with his military position. He had to get out of here. "Think, Colonel, think! You're a soldier!"

Hearns then realized his horse was not where it should have been. He called out to him with a whistle, and then sat in silence. Nothing. He whistled for him again and waited. Finally, he heard a faint neighing and ran frantically in the direction of the sound.

Hearns hopped onto his horse and spurred him into a gallop toward home. "When I return, I will bury the body if no one else has found it yet." Jumpy, he constantly looked back over his soldier. Colonel Hearns was scared. Flesh and blood he could stomach, but what he had seen this evening dashed away all the false notions of bravery he had tried to fill himself with a couple of hours ago. What he just experienced was similar to the stories he'd heard from Tanjee, and from now on he knew he would always be a believer. He would make one change: he was taking one hundred men instead of fifty.

Hearns wished he could sleep in Tanjee's arms tonight. She'd be the only one to keep the scene he'd just witnessed from returning over and over to prevent him from his quiet sleep. His only comfort was knowing that, soon, they would be reunited forever.

CHAPTER 9

THE GATHERING OF SPEARS

Looming, sharp spears tightly woven together formed the circle of death surrounding the arena. There was a hustle and bustle of activity as eager tribe members hastily hurried to their assigned posts. Each member of the council had a special seat of wood on which was engraved an insignia of his or her tribal caste. Gausje took her seat in the center. The memories of last night with Tanjee, the tribe member who had been caught sneaking out to visit her white lover at a plantation just ten miles from the camp, were still fresh in her mind. That Tanjee had a sexual relationship with Colonel Hearns during her years of servitude and had grown fond of him, despite her slave status and her lover's occasional mistreatment, still bewildered Gausje. He had even beaten her nearly to death one night when she refused to pleasure him and a visiting friend simultaneously, and she had suffered a most severe rape. It was in the weeks that followed that a mysterious man had befriended Tanjee and told her of the Maroons, people who had the power to rescue her. She later came to know him as a Maroon brother whose mission it was to seek out those who truly wished to be saved. She pledged herself to the tribe, and they fulfilled their end of the bargain. She was rescued without bloodshed, but her haughtiness had led her to be judged with blood of her own.

Tanjee's was the first punishment of its kind to be witnessed by the entire Maroon village. Most sessions were private, with only members of the council attending. In the case of inducting a new member to the Maroon tribe, the council was open to all; children, women, the old, and the young all made their way to the gathering of spears. The new member would either meet new family or cruel death, depending on how he or she responded to the terms of initiation.

All believed that the newest member of the Maroon tribe, Jakeel, would fare much better. Isiki was quite curious to see Jakeel under normal circumstances. His first memory of him was as a bloody conglomeration of tissue, his true features a deluge of disfigurement. Isiki had taken his position as chief of the warriors when he finally caught a glimpse of the one whom Gausje had risked the lives of his men to save. He thought Jakeel had noble features: a broad nose, thick hair, a muscular frame, sharp eyes like a hawk, and a humble disposition. His black skin resonated power and purity and made his white loin cloth glow in stark contrast. Isiki believed that Jakeel could be trained to be a great warrior like himself.

Jakeel sat in the center of the gathering. All eyes were on him; all awaited the voice of their leader, Gausje, who sat in absolute silence until she was ready to speak. Finally, she gracefully gathered her robes about her and stood amid the council. The fluidity of her actions worked wonders to soften that fact she was absolutely bereft of beauty.

"Today we have among us the one I've dreamt about, the one whose name was whispered in the night's song of freedom, death, and new life— Jakeel." She paused and fondly cast a glance down on Jakeel's lowered head. He lifted it, and their eyes met as she addressed him directly. "I am happy to welcome you to our humble habitation."

"How modest," Isiki thought.

"But I must ask you to make a promise in order for your presence here to be accepted." The audience remained hushed. They hoped he would accept the terms for fear of another execution. The community, although they agreed with Gausje's decision and subsequent explanation of Tanjee's execution, had not totally recovered from what they had seen.

Jakeel sat still as stone, his eyes riveted on Gausje, a pang of trepidation piercing his heart as he feared her request might be more than he could fulfill. Unknown to the Maroons, he had witnessed Tanjee's demise as well, and though he feared Gausje, he had certain standards he would never break. He felt his sacrifice at Jared's plantation was sufficient. He knew the Maroons could have rescued him sooner, but Bella had told him in order for the gods to be pleased, they required blood. And so his blood was shed, and he had received his reward. Or so he thought. What more could the tribe want from him?

He noticed a hulk of a man rise from where the warriors were sitting. His skin was not black but fair and reddish, which stood in great contrast to the pure black hair that draped across his shoulders as neatly as a woman's. He looked to be middle-aged but as fit as the one who rescued him. On both cheeks were two tattooed stripes of red, and a white stripe of paint ran down the length of his aquiline nose. He wore a leather loincloth and had on his back what looked to be a sheath with a leather strap crossing over his right shoulder. Jakeel observed that the man's muscles flexed without effort as he walked and took a position directly behind him. Gausje continued.

"You must swear a vow of silence of our existence, of our community and its whereabouts, and our system of order. You must not speak of the strange events you will witness and have witnessed here already." She allowed him to catch a glimpse of a smile. Had she known he was watching the execution? He felt childish, as if he had been caught doing that which he shouldn't have been. The crowd sat ignorant of the secret the two shared. "You must reveal nothing of our village to any outsider, black or otherwise, lest you open yourself to death. This may mean you may not see your family again. But you will have the full protection and embrace of your new family here, and the powers that bind us. Do you swear to this, Jakeel, former slave of Jared?"

Jakeel sat; all was acceptable except not seeing his family. He wanted to see them so desperately, and, even more, he wanted them to be delivered from the vices of slavery, even at the risk of life. Jakeel had two daughters and a wife back at the plantation. He considered his options, then raised his head and answered the tribal leader.

"Yes, Gausje, I will do all you have asked."

"Well done, Jakeel." The large man returned to his seat. Jakeel realized that if his answer had been no, he would have promptly discovered what was hidden in the leather sheath on the man's gigantic back. He wondered how a man could get to be so big. Jared thought about his next move and then dared to make it.

"Ma'am? Permission to speak?" Jakeel spoke in the humble way taught him by his master. Gausje looked upon him with contempt, then sympathy.

"My name is Gausje, Jakeel. You may address me by my name. You must work to forget the patterns of servitude. In our village, all are equal. And soon you will play a significant part in the liberation of this wicked land. What is it that you want to say, Jakeel?"

"My family—would it be possible to rescue them as well?"

"That depends on you, Jakeel, but we shall speak of that later."

"Thank you ma'am—Gausje. Thank you." Gausje made a motion addressing the whole community.

"Jakeel shall now be part of us. He is to be treated as a brother and a friend. Keigei, you shall teach Jakeel the ways of the Maroons, all her secrets and the power of the spirits."

Another man, who was not black like Jakeel, stepped forward from the council. He, too, had long flowing silky black hair. His frame was well suited to hoist the muscular build he obviously developed through many years of arduous work. He wore a cloak of deerskin with feathers symmetrically embroidered in the pattern of an eagle. As he walked straight toward Jakeel, his cloak parted to reveal a pattern burned into his chest. It appeared to be two jagged lightening bolts intersecting each other inside a circle. Jakeel figured the man had been branded, like most slaves. Jakeel had never seen this type of people before, but he imagined that they were former slaves, and that explained the secrecy of the community. He didn't even remember how he had gotten to this place, but he did know that everyone had treated him well. In fact, he had never been treated so kindly in his entire life. Keigei offered his huge hand to Jakeel. Jakeel reached out and clasped Keigei's hand, and Keigei promptly picked him up without effort. Keigei took him to the council seats and they both sat down—Keigei in his seat and Jakeel on the floor.

Isiki remembered what it was like on the day he first became part of the village when Phoenix Sun had taken him under his wings. He knew Jakeel would have much to learn in the days to come, but he looked like a capable pupil. Eerily, Isiki's mind went back to the naked woman on Jared's plantation. She knew his name and his mission. She even knew of his personal vendetta against Jared. He knew only the spirits could have told her of these facts, but he marveled at the fact that this obviously powerful woman was remaining in a state of servitude. Why? Surely, with her power, she could escape. Why did she remain under the oppression of Jared? What was her relation to Gausje? Did the Maroons purposefully place her on Jared's land? Why is Jakeel so important to Gausje? All these questions were about to drive him mad, but he was guided back to reality by the sounds of the crowd.

The community rejoiced. Here was one more person who would no longer have to experience the hardships of slavery. Thinking that all was well, they sang and danced around a big fire in the center of the circle of spears. Even Gausje, who at many times seemed aloof from the others, danced with the children, and sometimes alone, but smiled all the time, showing flashes of love and good will through her hideous face. It was amazing how the children didn't even flinch at the sight of such ugliness; they reciprocated Gausje's love unabashedly. This truly seemed to be paradise.

As the fires died and the people sauntered home, Gausje called a meeting of the soldiers. Everyone was there except Keigei and Jakeel. They were sent to the Kalehari forest where Jakeel was to complete the lessons first started by Bella.

"By noon tomorrow, an army of white men will be in the swamps in an effort to attack and destroy our village. This is a result of Tanjee's treachery, but her sacrifice has been accepted by the gods, and I have discovered his plan."

The soldiers sat in eager anticipation of their method of counter attack. It was almost unfair for their opponents because they were always a step ahead of them. At times they wished the elements were even, but then none of them asked to be here in this country. They would have been content to be in their own homes in their own lands, with their extended family and their own soil to till. They had been pillaged of all rights and desecrated from their once-lofty human existence, relegated to the level of beasts. They and their loved ones had been raped—both men and women—by their white masters, beaten, and killed. It was good that the tables had turned. Now the white man would get a taste of his own evil. The Maroon warriors also had to consider that, although they now had an advantage, there was always the price of blood that had to come from one of their own. Was the sacrifice worth it? No one really hesitated in his or her response to that question. Of course it was! They had seen so much senseless bloodshed that bloodshed for a worthy cause seemed more than reasonable.

"We will know when these murderers will be coming. Their leader is awaiting a signal from Tanjee. We will give him the signal and allow him to enter the city. Phoenix, you will tell the tree guardians to do no harm to the men and not to impede their advancement on our refuge. I want the enemy to walk right into the city. Tanjee gave the soldier directions to get here and the key to the great doors. Isiki, you and your men will all be here in the circle of spears." Isiki nodded. He was uncomfortable with that command because it placed his men and him in a trap. If Hearns entered the gates without conflict, Isiki and his men would be easy targets from firearms.

"Have your bows lined up and pointed to the sky and fire at the hawk as soon as it screams. Wait until it screams again, then pour out of the circle and lead your attack toward the city gates." Isiki's confidence returned as he began to see the brilliance of Gausje's plan. There was a slight commotion among the soldiers as they nodded at each other silently with an air of confidence and assurance. At that moment, Keigei and Jakeel joined the group and bowed before Gausje. The mixed emotions of pleasure and irritation at their unannounced presence flickered briefly over Gausje's face but ended before anyone could determine her true emotion.

"Forgive me, Gausje, but Jakeel insisted that we be present at this meeting when I told him it was about plans for the battle tomorrow." Raising an eyebrow at Jakeel's boldness, Gausje smiled faintly.

"The gods are wise in their choice of you, Jakeel. You are brave."

"Gausje, I don't know what the gods want of me, or how I can be of help to your village—" Jakeel was interrupted.

"Our village. This place is as much a part of you as it is of me, my son. That is why we are here. We must protect it and the service it renders to the rest of our impoverished brothers and sisters."

"I want to help protect it, Gausje, yet I cannot do that in the forest of Kalehari. I want to be involved here!" Jakeel spoke rather forcefully. Looking at him with a deep penetrating glare, Gausje took his face in her hands firmly.

"Then so be it. You and Keigei shall resume your training after the battles, for there shall be two. Be seated; Isiki will catch you up on what we have discussed so far."

Isiki was incredulous! This newcomer had just barged in on their meeting and shown disrespect to their leader, and she had done nothing about it. If he had done the same, he would have been punished. But instead Gausje took Jakeel's face in her hands like a loving child. Isiki thought that for Jakeel to receive such treatment, he better be able to walk on water and through fire!

"At the second scream of the hawk, a dark cloud will descend upon the city; it shall mask the shower of arrows that will return to our earth with a vengeance. The men will be struck down, scared and confused. Isiki, you take the charge and wipe out every last soldier possible. This, perhaps, could be our biggest kill. Save all the bodies and take them to the circle for a sacrifice. The moon will be blood red, and our sacrifice will be accepted. We must not hesitate in favoring and responding to the blessings of the gods. The time is now for our liberation!"

The men shouted and raised their swords, excited and confident that the gods were on their side and that they would suffer little loss. All, that is, except Jakeel. He just sat and absorbed the import of what was to happen tomorrow. He'd seen enough killing, whipping, and dying. Was there no limit to the amount of blood the earth would have to drink? He wanted to be a part of it, but not in this way. This was too much like what the white man had done to him, and it was now leading to their revolt. Might not an act like this result in retribution from the white man, causing the cycle of death to never end? There had to be another way. Jakeel's mind was moving frantically, attempting to identify a viable solution that would not send him floating onto a spear of Gausje's anger.

Isiki noticed the contemplative and apprehensive look on Jakeel's face. It took the spirit out of his celebration as he felt anger swiftly overtake him. He hated that about his character. Phoenix had tried to exorcise it from him during his training but had failed because Phoenix had a few demons of his own to fight. But Phoenix had instructed and warned him about the benefit of discipline, and Isiki's lack thereof, when it came to controlling his temper and passions. Phoenix warned him that if he did not learn to manage it, it would be his undoing; Isiki had been working ever since to overcome it, but he just couldn't help himself. He had failed by trying to kill Jared, had failed by accosting Tanjee and getting angry and jealous because of her choice of men, and now he was failing again because some quality about Jakeel made him uneasy. He tried to keep silent and continue with the celebration, but Jakeel's morbid stare just angered him. He wondered why Gausje didn't notice it and make a comment. Perhaps she did and was just ignoring him to later make a point of her power. And why her recent need to constantly demonstrate her power? Everybody knew she had great favor with the spirits; there was no need for her to prove it. She was respected and feared— for what more could she ask? She was being greedy.

These thoughts built up in Isiki in a matter of seconds and, before he could stop them, he blurted out, "What's your problem, Jakeel? You can't stomach a little bloodshed?" Isiki's men chuckled. "You should have stayed in the forest. Can't no trees hurt you there." The chuckles turned to outright laughter. "I guess after your last tree incident, you're probably scared to death of trees, huh boy?" Isiki sneered and glared at Jakeel. He'd called Jakeel a boy, and Jakeel had ignored it. He was weak. But Isiki's glowering was cut short as Gausje bruskly smacked him across the face. It stung fiercely, but what stung more was the public reprimand and humiliation he suffered from the one he respected so much.

"Once again you disappoint me, Isiki. There is lesson to be learned from Jakeel. Taking the time to think about an action is more beneficial than time spent in regret once an impulsive response is made. Jakeel, what is on your mind?"

All eyes pivoted toward Jakeel. He still sat humbly before Gausje. He paid them no mind, just as he had ignored the taunts of Isiki. Years of slavery had taught Jakeel to disregard the calloused words of hate. It was because he had reacted to words that he was put on the tree in the first place. He looked directly at Gausje and spoke slowly, hoping the answer to his dilemma would come as he spoke.

"Gausje, you are wise and have the gift of magic that most will never attain. I could only hope one day to possess your foresight. But this act that you speak of—this grand sacrifice—I feel it's wrong. There has been too much bloodshed already. Are we not becoming like our white oppressors? I sense evil and feel there has to be a better way."

Phoenix spoke. "The enemy is going to come to us, young one. We didn't invite this bloodshed; he is bringing it upon himself. What are we supposed to do? Let him come in and take us willingly?" Although Phoenix was upset at Jakeel's inquiry, he did not allow his voice to reveal it.

"No, we should defend ourselves. But to kill Hearns and all his men and offer them up as a sacrifice, that's brutal, and it's just like what the white man did to us. Then he will—" Keigei interrupted Jakeel's argument with a firmly raised hand, his dark eyes focusing unwavering on Jakeel.

"No, the white man came and killed many of us and made the rest of us slaves. He uses us for his pleasure as well as his labor. He destroys our families and our minds. We can no longer think right, and then we begin to turn on one another because of his curse. It is because of him that such evil exists. He gave my people diseases, sometimes killing off an entire tribe by giving them blankets in a gesture of kindness—but those very blankets were filled with disease, so that all in the tribe died. You must recognize that this type of evil must be wiped out entirely. And if the white man chooses to walk into the hands of fate, so be it." Keigei's eyes were glistening with hurt and hate. Jakeel was beginning to realize the cruel fact that hate begets hate, and hate's offspring would be hard, if not entirely impossible, to abort.

"Why not capture the leader and use him as ransom for peace between the Maroon tribe and the white man? Grant us peace and put it in writing. The white man puts much honor in his written word, right? Then there is not so much bloodshed, and we have a pawn to use in this war to finally put an end to it." Jakeel felt better about what he was arguing for. The ideas were coming to him, but Gausje spoke before Keigei had a chance to retort.

"Jakeel, you have spoken what you think to be wisdom, but you lack the benefit of experience or the advantage of maturity that I, Isiki, and Keigei have. I am dismayed at your boldness of speech in light of your ignorance. Be careful to think more before you speak in the future. You assume that we have not considered long and hard all that you have mentioned here today. Trust me when I say that we have. Keigei knows even more than I about the white man's treachery. His tribe was wiped out because they trusted the written words of the white man. They believed he would grant peace when instead he provided persecution. He tricked them into fighting each other, just as now I see the white man's influence on you as you speak in his behalf today."

"But—"

"Silence!!!" Gausje's raised voice caused the hairs on the backs of everyone's necks to stand at attention. "No bloodshed? Foolish boy! You'd ignore all the vices that he has put our people through, us through, you through! Have you forgotten how you were nearly beaten to death by your master? Jakeel, the only way to stop this cesspool of evil is total, unmitigated erasure. Nothing must be left behind, no stone unturned. We must let them know we are no longer going to take their oppression and abuse. But more than that, we are not going to allow them any longer to hurt our brothers and sisters who have yet to be liberated!" Gausje rose from her seat to address not only Jakeel but also the rest of the men before Jakeel interrupted.

"Can't God handle that?"

"He already has, son." Her eyes were bright with fury. "He already has, and tomorrow you will see and be a part of his handy work. We will stamp out this soldier's men and will sacrifice their bodies in the circle!"

Isiki couldn't help himself. He at first thought Gausje was softening up, melting in the presence of Jakeel, but he now realized that she was in full control. He let out a war cry that Phoenix, Keigei, and the rest of the soldiers quickly joined. Their cries rose up to the heavens, high enough for the gods to hear. Gausje stared at Jakeel momentarily, and she then raised a hand for silence, which came immediately.

"I've yet to understand your purpose here fully. I shall speak to the gods tonight in hopes that they will help me see more than what has been shown to me today, my son. Now, you listen to the plan that I've devised and be prepared to obey."

"Yes, Gausje." Jakeel spoke, humbly. Isiki relished the moment and, again, his love and admiration for Gausje was rekindled. He would give all he had for her in battle tomorrow.

Chapter 10

Sowin' Seeds

Bella crept back into her cabin without a soul realizing her coming or her going. Life had been quiet on the plantation ever since the massacre that followed Jakeel's escape and Zelia's death. Jared was visibly depressed, and his cruelness or kindness was dealt out with a monotonous indifference. Bella knew something significant was going to happen soon, even though the details were still unclear. The slaves on the plantation were enjoying a peace never before experienced in the Tolby generations, and she would relish in it, too, even knowing that it was the quiet before the storm.

Recognition came soon enough for Bella while she was working in the field planting soybeans that same day. After thirty years, she'd become accustomed to the routine of planting. On the Tolby field, one hundred slaves would work the rows. Five slaves were assigned to a row of ploughed field, their job being to fertilize, weed, plant, cover, and water. It was a constant up-and-down motion, and the Tolbys insisted on enforcing a certain rhythmic singing and swaying—it helped to keep the slaves moving. A leader would call out a phrase, and those working the row would respond.

Bella was working the thirteenth row when it came to her. The sun was a hue of orange in a bright blue sky, dotted by cotton ball clouds that moved at a sloth's pace, the wind barely noticeable. Bella wished for a gentle wind. She wasn't feeling well, and she began meditating to make the day go by faster and to lessen the weariness caused by the wet heat. Beads of sweat poured off the bodies of the slaves, causing their clothes to stick to their flesh.

Bella wanted a drink of water but was halfway down the row and knew returning to the front would result in a flogging, and being flogged during this blaze would result in sure death. No, she decided to bore ahead and rest in the shade of the trees at the end of the row. By the time the overseers saw her she could get up and start working her way back down the row. She prayed to the gods for just a breeze only to see a wave of heat shimmer in the distant end of the row, billowing toward her. She began to feel light-headed, her skull itchy and heavy, her mouth filling with spit. No matter what she did, she could not gain her equilibrium. Her feet were as heavy as stone. Recognizing that she was going to throw up, she began to swallow repeatedly. The green leaves blurred, cleared, and then blurred again. Bella fell down on all fours, her fingers digging into the earth. She touched a form that was cold and hard, and she clamped her hand around it as her vision cleared. She saw it was a seed. Tiny dots danced about her eyes like motes in a ray of light before they suddenly flashed into one bright, white light. All Bella could see was the seed in the bright light, but her dizziness began to abate. She wondered at the light emanating from the seed and saw tiny flints of green peaking in and out between the bright flashes.

Suddenly, a hot stinging pain shot across Bella's back, ripping her attention from the glory of the seed. Bella was slow to move, and her brain had not yet registered what was happening when she felt a warm trickle spilling down her neck. She shook her head to clear her mind and pocketed the seed but took time to look up to see the taskmaster holding a whip and pointing his finger at her. He looked to be shouting, but she could not hear his voice. Her hearing was muffled, and she only saw his mouth moving and flecks of spit flying from it as he shouted down at her while pointing at the row. She realized now he had hit her with the whip and was preparing to strike her again.

Slowly, Bella began to rise to her feet, but not fast enough for him. This time the burning sensation hit the side of her ear and lower jaw. At last, she got back to her feet and again began working the row. A tide of anger swelled and crashed on the beach of her soul. She knew she could not stop for even a second without the taskmaster bearing down hard on her, but the sharp pain of the whip never lost its surprise.

Now the whole side of her face was warmed with her blood. The other slaves continued to work the row as if nothing had happened, purposely not looking at Bella or the white man glaring down on them from his horse. They just wanted the day to continue without the shedding of their own blood. Bella used her anger to fuel her muscles into completing the task at hand, channeling her energies into regaining her equilibrium, and relishing her imagination of the sweet revenge she would have upon taskmaster Ivan. Oh, he sits high on his horse, savoring in his power, Bella thought, but Bella knew she needed to concentrate instead on the days ahead when Ivan would regret the hour he ever laid the whip on her flesh. Ivan made no effort to allow Bella to clean or fix her wound; he just whipped at Bella's feet if he felt she was slowing down.

Bella worked six hours more before the workday ended, an amazing feat to anyone who observed it, but, unknown to the others, every time Bella felt the slightest fatigue or illness coming on, she would put her hand in her pocket and touch the cold seed, and her strength would miraculously be renewed.

That evening Bella returned to her quarters, her clothes covered with dried blood and caked with the dirt and dust of the field. She only had one other pair of working clothes, and they had to last her all year. She removed her shirt and set it in a boiling pot of water, which she did nightly to soak out the debris of the day's labor. She removed the seed from her pocket and inspected it. Nothing magical happened. Bella raised an inquisitive eyebrow and pondered for a moment. She replaced the seed in her pocket and walked over the earthen floor to the center of her hut where she daily kept a small fire going. She sat there, reflecting over the strange feeling she experienced earlier that day. Bella again removed the seed from her pocket and began turning it over between her fingers.

Even though it was dark and the moon had fully risen from its hiding place, the air was still stifling. Bella fanned her face with her free hand, perspiration flowing uninhibited down her neck and cheeks. She placed the seed by the fire and prepared to say her evening mantras to the gods of her homeland, as she had been taught long ago. Unlike other nights when she would ask for guidance and deliverance and for the time that her service here on the plantation would be done, tonight she was interested in this seed, and she wanted the gods to explain to her its significance. She knew that a seed of this type had to come from the gods, which was the only explanation for what she experienced in the field that day.

She reached for the staff that was lying against the wall. It was a wooden carving of a python, the form her god at times took when communicating to its subjects. The rod quivered momentarily before it coiled down to the floor as a living serpent. It proceeded to wriggle its way across the floor to the place where Bella was sitting; it erected itself and again formed a solid staff ready for her embrace. She took the staff between her hands and knelt before the fire, closing her eyes and beginning her mantra, not seeing that the seed was beginning to glow and vibrate softly on the floor of her hut. The wooden staff was solid between her palms, and she felt the tiny crevasses in the woodwork as the wood became clammy and tenuous, transforming into the flesh and the muscles of a strong serpent, undulating underneath her firm grasp, creating an unnerving tension. Bella never quite got used to the cold-blooded feeling of its flesh; it just seemed unnatural for a living and breathing creature to feel cold.

Slowly, she opened her eyes to see her master before her. The snake hissed, its black tongue flickering in and out of its mouth. When she released it from her grip, it coiled to the floor like a feather falling to the ground, with grace. Its skin was bronze, and its eyes glowed like burning copper. She watched the snake intensely as she had been taught. The elders made it clear that when communicating with the gods, every movement indicated a message. The snake first swallowed the seed Bella had retrieved from the fields; Bella watched as the seed formed a bulge as it traveled down the serpent's throat. It took about ten minutes for the seed to become fully lodged within the snake's digestive system. Then the snake unhitched its jaws and gurgled as branches and vines scrambled frantically outward onto the ground, forming patterns. They squiggled on the earthen floor like worms exposed to light when their rock has been upturned, making them vulnerable. Bella noticed that the vines seemed to be forming into a shape. What she saw explained the cause that she must next fulfill—the branches had transformed into a ragged four-leaf clover. Many years of training in listening to the spirits prepared Bella for interpreting difficult messages, but this one was easy. It had to deal with what Irish people called a good luck charm, and Ivan was Irish.

A few more cackles from the serpent and all the vines were out of its mouth. It elevated the first seven inches of its neck, indicating it was ready to leave. Bella clasped her hands around it once again, lifted it until only the tip of its tail touched the ground, and as quickly as it had become a snake it was again a carved wooden stick. She knew instinctively that her wishes in the field would be granted. As she was walking the serpent rod back to its proper place within the shack she heard a strange sound—it was the vines. Bella ran back over to the fire to see all the branches and vines retreat into the seed.

Bella looked at it, an innocent seed yet one full of magic and power. Instinctively, she knew she needed to keep it safe for some still unknown future purpose. She sat back by the fire and contemplated what had occurred. This could be an answer to her prayer, the final act that would appease the gods, allowing her to escape this plantation and join the Maroons and her Gausje.

*****

Jakeel was sitting in a lavish hut that had been prepared for him by the tribe members. It had provisions for dispelling waste, a fire pit, a smooth floor made of wood, a bed hewn out of the large trees, a bow with a quiver full of arrows, and food to last a week, all at the behest of Gausje. It was comfortable, slightly better than most in the Maroon village, with the exception of the huts of the soldiers.

Jakeel was satisfied with his new accommodations, but Tanjee's death still haunted him. All the violence and strange occurrences were making him question whether it had been such a good idea to confer with Bella about collaborating with the Maroon tribe in the first place. Slavery was horrible, and he had no choice in leaving Jared's plantation because, if he had stayed, he would have surely been killed, but maybe it didn't have to be like this. The amount of blood the tribe was about to spill was significant, and all the events to which Jakeel had been exposed only led to confusion.

He remembered how he ended up getting flogged on the day of his deliverance. He had been caught reading, a habit he had acquired from his mistress, who taught him to read when he was a young boy. She did so against her husband's wishes and ran the risk of criminal prosecution; nevertheless, she was undaunted in her insistence on doing what she called "The good Lord's will." She used the Bible as her textbook, starting from the beginning. Jakeel enjoyed learning, and he definitely relished in gaining the power to read. He found the stories of love, failure, treachery, and deliverance quite fascinating, and it was the deliverance stories that most attracted Jakeel to the Bible, especially those of Moses against Pharaoh. He was intrigued by this powerful king of Egypt who enslaved a people and made them build his kingdom, but still God delivered them to freedom through His servant Moses.

Jakeel couldn't understand why Mrs. Tolby would teach him to read from a book that spoke out against the very enterprise she and her husband labored over so tediously. She was always so arrogant when she instructed him, smacking him when he couldn't pronounce a word that she felt was simple. Her temper was just as bad, if not worse, than her husband's. Jakeel wanted to talk about what he was learning, but he did not wish to incur her wrath. He struggled hard with the words and was full of questions. Finally, one day, he had been brave enough to ask his mistress about God, and her face lit up.

"Ma'am, God seems so nice and loving, even though people treated him mean; how could he stand it, being so powerful? Why didn't he just strike back at those who hurt Him?"

"Why, Jakeel, I do believe that's the smartest question you ever asked me! The Reverend Freemund says that God's ways are not our ways. He doesn't manage business the way we do because He is so full of love. He wants to save us and take us to Heaven to be with Him forever, so that meant He had to sacrifice His most precious son."

"Why sacrifice His son? Why not sacrifice all the evil men who did bad to Him? That makes more sense to me," Jakeel said in earnest.

"No, dummy, you wouldn't give a rotten tomato to feed your child as a gift, would you? Evil men are spoiled, and they would not do as a sacrifice that gives the gift of life! Jakeel, you have to sacrifice something pure in order to get something pure in return. That's why only Jesus would do." Mrs. Tolby smiled at herself, prideful of making her explanation so clear that even a nigger could understand. She saw the look of enlightenment in Jakeel's eyes, and she was proud that she had done her Christian duty to spread the gospel, but her gloating was cut short by another question.

"Ma'am?" Jakeel felt his lips quiver slightly.

"Yes."

"You taught me to love God, and to try to be like Him in all that I do." Jakeel paused to receive his mistress's response.

"Yes, Jakeel."

"And to practice walking in His ways."

"Yes."

"Now, from what you read to me in Exodus, it seems to me that slavery is not the way of the Lord. That's why He chose Moses to free the Israelites. It seems to me that slavery is all wrong, and I don't think God is pleased."

A stiff smack across his mouth interrupted Jakeel's speech. He hadn't seen it coming because he was so carried away in his argument. The salty taste of blood filtered into his mouth, and his thoughts were dashed away by his mistress's rude mistreatment. He stared at the floor, not daring to look at the vile hatred coming from his mistress's eyes. But curiosity overwhelmed his sense of self-preservation, and he continued to speak while looking at the floor.

"I don't mean you no disrespect, but from what you say this is wrong. Either you are wrong or the Bible is wrong, and from what you taught me, I'm willing to bet it's not the Bible. God don't like no slavery!"

Jakeel almost screamed the last sentence, his heart was so sure. Mrs. Tolby got up from her seat so abruptly it fell over with a loud crash. She nearly ran to the corner of her office where she kept a leather whip. She let the coils fall to the floor for only a moment before she rushed upon Jakeel and lashed at his face with three quick blows. The first two came so fast that he didn't have time to put his hands up in defense, and they left two welts under his right eye and across his bottom lip and chin. The third strike caused a wound right along the edges of his wrist. He fell backward, away from the oncoming attack, and curled up tightly on the floor, writhing back and forth like a wounded animal.

"Please! Stop it! I won't say no more. Have mercy!" Jakeel sobbed. What had he been thinking? He was angry with Mrs. Tolby but even angrier with himself for losing control of his mouth. He knew better than to speak this way; now, he was paying for it. She glowered over him, striking him three more times. Although he was fully dressed, the short cracks from the whip caused his skin to welt and bleed underneath. Jakeel longed to snatch the whip away from her, but he knew that would result in his death. He continued to plead for his life.

"Please ma'am!" he gasped, "Please stop! I'm sorry for saying that."

"You are the most ignorant nigger I ever met! That'll teach you to open you mouth when you don't have anything of worth to say!" The effervescing school teacher was gone, and the all-too-familiar Tolby was present.

"Oh, Lord, forgive my mouth for saying words that do not please you. And forgive Jakeel, for he knows not what he says." Mrs. Tolby's eyes bore down on him with a glare that spoke disappointment, and he gazed in return with amazement as the anger just displayed drained slowly from her face. Mrs. Tolby slowly gathered her composure before she spoke again.

"I ought to beat the devil out of you for what you said, boy! And you should realize that is it only by the grace of God that your exhibition of weighty ignorance was demonstrated in my presence only. Not everyone on this plantation knows and respects the good Lord the way I do. And you well know if any other person on this plantation were to hear you say a niggardly thing like that, you'd be headed straight for the grave!"

Mrs. Tolby coiled the whip and stood over Jakeel's body, her emotions stirred by his rousing question. His earnestness caused her great indignation, making her feel embarrassed. Remembering the words her pastor had said to her when in her own Bible study, she recognized now was the time to teach those words to Jakeel.

"Get up and bring me my chair, boy!" Jakeel obediently did as asked. He wasn't that hurt; he'd taken far more severe beatings for offenses far less than this one. What hurt him most today was the unexpectedness of the whip coming after what he considered to be a calm and interesting Bible study. He set the chair upright and held it in place for Mrs. Tolby to sit upon.

"I appreciate your lessons, ma'am, I guess I be makin' my way back."

"Sit down, Jakeel." Mrs. Tolby straightened her frock and attempted to put her hair back in place, but all she managed to do was make a neater mess, completing the metamorphosis back into her Sunday school teacher personae. "I apologize to you, Jakeel, for losing my temper. The ignorance of slaves is so appalling to me that I sometimes grow angry. I want to answer your question."

Jakeel was incredulous with disbelief. He didn't think there was a response to his question other than the admittance of guilt and wrong doing, and he could not believe he was about to hear Mrs. Tolby confess the error of her generations to him. He was also frightened, because if she told him, what would happen to him with that knowledge? Surely he would not be allowed to live.

"Ma'am, that's all right; you done taught me plenty. I'se just be going back to my quarters now. I done got you riled up mighty fine; don't want to say anything stupid and get you riled up again."

Jakeel slurred his words and did the "nigger" routine, which for others was genuinely the way they knew how to speak. Jakeel, on the other hand, had discerned the nuances of his white speech, and he spoke accordingly. There was a refinement to Mrs. Tolby's language that he wanted for himself, and he practiced it daily. But he knew that most whites did not like it when a "nigger" sounded intelligent. They would get annoyed and even violent because they, too, lacked education, so it would be best, like today, to talk in the ignorant manner to which whites had become accustomed. He turned to walk out the door when he heard the leathery sound of the whip coil brushing on the floor.

"Sit down." Mrs. Tolby smiled, but there was no warmth in it, the look in her eyes steely. Jakeel stopped right where he was, several feet from her.

"Closer, Jakeel, I'm not going to hit you again today. Sit down" He did as she asked.

"Jakeel, as I said before, there are matters you won't understand because you aren't God. I guess I should have added there are aspects of life you won't understand because you are a slave and simply are not capable." Her condescension did not go unnoticed.

"Slavery is an institution divined by God, Jakeel. Find Genesis 9: 20-27 and read it to me. Let's see how much you have learned." She handed Jakeel a huge family Bible, and he located the verse. He had become very adept at finding scripture and prided himself in memorizing all the Old Testament books in order.

When he finished reading, his mistress spoke.

"Jakeel, this story is about Noah. You see, Noah had successfully survived the flood due to God's divine intervention. He was now starting life over. He became a farmer of grapes and maker of wine. One day, he had a little too much to drink and passed out naked in his tent. Noah had three sons, Shem, Ham, and Japheth. Your ancestors are the descendants of Ham, Jakeel. Well, Ham, acting like a typical nigger, went to his father's tent and saw him lying there drunk and naked, and he made fun of him and went and told his brothers. But his brothers—from whom the white race is descended—were dignified men who did not find humor in Ham's joke. They took a garment and laid it upon both their shoulders and went backward into the tent, covering the nakedness of their father; as their faces were turned backward, they did not see their father's nakedness. When Noah woke up, he realized what his younger son had done. Now this is the important part. Read to me verse 25."

"And he said, 'Cursed be Canaan; a servant of servants shall he be unto his brethren'." Jakeel could hardly believe that his life and the life of his people could be so doomed! But here it was in the Bible, the word of God!

"Yes, Jakeel, a servant, but not just a servant, a servant of servants! Because of Ham, you work for me, and so will your children and your children's children. The Bible goes on to say that Noah blessed his other sons and that Ham was to serve them. So, Jakeel, I am only fulfilling the word of God, as are you by being my slave. Don't let the story of Moses get in your head because it is your destiny to be a servant. What you have to focus on is being a good servant, so that when God returns, you will be found righteous, and He will look favorably upon you. That means strict obedience to me, my husband, and any white person who commands you to do his or her bidding. It's divine, and it comes from God. I hope you have sense enough to understand that."

Mrs. Tolby held out her hand to receive her Bible. Reverend Freemund would be proud of her discourse. She'd almost missed this opportunity to witness, but she had managed to recover from her mistake. She would thank God in her evening prayers tonight for the opportunity to turn yet another dark soul to the light. Jakeel sheepishly held out the Bible to her and asked permission to leave, and she obliged. As Jakeel walked dejectedly back toward his quarters that day, he ran into Bella. So it was to be that even though he continued his Bible study with Mrs. Tolby, it was Bella who had become his true teacher.

Jakeel now understood his purpose. He involuntarily shuddered at the ignorance he exhibited in the presence of Gausje with his self-righteous mannerisms that his mistress had taught him. Jakeel now understood more of Gausje's words and how he had embodied the principles indoctrinated into him by the white man, thereby insulting everyone in that tent. It was this God about whom his mistress so fervently spoke, and His entire population, the descendants of Canaan, who indeed must be wiped out.

Ever since he had been taken into the village, Jakeel knew he was experiencing life the way it was supposed to be lived. This world was the opposite of what he had known as a slave. Where before there was slavery, here there was solitude; where before there was rape and violence, here there was respect and serenity; where before there was an ambiguous God who delivered a certain people but condemned another to eternal servitude, here there were forces who accepted Black, Indian, and the offspring of the two. And although there was room for improvement, Jakeel knew there would be no going back to his life of servitude and false doctrine.

CHAPTER 11

THE BLOOD

Reverend Freemund coiled back on his podium like a venomous serpent waiting to dispense another litany of spiritual diction from on high. His gaze caught his captive all-white audience as the room murmured with "Amens" and "Tell its" from those whom he called his flock. Beads of perspiration dangled from frizzled strands of graying hair that had fallen into his face, and he instinctively swiped his hair out of his eyes with a big, calloused hand. His gesture pronounced much about his character: control, arrogance, and confidence. Springing forward, he emitted another barrage of fire and brimstone to his entranced congregation.

"I'm talking about sacrifice, saints. The sacrifice must be precious; it must be sustaining to your very essence, big enough to gain the attention and approval of an almighty God! Since the beginning of earth's history, God has required living sacrifice. I said living sacrifice!" The whites of Reverend Freemund's eyes glistened with intensity as he paused and stared at his flock for emphasis; he did not want his point to be lost. The congregation, eager to hear what Reverend Freemund would say next, yelled out the responses that usually kept him moving.

"Preach it, Reverend! Tell it! Amen!"

"He required it of Adam and Eve before they left the Garden. You see, God wanted Adam and Eve to know that He was not pleased with their actions, that he was not pleased with their distrust, that in order for them to see His face in peace again, some person or other living thing would have to die!"

"Amen, Reverend!"

"God made them kill a dumb lamb, a creature of ineptitude, a creature that requires a master. God could have chosen an ape, a creature of significant intelligence, or a parrot, a bird that could be trained to speak! He could have chosen the serpent, which was the cause of their fall in the first place! But he chose a lamb!"

"Now, I know most of ya'll are farmers, and you are well acquainted with nature. I still live on a small farm, and some of my childhood memories are applicable to this here message. When I was a boy my brothers and I would play a joke on our pets. We would take our dog and put him in a bag and place him on the back of our daddy's wagon, and we would take that wagon miles away from home. Then we would take the sack filled with our dog and spin it round and round and round until the poor dog could barely stand. And then we would high-tail it home, leaving the poor brute alone to find his own way!" The congregation laughed quietly at the reverend's juvenile history.

"And I tell you, no matter how dizzy, confused, and distanced that dog was from home, he would always manage to make his way back to the farm. If you take a cat, and take that cat through the same process, it may take days, but that cat will find its way back home." His southern drawl became more pronounced.

"That's right! Say it!" The congregation affirmed.

"That goes to show you the intelligence of a cat and a dog. Now, on that same farm you could take a sheep from the front yard and move that sheep to the backyard, and that dumb sheep could not find its way back to the front of the house!" The audience laughed out loud this time; many of them knew that the reverend was right. They awaited the punch line.

"God required it of Cain and Abel, so Abel offered up the lamb as God requested, but Cain offered up fruit, and God accepts no substitutes! Cain was cursed for his belligerence. Is that what you would want to happen to you?" The congregation sat quietly, waiting for more wise words.

"Saints, we are now masters, granted that privilege by God Himself. And when we do wrong, we have got to make a sacrifice, but we got to sacrifice that which will please God. God does not want us to sacrifice what we think He wants, no—he has been specific. He wants the creature that has been given our charge, the creature that does not have the sense of a cat or a dog but needs our leadership, our guidance, to be the bearer of our sins. We are shepherds, our black slaves our sheep, and if we are to please our God, we will not hesitate to sacrifice those put in our possession by divine right to the God who gave them to us in the first place!" Sweat streamed down Freemund's face, his brow furled in an intensity of conviction.

"You see, saints, we have a deeper responsibility than you realize with the ownership of slaves. They are in our charge. We must teach them, lead them as dumb sheep and driven cattle, to do our bidding that has been given to us by God, and we will be rewarded in heaven. We must teach the slaves the Bible, teach them God's lessons, and the Lord will be pleased. Teaching black slaves the Bible makes them more manageable, more humble, and more fit for their place in the kingdom." The reverend was slowing down now, smiling lovingly on his flock as a father would his child.

"Now, we don't always have to kill our slaves as a sacrifice, although that may at times be required. But for the most part all that is required is the blood! The blood can be offered up in many ways—flogging, sacrificial cuts, and beatings."

"Preach, Reverend!" A man with an angry red face nodded his head in agreement.

"Ya'll know that our task is hard! Our burden is heavy, and black slaves can at times be intolerable, but with God's divine guidance, and a strong arm, we can make them into the servile creatures that they were designed to be! And when we do this, the Lord will be pleased."

The congregation rose to its feet, filled with the message Reverend Freemund had delivered to their malleable minds. As they filed out of the church by noon, they felt the euphoria of the chosen, their consciences clear.

Mrs. Tolby waited patiently in the back of the line as the people proceeded through the two large doors of the church to shake the leader's hand. Freemund was favored among the citizens of Carolina as a respected pastor, partially because of his religious stance on slavery. He owned one hundred slaves and was known for his firmness and Christian home. His piety reigned throughout the state, and he was loved and revered for it by all whites.

Mrs. Tolby had always been committed to her church and her religion. But now that her daughter had died, she felt the need for more than promises—she craved answers, and she planned to ask Reverend Freemund for them.

Life had changed drastically on the plantation after Jared's mistress Zelia had been killed. Elizabeth knew all about her husband's affair, but she kept it a secret to protect the family name and maintain an air of dignity around her daughters. Unfortunately for her, the slaves did not have the same intention because they were bitter that another one of their own had to die at the whim of their master, and they were more than willing to defile his name at any given opportunity.

When her youngest daughter, Emily, went out to the garden to pick strawberries for an evening dessert, she overhead one of the slaves talking about her father and his mistress, Zelia, and how he hated having sex with his own wife and loved this slave more than the plantation, but his wife could die any day and he wouldn't shed a tear. Emily had pretended not to hear, but her shock could not disguise her anguish at such horrible news. When the field hands realized that she was in earshot and was indeed listening, they grinned and embellished the story with lurid details. Emily had dropped the strawberries and had ran home to confront her.

As much as Elizabeth tried to hide the truth, her face said it all, and that had changed Emily for the worse. When she sought to avenge her mother, she was brutality killed by one of the slaves. That day, the Tolbys lost much. Ever since that moment, Elizabeth began to reckon with the way her husband Jared conducted himself. She promised herself she wouldn't scold him anymore and would do more to understand his feelings, but first she needed to find answers to questions that her daughter's death had revealed. And that was why she was here, waiting in line to speak with Reverend Freemund.

When Elizabeth's turn finally arrived, she extended a soft, warm greeting to the pastor.

"I really enjoyed your message today, Reverend Freemund. You describe slavery in such convicted terms. You make it sound as if it's right to own slaves."

"It is right, my child, it's ordained by God." Freemund nodded his head toward Elizabeth in his most southerly manner. "But what is troubling you, my child? You are a faithful follower, but I sense you seek counsel."

Several members who were exiting overheard the reverend and looked back with inquisitive eyes; Elizabeth blushed with embarrassment, and the keen preacher promptly responded. "Why don't you come ovah for dinner, Mrs. Tolby? My wife Rebecca would be happy to have a new guest in our humble home. I live on a farm, as I mentioned in my sermon today; it will not measure up to your earthly comforts, but it is a home where God dwells."

Freemund warmed a smile towards Elizabeth, his slightly coffee-stained teeth fully revealed as his lips peeled back farther than normal. Elizabeth thought he may had once been an attractive man, but time had regulated him to just being rather ordinary looking. She imagined that he probably struggled with temptation of another sort from female members of his flock.

"My wife is in my office. Won't you meet her there, and she will carry you home. I will be there after I attend to church business."

"I am much obliged to you, Reverend, and I accept your offer." With that Elizabeth turned on her heels and headed for the office.

The ride home with Mrs. Freemund was a bit uncomfortable. Elizabeth wasn't sure, but she felt as if Mrs. Freemund were evaluating her body. Every time Elizabeth would glance over at her hostess, she would find Rebecca's eyes probing. Elizabeth tried starting small talk, but her conversation just led to one-word responses. Eventually Elizabeth gave up and tried to enjoy the country landscape. When they got home, Elizabeth assisted with dinner preparations as both women patiently awaited the arrival of the man of the hour. Finally, Mrs. Freemund spoke.

"So chile, what do I owe the pleasure of having yet another pretty face in my home?"

"Reverend Freemund invited me here for lunch, Sister Freemund. I have important questions about life after death. I have endured a great tragedy, and I hope Reverend Freemund can help me understand its purpose."

"Life after death?"

"Yes, I lost my youngest daughter, and I just have a feeling that this isn't the end of it. I grieve for her so deeply. I just need answers." Rebecca stared at her without emotion, silently tapping her toe on the hardwood floor.

"And what exactly is it you expect my husband to do, child? Resurrect your girl?" Just as Elizabeth was about to respond, Reverend Freemund stepped through the door.

"Emmpph, emmph, empph! Sure smells good in heah! Just what does my favorite lady have cookin' on the stove?" Rebecca just stared at him for a second before she showed a weak smiled.

"Just what you like, Reverend." Elizabeth thought it queer for Rebecca to refer to her husband as "Reverend"; it just seemed so impersonal. He ushered them all into the dinning room, and they sat down to a wonderful meal. Rebecca could cook a mean stew, and her greens where the best that Elizabeth had eaten since her grandmother died. When they finished, Rebecca stayed to oversee the servants who were cleaning the dishes while Elizabeth and Freemund retired to his study.

The large study adjoined the dining room through two large doors that slid open to reveal a room lined with bookshelves. An imposing mahogany desk sat in the middle of the floor and a wooden oak chair in front of it. Reverend Freemund walked behind his desk and pulled out a cabinet that contained beverages of all sorts and offered Elizabeth a drink. She accepted a glass of water while he poured himself a bourbon before slowly sitting down behind his desk. Elizabeth noticed his smooth movements and southern courtesy. She was ready to finally get answers. She didn't want to seem anxious, so she decided she'd break the conversation in subtly, asking a question to which she already knew the answer.

"Reverend, I enjoyed your message today. I believe it is Biblically acceptable to make blacks our slaves?"

"Not only is it acceptable, it is mandatory. Remember the story of Noah, Elizabeth?" Elizabeth nodded her head in affirmation. As a little girl it was one of the stories they told in Sunday school, and she had also been reacquainted with it through her Bible study. "Well, what you probably don't know or remember is what took place after the flood."

"But I do, Reverend. His own son's disrespect has brought the curse of slavery to the world. May I see your Bible, Reverend?"

Freemund handed her his Bible, and she turned the pages to find the passage she wanted to read. "I now put a curse on Ham! He will be the lowest slave of his brothers. I ask the Lord my God to bless Shem and make Ham his slave. I pray that the Lord will give Japheth more and more land and let him take over the territory of Shem. May Ham be his slave." Freemund's eyes were again glistening at the power of his text. Elizabeth could hear the blood rushing through blood vessels in her brain as the full import of this text began to take root in her heart. All the guilt that she had possessed from the murders, the beatings, and the cuttings of slaves out of anger had been assuaged by this passage.

"Elizabeth, whites are the supreme race by the blessings of Noah. We possess high intellect, power, and land. Were these words not applicable to our race, we would not have been able to establish this country as quickly and sturdily as we've done. In addition, the Africans, Blacks, Negroes— whatever you want to call them—wouldn't have suffered such a low social caste were it not for a curse on them from the same lips that blessed us. And I don't feel sorry for them. They were not worshipping the true god but false idols such as bark, trees, the stars, and the moon, everything the Lord commands us to refrain from within his Ten Commandments."

"Well, why not let them just suffer then, Reverend? Why not let the curse take its full measure upon this wayward race of people?"

"Our making these lowly creatures slaves and teaching them the Bible is doing just that: letting the curse take its full measure, as you put it. You see, with our leadership, our wealth, health, and prosperity is increasing faster than our brains can comprehend. Teaching Negroes the word of God has two positive results. First, it lets them know of the error of their ancestors and helps them to better understand why they are in the situation they are in now. Second, it makes them better workers. Once anybody comes into contact with the word of God He makes a change upon their hearts—

teaching slaves the Bible helps them to better appreciate our role as masters over them."

Freemund relaxed back into his chair now that he had fully explained his beliefs. Elizabeth was nodding her head with acceptance and reverence. She felt confident that she and her husband were doing right. But if they were doing right, why did God let her child die? Why did He allow such a horrible massacre on her plantation? Her face twisted in pain, bringing Freemund out of his reverie. He set down, swallowed what was left of his bourbon, stretched his hand over the table, and lifted Elizabeth's face.

"What's paining you, child? We didn't come here to talk about slaves. How can I be of service to you?"

"What is troubling me, Reverend, is the fact that my daughter is dead; I have to know that there is a way we can be together again. I thought I was being cursed for mistreating the slaves, but after your explanation I realize that I have done more than my part to measure up in God's eyes in terms of leading his wayward flock and fulfilling prophecy." Elizabeth fought back tears and anger as she spoke.

"Why don't you tell me exactly what happened?"

"It started after the Maroons struck our plantation, killing several neighboring plantation owners and making an attempt on my husband's life. It happened on the night of the blood burning moon. There—"

"Wait, the blood burning what?" Freemund asked, puzzled.

"The blood burning moon. The slaves talk about it with fear, but they welcome it because they believe it could mean their freedom because it means someone evil is going to die. Their superstition insists that on a night when the moon has a reddish coloring, there will be violence."

Elizabeth paused as Freemund raised his hand. She could see the machinations of his mind at work. He poured himself another drink. Elizabeth took up her glass and drained it completely; without waiting for her to request a refill, Freemund almost absentmindedly refilled it.

"Sounds like Revelation, Elizabeth, when the stars fall out of the sky, the sun becomes dark, and the moon turns to blood. Go on, tell me the rest."

"Well, in the process my husband's slave mistress was killed. He doesn't know that I am aware of this affair, but I knew it was going on almost before it began. Our relationship has not always been even remotely ideal."

"Ever since the attack he has been obsessed with avenging the murders that took place when the Maroons came, even though I know he doesn't give a damn about the whites who died; he really wants to avenge the death of Zelia—his mistress. He hasn't even mentioned getting back Jakeel, the slave they stole right from under our noses while he was getting flogged!" Elizabeth's voice was beginning to get raspy. Freemund felt his anger grow as he listened to the incredible tale about Negroes being so bold as to attack a white plantation and actually be successful in rescuing one of their slaves from that slave's just reward—a lifetime of servitude.

"Elizabeth, you mean you expect me to believe that a group of dumb niggers walked onto your plantation and took one of your slaves from the whipping post! I find that hard to believe!" Freemund started to chuckle, but Elizabeth's piercing gaze stopped him.

"Believe it, Reverend! And ours is not the only plantation that has been hit by these bad-blooded niggers! There are at least two others that I know about in the adjoining counties. Anyway, my little girl found out about the affair, and she was determined to avenge me despite my pleas for her to stop, and those damned niggers on my plantation brutally killed her!"

Elizabeth's eyes were red and shiny; only her prodigious anger kept the tears from flowing, and she allowed that anger to grow deep within her soul, festering like an open sore. She did not want the pain to go away with time; she wanted to wash it away with the blood of as many niggers it took to make her feel whole again. She looked into the reverend's eyes, and she saw the same hate within them. She knew she had come to the right place. Just then the doors to the study opened, and Rebecca stood in the doorway; Elizabeth could not read her face.

"I heard noises coming from this room. Is everything okay, Reverend?" Freemund did not take his gaze from Elizabeth's face when he spoke.

"Yes, we are fine."

"Are you sure that—"

"Yes, Rebecca, I am certain of what I just said to you. Now, please don't be rude to our guest." Rebecca closed the doors quietly and, for the first time, Elizabeth could see the jealously and anger on Rebecca's face. But surely a reverend wouldn't—her anger wouldn't let her finish the thought, as the image of her husband inserting himself into a dirty, black whore to find pleasure flashed into her mind. She could barely remember times when he would want her. She wondered how often he had defiled his penis in a nigger woman. Elizabeth doubted herself sexually. Her husband rarely looked at her, and now her daughter was dead trying to avenge an act that should have never happened in the first place.

Freemund got out of his seat and motioned for Elizabeth to come over to a couch that sat under an oil lamp near a bookshelf that reached all the way to the ceiling. He lit the lamp; while it was still sunlight out, that part of the room didn't get as much of it as his desk did. They sat down, and he patted her knee softly.

"Elizabeth, what I am going to ask you is going to put you through pain because you are going to have to relive the events that led up to your daughter's death, but I need these details in order to help you. You came to me asking about life after death, and I am here to tell you I have the answers you seek." Elizabeth's face lit up as she realized she would get the answers she sought.

"Child, not only am I going to give you the spiritual lessons you requested, but I am going to offer my services to help you rectify the gross wrongs that have been done to you and your husband on your plantation. You see, it is a spiritual battle that we are fighting and sometimes, like the Israelites against the Philistines, we have to take it to a physical level to teach those who are wayward and do not follow the law of God that theirs is the blood that is to be spilled! No nigger kills a white man and lives! It simply goes against the curse. The devil is crafty and works his witchery on those who have been cursed by God, but God is on our side, child, and your troubles are about to be over."

Veins protruded from Freemund's scalp, revealing his outrage. He had never before heard of such belligerent niggers who would actually attack whites openly and successfully, who would kill the daughter of their white master. What was the world coming to? Surely he was living in the last days, and he would fight tooth and nail for what he believed to usher in the apocalypse and make those who chose to follow the whore of Babylon drink from the blood of her cup. The blood; it was all about the blood. He took another shot of bourbon and listened while Elizabeth revealed to him the events that led to her daughter's death.

CHAPTER 12
THE SACRIFICE OF EMILY

Elizabeth could hear her daughter's voice. "Mother! Mother!" Emily was running as if the devil were chasing her. Her hair flung wildly, caressed rudely by the summer wind. Tears streaked down her face and mixed with the strawberry stains that embroidered her linen dress. She was seventeen and filled with the emotional tirades of adolescent humiliation. She ran up the steps to the big house and nearly tore the screen door off its hinges when she flung it violently open.

"Mother!"

Elizabeth was upstairs looking over the books, making sure Jared wasn't squandering away more of their money. She never wanted her daughters to have to struggle in life; she would ensure her family would live in luxury for the next five generations, and she would be damned if her dumb husband would throw it all away because of carelessness. Jared really wasn't all that dull-witted, but she seemed to want to believe he was. Indeed, for her, her own expectations made his stupidity real. She barely heard her daughter's screams because she was so deep in concentration. She had just turned another page when the door to the room burst open, and Emily flung herself in, her face red, her voice aggravated.

"Mother, them niggers in the garden say Daddy's been sleeping with one of our slaves! Says he loves this nigger whore more-n-you! Tell me that ain't true, Mother, please tell me!" Elizabeth's pen fell loose from her grasp, and she saw in her daughter's face a myriad of emotions dancing on her quivering lips and dilating pupils.

"First of all, don't you ever come into this house with that type of language again! I taught you better than that!" Elizabeth's shouting momentarily disconcerted her daughter.

"I know, Mother, I'm sorry, I just—"

"And how are you going to take what one of them foolish nigger-crows say for anything other than pure lies, Emily? You should know better than that! You are an embarrassment to me and this family by giving them that much credit!"

Emily was shaking. She hadn't known what to expect from her mother once she confronted her; as a matter of fact, she hadn't even thought that far ahead. She just had to know the truth. She tried desperately to modulate her tone.

"Mother, I'm sorry, but don't treat me like I'm a child! I'm seventeen, and I am a woman! I wouldn't have questioned you if what those damn—if what those niggers were saying didn't sound so convincing. I also know you and Daddy haven't slept in the same room since I was eight." Her voice had dropped, but her tension mounted.

"Watch your mouth, Emily, or I swear to God I will slap you!" Tears welled up in Elizabeth's eyes. How dare those niggers tell a child about the secret sexual affairs of her father? Didn't these savages have any propriety? Now she was sitting here in front of a child who just had her dreams about her father shattered, and if she didn't handle this right, those dreams would never be repaired. Elizabeth was angry with herself for losing her temper so quickly. What was it about her daughter that was bothering her, that was making her feel manipulated? She couldn't quite put a finger on it, but there was a quality about her daughter that disturbed Elizabeth.

"Are you going to hit me like you hit them, Mother? Is that it?" Emily queried.

"How do you know that your father and I haven't been sleeping together, Emily?"

"Because I would overhear you arguing with him, that's how! I would want to come and sleep in the bed with you and Daddy, and I heard you arguing. You told him to go sleep in the guest bedroom, and I went there to sleep with him. So help me, Mother, I better not find out that your defiant attitude forced Daddy to sleep with a nigger!"

That was it—before she could tell herself to stop, Elizabeth slapped her daughter hard across the face; the shock and pain sent Emily stumbling back toward the door. Elizabeth tripped and fell to the floor a little way from Emily, but she quickly got to her feet and stood, glaring, over her daughter. Emily forced herself up on her elbows, blood spurting from her nose, hate in her eyes. She turned her head and spat onto the floor, not even trying to stop the blood. She just let it flow, warming her mouth and neck, tasting its saltiness, letting it run down her chest, her eyes never diverting from her mother's.

"You little wretch!" Elizabeth turned away from her daughter and called for one of the house servants to bring a wet towel.

"So, it is true, isn't it, Mother?"

"Yes, Emily, it is. Your father and I had problems, but it's still no excuse for what he has done and the shame he has brought upon this family."

"Perhaps, Mother, it is you who has brought shame upon us by being so intolerable to your very own husband. And why didn't you tell us? Do my sisters know?"

"No, they do not, and I don't expect you to tell them either. I was trying to protect them from the feelings that you have now."

"Looks like you've done a fine job of being discreet." Emily hissed. "How long do you think you can keep this a secret?" At that moment one of the servant girls arrived with a warm towel on her wrist. Elizabeth took the towel and shooed the servant girl away.

"Something must be done about this. I can't believe you allowed Daddy's affair to carry on for this long. Had I known, I would have done acted already. It would be better for our father to be sleeping with a common white whore than with one of these animals!"

"Your ignorance darkens the walls of this home the more you speak, child. You have no idea! No idea! By the time I realized how I pushed your father away, it was too late. It didn't matter how much I tried to get him to love me, he was consumed with Zelia!"

Hot tears burned molten streams down Elizabeth's face. This was why she hated Jared: not because he was an inept bookkeeper, but because he desired another woman more than her, and to add insult to injury, a woman she considered no better than a dog. Her blind faith dissipated and reality set in. Her husband had enjoyed another woman—a Negro slave.

"Mother, I will not stand for nigger slaves insulting me and my heritage! We must make them suffer, make them understand that to insult a Tolby means death!"

"Daughter, by making such a fuss in front of the whole lot of 'em you have made matters worse. You should—"

"Are you going to do something, or do I have to?" Emily's indignant temper was unstoppable, its force wielding her mother's to her own.

"Wait until your father gets home, and let's make a smart decision about all this, Emily."

"No, Daddy is without reason, no thanks to you, I'm sure. It's time we put affairs back in order the way they used to be when the Tolby name was feared." Elizabeth recognized what she had been sensing all this time—the trait in Emily that commanded her attention and respect, despite her maternal position, was that Emily was the spitting image of her grandfather, Jared's father, and she had his disposition and temper as well.

"No, Mother, I will take this matter into my own hands; the slave who mocks a Tolby will be flogged. Tonight ain't no burning moon either, so get that superstitious look off your face. I don't know why all the older people around here believe that jumble to begin with." Elizabeth stood within her daughter's way momentarily, but the angry, sullen, bloodstained visage that faced her caused her to move aside.

Emily stepped past her mother and went down to her father's study. She walked to the wooden standing closet that sat next to his desk, grabbed the handles protruding from the door, and pulled the two doors open. Inside there were all manner of mechanisms for torture: mouth bits and iron rods for branding, paddles of different sizes and lengths, and shackles. She picked the one she had seen her grandfather wield as a little girl, the cat-o-nine tails. She remembered her first lesson from him on how to use it came when she was just ten; he had flicked an eyeball right out of the socket of ole' Rusty, the dog that had contracted rabies. He did it so fast and from such a distance that it almost didn't seem real. She remembered the dog being stupefied at first, and then the frantic pawing of its eye as the socket slowly began to gush forth blood. Her grandfather shot the dog to put it out of its misery. She remembered him saying, "Had this dog not been out of his mind, this one action would have taught him to fear and obey me until the day he died. Emily, darlin', sometimes it takes a mean stroke to set matters right. You'll understand me one day."

"A mean stroke—" Emily mumbled. That's what it was going to take today. One mean stroke to let these darkies know that the Tolby name is to be feared and respected. She was going to show them. She could not, would not, wait for her father to come home; this would be a lesson she would teach the niggers herself.

Emily took hold of the leather handle and removed the whip from its resting place. It still sparkled from its last cleaning. She reverently closed the doors and walked briskly out of the study, down the hall, and through the dining room toward the vestibule. Emily continued onto the front porch and down the steps toward the slave quarters. Every slave on the plantation nervously tended to his or her duties, trying desperately not to make eye contact with Emily. She looked infuriated and, although Emily had never before used the whip on them, no one wanted to be the first to taste its bloody fury.

Ivan the taskmaster and Jared had taken the day to travel to neighboring plantations to warn of the Maroon attack. They had assigned two Irish farmers to watch the slaves and make sure they did their duties. But William and Harvey were also lovers of moonshine whiskey and took every moment they could manage to steal away for a sip or two. By late afternoon, when Emily consummated her tirade with her mother, they were inebriated. They figured that with two pistols and rifles, they wouldn't need to have the full command of their mental bearings. They couldn't have picked a more inconvenient time to make such an assumption.

Emily's pride and anger propelled her on without even considering that a slave would resist punishment, and if so, she had no recourse as to what she would then do. When Emily's grandfather was alive there could be a hundred slaves working side-by-side in silence so pronounced that the flicker of a dragon fly's wings was as clear as a bell. There was fear, respect, and order, and never, never, would a slave be caught in mindless chatter such as that Emily had overheard in the garden today. Emily's mind brought to conscious the sneer; was that it? Yes, a sneer, a look of gloating contempt that stretched itself across the cruel, smiling lips of the slave who told her of her father. She wanted to erase that smile, whatever the cost.

In comparison to the way life used to be, this plantation was becoming a disaster; work production was low because the slaves would claim that they were sick and her father would give them a glass of water and, on occasion, even allow them to rest. The noise was unbearable—the singing, the dancing, the goofing off in the fields. Jakeel's scourging should have sent fear through the fields, but his escape had only encouraged the remaining slaves to become more insolent. Now she was going to have to set things straight. This was not how a plantation was to be ruled, and her Tolby blood demanded that she make amends and honor the family name.

When Emily reached the center of the plantation, she called out to the two field hands who insulted her earlier that day. She flailed her whole arm and cracked the whip with acute deftness. The wind parted violently against the leather's slice, uttering its resistance with a booming thunder. The loud crack brought bewildered eyes to the holes that served as windows to the slave huts.

"Yemanja and Vashti, come out here this instant! You're women enough to talk about my daddy; let's see who is a woman now!"

A little slave girl barely four years of age was playing between two shacks a few feet from Emily. When she heard Emily's angry voice, instinct commanded her to her mother's arms. She ran from between the two buildings and into the dirt path that served as a road down the length of the slave quarters. Her movements and fear were not lost on Emily's gaze. Her eyes followed the tiny girl, waiting for the right moment. The girl was barefoot and had only a short tweed shirt, which barely covered her naked bottom. Emily remembered the dog and her grandfather's first lesson to her. She uncoiled the whip and let its heavy leather fall to the ground. The little girl's pigtails bounced up and down, her eyes full of fear. "A mean stroke, darlin', sometimes it takes a mean stroke to set matters *right*." Emily remembered her grandfather's words, and she committed herself to following them.

The little girl just crested what would be considered the front porch when Emily released the most calculated lash of her life. The whip tore through the air, splitting asunder time and space as its tip arched its way directly before the little girl's face. Sweat glistened on Emily's brow as her arm extended firmly to control the blow she threw. Just before the tip of the whip struck her eye, the little girl instinctively held up her hand as a shield. The whip cracked ominously, missing its mark, burying itself in the child's two middle fingers, tearing off flesh and sinew. Emily's eyes momentarily caught a glimpse of the stark whiteness of exposed bone before the child fell to the ground, startled. The little girl stared bewilderedly at her hand for a moment before quickly dashing up into the house. Emily waited. "True pain takes time," she remembered her grandfather saying. "It starts from deep within before workin' its way outward toward mental recognition." It was only when she heard a blood-curdling cry come from the cabin into which the little girl had rushed that Emily's anger subsided.

Unknown to Emily, the slaves all had knowledge that Jared and Ivan were gone. George, the horse groomer, was the one who had supplied William and Harvey with the moonshine he had wisely stolen on one of his journeys to Salem. He knew they would drink themselves silly, and that would allow the slaves to let down their guard while the real master was away. The act Emily just committed, however, broke a dam of pent-up emotions that she could never conceive, and what occurred next would seem impossible. Emily didn't realize that Bella had already put into motion irrevocable plans.

Vashti and Yemanja now came out of the house.

"Missus Tolby, ma'am, please don't hurt that chile o'no one else, please ma'am!" Yemanja pleaded and genuflected. Emily mentally glowered as she thought, *"That's better, nigger."* Yemanja just looked at her. Emily regarded her stare—did she see hate? Perhaps, but it looked more like defiance.

"Dat was a chile, ma'am. Ya tore her future away from her. Now what do ya suppose she will do that is worth some'in? She might not have no mo' use of de middle fingers on her left hand!"

It was obvious that Yemanja was upset, and rightly so. That's the reaction Emily wanted to conjure; let them know who's in charge. Yet she didn't like that this woman had the audacity to stand before her without apparent fear while she had a whip in her hand. Her father had let affairs go too far. She had to restore the plantation to the condition her grandfather would want.

"William! Harvey! Get down here this instant!" William and Harvey had been sitting up under the whipping tree, quietly enjoying the summer's day in the shade with a jug of cool moonshine. When they heard their names being called they were agitated. Why did this girl have to ruin a perfectly good day? What was the damn problem? Work was being done. They'd noticed her bossiness around the house lately with the slaves, and even with them, and they resented it. But her father was paying them well, so they decided that pride could take a back seat in the face of financial gain. They ambled down the slight decline toward the servant's quarters to see Emily with a whip and Mrs. Tolby running out of the house, a pistol in her hand. They all convened at about the same time.

"William and Harvey, grab those two wenches and hold them tight!" William and Harvey looked at each other with surprise and delight. Perhaps this day would get better after all. A little excitement couldn't hurt, and that Vashti was a pretty little wonder. Harvey made sure he grabbed her first, allowing his pelvis to feel the softness of her behind. She struggled against him violently. His hands rudely brushed the side of her breasts as he firmly pinched her arms in his grasp, trying to hold her still. William caught Yemanja before she made an attempt to flee. He sloppily wrapped his arms around her waist, roughly pulling her to him. They all heard the pistol being cocked, and Emily smiled when she saw her mother standing by her side with the gun aimed at the face of the women who dared bring shame to her family.

Emily cracked the whip and popped a piece of flesh off the pretty face of Vashti, near the corner of her mouth. Vashti's scream broke the silence that had taken hold of the plantation.

"It's not so easy to smile at what's not funny, is it, whore?" Emily didn't expect an answer; she just glared at Vashti and Yemanja. "You thought you'd make fun of my daddy's name and that you'd embarrass me with your gossip, didn't you? Didn't you?" Emily screamed and then laughed harshly.

"Emily, I say you teach them how to watch their mouths by giving them a couple of lashes from that whip!"

"I should, Mother, but then I wouldn't want to scar up that pretty face too much; it might make it harder for William and Harvey." Elizabeth, William, and Harvey stood silently as they contemplated what Emily planned to do.

"No, Mother, these girls here say that my daddy ain't respectable, that he sleeps with niggers! They are trying to embarrass our family by false accusations."

"Then strike them down with the whip, Emily! We have money; we'll buy more." Elizabeth suggested.

"I want these niggers to realize what it feels like to be whores. I don't think they realize it, Mother." Emily's raspy voice was quiet yet firm. "I think they believe they are better than us because they believe Daddy loved a nigger woman. I'm going to show them what Daddy did to Zelia, and then they can tell me if that's love or not. William, Harvey, take these women to the horse shed."

Emily turned and began her way to the horse shed. The two women frantically dug their heels into the earth, vainly resisting that to which so many other women succumbed in the past.

"No Massa! Please! Ise sorry for jibbin' with ya! I didn't mean no harm! We is low creatures unworthy of your kindness! Please forgive our ignance, Missus Tolby! Please!"

Vashti's eyes were wild with fright and contempt. She tried to make her last blurt sound helpless, but the venom of her hatred poured through and it ended up sounding like a command. Although they both were trying to maintain composure and placate with their best "nigger" dialects, Vashti and Yemanja were quivering with fear and wrath. Vashti was the first to break down and began to cry. Yemanja, though frightened, maintained an air of dignity. She knew Bella would have devised a plan as soon as she heard about Emily taking off the little slave girl's fingers.

In fact, Bella peered from her window at the procession that was making its way to the barn. The other slaves, conditioned by the strong yolk of fear, resumed their daily patterns of work, not wanting to involve themselves in the punishment that was administered to those who proved unruly. They feared for their meager lives, and this made Bella almost sick to her stomach, but she knew what would happen, and it facilitated her plan.

Once the six had reached the horse barn, Emily's furor only grew stronger.

"Strip them!" She ordered William and Harvey, but she heard a quiet moan of displeasure from her mother. William and Harvey, although excited at the prospect of what might occur, were starting to get a little nervous because they didn't have a plan of action but were just acting at the behest of this out-of-control young girl. The situation could go fantastically well or drastically wrong, and there would be little they could do about it. They were both armed, but their weapons were in their holsters while Mrs. Tolby had her pistol pointed in their direction.

"Ma'am?" said Harvey.

"Take off their clothes! I want them naked. Wouldn't you like that, Harvey?" Emily quickly licked her lips and smiled. She gave him a wink, and he felt his organ begin to inflate with blood. Yemanja resisted, but William punched her hard on her right temple. When she crumpled to the floor, he frantically began tearing at her garments, which were merely a slight cotton skirt and thin, ragged top. Because she wasn't wearing underclothes, she was soon naked. She tried to cover her pubic thatch, but William yanked her arms painfully behind her back and held them there, bending them to arduous degrees of discomfort.

Yemanja twisted and spat; Vashti gave little resistance to Harvey, and she collapsed to the floor out of pure despair and helplessness. Her dead weight made her body hard to manage, but he finally had her completely disrobed. Both William and Harvey were now sweating profusely, the alcohol slowly working its way out of their system. Harvey took in a deep inhalation of Vashti's hair like a dog trying to sniff out a scent of a runaway. His hands were shaking uncontrollably with excitement as he looked at these two beautiful nude women. As far as Harvey was concerned, a beautiful woman was good for one thing, no matter what her race.

"Rape them." Emily stared coldly at the women as she gave the order.

"What?" queried Harvey.

"I said rape them! You two gents deserve it. Sitting up under that tree has really worn you out. Now pull down your trousers and—rape—them." Emily uncoiled the whip as if to punctuate her last sentence. "I'll make sure they cooperate." She took the whip and flicked it lightly at Yemanja's exposed breast, gouging a fresh wound across her light brown nipple. Yemanja screamed.

"Bella! Bella! Get in heah now!"

"If that voodoo wench so much as steps into that doorway I'll have her shot! You understand me, nigger? Get started."

"Ma'am, I can't do it in front of the Missus." Harvey's eyes had a pleading in them that further infuriated Emily. Elizabeth was astonished at her daughter's cruelty, yet her hatred for the two women who told her daughter about her husband's nasty deeds with a nigger whore kept her from resisting the urge to run out of the barn to the house so she wouldn't have to witness this act. It was barbaric, and she was from a higher class of family than this. This was how the Tolbys managed affairs, not she, but yet she held steady.

The two slave women were now pleading and crying; Yemanja had held out as long as she could, but the prospect of getting raped by either of these men caused her to lose control. She reached up and felt her temple; it was bleeding, and her head was beginning to throb.

"You'd better get undressed or you won't leave this plantation a man. Mother, show them what I mean." Elizabeth pointed the pistol towards their groin. Both Harvey and William lost their erections and started to tremble.

"You two take off your trousers." They obeyed. Elizabeth was disgusted by what she was involving herself in.

"I tole you, ma'am, I can't do it like this. Can't you two go out the barn? William and I can handle these two niggers from here on out."

"I want to watch you do it." Emily sneered. "We'll get you ready. Vashti! Yemanja! On your knees." Emily punctuated her command with the crack of the whip. The women looked at each other hesitantly, hot tears trailing down their faces. Yemanja turned on her side and slowly pushed herself into a praying position, her knees and the top of her feet pressed to the dirt floor. Vashti followed her lead, her lips quivering, crying. Vashti's legs were stained with her own urine, a steaming puddle forming around her knees.

"Put your penises in their mouths." The women both moaned in protest. Emily ushered her mother around to the kneeling women and placed her hand on her mother's to guide the pistol to their heads. The men took their limp members and forced them into the girls' mouths. Yemanja started to involuntarily gag in pure disgust and hatred, her body lurching forward as spit began to dribble from the sides of her mouth. Both men now started to become erect and to lose their inhibitions. Emily seemed almost excited. Her eyes were electrified as she watched the scene. Elizabeth wondered what had happened to her daughter to make her like this. Elizabeth realized just how out of touch she had become with her own family. She'd focused so much on wealth that she lost sight of flesh and blood.

William and Harvey were now forcefully ramming themselves into Vashti's and Yemanja's mouths. Emily walked briskly behind Yemanja and grabbed the woman by her hair, jerking her backward so she fell down in the hay-laden floor. She stepped back from Yemanja and looked at her mother. She nodded her head to the floor to indicate that she wanted her mother to do the same. Vashti, a quick study, was watching Yemanja and saw what happened, and she lay down on the floor.

"Take them." At that William and Harvey fell on top of the women. It no longer mattered that two pretty white women were watching them do this. Strangely, it now added an intoxicating tinge of pleasure to the sexual act, and they were hard enough to forcefully penetrate the two girls. Harvey had experience with this act before and quickly negotiated himself into his victim.

William, on the other hand, was so excited he hardly knew how to begin. Holding Yemanja to the floor with his fist and forearm planted firmly on her chest, he investigated her body with his other hand. He felt the tautness of her breasts and pinched them in turns between his palms; then he moved his hand down her stomach and into the tuft of hair between her legs, rough and thick like the hair on her head. He impaled her coarsely with one finger. Yemanja moaned her distaste, turned her head, and screamed out of anger. She was being violated. The smell of moonshine and tobacco was unbearable to her as he heaved his stuffy breath into her face. William smiled at her with wretched stained teeth and, with a tongue blackened with tobacco juice, licked her face, leaving a dark trail of tobacco slime in the dust that caked her cheeks. He was so stiff it pained him. He forced her open and rammed himself in her, but the dust and the absence of pleasure on her part made doing so difficult. He took his free hand and spat on it repeatedly until is sloshed with saliva and rudely rubbed the moisture between her legs. When he shoved his finger inside her again, she gurgled out a cry of anguish. That only urged him on. He took his free hand and tried again, and this time the moisture assisted and he slipped in easily. William was a bit dismayed at the ease with which he entered her. He was hoping to violate a virgin and cause her physical pain, but he realized the pain she felt was only that of being forced to do what she had no desire to do. Another man had had the pleasure of opening up this vessel. William shoved himself in as hard and as far as he could and began raping her viciously. She hated the feel of him moving in and out of her; his panting was suffocating. He ejaculated in her quickly, and the warm fluid draining out of her vagina made her feel sick.

"You know you liked it, wench!" William said. He got up clumsily and started to put on his trousers. He looked at Emily and Elizabeth out of the corner of his eye, hoping he could move quickly enough before they caught a glimpse of his exposed organ. Harvey was still going, but William knew he could not hold out much longer. He panted with excitement, his face creased with intense pleasure.

Emily's thirst for vengeance was nearly quenched. "Stop, Harvey. I want you to put it—" Harvey was momentarily distracted by Emily's voice, but the culmination of his pleasure was too far gone to be stopped. Harvey's body jerked violently as he climaxed, and he collapsed face down into the floor, his deflated member still in Vashti. He lay momentarily in fatigued bliss, then pushed himself up and hobbled on his knees to a defeated Yemanja.

But just as he did an arrow lodged itself in the base of his skull, and Harvey fell to the ground, dead. Emily turned around to see from where the arrow came but only saw a figure disappear fleetingly past the door. William frantically grabbed at his holster and fumbled with his gun, but it slipped from his sweaty grip and fell to the floor. He scrambled down in the hay to find it and got clumsily back to his feet, pointing the gun in all directions as he tried to comprehend what was happening.

"Mother, William, shoot whoever is on the outside of this barn!" Vashti and Yemanja saw the opportunity and dashed toward an empty horse stall. William shot at them but missed just as another arrow whizzed in and struck Emily in the arm. She dropped the whip to grip the arrow and yanked it out with a yell, then she held her arm firmly to stanch the flow of blood. Elizabeth fired two shots in the direction of the door, but there was no one there. Vashti and Yemanja continued to huddle in the empty horse stall, hoping desperately for deliverance. Yemanja suddenly felt a funny, dizzy sensation in her head and tried to reach out and grab the side of the stall for support. Her chin was shiny with fluid, and she looked confused.

Suddenly, Emily, Elizabeth, and William heard a raspy noise and saw a form moving under the loose hay on the floor.

"Oh, no! It's them voodoo spells!" William shot at the floor to try to stop what was coming at great speed for them, and Elizabeth followed suit. Emily just stared in total disbelief. Finally, William had enough; he threw down his gun and ran to the back of the horse shed to a little area where the boards had rotted away and no longer came all the way to the floor. He flopped down on his belly and scrambled out of the barn until he could go no farther, never looking back.

The shape under the hay was nearly at Emily's feet when her mother fired her last shot. For a moment, all stood still.

"You got it, Mother, whatever it was!" Emily was breathing the breath of relief; she looked at her mother and smiled, and Elizabeth felt warm inside. She'd done something great, something that her daughter would appreciate and never forget. This would be the beginning of a healing of their relationship, and all would be well. Elizabeth smiled back.

"Thank you, Mother. I was starting to wonder about you. Now let's get the two whores and see that all the slaves witness—" Her voice was caught in her throat at the huge snake that sprung up from under the hay and struck her pelvis. Emily screamed as Elizabeth fired on the serpent, but her gun was empty, and she'd not thought to bring extra bullets. She angrily threw her gun at the snake without effect. The giant serpent reared back, its body coiling forward to wrap itself around Emily's ankles. The snake fastidiously wound its way up to her neck as Emily staggered backward toward a huge supporting beam near the stall where Vashti and Yemanja where still hiding.

"Oh my God!" Screaming, Elizabeth ran to her daughter and pulled desperately on the snake, but her hands kept slipping from its damp muscles. The snake wound itself around her daughter's neck and the supporting beam before the snake mystically turned into a smooth piece of wood. Emily was trapped, pinned to the beam by a snake that was obviously the product of forces she'd once doubted and couldn't understand. She struggled.

"Witch! Mother, run to the house and get Daddy's shotgun! This is the doing of Bella, that voodoo witch. Stop her!"

"I'm not going to leave you, Emily! William! William!" But William was long gone.

"Go, Mother." Elizabeth ran toward the front door but stopped just as suddenly as she had started. Outside stood Bella and ten field hands, all with eyes filled with hate.

"These are the women who ordered the rape of Vashti and Yemanja. Now what would the white man do to you if you dared rape a white woman in this fashion?" Before Elizabeth could began to process how this slave woman could talk so elegantly, the men rushed forward and grabbed her and took her back to her daughter, who was struggling and gasping against the coiled, now wooden, snake that held her captive in the horse shed. Elizabeth's heart sank with despair because she realized that there was no hope. Jared wouldn't be back until tonight, Harvey was dead, and William had run off like a coward. "Maybe he was going to get help." No, she had seen the look of fear in his eyes and knew he was not coming back. She and her daughter were stuck, and they were about to reap what they sowed.

A hulking man with a heavily scarred back walked over to Emily and ripped off her bloodstained top from between an opening in the serpent's coil. Her breasts bobbed like white buoys in a bay.

"Go ahead, nigger, steal what you can never freely have." Emily spat at the man, but he quickly moved out of the way.

"Let her go! Take me instead! I'll give you whatever you want! I'll even write you freedom papers. Just don't rape me or my daughter. There is much to be gained if you heed my words!"

Bella looked at Elizabeth and laughed, but the men did not laugh; there was nothing amusing in their expressions, only loathing.

"My men don't want to rape you or your useless daughter; she is not worthy of such an act. And the emptiness of your offer is so pronounced I can only laugh at it. I don't for one minute believe anything you'll ever pen on our behalf will be legitimate. No, Elizabeth, today we only require compensation for what you stole from Vashti and Yemanja and all the hundred other women that have had to lie—devoid of pleasure—under corrupt men, men only interested in deriding a race to make themselves feel of higher value."

"What do you mean an eye for an eye?" Elizabeth was frantic now. "Take me! Rape me! Rape me!" Elizabeth scrambled out of the clutches of one of her male captors to raise her skirt and pull down her undergarments, grabbing his hand to force him to touch her, but he recoiled as if she were poison.

"No, Elizabeth, compensation for what you have done today requires a life, and Emily's will do just fine." At that moment a slave came forward with a pitchfork used for lifting heavy bails of hay. He looked at Bella, she nodded, and without hesitation he hefted the heavy pitchfork in his strong, capable arms and shoved it into Emily's abdomen. Emily let out a blood-curdling scream. He pulled out the pitchfork, backed up two steps, and lunged forward, this time pushing it into her rib cage. Elizabeth heard tiny whistles of air escape as her daughter's lungs deflated. She watched in horror as a dark and ropey object fluffed out of Emily's slowly heaving abdomen. It was too much; Elizabeth fainted at the brutality of what her daughter was suffering.

Emily died slowly, but Bella stayed and watched. Once Emily was dead, the wooden snake sprang to life and uncoiled itself from around her body and fell to the floor on her side. When Elizabeth awoke she saw her daughter, blue in the face, covered in her own blood, the pitchfork pinning her to the beam. Elizabeth screamed for help, but no one came. She ran outside to discover the plantation totally deserted. Only a few loose roosters, stray dogs, and birds walked around, aimlessly pecking and sniffing for food.

Elizabeth called for her servants, but there was no answer. She ran into the house and paced back and forth until the sun was nearly set. Finally, she grabbed Jared's shotgun and ran to the slave quarters to find any sign of life. To her dismay she discovered that all five hundred slaves were gone. Her world had collapsed in a day. There were just a few taskmasters and field hands roaming about the slave quarters in a solemn stupor. The pupils of their eyes were milky white, unresponsive to the threatening presence that had only recently spooked them. Elizabeth felt her head grow rapidly light. The ground beneath her feet seemed to heave, and she slowly knelt in total defeat.

But she had been wrong about all her slaves escaping; she didn't feel the cold eyes of Bella staring at her from within the confines of her slave quarters, the slightest smile on her face.

CHAPTER 13

EXODUS

Jared was incredulous. "What do you mean, they're gone? How the hell can five hundred slaves just disappear?"

Jared was pacing back and forth across the threshold of the horse stable like an angry lion. Elizabeth had never seen him this angry. His eyes looked like those of a lunatic, and his hair was clotted with dust and perspiration. Jared had just returned from the neighboring plantations, and luckily he had been able to gain a prize to replace Jakeel, a house slave named Pluto, who stood by gazing dopily at the grotesque, stiffening corpse of Emily. She was still stapled to the barn post by a pitchfork, her arms hanging low by her sides, palms falling below her waist. Her spilt blood had taken on a purplish hue and had congealed into a dark sticky substance that was a far cry from the vivacious red it bore earlier.

As Jared paced back and forth, Pluto lowered his head in fear, his eyes darting from left to right as if reading an invisible message written in the air. Elizabeth was stunned at Jared's cold reaction to their daughter's death at the hands of slaves.

"Jared!" she screamed. "Don't you realize our youngest daughter is dead?"

"Yes, I do, got-dammit! And I am trying to figure out just how the hell you managed to oversee such a loss in my short absence! And you tell me I'm incompetent! Hell—in all my days I have never done or witnessed the incompetence that I've seen today! Five hundred slaves gone, along with our youngest chile. It's good that Susan and Ester are away visiting your damn sister, or else our entire generation would be snuffed out under your watch!" Elizabeth stood, stunned momentarily, then her fury took precedence.

"Well, if you had been here doing your job in the first place before Jakeel was stolen under your watch, maybe we wouldn't have suffered to begin with, Jared!" Elizabeth's face was a hurricane of rage, but Jared was not backing off, not when he was winning. He took his time, wiping his brow of perspiration before responding.

"Woman, shut your mouth." His voice was calm but steady. "You know well as I that the loss we suffered that day was due to a voodoo spell beyond our control. How about today? Was the moon red, Elizabeth? Did dey blow some powder in your face or something? Please tell me that's what happened, Elizabeth! Please! Or else just face up to the truth that you managed to lose all our profit over da years, and our youngest chile is hanging off a damned pitch fork 'cause of it!" Jared was staring right into his wife's face, his finger pointing at her nose. He held his pose for a moment before roughly flicking her cheek with his index finger, pushing her away from him. She was too angry and stunned at his resilience to mention the serpent.

"You ever put your finger on Zelia's face like that, nigger lover?" Jared balked briefly and looked at Pluto, who quickly turned. Pluto took his time formulating the best response in this awkward situation. He licked his pursed lips and carefully looked toward the earth.

"Massa Tolby, I bes' be meetin' the head nigga inside so I can bes' acquaint myself with da chores of da place." Pluto started to back away from the escalating hatred between the couple. He wanted to get out of the way before the flying sparks managed to start a fire under his tail. He did not expect his first day to be like this, and he wanted to last a little while before the real slave torture began.

"You stay right where you are, Pluto. Ain't no head nigger 'cause this here incompetent excuse for a wife let 'em walk away. Ain't you in the best place for a nigger, Pluto?" Jared looked at Pluto but did not move out of striking distance from his wife. He waited for an answer. Pluto stood, silent. "Pluto, if you ever try to walk away from this here plantation while you'se my boy, I'm agonna cut off your balls and feed 'em to you on a plate. You understand me? And I will find you, boy. I'll find you. Just like I'm gonna find Jakeel and the rest of my damn property."

Jared turned to his daughter and caressed her dirty face. He stepped closer to her and inhaled, smelling her hair. His hands were trembling. Pluto had no idea what his new owner was going to do next; he knew being sold was going to be bad, but he had hoped it wouldn't turn bad so quickly. He and his new master had a quiet ride from Salem home, and as soon as his master pulled into the dirt road that led up to his new abode, he knew his life was going to be a living hell. Pluto watched intently, although to an observer he was simply staring at the floor, as he and Jared arrived at a starkly quiet plantation. Not one black face was to be seen. The plantation that Jared had bragged about as teaming with activity was like a ghost town.

Jared was now weeping, his shoulders heaving violently as he clutched his dead child. He was mumbling words, but Pluto couldn't quite make them out. He had been too busy watching to see what Elizabeth was going to do. But when Jared broke down it changed the whole atmosphere for the worse because Pluto could not predict what was going to happen next or to whom it was going to happen. At this point, Jared's anger could be taken out on his wife or his new house nigger. Pluto hoped it would be the wife. What was he saying? Then he heard it. Jared was blurting a phrase repeatedly as if he were saying a mantra. "I'm sorry, Daddy, I'm sorry, Daddy, I'm sorry—" He repeated the words in a barely audible whisper.

What happened next caused Pluto's stomach to ache in distress. Jared stepped back from his daughter and gave her one last look. He then placed his hands on the handle of the pitchfork and jerked his body backward, pulling the instrument of death from his daughter's corpse. Her body fell forward like a small tree hewn down in a forest of giants. Her cheeks collapsed, then jiggled, against the crushing embrace of the floor before slowly pinching up. Elizabeth emitted a soft moan as Jared, still carrying the pitchfork, walked over to her.

"Get off my father's land, or I'm going to send ya to hell where ya belong." The look in his eyes conveyed the seriousness of his threat; Elizabeth needed no further instruction. She got up from the floor where she was kneeling and ran out of the barn. A few minutes later, Jared and Pluto heard a horse galloping away. Now Jared was alone, back at square one with his one and only slave, and he actually felt a huge sense of calm and relief.

*****

Reverend Freemund pinched the bridge of his nose, squeezed his eyes shut for a moment, then poured himself his fifth cup of bourbon. Elizabeth sat in front of him, tears slowly crawling down her pallid cheeks. For the first time in many years, Freemund didn't have any words to say; he just continued to pinch the bridge of his nose and twirl his glass of bourbon as he watched it swish around his glass like a miniature ocean. After several moments of awkward silence, Freemund spoke.

"So where have you been staying, child?" Freemund queried.

"I've been staying at the Wilmont Hotel, about a two-hour ride from your church. I have money, and the hostess of the hotel has been very accommodating until I find a new place to live."

"Umhmm." Freemund nodded his head. "And what about your two daughters? Won't they be returning home soon?"

"No, they are getting ready to attend a private school near where my sister lives. I had them sent there to see if they would like it and would enjoy living under the care of their aunt. So far that has been a successful endeavor, and it will give me the time I need to straighten matters out before they return home."

"And you have lost your home, your husband, and five hundred slaves?" Freemund's voice inflected on the words *five hundred slaves*. Elizabeth could tell he was struggling with her story. Maybe he thought she was a dunce as well, just like she used to think of her husband.

"Yes, Reverend, five hundred slaves. Our primary source of wealth is gone, and I have to find a way to start over. I won't be a pauper."

"No, you won't, my child, you've got too much spirit. I'll tell you what; you will stay with my wife and me until you get yourself back on your feet, and I won't even consider any objections. We'll send our trusted servants over to the hotel to bring your belongings back here and settle your bill with the Wilmont." Elizabeth opened her mouth to speak, but Freemund held up his hand and spoke softly.

"We are also going to get your wealth back, Elizabeth. The devil is at work here, and I know just how to fight him. I've got a greater power on my side."

"You are going to get back my slaves?" Elizabeth repeated, doubtfully.

"All five hundred of 'em." Elizabeth liked the note of confidence in his voice. "First, I need you to tell me more about this woman named Bella. She is crucial. I've learned never to underestimate the enemy and, in this case, one of the devil's puppets. That's how you and your family got into the mess that you're in now. I know you'll disagree with me, but I'm telling you it has nothing to do with you or your husband. Even the most incompetent idiot can manage slaves without losing five hundred of them at one time. These niggers had help, special help." Just then Rebecca opened the door.

"Reverend, there is someone here to see you! It is Colonel Hearns!"

"What the hell?" Freemund blushed as he realized he had used an expletive in front of these women. "Pardon me, child, I just have to see this to believe it. Wait here." Freemund rushed out into the living room where a muddied, bewildered-looking soldier was sprawled, panting, on the floor.

"The devil's at work, Freemund! Something is not going right! Something's not right! They got strange ways about them, Freemund. Strange ways!" Hearns screamed only these words before he passed out.

"It's good to see you too, Colonel!" Freemund sarcastically retorted. Freemund, Elizabeth, and Rebecca quietly situated the fallen soldier in a comfortable position on the floor and waited for him to return to consciousness. After a few minutes, and Rebecca's consistent dabbing of his sweaty forehead, Hearns groggily opened his eyes. Rebecca went to another room and returned with a pitcher of water.

"Here, Hearns, you must be thirsty."

"Thank you kindly, Becca." She went to pour him a cup, but he grabbed the pitcher with both hands and began to drink like a wild beast. He nearly emptied half the pitcher of water, spilling only a few drops on the floor. "My horse is probably near dead of dehydration. Would it be possible to bother your servants to attend him, Reverend?" It wasn't a question really, and Freemund recognized this, but with all the turmoil of the day, he was willing to let this pass.

"Certainly, son." Before Freemund could muster a request, his wife was already out the front door to carry out Hearns's wish.

"Sounds like you have a partner in here whose faith is also being tested, Elizabeth. Hearns, have a seat and relax. You look like you've seen the devil. We are most anxious to hear your tale."

"Reverend, I have seen many horrible, horrible atrocities during battles, but nothing like what I've seen here today. You must believe me and hear me out before you begin to doubt what I am telling you. You are the only one I believe can help me with this situation."

Slowly, Hearns began to weave a plot similar to what Elizabeth had just told him, and Freemund soon began to realize that these happenings were definitely amiss. It was nearly dark before Hearns finished his tale as Rebecca, Elizabeth, and Freemund listened intently. Hearns normally would not have revealed the true nature of his relationship with Tanjee, but he did not care anymore about hiding secrets; he was only interested in a solution.

"So I sent her there with a plan. If what she said is true, my men and I will catch the signal and root them out. Fortunately, she did give me information as to where this Maroon city is and how to get in it. She said it was perilous, filled with traps of all kinds. She says they have a religious priest who commands great power. And Freemund, after what I saw today, I believe. If this God you speak of every Sunday is half as powerful as you say he is, then that's what I want before my men and I go in for the kill." The sun had completely set now, and the room was dark except for the light shimmering from the lanterns lit at evening. All was quiet for a few seconds before Freemund spoke.

"This is the Lord's will. He is trying to teach us all a lesson here, and it's important for us to listen. I find it no strange coincidence that you both were brought to me here today. You were led by God to show me the truth about what great evil is assailing our land. I will help you. I need time to formulate a plan and to meet with important associates of mine who are well versed in this type of spiritual dynamic. You are welcome to rest here, Colonel. Once I have my men and plans gathered, we can launch an all-out assault on this city. I believe your story, Colonel; yours too, Elizabeth. We must be careful, however. Our lives and money depend on the outcome of this conflict." Freemund suddenly looked tired, as did the rest of the party. Rebecca spoke.

"I think we have had enough excitement for one day. Why don't I show you both to our guest quarters so you can get a good night's rest? You can talk more about this matter in the morning over breakfast if you wish." She smiled weakly, but her face held a look of concern, even as Reverend Freemund took her hand and gently caressed it.

"My wife is right. Our souls need rest for the war that is about to come. Don't fear, though, we have a greater power on our side." Freemund looked up at his wife, then at his guests.

"Then let us not delay. Follow me." With that Rebecca turned and started to head up a flight of stairs that led to the guest bedrooms. Elizabeth and Hearns followed tiredly.

Freemund sat still on his couch, rubbing his forehead thoughtfully. If only they knew the truth about him they wouldn't dare step foot in his house. If only they knew he believed in God as much as he believed pigs could fly, they would not put their trust in him. And that was exactly why he got into this profession of "saving" souls, because of the amazing power of trust he could gain from people by simply telling them old fables. He chuckled to himself. The Guild would be amazed to hear what he had to say; the time of fulfillment had come—the time for Armageddon and the purging of all Negroes from the land.

CHAPTER 14

JARED'S NIGHTMARE

Jared liked Pluto. Jared couldn't quite put a finger on it, but there was a quality this Negro possessed that made Jared feel relaxed, comfortable. Maybe it was the slothful way in which Pluto carried himself, or the funny sayings that Pluto often used. He was so comical looking with his tiny head and mammoth body! Jared found himself wanting to talk to Pluto just to hear what silly phrases would come out of his mouth. With his wife off the plantation, Jared had found peace. Pluto fixed him dinner at night, and he was pretty damn good in the kitchen, much better than his wife ever could dream to be. And although Jared could not possibly see how a being as dumb as Pluto could escape him, he decided to take precautions with his one slave.

Pluto would sleep in the big house in Jared's room chained to the floor at the foot of Jared's bed like a giant gothic martyr. Jared thought of the mechanism himself and had forced Pluto to build it, but Pluto did not protest. The mechanism simply followed the same pattern as the whipping tree, with four metal braces fixed to the floor with manacles to fasten the wrists and ankles. What amazed Jared most was Pluto's acquiescence to making the device to which he himself would be chained; eerily enough, what drew him to relax around Pluto was that Pluto never complained.

That night Jared laughed himself to sleep; he was tickled by the look on Pluto's face when he told him to get ready for bed and he pulled out his pistol and pointed it at the four braces on the floor. It was only a second before Pluto responded by asking if he could put on his night clothes first. Jared obliged him with a pair of his own pajamas and made Pluto put them on in his presence. Jared hollered when he saw how far his pajama pants stopped short of coming to Pluto's ankles, and how the back of his shirt ripped when Pluto tried to fasten the front buttons. Then Pluto laughed at himself clumsily and said, "Dat's right fine, massta, thanky. I'se just be gettin' to bed now." And he then had lain down on the floor as if he had done this every day of his sorry life. Jared almost felt compassion for him, but when the thought of his deserted wealth resurfaced, he hurriedly chained Pluto to the floor. As Jared got in bed, he shook uncontrollably with laughter at the memory of what had just happened. This was what his father would deem a good nigger, sort of like a pet.

Jared had not thought much about his daddy in a while. Before the day of Jakeel's scourging, Jared's mind had been nearly torment-free, except for the constant nagging of his wife. He had not had nightmares for the longest time but rather pleasant dreams of his conquest of Zelia, or he simply dreamed nothing at all. He hoped he would have another one of those dreams tonight where the feel of Zelia was the primary focus. He appreciated his mind's vivid imagery, the sinewy way his brain elongated the limbs of his women, the bulbous swell of their breasts, much like his memories of his old Nanny, and most of all the intense grit his mind placed on the actual copulation. For him, these dreams were often better than real experiences. Their realism made them magical.

Jared now closed his eyes, wet with tears from laughing so hard, and slowly fell into a deep sleep, his chest rising and falling with the smooth cadence of an orchestrated dance, not a care in the world. Pluto shifted a little uneasily on the floor, rattling his chains quietly while trying to find a comfortable position of rest. This noise did not disturb Jared but rather sent him deeper into a liquid state of unconsciousness—a place where dreams are made. And dream he did.

His dream that night took him back to when he was young and desperate for his father's approval. He looked at himself in his boyish image and decided that he really did look as funny as everybody said. Skinny and gangly, he grinned stupidly as his dad walked into his bedroom and told him to get dressed because they were going out.

"Big night tonight, son. Sometin' I want ya to see. Ya dress warm, ya hear me, boy? Don't want ya mammie getting' on my back about how I gave ya a cold."

Jared watched his father half smile and heard him click his tongue twice, insinuating that the boy should make haste. Jared watched himself amusedly in his dream. What was this all about? He tried to remember while dreaming but could only follow the course his dream took. He watched himself go to his closet and pull out his favorite outfit: brown trousers with a cream-colored cotton shirt and black suspenders. His dad always said Jared looked handsome in this get up. He went to the mirror and combed his hair back, liberally applying the hair oil that made his hair shine and slick back in place. Then he ran out to the kitchen in a flurry of excitement because he was actually going somewhere with his dad. His father was so absorbed in his daily dealings with the family business he never took time for Jared except to discipline him.

Jared dashed down the hall that led from his bedroom and took a sharp left, which brought him to a huge flight of twenty stairs. He'd gone though this routine so often that it was second nature. He arrived in the living room just in time to see his daddy kiss his mother good-bye on the lips. The evening sun cast dim shadows throughout the living room, and pale orange shafts of light softly glowed on the polished wooden floors, seemingly catching tiny motes aflame as they danced in the sun's fleeting rays.

His father roughly grabbed young Jared's hand and walked him outside to the horse and buggy, where a gentle slave waited for them, holding the reigns. There was a deep sadness in this slave's eyes, but he nodded at Jared's father and at him and said a courtesy. Jared's father just snickered, hoisted Jared onto the buggy, and then ran around the front of the horse to his side and hopped in. When the slave walked over to his father and handed him the reigns, Jared watched how his father harshly snatched them away as he whistled for the horse to move.

"Where are we going, Pa?"

"To see a nigger hanged, son. Hanged the proper way." Jared's belly shifted its position inside his abdomen. He had overheard his father talk of these matters but never imagined that he would see such an event for himself.

"It's time you become a man, son, learn how to do things 'round here. Ya going to take over this plantation one day, and I wants ya to be prepared."

Jared was sleeping comfortably now while watching his younger self bask in the warm acceptance of his father. He couldn't imagine why he never had these thoughts before. It wasn't a dream about communing with Zelia, but it was a comforting dream nonetheless. How old was he here? Eleven? Twelve?

In his dream Jared and his father rode in silence as evening turned to dusk and dusk turned to dark. The stars leaped up into the early night sky, and the moon glowed at half-mast, still reflecting the orange tint of the sun. The night was cool, and a gentle breeze cooed them toward their destination.

"Just enough breeze for the flames," his father said as he held his hand up to test the air.

Now Jared's dream took him back to his Nanny. His skinned rippled with goose bumps as he remembered stories of "bad-blooded niggers," their eyes glowing red. Perhaps Nanny would be in the woods, waiting for him and his dad, waiting to spill their insides over their neat little wagon in payment for the deed they were about to witness. Jared closed his eyes, trying to squeeze away the stories Nanny had told him, but the tighter he squeezed them, the clearer the image of her became. She was looking straight at him as she held a broom stick, rough and hardened with stumps of twigs roughly torn off, viewing him with venomous hate. She gripped the broom with one hand and with the other ripped open her shirt, revealing one breast. "Come and get it, Jared." Young Jared, frightened and excited at the same time, produced a meager erection, but he clumsily tried to conceal it by pushing his hand between his legs. His father looked at him daydreaming, disgruntled.

"Ya all right, dammit?" Was that concern in his father's voice, or irritation? Jared tried to decipher it but could not. Opening his eyes, Jared looked straight ahead, no longer wanting to be a part of what was waiting for him in the woods. He very much wanted to lie across his father's lap, to be comforted, to be loved. He scooted closer to his dad.

Jared timidly glanced at his father, who peered straight ahead. Cautiously, Jared began to lay his head down on his father's lap. He never usually initiated acts of this type with his dad because the only affection he received from his father was typically tainted with disgust. He'd learned early not to go to his father for that type of support—unless he wished for a beating or harsh rebuke. He didn't know exactly why he did it this time. Perhaps it was fear of what they passed on the road, or fear of what they were driving to witness, but whatever it was, Jared wanted it remedied by the one person in the world he believed was in control.

To his surprise, his father did not smack him or tell him to sit up but allowed him to lay his head on the thick of his thigh, and Jared felt safe. Jared's father began to ruffle the black, slick hair he'd inherited from his mother. Then his father began to whistle an old tune Jared often heard when the day was going "dandy," as his father used to say. It was a song the slaves would sing every Friday evening.

"I looked ova Jordan, and what did I'se see?
Coming for ta carry me home!
A band of angels, coming after me.
Coming for ta carry me home!"

Jared didn't realize it, but he was moaning the song in his sleep now, muffled between sobs and spit. Pluto was awake, staring wide-eyed at the ceiling. He wasn't sure what was going on, but he did not like the feel of it. And the fact that he was chained to the floor didn't make it much better.

"Swing low, sweet chariot, comin' for ta carry meeeeeee home."

Jared now relaxed under his father's heavy hand as it rested on top of his head. The wagon bounced as it rolled onward, propelled by the steady clop, clop of the horses' hooves on dry earth. Jared looked up at the sky that had now fully bloomed into night. The cool breeze carried a soft yet tart scent of smoke, and Jared realized that nearby an open fire was burning. His eyes began to soak up all he observed—the stars, the upper parts of the trees, their leaves bathed in moonlight, the hind parts of the horse, muscles rippling as they worked to pull the weight of their burden, the whelps on its back from his father's whip when the horse didn't move quite fast enough. He liked it when his dad whistled. He sounded like a bird, pure and shrill, every note on perfect pitch, just like the slaves in the fields.

The wagon hit a bump in the road, and Jared's head bounced in his father's lap, closer to his waist. He could feel the steady movements of his father's breathing against the nape of his neck now, and he thought he'd be able to catch a little sleep before he watched the nigger burn when he felt an odd sensation against his left cheek, something hard and warm. Jared tried to move his head but his father's hand held him steady, pushing his head closer to the source of that warmth. Suddenly, Jared felt his father's hand tighten like a vise around his neck, slowly twisting his face downward toward the middle of his crotch. Jared now frantically scrambled to sit up, but he was helpless. His body would have fallen from the seat were it not for his father's strong grip holding him in place. Twisted like a gnarled limb, he grunted in protest.

"Stop, Daddy!"

"Easy son, sit tight, we're almost there." There was a strange sound in his father's voice. Jared felt the warm hardness rise up, brushing roughly the edge of his nose. He did not like this feeling at all, and a strained cry emerged from his throat. His father continued the song.

"Swing low, sweet chariot."

"Daddy?" Dad?" Jared's voice was muffled, his face pressed so hard into his father's lap he could barely breathe. Hot tears rolled down his face.

"Easy boy, we almost there." Jared could feel his father's breath becoming irregular, his stomach heaving in and out a little harder. "Almost there, son." His dad coughed and grunted, then suddenly he grabbed the back of Jared's head and flung him over to his side of the wagon.

"I don't know what ya think ya doin', boy! Putting your head in my lap like that. Ya been hanging around ya mom so much ya startin' ta act like a girl!" Jared was crying now. He felt nauseous. His father looked at him fiercely. "We're almost there boy, now shut up!" Jared's father shouted as he smacked Jared across his lip. It stung, and he sucked it in, trying to stop the moans that wanted to escape.

Jared folded his arms around his waist and rocked back and forth on the wagon seat. Watching his father out of the side of his eyes, Jared saw him grab himself in the middle and readjust his member. The woods began to thicken around them, shutting out the moonlight and the stars. Jared's mind again returned to tales of the unknown and the known given to him by Nanny, and the fear returned, but he was comforted because his apprehension was better than the cruel solace of his father's embrace.

"Now ya say anything about what happened here today, son, and I'll just as soon treat ya like one of my darkies. Ya understand me?" Jared could not speak, so he only nodded his head in agreement. "Wipe dem tears off ya face," his father whispered harshly. They were nearing people now. His father jerked the reigns, and his horse obediently slowed down. His father found a place to park their wagon and harnessed their horse to a tree. As they started walking forward, they ran into one of his father's friends.

"How ya doin', Pap? See ya brought ya boy with ya. Good thinking. The missus at home wouldn't let me get my boy up to bring him out. Says such acts are for barbarians. I tell her ya wait 'til one of dem black bastards get they'se hands on ya, and we'll see what ya think of our lynching ways then!" The man chuckled at his remarks, and Jared's father humored him with a grin. The man's gaze went to Jared, and once again he took on that awkward look and that gimpy smile. But his face was swollen from crying, and no matter what was said, anyone with a lick of sense could look at him and see his ailments.

"And what's the matter with you, boy? Didn't want to come out and be a man, huh?" Jared looked to his father, but his father sent back a cold stare that meant for him to keep his mouth shut.

"It's all right son! My little tyke didn't want to come, neither. Least ya gat a daddy man enough to stand up to the missus to teach ya what's important." At that the man ruffled Jared's hair and turned to walk toward the smoke. Man enough? Jared's stomach curdled at the thought. Is that what a man did? Take his own son and push his head between his legs? If that was so, Jared was determined to stay a boy!

His father looked at him and smiled. "Come on, son. There's a nigger to burn." But when he reached for Jared's hand, the boy retracted his whole body a full foot from his dad.

"Dammit, I tole you to act normal! One more move like that and I'ma gonna give ya more than what ya mother gets on a regular basis." Though his words were hushed, they fell like hot coals on Jared's back. He could not understand why his dad hated him so but was willing to make him into a man.

The walk took them down a trail about fifty feet into the woods that opened up into a clearing. Jared expected to see men toughened by vices and years of banal cruelty dealt out to slaves, so he was not surprised when he saw their glaring faces as he and his dad approached the flames. But what caught him off guard was seeing cute little girls, younger than he, running around in pretty white petticoats, and their equally pretty mothers looking as if they were at a Sunday picnic. There must have been at least a hundred people there. The smell of roast pig, mashed potatoes, and freshly baked bread was in the air, and he saw spread out on the ground blankets covered with enough food for a feast. Women relaxed on the blankets by their husbands, and children dozed under doting mothers after filling their bellies with food. Lightening bugs danced a ballet in the cool night's breeze, flashing on and off their abdomens in perfect cadence.

A little girl suddenly ran up to Jared and handed him a piece of homemade pound cake. She smiled at him and ran back to her mother. His father looked at the mother politely, tipping his hat, although Jared hardly had a chance to say thanks to the girl. He realized he was hungry and found that he had nearly forgotten what just happened with his father. He guessed it was a good he had. Wanting to forget, he tore into the cake, its sweet taste filling his mouth. Its texture was mildly moist so that no drink was necessary to wash it down; his saliva took care of that. Just then, he heard a big man's voice bellow out to the crowd, "The nigger has arrived!" and the crowd responded with loud cheers of expectation.

The relaxed atmosphere quickly changed as women giggled to each other and frantically grabbed their children and made haste in picking up their belongings and moving closer to the fire, which was burning hot. Jared felt his father's rough hand again on his neck as he swallowed his last bite of pound cake. He nearly choked, but what was worse was choking back his flesh's instinct to quail against the touch of his own father. The crowd began to thicken and draw closer to the fire. Jared's new friend walked back with another gift in her hand for him as Jared looked up at this father.

"You stay here, son, with the little lady. I'm going to find us a good spot and be back for ya."

"Momma said you'd might a piece of dried ham to eat while you watch the nigger burn." The little girl handed him a napkin filled with five weighty pieces of dried ham. They smelled so delicious that Jared immediately began to gnaw on them, one at a time. The little girl smiled at him in delight, grateful that he had accepted her gift. Jared surmised that she was about six years old, maybe seven. She was shorter than he but carried herself in a certain way. Jared looked at her while he chewed on the dried delicacy and decided it might be polite to speak to her. His mother had always harped on him about being proper when in public.

"Why are they burning this nigger? What'd he do?" Jared asked.

"Momma says he got too familiar with Mr. Fowler's woman." The little girl spoke with absolute clarity. Jared heard the fire roar and the glowing ashes at its base occasionally pop. He noticed how the fire's glare, slightly blocked by the bodies of eager men and women, cast intermittent displays of shadow and light across the little girl's face. "Momma says he might have gotten away with it iffen Mrs. Fowler hadn't liked it so much and gone back for more!" She giggled and covered her mouth as if what she had said were bad. If it hadn't been for the shadows and the glare, Jared would have noticed a slight blush in her cheeks, although he didn't quite understand what she meant. Anyway, she looked cute and was nice and he liked her. He wanted her to talk more.

"Have you ever seen a nigger burnt before?" Jared inquired.

"This is my third nigger burning!" She spoke this fact proudly as she held up three stubby fingers. "They are lots of fun. Mommy always bakes such good food, and everybody comes out. And I get to stay up late! The smell's bad though. I don't like that part. And sometimes I want to turn my head when the nigger starts bursting."

"Bursting?" Jared nearly dropped his last piece of dried ham. "I didn't know niggers burst!"

"They don't, silly, but they eyes pop out sometimes, and one time, this nigger's belly blew open. It smelled so bad. But Mommy says I'll get used to it after a while." Jared had finished his last piece of ham and opened his mouth to speak again when his father came back.

"Hey, son, I got us a good spot right up front! Hey there, little missy, thanks for keeping Jared company, but he has to go now. You'd better hurry and find your mom and pap, else ya going to miss the fireworks." His father chuckled and picked Jared up, hoisting him onto his strong shoulders. Jared was shocked at how amiable his father could be. The little girl waved bye to him, but he was so caught up in a storm of confusion that he didn't notice. His father waded through the crowd right up to the front where the fire made him, and all those present, break out into a heated sweat.

The Negro was chained in the top of a horse-drawn wagon, his eyes wild and white with fright. He was so dark that his eyes were the most distinct feature Jared could see. Jared found himself staring in awe and excitement at the creature chained to the top of the wagon. A man, who Jared would later come to know as Mr. Fowler, was ranting about how everyone's sins would find them; next to him a woman stood with tears streaming down her face. Everyone, especially the men, looked upon her with scorn and contempt. Jared saw the man rant and point an accusatory finger at the woman and then the Negro. Jared noticed that the Negro was bleeding profusely about the face and ribs, and Jared saw a gaping hole in the man's side that looked as if someone had stuck him with a spear. Blood puddled beside the Negro in one huge pool, and his face was badly bruised. The white cloth in his mouth was slowly turning red as was his white tunic, which was all he wore. His face was a visage of pain and fright.

Mr. Fowler stepped closer to the wagon and addressed the crowd. "Who is ready to see this nigger burn for his sins?" The crowd yelled in unison their acceptance of this sacrifice. Two burly men hoisted the Negro off the wagon, and one pulled the gag out of his mouth. Immediately, the Negro began to plead for his life.

"I'se swear, I didn't know dat dis woman was attached to anybody. I'se so sorry! Please don't kill me! Whip me, cut me, but don't kill me, please, sir!" Spit burst from his swollen lips and mingled with the blood that ran freely from his nose. Mist came from his mouth in spurts every time he spoke. Finally, he stopped with a gurgling cry and began mumbling to himself, which to Jared sounded like a prayer. The men just stared at him in cold silence.

Mr. Fowler turned his back on him and started to walk away, then suddenly pivoted and ran at the Negro and kicked him fully in his privates, causing the Negro to collapse on the ground, but Mr. Fowler ordered the two men to pick him up. Jared noticed that one of the Negro's eyes was swollen shut. The crowd roared its approval at the unfolding drama.

Until this point, with the exception of the trip, Jared had enjoyed himself at this gathering. He met what he hoped would be a new friend, had eaten good food, and had been absolutely fascinated by the show, the fire, the smells, the fireflies, the moon, and the night. But what happened next no one, not even Nanny, could have prepared him for. Mr. Fowler produced what looked to be a huge machete, cold steel glistening in the light that was cast from the fire. He held it high above his head as if in ceremony. The crowd was now nearing a frenzied state. His father shuffled a little to keep his balance as he hollered, "How ya doing up there, Jared?"

"All right, I guess."

"Good. Ya be sure to watch carefully, son. Don't want ya to miss nothin'!" His tone was more of a command than one of fatherly concern for his child. Jared wished he'd stayed home with his mother, but he wanted to spend time with his father, so he watched the Negro. Mr. Fowler turned away from the crowd to abruptly yank the Negro's loincloth from his body. The Negro moaned in resistance, but the rough-looking men who held him up just sneered. The Negro's body now glistened with sweat, and his privates dangled loosely from his body. A few of the women turned their heads while others looked on, unflinchingly.

Mr. Fowler reached down and deftly lifted the Negro's privates in his hand, smiling while looking at the crowd. Then he tightened his grip, causing another howl to emanate from the Negro's swollen lips. Without hesitation, Mr. Fowler turned back to the Negro and, in one fell swoop, hacked off his penis. Mr. Fowler turned to the crowd, holding the penis in the air in adulation, causing the multitude to cheer even louder. Hands fought for the organ as if it were a trophy, and people began to get frantic as they pushed and shoved each other in an effort to reach the prize.

Mr. Fowler's eyes caught those of a woman who had a large mason jar used for canning. Jared noticed it was filled with fluid. She eagerly held out the jar, her eyes as wild and frantic as the Negro's had been while chained to the wagon. Mr. Fowler threw her the penis, and though she had to fight against others, she managed to grab hold of it and put it into her jar. She howled in a fury of triumph before settling back into her place in the crowd, clutching her prize to her breast.

By now the Negro was unconscious, his head just bobbing around on his neck like a rag doll. Without his penis he didn't look human. "It's time." Mr. Fowler growled, and Jared watched as the men took a bottle of liquid and poured it on a cloth that they held under the Negro's nose. The Negro's head jerked up, and his feet kicked out frantically, nearly knocking Mr. Fowler over before he took several blows. But Mr. Fowler was a sturdy man and stood his ground.

"Let me die!" the Negro pleaded, his voice barely audible.

"On my time, nigger! On my time!" The men now produced large poles that looked like ten-foot pitch forks, except the ends of them were shaped like a "U." They gave the forks to five men standing on the frontline who used them to pick up the Negro and throw him in the fire. Jared had never in his life heard a howl of pain as he did that night. It made the hairs stand up on his skin; his belly bubbled in disgust, and a taste of bile permeated his throat. The Negro tried to scramble to his feet, but the hot coals kept giving away. Thunderous billows of smoke flailed about his body, and the stench of burning human flesh was horrendous.

Jared saw the hairs on the man's body singe quickly and then melt into his flesh, which was cracked. He saw the Negro's melted fat running like oil in every direction. Then the Negro called out the name of the Lord, turned his head, and Jared watched the man's eyes burst out of his head like egg yolks, leaving two deflated white blobs on the tops of cheeks that were quickly devoured by the flames. That sight made Jared wretch, and all that he ate came tumbling out of his mouth in a torrent onto his father's head. By this time the crowd was in too much of a frenzy to even notice. Jared slumped down over his father's head and emitted one last purging of food as his father nearly slammed him to the ground.

"Hot dammit, boy! What the hell did you just do?! What did you just do? You little shit! You puked all over my head! Hot damn!" His father pranced around, trying to wipe the vomit off his head and onto his sleeves. Jared just slumped to the ground. The men with the pitch forks prodded what was left of the Negro and pulled him out of the fire. He was long dead. Jared saw people with knives come up and cut pieces from the burning carcass. One woman cut off a toe; a man, an ear. Jared couldn't even tell that this had once been a man.

Jared could take no more, and he felt himself lose consciousness. When he woke, his pants were around his ankles, and he was tied to a tree. The bark scraped his naked penis. He frantically looked around, but the fire was gone, though he could still smell smoke and the lingering stench of burnt flesh. What was happening? He heard his father's voice from behind.

"Didn't I tell you if you didn't straighten up I was going to treat you like your ma? Well, as it stands you just don't like to listen, do ya, boy?" Jared smelled whiskey on his father's breath and felt warm oil being splashed on his naked buttocks.

"Daddy, please, I didn't mean—" He was abruptly cut off.

"Daddy, please, I didn't mean—" His father mimicked him in a most piteous voice. "I'll teach you to not mean, boy!" And at that moment Jared felt more than heard a tearing pain rip into his anus as his face was crushed against the tree. He heard his father grunting and, right before he lost consciousness again, he saw Nanny in the distance, her hand slowly rubbing her big, black nipple as she said, "Ohhh, Jared's such a dirty boy." Then all went black.

Jared woke from his dream with a yell and cried unremittingly. Rocking back in forth in his bed, he looked like an infant. Though grief racked his body, oddly enough he had an erection. Jared's restlessness had unnerved Pluto, and his chains rattled on the floor as his head darted left and right, trying desperately not to panic. He wished he could see, could somehow escape.

"Massa Jared? Youse' all right? Massa? Massa?" The only sound was the wailing of his master, and he just wanted it to stop. From what he heard escaping his master's lips during the night, something horrible had happened to him when he was a child. Jared sat up in bed, his eyes swollen with tears and grief. He had forgotten about that terrible night all these years ago until now. Why? What had brought it out? Then he heard chains rattling, and Pluto's querying, and decided that was it.

"It's your fault, ya damn nigger! It's all ya fault!" Jared got out of the bed and stood over his new slave. "But I'm going to teach you to mind me, boy!"

"Massa, what you talkin' bout? I'se always mind you!" Jared continued as if Pluto hadn't said a word.

"I'm going to teach you to mind me! Just like I teach all them nigger wenches." And with that he ripped off Pluto's pajama bottoms and fell on top of him, and in that moment he came one step closer to being like his dear old pap.

CHAPTER 15

THE GUILD

Elizabeth sunk into the warm embrace of the goose-feathered mattress. Rebecca dotingly pulled the bedspread up close to Elizabeth's chin without so much as a word, though Rebecca's lips quivered lightly as if she wanted to speak. Instead, she just looked at Elizabeth for a moment and then turned quickly toward the door, blowing out the candle as she went. Her lithe fingers pulled the door closed, but it didn't catch in the latch and fell back open, leaving a tiny trail of light from the hallway lamps. Elizabeth was too tired and comfortable to get out of bed to close the door, even though she wanted complete privacy. She figured she'd be asleep in no time. The day's events had been quite tiresome, and her eyelids were already beginning to yield to the weight of slumber.

The episodic tales played back eerily through her mind's eye. Could it have been coincidence that Hearns and she both came to Freemund's house on the same day with similar stories? What was going on? Her mind began to race with questions and scenes from the past. She thought of Jared, her husband. She thought of sharing a bed with him for so many years; she thought of the children their coupling produced. In an odd way she missed him, despite his constant fumbling with the finances and the mismanagement of his father's inheritance. But could she really blame Jared for her current plight? Had she not lost all the slaves and their daughter Emily? The pain of her loss crushed her like a heavy stone, and a muffled cry escaped her lips. Her lungs were on fire, and she felt that her chest would collapse from grief. Hot tears rolled down the side of her face into the soft cotton pillowcase.

Rolling to her side, she tried to focus on the encouragement that Freemund had given her that day. He promised she would get all of her slaves back, and she enjoyed his sense of confidence. Elizabeth wondered why Rebecca was so awkward with such a good, confident, competent husband. She wished that she had a husband who could manage like Freemund. Elizabeth had no idea how long she'd tossed in bed, pondering her thoughts, but she imagined it'd been awhile. In her final moments of consciousness her mind turned to Hearns. She noticed the shadow of a muscular frame beneath his dirty shirt and trousers. She wondered what his story was. Soon, however, her thoughts led to sleep as she snored softly, the crescent shape of her curled body rising and falling with deep breaths.

Unknown to her, however, at her door stood a silhouette that stared at her slumbering posture, the bourbon wafting corrosively through his veins, making him feel warm all over. Freemund gazed at his guest lying in sweet repose while he rubbed a thick hand over his belly and down the front of his trousers, sensing his arousal. He was going to help Elizabeth, in more ways than one. As he turned to walk to his room, he caught sight of his wife's hateful eyes. She was so simple to him, just plain and ordinary. But she fit the image he needed to maintain with his church flock until his ultimate mission was complete, and then he would divorce her without any remorse.

Instead of going to bed, Freemund decided to travel to the lodge to review a few notes before he met with the elders. They depended upon his leadership, and he would be remiss to let them down. Who ever heard of a Negro leading a successful revolt? Just where did these black beasts get the sense to be able to pull off a feat like that he had heard of today? He figured it must have to do with the prophecy and knew if he was to get extra help, he would need to get started right away. He treaded softly down the steps to the coatroom and retrieved his hat. His wife walked to the top of the stairs and stopped, staring down at him.

"You just can't get enough, can you? You dog!" It wasn't as much a shout as a harsh whisper. Although Freemund winced at the venom in her voice, he felt anger coil up in his stomach. Forcing himself to subdue the hate within him, he spoke softly.

"Honey, we have guests. You might try keeping quiet so others can sleep. I'm going to the lodge, if you must know, but in the meantime, why don't you make yourself useful and go to bed." Freemund didn't wait for a retort; he simply turned and walked out the door into the cool night's air.

Under the porch he kept one of his rifles and a cardboard box of bullets. Gingerly, he reached for them and loaded his weapon. He took a few extra shells in his coat pocket, although he didn't know why. He was well known around his parish and never feared being robbed. But a feeling chilled his spine just briefly as he stepped out of his warm home, and it wasn't the late evening breeze. Freemund learned long ago never to ignore premonitions. Once armed, he began his journey, thinking to himself that tonight was a good night for walking. The lodge was a ten-minute journey from his house, and the exercise would help ease the noxious effects of the bourbon. No one would be there, and that was good. He'd be able to read the secret manuals undisturbed.

The lodge was hidden in a cloak of trees away from the commonly trodden road. It was just far away for privacy but close enough for welcome guests who shared the unity of the Guild. Many had come upon it accidentally and wondered at the designs upon its walls. Made of ashlar, it had Latin inscriptions above the door and at each cornerstone. *Annuit Coeptis* was the inscription above the door and *Novus Ordo Seclorum* at the four corner stones. The only window, five feet above the door, was in the shape of a hexagon with a glass-stained portrait of a serpent. Freemund pulled the keys from his vest pocket and unlocked the heavy doors.

Inside, the main auditorium looked quite similar to his church. There were oak pews, forty in all, twenty to the left and twenty to the right. In front was a pulpit with two pews set neatly behind to the left and right. At every fifth pew on the main floor was an oil lamp placed high on the wall, and these lamps burned continually. No one saw the keeper who kept the lamps full, but all Freemund ever remembered during his twenty years of membership was that they were never out. The floor was barren, and the ceiling was high and vaulted. Freemund made his way down the aisle toward the pulpit and turned right to walk across the front row. He entered the door to his left that led behind the center stage. Immediately behind the door were spiral steps leading down to the first level. There were two other levels beneath that one, but only the chief elders were allowed entrance to the third; Freemund himself, who'd been a part of the Guild for twenty years, had never seen it—and dared not try. The first level housed the library, and that was where he needed to go.

One of the most intriguing aspects of the library was the documentation on those of the Guild who had made significant contributions, philosophically, to the organization. Freemund hoped to one day have his name on the spine of one of the hardback books for others to read and admire. He had spent hours of devoted study to sanctifying the servitude of the Negro. In his own mind, he knew he'd stretched the truth a little, but his work had made him legendary in his own right. He'd been accepted into the Guild and was immediately given high-rank. His congregation would follow him into the depths of hell, and he had successfully brainwashed every slave he had ever owned into believing that it was God's divine blessing that they be in servitude to the white man. That would definitely place him in the books after he had left this earth.

One of the reasons he wanted to get to the library as soon as possible was one of the features Elizabeth mentioned about her husband's plantation: the whipping tree. Freemund faintly remembered the elders referring to a mysterious tree that bridged the gap between mortal and spiritual realms. Freemund searched the stacks, looking for the magical book. At the moment he couldn't remember the title, but he'd recognize it when he saw it. Every book had an enchanting presence about it, having the best-tailored leather covers and gold-embossed lettering. Once opened, the pages felt like silk underneath one's palms, and the manuscript simply flowed and ebbed its way across the pages like an evening tide.

Finally, Freemund found the book for which he was looking, *The Book of Divination and Spiritual Communion*. He briefly scanned the table of contents, which consisted of prayers, spells, sacrifices, and spiritual relics and symbols. What he wanted was under spiritual relics and symbols. There were all manner of visual assortments that were drawn in pencil or ink stencils. The one that appealed to Freemund dealt with the tree. He carried the heavy book from its shelf and sat at one of the huge tables where he began reading slowly, trying to absorb every word.

The results of his search amounted to this: Biblically, since the beginning of time, there have been objects on earth to put man in contact with spiritual forces higher than his own. In the Garden of Eden, when man was reportedly perfect, there was God and the Tree of Knowledge of Good and Evil. At that time, Adam and Eve only had a one-dimensional interaction with the divine, and that was with God and his angels. But in all fairness, God, in wanting unmitigated loyalty from his followers, made it possible that Adam and Eve could also have exposure to the underworld— those who had been expelled from heaven. According to the text, one had to go to the tree and engage it or its inhabitants in order to have this experience. Of course, as everyone knows, the serpent was the first inhabitant of this tree and communicated with Eve. The serpent was this very organization's emblem of spiritual communion that served as their contact with other-worldly powers. According to the text, at the time it was not necessary for man to have access to the dark spiritual world because mankind had divinity keeping him company in the garden. However, after the fall of man, his ability to commune with the purity of God became estranged, while the forces of darkness increased their presence on the earth. Those forces desired to commune with man, as did the serpent in the Garden.

What was interesting to Freemund was the reported location of the Tree of Knowledge of Good and Evil. Scholars had deduced that the landmarks given in Genesis placed the Garden of Eden in Africa. No other race or people other than his organization knew of the import of this tree. Also, many whites underestimated the power of the spiritual world and, consequently, did not accurately appreciate the power of the Negro who, if properly directed, would have access to this kind of supernatural strength.

Freemund understood more than he allowed his counterparts to see. For one, he knew that slaves were not the stupid imps that even he himself had portrayed them to be; they were intelligent and capable of much power if they were ever allowed to realize their potential. He knew that if that day ever came, the paradise that he and all whites were experiencing now would end. Furthermore, the slave who had access to the nether world would be mightier than any man without spiritual help, thus Freemund would never underestimate any black person. His duty to his wealth, his generations, and his career depended on his intellectual ability to stay several steps ahead of everyone, especially the Negro. It seemed that through the tree, mankind continued his communing with the dark but powerful forces, especially when his fate and the fate of all his kind seemed destined to be extinguished at the hands of Anglo-Saxons. Who better fit this situation than the slave? But the text only mentioned that one such tree existed some place in Africa, and its exact location was uncertain, although there was speculation that it was near the river Euphrates in northern Africa.

For Freemund, who had studied this tree before, a feeling of clairvoyance suggested that, indeed, this was the source of power for these wayward Negroes. So the puzzle was how the slaves had managed to bring its power here. He'd seen the slave ships and knew that those voyages thoroughly stripped the slaves of all they held precious. What usually arrived on American shores was a stark, naked echo of what left the Dark Continent, which meant that the slaves they were dealing with were of superior ability and intellect in comparison to the thousand others he'd seen on the auction block. Solving this mystery was going to take the aid of the serpent and a lot of firepower; magic did have its limits.

When Freemund glanced at his watch he realized that it would soon be dawn; he needed to get home and work on a plan. As he was getting ready to close the book his eyes fell on footnotes at the bottom of the page. The tree did bear fruit once a year, which meant that the tree had the ability to reproduce. Legend had it that the fruit was consumed only by the priest who guarded the tree, and that the seeds were offered as sacrifices to the gods. One could only speculate what the result would be if the seeds were planted in other regions of the world. The Africans kept the tree safe from outsiders, so the possibility of the seeds being somewhere other than Africa was slim, unless, upon the threat of being sold into slavery, the seeds were distributed to certain members for use at a later time. Perhaps this is what had happened. A whole plantation had basically been delivered from bondage; once word got around to other slaves, revolt would be imminent.

Hearns had mentioned roots vomiting out of the mouth of the man who was in the cane field. "Strange ways." Isn't that what Hearns reported the poor man as saying before he died? There had to be a connection. To defeat this power the serpent would have to be appeased, and Elizabeth seemed ripe for the taking. Such a beautiful vessel would grant him and the Guild the leverage needed for spiritual assistance.

Freemund closed the book and replaced it on its shelf, then retraced his steps and climbed back to the main floor to exit the lodge. As he walked home his mind worked through various scenarios. He would talk with Hearns in the morning. Together, they would ensure the downfall of these pernicious rebels.

CHAPTER 16

THE PROMISED LAND

They remembered the earth. Of all they could have recalled at this moment, it was the earth of their homeland that captivated their thoughts, their memories. The magus had often told them stories of the grandeur of the magic the earth possessed. Indeed, it was quite beautiful to look upon: fertile soil, rich, dark, moist, and always yielding the most bountiful crops in their region. The verdure of the trees held such a lush green that visitors often commented that the leaves glowed. Yes, the soil is what Yemanja and Vashti meditated on while in the perils of an angry god. The gods had to be angry, or how could one explain their predicament? Weren't they supposed to be blessed? Chosen? Wasn't that what the magus had told them? But here they were in the hull of a strange vessel, shackled to strangers, the locks of their hair swimming in the feces and vomit that had escaped the cursed bowels and mouths of those whose spirits were about to be broken.

Yemanja and Vashti concentrated and focused their minds on the object that would give them the power to survive as they had been taught in the village school. They wished they had concentrated more like their magus Bjerre. Then they would not have been caught and dragged upon this demon that walked the waters. Bjerre sensed that something was wrong, but they did not listen. Instead, they laughed and giggled as they always did when talking about mysticism or the spirits. Now they were beginning to have their first real-life lesson in demonology, and they knew they were unprepared.

The vessel rocked relentlessly as it creaked against the harsh clap of the waters. Thunder boomed, and rain pelted the deck. The groans of men and women clamored against each other, each fighting hopelessly for air, for an audience with the gods, begging for deliverance. Yemanja and Vashti knew there would be no response to the anguish, so instead they meditated and finally found moderate reprieve in the earth. That was one lesson they were thankful they had learned. Of course, it was at Bjerre's insistence, but it was working, and they became instant believers. In the bowels of the ship, Yemanja and Vashti swore they would never again doubt the teachings of the magus and would seek instruction at the first given opportunity—if such an opportunity ever presented itself again.

As they clung to each other their minds settled upon the earth of their homeland in Africa, their village, to their past when they were children. Were they having the same dream? They could not know that they were, for they both had their eyes closed tightly, their breathing regulated, their senses focused on a better place, momentarily leaving this evil vessel for richer, cleaner territories. Yes, their bodies still lay chained in filth, but the most sacred part of them escaped, briefly, to another time, another place. If any of the other victims on the ship would have rolled over to look down upon them, they would have been shocked to see Yemanja and Vashti smiling, their eyes closed.

"Yemanja, wait for me!" Yemanja's feet pounded the earth rapidly, her hair flowing in the wind. She felt as if she were floating with the grace of gazelles. Vashti, whose legs weren't as long, raced as fast as she could behind her friend. She could never keep up. They were on their way to the village river to bathe. The morning air was crisp and had not yet taken on the tepid heat of early noon. The sun was just peeking her eye over the eastern horizon, and the morning dew reverently withdrew in respect of her quietly fierce gaze. Vashti always liked to watch the earth and grass speed by her feet, continually amazed at how it blurred then came back into focus with each pounding step. One day it would all be a blur when she would be able to keep up with Yemanja.

"Slow down, Yemanja! My lungs are starting to fire!"

"We're almost there, Turtle!" That was Yemanja's name for Vashti because of her slothful feet. Vashti and Yemanja laughed together as their progress took them up a small hill that sheered off into a quiet pool fed by the river. Vashti was impressed with how gracefully Yemanja lunged off the cliff, her legs still peddling her body forward on air, her arms swinging roundabout her head, before she plummeted out of sight. Vashti's heart raced in her chest, beating out a warning cadence that said, "Don't push it!" She looked up from the earth, saw that the drop was approaching, and concentrated on the jump. She wanted to be as elegant as Yemanja, but she knew that she wouldn't be. Almost there, she heard the splash of her best friend plunging in the pool below and, then, she too was airborne. She twisted in the air and looked down and back to watch the ground retreat from her body, which was now fully floating in open space between earth and sky.

All seemed to be happening in slow motion. She swung her head forward and saw the green hills on the opposite side of the river in which she would land. A floating braid fell into her vision then bounced back out of it with the same speed it entered. She looked down past her still-peddling feet and saw Yemanja gazing up at her, smiling. Her stomach was beginning to take on that funny feeling she always enjoyed, as if it, too, were trying to set itself free and float up and through the top of her head because her body was making its descent so rapidly, even though it appeared as if she were a bug swimming through tree sap. Yemanja was speaking to her, but she couldn't hear. She could see the water ripples still slowly emanating from Yemanja's body as her free fall brought her closer to her destination. She looked down just in time to see and feel the cool water embrace her body, and then she was fully immersed, baptized.

The girls splashed about the water frantically, shrilling in delight. Whatever peace nature experiences in the morning was broken by the joyous cries of these two girls. They were the vision of happiness, innocence.

"Let's see who can touch the bottom first, Yemanja!"

"Okay." Yemanja panted. "But let me catch my breath first."

"Okay, me too." The two girls bobbed up and down in the water like bark.

"Now!" Yemanja exclaimed mischievously, quickly flipping so that all Vashti could see was the tip of her ankles disappearing under the surface.

"No fair!" Vashti took in a deep breath and plunged her head into the water. She pumped her feet and legs like a frog and pulled the water toward her as she struggled to find the bed of the pool. They both swam with their eyes open, watching each other's blurry forms. Vashti observed there weren't many fish swimming here today but thought nothing of it; she was intent on beating Yemanja to the bottom. Vashti exerted all of her energy and swam past Yemanja, downward. She turned to her friend and blew a few bubbles of air toward her, taunting. Vashti touched bottom first, then flipped and pushed off the soft underwater earth toward the surface. The cool water rushing past her body made her feel powerful as she stroked toward the surface. Vashti burst from the water with a gasp, her body emerging from the water all the way to her waist. Seconds later, Yemanja did the same. She was becoming a better swimmer. Vashti was momentarily struck with jealousy. She wanted to have at least one skill at which she could far outperform her friend. That skill used to be swimming, but she sagaciously knew that era was ending. However, she would never let it interfere with their friendship. She just had to work harder than everybody else, and that was all there was to it.

After frolicking in the warm sun for nearly an hour, the two swam to shore and began their walk toward the village. The magus was not lenient on tardiness, and neither Yemanja nor Vashti wanted to experience that lesson again, so they decided to race to their meeting. The bronze-colored temple was situated in the middle of a dense forest. The dirt path leading to it widened out into a hardened-clay spread where trees and shrubbery had been replaced by circular buildings with thatched roofs and packed earthen floors. This was the only part of the village that had two-story edifices. Yemanja remembered her father talking over a meal about how a priest had invented a masonry mechanism using trees and ropes to bind and form anchors over which mud walls were laid. The builders cut down trees and measured them all the same length in order to make wooden floors above the earth. It amazed her every time to walk into the temple to look up and see another floor above the earth. The center of temple was the only building that held the pool of reflection through which the magus could see the future. Many students under training at the temple would be chosen to visit the magus by appointment to have their futures revealed to them. Today was Yemanja and Vashti's turn.

Bjerre, the eldest magus, turned to face the oncoming patter of feet as the two jovial girls crashed through the doorway. They were laughing, and their laughter was contagious. Bjerre's wizened gray eyes twinkled with joy at his two favorite pupils. Bjerre wore only a white skirt about his waist that flowed to his ankles. The bottom embroidery was a beautiful tapestry of symbolic figures that delineated his family's history. All elders earned the right to wear such a robe, but it took many years to deserve it. Once an elder had received a robe, he had new embroidery added to it every ten years. In the days of old, priests often had up to three robes in order to detail the span of their history. But that was before the war, when priests lived much longer.

Although Bjerre's face bore signs of age, his body was as fit as a thirty-five year old's, and no male student dared to challenge him in a wrestling match. His undefeated status exhibited proof of that fact. Bjerre raised his hand to shield his eyes from the rising sun but only momentarily, for dark, cumulus clouds were making their way through the sun's rays. The murky scent of imminent rain filled his nostrils as he inhaled the balmy atmosphere. The sight of his students, the village, the trees, and the rays of light dancing off the morning dew brought him immense gratification. He wondered how anyone could be unhappy when such simple pleasures gave such joy.

"We're early today, Magus." Yemanja said elatedly.

"As well you should be, children. The future awaits." Bjerre gestured silently toward the pool of reflection as a crackle of thunder shook the cloudy sky and a gust of wind picked up a few stray leaves in the temple doorway and carried them to the heavily foliaged outskirts of the village. Yemanja and Vashti stepped within the comfort of the temple and walked over to the reflection pool where six knitted mats lay around it on the floor. The pool, which was more like a huge cup for a twenty-foot giant, was made of hardened clay and was emptied by dipping large, wooden buckets into its depth. The water had to be renewed every full moon in order for the priest to see clearly. The old water, considered to be blessed, was taken to the villages and used to irrigate the gardens.

"The waters have been unusually still this morning." Bjerre said with a sudden grimace. Yemanja and Vashti settled on their mats and regarded each other with anticipatory excitement. Bjerre glanced at them with a subtle frown. When Yemanja looked up at him, she noticed the emotion in his face.

"What's wrong, Magus?" Yemanja asked, honoring the priest by not using his birth name. Bjerre quickly caught himself; he was letting his emotions show, and that was inappropriate for a priest. His was a huge responsibility as his position allowed him to see what was out of reach for all but the priest: the future, and sometimes alternate destinies. That's what made Bjerre keep his station as a magus—he felt a tremendous obligation to undertake this great responsibility.

"My apologies, young learners, but the atmosphere today troubles my spirit. Something is amiss; however, it was sharp of you to be aware of my emotions, little one, or clumsy of me." Bjerre pointed a thick, sturdy finger at Yemanja, his face stern but his eyes now full of laughter. "Many priests quit the service almost as soon as they start because the burden of seeing the future and advising our people proves far too heavy. There are times when seeing the future is not always pleasant."

He remembered his teacher Gausje. When he was twelve she had told him a story that he now related to the girls. Gausje had foreseen the gruesome death of one of the magus at the hand of his own son. She wanted to warn him, but she also saw more. The Magus Tetati was blackmailing his son's chief wife into working for him. He gave her a potion that would make her less inhibited, and when the herbs had their effect, he had sex with her. This had occurred one month before his son was to wed her. The dilemma Gausje faced was that African tribes were chauvinistic. If a woman was caught in the act of adultery, she could be put to death, which was usually the case—even if she had been raped. African culture believed that once a woman's body had been violated, she was unclean and thus unworthy to be taken as a wife to bear children. Bjerre, now sixty-three, was glad life had changed. He remembered Gausje had been banished from the tribe when another member looked into the pool of reflection and discovered that Gausje had seen the future and withheld it from Tetati, who indeed was murdered by his son. The tribe claimed that because Gausje was a woman, she felt undue compassion for the woman with whom Tetati had slept and, consequently, unnecessarily compromised the sanctity of the magus order by causing one of their members to be slain. She had been the only female to ever hold place as magus or been a pupil in the great temple.

"Is that why some of the priests don't call you Magus? Is it because they are angry that you have two girl pupils?" Vashti queried.

"You are very observant, my child. And, yes, that is why there is such disrespect. Gausje was the greatest magus in the history of our tribe. Yet her family's history has been totally erased except from my memory. She became greater than her teacher, who thought it right and proper to teach anyone who was willing to learn."

"Is that why you have chosen us as your pupils? Because you know that soon we will be better than you?" Vashti asked with a slight grin on her face. She looked over at Yemanja, who was struggling to keep a smirk off hers. Bjerre laughed heartily. Yemanja and Vashti both joined in, unable to control themselves. They had never seen Bjerre laugh like this.

"So you believe you are a good pupil, eh? Actually, you are right. I do believe that you are to serve a great purpose; what it is, I don't know, but perhaps today we will see. But Gausje taught me that everyone deserves a chance, and I believe that, despite what some of the other priests think, banishing my teacher was wrong, and one day her misfortune will be avenged."

"Perhaps you taking us on as your learners will be a part of that vengeance," said Yemanja.

"Perhaps. Magus Gausje strangely disappeared one night. Her hut showed signs of a struggle, and all her belongings where there except for the magic runes of her family, which she kept on her at all times in the most peculiar way. The day before she left she took me on a walk down to the river and told me to study hard and become a magus, because her life and mine had a deeper purpose than what we both could imagine. It has been years since, and I have held my part of the bargain, but I've no idea about my former teacher. Now, enough chatter. Let's do what we came here for, shall we?"

Bjerre's eyes lit up. He went to the pool and stood opposite where the girls sat. He closed his eyes and raised his hands directly above his head. A glass eye was embedded in the temple's ceiling. At high noon the sun's rays blazed a brilliant shaft of light through the eye directly into the pool of reflection, setting it ablaze. It was amazing to see. The first set of priests purchased the glass from Egypt, where Egyptians had been using glass for centuries. In Egypt, the sun's glare was so intense it could melt sand into this the object the priests called glass. But today, the thick, black clouds covered the sun's rays, and, as if in retaliation, bright lighting streaked across the sky instead. When the thunder clapped loudly, the girls shrieked in excitement. They giggled and held onto each other, momentarily using one another for support to maintain an air of dignity in front of the magus, yet they could barely contain themselves.

The shaft of light that normally blazed through the roof into the pool of reflection added clarity to the visions. Priests could see everything clearly, and it at times added a sense of palpability that was inordinately tangible. But the priest could still see, even on days when the sun did not shine; on such days the images were quite murky and hard to make out but appeared nonetheless. But Bjerre was gifted and could see better than any other of the priests. Today, though, he felt an ominous twinge of negativity, as if he shouldn't look into the future.

"Well, Magus, what do you see?" said Yemanja.

"Yes! How great are we going to be?" Vashti chimed in.

Bjerre decided he was being unusually unnerved today. He would look into the future. He repeated the chant that always brought truths to light, letting the rhythmic words roll off his tongue. He closed his human eyes, the water rippled, and his spiritual eyes began to slowly open. Although his human eyes were closed, he could still see the pool of reflection and the two girls sitting before him. As always, all was clearer, brighter. The wind outside had escalated to a howl, and the trees genuflected and swayed. The temple, hardened by years of sunlight and care, remained a rock, unmoved by the elements. Bjerre shut out the howls and focused on the pool, the chant, and the future. Suddenly, the waters rose around the edge of the pool in what looked to be tiny ripples, as if someone had dropped dozens of tiny pebbles into the water. Yemanja and Vashti, sitting at eye level, could see the water rise silently, forming an upside down tear, but it never returned to its place. The water rose and stayed right where it was, frozen in time.

"Amazing." Yemanja whispered. Vashti was speechless. She had heard how the priest could make the elements do that which was unnatural, and she thought she had prepared herself to see it, but actually being here in the presence of magic, witnessing water defy gravity, left her speechless. All inside the temple was at peace while the elements stormed outside as if in angry protest. Then, Bjerre gave a little grunt, and the girls saw his body grow rigid as he stretched his hands over the pool, beads of perspiration rolling down his shiny head. Bjerre was in vision.

Not even the disappearance of Gausje could match the horror to which Bjerre was now to be exposed. He saw the two girls walking home hand-in-hand. He saw them go inside their hut and speak to their parents, saw them all embracing, crying? He wasn't sure, but he thought he saw a look of sorrow on the face of the parents.

Then that scene rippled away and another came into view. Yemanja and Vashti were older now, nearly grown. They were beautiful, the most beautiful girls he had ever seen. Their skin was flawless, and their breasts and hips were full with womanhood. Bjerre's heart swelled with pride at what he saw. He noticed that around their ankles they both wore rings of brass, which meant they had passed the rites of passage and had been fully accepted into the school of the magus. They were happy, and once again he saw their parents standing proud.

The water rippled again, and he saw a scene that was unusual and ominous. He saw huge vessels riding the sea like demons. He saw strange-looking men with pale flesh and straight yellow hair being carried by these vessels. Their eyes held the look of greed and hate that he had seen in the jealous priests and in neighboring tribes against whom he had to defend his village. The scene swooshed away to show the men walking out of the water and coming onto shore. They carried objects made out of metal, and they pointed them at his tribesmen; fire and smoke blew out of these devices, and several of the tribesmen dropped to the ground, bearing holes where their chests had once been.

Bjerre then saw the men meeting with the Watusi, archenemies of his tribe. The Watusi gave the pale men gold and gifts, and the pale men gave them the stick that shot out smoke and fire—the stick of death. The waters rippled, and Bjerre saw his village in flames, saw Yemanja and Vashti being taken captive. They were screaming and crying. Bodies filled with holes lay strewn over the village floor. His people were tied to thick logs and hung upside down like animals after a big hunt. Another huge ripple in the water and Bjerre saw Yemanja and Vashti and many, many others being hauled onto the ship. Bodies were stuffed into the belly of the vessel, and Yemanja and Vashti were chained together. The vessels departed and headed away from the sun.

Bjerre had seen priests float off the ground for minutes before coming down; he'd seen priests touch wounds and when they removed their hands, the wound was gone; he'd even seen priests speak to animals, and the animals would do whatever they had been commanded to do. He himself had mastered and could do these wonders, but never had he seen a beast that could walk the sea and carry people with it.

The waters rippled again, and Yemanja and Vashti stood on a platform, beaten, striped naked, sweaty and humiliated before hundreds of pale-fleshed observers who had the look of the devil himself in their faces. Another ripple of the waters, and he saw a village that looked like the one he was in, then he saw the back of a woman; she had a certain look of familiarity about her person. He saw red-fleshed men and women and African men and women walking about her. She wore a regal red robe about her waist. She looked extremely old, but he could swear that he knew her or someone from her family. When the woman turned slowly around so that Bjerre could see her face, he let out an audible gasp. It was his old teacher, Gausje, smiling at him. She mouthed a message to him, but he could not quite decipher what she was saying. His closed eyes squeezed out droplets of tears, and his throat became filmy with spit.

Gausje was alive, but she was no longer here in Africa. She was in another unfamiliar place. Gausje mouthed the words to him again, and this time he understood. She said it is destiny. She then held out her hand to him, palm turned upward. In it was a white stone. She turned her hand face down, and the three of them heard a plop in the water. Then Gausje was gone; in her place were a much older and haggard-looking Yemanja and Vashti, standing together, besmeared in a substance that looked like blood on their flesh, but the look of triumph was on their faces. The water rippled again, and Bjerre saw the words, Give the stone to Vashti. Instruct her in the ways of the priest. And then it was over. The raised droplets of water quietly returned to their resting place as Bjerre opened his eyes. Lines of tears streaked his troubled face as Yemanja and Vashti looked up at him in wonder.

"We heard an object drop into the water, Magus. Shall one of us retrieve it?" questioned Yemanja.

"No, child. Do not touch the sacred waters while they are in the sacred temple. Only a magus can do so and remain whole." Yemanja and Vashti looked astonished but did as they were told. Bjerre's body quivered involuntarily, and his face looked ashen, his skin pimply because the tiny, nearly invisible hairs on his smooth skin were standing straight up. "Maybe," he thought to himself, "maybe it was just a false illusion. Maybe the thunder and the winds and the lightening were just signs telling me not to look into the future today because I would be wrong."

Bjerre knew was that the stone he saw Gausje drop into the pool was one of her magic rune stones. And if it was in the pool, then all this was real. He plunged his hand into the pool but had to immerse his entire upper body into the water in order to touch the bottom. He fished around until he felt the smooth and cool object fill his hand—sure enough, it was one of the rune stones that Gausje always kept with her. She was passing the stone onto Vashti, a tremendous honor. Gausje had given only one stone away, and that was to him. And he remembered his responsibility. Although grim, the future must be delivered once inquired. And, most importantly, these young ladies seemed destined for greatness—it would just come at a terrible price.

CHAPTER 17
RITES OF PASSAGE

Yemanja and Vashti awoke amid a thundering boom that was followed by fierce lightening. They were still in the hull of the ship, but the memory of Bjerre and their vision worked to help them cope with the rancid stench that stung their nostrils. The heaving and quaking of the vessel kept them in a constant state of nausea, and prisoners wailed helplessly at the horrid conditions in which they found themselves. When Yemanja thought about it, there was nothing that could have gotten them out of this situation. No planning or learning from the temple at the foot of the great Bjerre could have averted the inevitable. As he had said, it was destiny.

Yemanja looked to see a fellow prisoner chained above her open his mouth and spew out a trail of putrid vomit. She had just enough time to close her eyes and tighten her lips before the foul mixture splashed on her face and ran sluggishly down her cheeks and chin, getting into her hair. Most of the prisoners on the bottom row had yellowish stains on their necks and faces where the bile and stomach acid released from the sick and dying had slowly begun the decomposing process of digestion.

Vashti looked over at Yemanja, quickly turned her head the other way, and burped loudly. She was dizzy, and though bile rose up in her throat, she swallowed hard to keep it from falling on another prisoner. She felt her stomach heave and gurgle. Her sphincter muscles wetted, then loosened, as her bowels gave way to the pressure. The stench nearly caused her to pass out, and she heard someone curse in fierce retaliation of the smell. The anger, the frustration, the pity, and the helplessness created a sense of confusion that was nearly tangible. Suddenly, a loud noise and a burst of light resonated in the hull of the ship. The clanging of chains woke the sleeping and startled those already awake.

All the prisoners had shackles on their wrists and feet; everyone was stretched out to his or her extremities in order to create enough room for more than four hundred slaves. There were three-tiered cages below deck in the hull of the ship, allowing only twenty inches of space from one to the next. One foul aisle ran between them for shipmates to chain the prisoners, douse them with lye to help fight damaging infection, or drag out the dead corpses of those who sought an alternative to a life of misery. Those who were on the bottom tier lay face up, then those above them lay face down, and finally the uppermost tier had the slaves face up. The latter ones might be considered lucky because they escaped having vomit and feces dropped upon them. However, they nearly suffocated from the awful stench that rose from the belly of the ship. Until one rode in this vessel, he or she could not even fathom how such a horrible odor can kill one's spirit to live.

The boy at the door was named Richard. He held to his nose and mouth a white cloth soaked with bourbon to stifle the stench. It was the odor that was worst of all, more than the haggard look of humans who were relegated to extreme levels of savagery. He quickly unlocked the deadbolt and gave a hard pull on the chain to get it loose. At times the rotted flesh of a dead slave's hands or wrists stuck to the metal. Yanking the chain set it free, allowing him to turn the knob of the joist that would wind the chains around a large wooden spool until every manacled hand was released. It was Richard's job to check on the slaves, drag away the dead, and bring those still living on deck for cleaning. Yes, he had help. The captain dared not send him down alone lest the angry beasts below quickly overrun him and take control of the ship. Richard faintly smiled at the thought. That might not be such a bad idea; anything had to be better than this. There were usually four men who followed behind him with drawn pistols or whips, but they took pleasure in watching the reaction of the first to catch the pungent stench of death. And it didn't matter how long a person smelled it—one could never get use to the horrible combination of death and shit and vomit.

Richard staggered against the stench of decay as he felt his stomach heave and his eyes immediately start to water. He turned around to meet a cold pistol set against the bridge of his nose. It was Jericho, and the guards laughed.

"Look at ye, little bitch! Can't hardly keep ye lunch, can ye matey?" Their laughter was harsh and insufferable.

"Go on, cupid, them niggers below are a smelly bunch. I'm goin' back up. Take this." The guard threw him a leather whip. "I'm goin' ta set me britches right a top here by the steps. If I catch a feelin' that even the slightest mischief is a foot, I'm goin' ta fill ye arse with lead! And dem niggers, too. Taint like we ain't got more 'nough to spare!"

Richard's red face, potted with terrible acne wounds that ran deep and ragged, twisted in anger and disgust as he turned back to the horror below deck. His yellow hair stood out in stark contrast to the messy visage. As for smarts, he hadn't done well in school and had run away from home, hoping to find a life of adventure on the seas. He snuck aboard this particular slave ship, the Marietta, which often ported in Carolina. He had sailed to Africa and now was on the return voyage to New Orleans.

Richard stood staring at the naked slaves. Their plight had placed them beyond the realm of shame, and they made no efforts to cover their nakedness; they were focused too much on living or dying. He shook his head and slammed his fist against the door plank. He thought that life aboard the ship would be easy, fun, even dangerous, but he was horribly disappointed. Once, he was discovered taking a midnight piss overboard, and the crew beat him and made him dress like a woman and prance on the deck while a sailor played the flute. He tried to laugh it off, but it stung him deeply that for the first time in his life he was powerless to defend himself. He also didn't like the way some of the sailors looked at him and held him while under the auspices of "just playing." These men leered at him as if he were actually a woman, and that made his skin crawl.

When he was found as a stowaway and brought to Captain Newton, the captain regarded him with seasoned, veteran eyes and told him that he had committed a crime and he was likely to have his men throw him overboard. Richard broke down and started crying once he saw that this was no joke. Just as he began begging for his life, the captain informed Richard that he would allow him to live and spare him future embarrassment if he promised to work aboard the Marietta for free. Richard reluctantly obliged. His job was cleaning out the slave decks, and he dreaded every second of it.

The moans of the slaves rose louder than thunder in Richard's ears. He absolutely hated this part of the job. The women and men were brought up separately, the women always first. Once the chains were released from their hands, Richard had thought they would get up and start running, trying to get out, but it was impossible to do as their legs had been tucked under them for long hours and so felt numb. The cargo were chained in the galleys for twenty-three hours at a time and were brought up on deck once a day, usually for an hour, to get hosed down, to dance to keep their muscles from atrophying, and to get a little sunlight so they would not suffer from rickets. But their hands—it was their hands that disturbed Richard the most. The touch of just one of them made him want to wash himself with lye. And they inevitably did touch him, grope for him, while he told them to shut up, while he whipped their hands away from him. Richard ran down the aisle amid the cries for water, for food, for death. The black hands slapped against his pale flesh, leaving dirty streaks behind. He could hear the floor splashing beneath his feet, and it seemed like the aisle was an inferno in hell that would never end. He reached the very end and turned to holler.

"Get up and out, ye arses!" He cracked the whip on the filthy floor, which looked to move as if it were alive, the different colors and floating objects undulating against the sway of the whip. He hollered again, and when they heard the music of the flute, they slowly began to inch out of their crawl space. "Damn if I do this much longer," Richard said to himself. The females oozed in slow motion into the aisle, their breasts jouncing against each other like pendulums. Their nakedness at one time would have aroused Richard to climax, but now it only produced disgust. On one woman's face he noticed a yellow spot growing. He remembered seeing it three days ago, but then it was the size of a pea; now it was the size of a quarter. Many of the females' hair was starting to fall out, and some of the younger girls' ribs poked defiantly against their skin. They were ghosts in human shells, waiting for the final metamorphosis of rot that would set them free. Richard determined at that moment he would end this, either with their death or his; he could not endure this much longer.

Once, when the Marietta docked in Africa, Richard contemplated running away. He didn't give a cat's ass if it wasn't his country; any life had to be better than being held captive on this ship. He packed a small sack of clothes and moldy bread that he had saved. He was standing in line, getting ready to disembark, when Captain Newton came on deck and walked directly toward him. The captain wore a fine, white suit, and had a shiny pistol stuck in his belt. The captain tapped the butt of the gun and calmly smiled at Richard.

"You don't get to leave the ship, lad. Stowaways are without privileges."

"But Captain—" Richard heard the crisp slap from one of the mates of the ship before he felt it. He couldn't understand why he didn't see him standing just a little behind him and to the left. The humiliation stung more than the actual hurt.

It was Jericho, named so by his Bible-toting mother who said he would grow up to be a strong fortress like the Old Testament city. Richard hated him; he was always bossing Richard around, and he treated the slaves worse than scavenger dogs. Richard realized Jericho was absolutely out of his mind the day he took his own excrement, put it in a loaf of bread, and fed it to a slave. The man had already taken two swallows before his brain registered that he had eaten shit. Richard didn't care how much hate one felt, there were certain acts that were just plain sick and intolerable. Jericho and the other shipmates roared with laughter as the man gagged and coughed up the half-chewed bread stained dark with feces. They were hardly prepared to stop him when he suddenly tried to hurl himself overboard, and he would have made it, too, were he not so weak. Richard remembered wishing silently for the poor rascal's death. He wondered how long it would be before it was his turn to eat human waste. He remembered looking at Jericho with profuse anger but feeling too damn scared to do anything about it.

"You watch ye mouth when talkin' to ye captain, mate!" Jericho sneered. He emphasized the "t" in mate, and a spray of spit puffed out his mouth when he said it.

"Richard, you will stay aboard the ship and wash the deck and sprinkle lye down in the hull."

"Yes, Captain Newton, sir."

"Jericho will supervise you and keep you company until we return. I trust he will make sure you don't try to escape like you did when you snuck aboard this vessel." Captain Newton looked at Jericho and gave a slight smile. Jericho nodded in return, the sides of his lips turning upward in an evil grin. "The both of you see to it that no one boards this ship." Captain Newton then turned away.

"Damn." Richard whispered furtively under his breath. He turned to go back to his quarters, a little crawl space of a room, which was supposed to hold artillery. The captain said that these days no one would be crazy enough to try to overtake a slave ship, and besides, there was enough bounty for all so that they had no need of artillery to defend their ship. Jericho followed close behind, chuckling.

"Damn." He mimicked. "After ye put ye shit back, little fooker, I want ye to get down in dem galleys below and make sure lye is everywhere. I want that place white as me skin, ye hear mate?" Richard nodded in response and did as he was told. He didn't want to rouse Jericho in the least bit, and he hoped Jericho would find another to pay attention to.

"Hurry it up, matey! We don't have much sunshine left!" Jericho's words were like the shrill bark of a Doberman pincher. They jolted Richard back to the present as he uncoiled his whip and took aim. Richard cracked the whip, accidentally hitting the buttocks of the last woman in line. Her flesh gave easily as she let out a small whimper. Blood flowed down the back of her leg, and the shock of her pain caused her to butt her nose against the back of the head of the woman in front of her. She didn't even cry; she just shook her head, violently, from side to side, her arms flexed straight down by her sides, her tiny hands balled into tight fists, and kept shuffling forward. Richard threw the whip to the floor. From now on he would just use his voice. "Get up and out, ye arses." But his fervency was gone.

On deck the sun was just getting ready to set. Because it had been raining most of the day, everyone had been in quarters. One week before, while eating stale bread and flat beer, Richard had overheard one of the older shipmates talking about the last time they brought the slaves up during a storm. Supposedly, a group of five bearing circular tattoos around their thighs did a kind of chant while dancing. The shipmate described them as having a look of earnest peace about them, and they danced to their own rhythm. This went on for about an hour when they suddenly stopped dancing, huddled together, and knelt on the deck in a tight circle. One of the shipmates was about to whip them back into action when a red bolt of lightening stuck them and that one shipmate, killing them all instantly.

"The flesh! It stank 'nough to make ya eyes water," Richard overheard the shipmate say. "Dey had da look of pain, and joy, in dere flashin' eyes as the bolt hit dem. Dey fell smoking on de deck. Dat po' ole boy with da whip looked de worse. His mouth was black, and his eyeballs had sunk in his sockets and smoked like steamed crabmeat. Everyone was scared dat night— da niggas and de whites—ya see, fear knows no color." At that the creaky shipmate lit his pipe and blew out a slow stream of smoke. Those who were there to witness bore proof of the story, but several of the newer shipmates shook their heads in disbelief, while others disregarded it as but a sailor's tale.

This evening was unusually humid, and the sun was a dark red, but more unusual than that was the color of the moon, which was quite visible in the evening dusk. It was red, blood red, and its glare made Richard think back to the strangeness of that night about which the old shipmate had talked. The captain got wind of the stories and forbade anyone to speak of what they had witnessed when the lightening streaked from the sky as if in direct command of these savages' cries. He said it would cause superstition.

Richard had finally gotten the Africans assembled on the deck and removed their shackles. Richard watched, mesmerized, by the perseverance of broken humanity while his mind wondered back to Jericho. Jericho—the man who, physically, had lived up to his mother's expectations by age sixteen, weighing two hundred and thirty pounds on a six-foot three frame, and it was mostly muscle, except for a gut that came as a result of heavy drinking. Richard mused over the fact he doubted Jericho's mother had completely read the Bible story, else she would have found a name with a happier ending. But come to think of it, most Biblical cities did not last long. Even Jerusalem, God's chosen city, had been burnt to a glowing crisp.

Richard found himself reading a lot more of the Bible after being stuck on this God-forsaken ship. After witnessing horrifying storms, human brutality, and death, he'd become a devout Christian. He'd secretly wished that what happened to the city of Jericho would happen on board this vessel; however, as far as he could tell, there was no one on board who would play the role of Joshua and knock Jericho on his ass. And God obviously was too busy elsewhere to care about what happened on board the Marietta.

CHAPTER 18

THE FALL OF JERICHO

Jericho felt the blood rushing to his privates in a way that was most pleasing. He absolutely hated these beings but was wildly attracted to the two who stood before him. Maybe it was the power, the many months at sea without a woman, their unmitigated beauty, or a combination of all three, but he intended to have these women. However, he wanted the crew to see that he was above sleeping with beasts. No, he would just play with them for a bit, see what their insides felt like with his fingers. He wondered if women got aroused from fear like men sometimes did. Did they get wet like men get hard in the face of death? He was about to find out. The heavy breast in his hand gave way to his grip while the lump in his crotch hardened. He saw the woman look at him with disdain, but that only made him want her more. When he placed his other calloused hand roughly on the thatch of black hair that hid her privates, Vashti let out a throaty groan of displeasure. The other slaves danced to the music of the flute, not even stopping for a second to see what was happening, as such events took place nightly aboard the Marietta. Women and men alike worked hard not to attract the unwanted attention of a lascivious sailor who had no qualms whatsoever in taking what was unrightfully his. Jericho looked around at his comrades and laughed.

"Eh? Someone want to split this one with me?" The men chuckled as Jericho danced back and forth with the woman, his hands between her legs. Sweat protruded from both their bodies, hers still having the stench of waste clinging to it. But Jericho didn't seem to mind getting soiled. Richard's red face glared from under his yellow hair. He was boiling with anger. A voice inside told him that if he did not act, Jericho was going to taint that which should not be tainted. Jericho never starved for flesh. At every port he bragged about how he got women to sleep with him, but Richard knew more about Jericho than the other shipmates did. Jericho wanted flesh, plain and simple, and it didn't matter to him what creed, race, or gender, as long as it was under his power.

The hair on Richard's neck stood up as his mind involuntarily took him back to the past, to the day his life changed forever, to his foiled escape. He had been filling the heavy metal bucket with lye when he had the strange feeling he was being watched, but when he turned around there was only the wind and a few seagulls riding her current. Why of all people did the captain have to leave him on board alone with Jericho? The boy with the flute never talked much, but Richard observed that he was obedient and a hard worker; why not leave him behind so the two of them could become friends? But Richard knew the answer; the flute boy was being rewarded for his good behavior, while he himself was a stowaway. He remembered talking to himself.

"Damn, Captain! You'd think I'd paid for my wrongs by now. It has been two months since I've been aboard this ship, and all I get is hell everyday!" Salty tears of anger stung his eyes. That always happened to him when he was mad. He blinked to hold them back, but two tears spilled down his face, and he didn't even bother to wipe them away. His vision blurred as he picked up the bucket of lye and walked down into the galleys. He began to swing the bucket at half angles, arcing sweeps of lye down on the hard wood. The lye puffed up in white dust clouds when it made contact, and soon the place had a foggy look to it.

Richard started to think about home and going back to school. He'd learned so much in the two months he'd spent aboard this vessel, and he believed he had the capability to learn even complicated skills. All the crew had to know various terminologies for equipment and how to use it. In the pubs, he'd listened to old shipmates tell stories about places they had been and the marvels they'd seen. It could be boring, but most often it was quite interesting. When he thought about it, he was basically sitting through a lecture as he would have to at school. It was funny how life was going to teach him one way or another. He was so caught up in his rapture of home and school that he did not hear the door to the galleys shut, or the soft footsteps come up behind him, until he felt hot streams of breath puffing on the back of his neck.

"What the—!" Huge, hardened arms wrapped themselves tightly around Richard, pinning his two arms tightly to his sides. He dropped the bucket of lye to the floor with a piercing thud, and Jericho kicked it away.

"Sit still, lad. This won't be but a moment. Did ye think ye was going to make this trip without one of us gettin' to ye? Ye must be mad!" Jericho grunted a chuckle. His hot breath stank and curdled against the nape of Richard's neck.

"Get off me, you bastard!" Richard's voice cracked as he screamed. He sounded so weak. He kicked his legs wildly against Jericho's shins, but Jericho rushed him forward to the end of the galleys and slammed Richard's body into the wall. Richard had just enough time to turn his face, sparing his nose but not his cheek. He heard a crunching noise and realized that he would be missing a few teeth once this was all over. When he felt the rough edges of Jericho's abrasive tongue tear at his neck, he screamed in retaliation.

"Help! Help me! Somebody! Please!!!"

"Ain't no one to hear ye scream lad, but meself." Jericho spoke in calm tones. "But to tell ye the truth, I kinda like it. Why don't ye scream a little louder? Eh, lad?"

Richard took his two feet and pushed a little way from the wall, giving him just enough room to plant the soles of his feet firmly against the plank. Then, with all his might, he pushed himself backward, throwing Jericho off balance and sending them both flying. Jericho landed on his back with Richard on top of him, but he had not released his tight grasp. Richard quickly bent his head forward until his chin touched his neck, and then he brought it back as hard as possible. Jericho let out a loud yell and squeezed Richard even harder, but Richard brought his head forward and repeatedly banged it back into Jericho's face. Finally, Jericho released him, and Richard rolled over onto the floor away from Jericho. Both of them were now covered with white powder. There was a little red streak of blood on Richard's lip; he felt his cheekbone, and the flesh was spongy to the touch. He looked at Jericho and was satisfied to see a bloody face protruding through the white ghostly image. Jericho was holding his nose, and blood was pouring out between his fingers.

"I'm going to kill ye when I'm finished, little shit!" Spurts of blood sprayed out of Jericho's mouth when he spoke. He charged at Richard, but Richard just stood there, paralyzed. He didn't know what to do or why he did what he did next. Maybe it was instinct, but when Jericho came within striking range, Richard lunged at him again and crashed his forehead in the middle of Jericho's face. Jericho's arms splayed out in a silly fashion, and were they under different circumstances, Richard would have laughed. Richard ran past Jericho and picked up the bucket, which he swung with all his might against the back of Jericho's head, and the giant went tumbling face down. Richard observed the slow spread of a small pool of blood emanating from Jericho's head. Richard hoped Jericho was dead, but he wasn't about to examine him to find out. He dropped the metal bucket and dashed toward the door, opened it, and rushed up into the light. Now was his chance to escape.

Richard looked frantically around the ship and was relieved to find it was still empty. Would he have time to get his bag? "Hell no! Just get off the ship!" His mind screamed. As he ran to where the plank led down to the dock he glanced at his outstretched hands and saw splotches of blood staining the white powdery crust that had encapsulated his skin. The contrast of red and white was stark; he couldn't go on land looking like that or else some of the captain's friends would see him and report him. He looked back at the galleys where he had left Jericho, but the door did not move. He listened for movement and heard no one. He decided to change his clothes quickly and leave the ship before anyone could realize he was gone. He ran to his quarters, pulled off his shirt, and stumbled out of his pants. He grabbed a shirt and a dirty pair of pants and quickly pulled them on. When he heard a creak behind him, he turned around expecting to see Jericho, but it was just the give and take of the ship. In less than two minutes, he had changed his clothes, gotten his bag, and was racing out back toward the plank.

Richard could now taste freedom; he could see it. Even in this foreign land, he would manage to survive and eventually make his way back home. Life on the ship taught him he could learn whatever he put his mind to. The wind raced against his face and hair, both still stained with lye and blood, but he didn't care. He would wash at the first opportunity. His feet clanged down the plank and onto the dock. He could hardly believe he was going to get away. He looked back at the ship expecting Jericho, but still there was no sign of him. Richard turned forward, running hard, putting as much distance between the ship and him as possible. The dock seemed to go forever. His heart beat rapidly; he knew that once he got his feet on dry land, freedom would be his, and there would be no turning back.

Richard raced, straining to shorten the distance to his liberation—thirty feet, twenty-five feet, ten feet; his heart skipped a beat; five feet; he looked back while still running forward. No Jericho! *"Damn, I must have killed him! Alleluia, old pervert!"* But when he turned back he saw Captain John Newton and his crew walking toward the ship. They had left but an hour before. Confusion blared into his brain and confounded his feet in a tangle. He tripped, skidded, and rolled on the dock, nearly falling into the shallow water. The noise caught the captain's attention, and he and his crew started running toward him. Richard screamed, "No!" as he leaped off the dock into the water. The shallow water came just to his chest; he dove under and tried to swim away from the captain and his crew, but his bag of clothes was buoyant and kept him above water. He ripped himself free from the bag and slung it toward the shore. He could retrieve it later.

There was a small boat tied to one of the poles on the dock. *"If I could just get to that boat, I could hide on the other side of it until I get a clear chance to run,"* Richard thought, but his hope for freedom was already waning. What he heard surprised him: shots. Diving under the water, he turned his head in the direction of the sound and saw a white, bubbly streak shoot past him. *"These bastards would rather kill me than let me escape!"* Richard was incredulous with disbelief. He wanted to escape, but he didn't want to die. His air was short, and he came up for a new gulp of oxygen.

"There he is!" shouted one of the shipmates. The captain looked and fired another shot in his direction. Richard splashed backwards, losing his balance, and knocked his head against the boat. He struggled to regain composure when he heard the distinct and authoritative voice of his captain.

"Richard! That was a warning; the next one will find your heart." The captain was calm but had his pistol pointing straight toward Richard, who looked frantically from left to right. People had stopped and were watching. Richard glanced toward the Marietta and saw the imposing figure of Jericho, standing portside, holding his face. Richard's hope was gone, so he raised his two hands out of the water while two shipmates jumped in to retrieve him. Was he now their "cargo," too?

Richard cursed in frustration. Not only was he caught trying to escape but also his archenemy still lived, which meant that he was going to pay double. Perhaps a bullet would have been better, but his body shuddered at the thought. Richard looked up for the captain, but he had already made his way on board the ship. Richard was thankful, for he didn't want to face the captain immediately, although he knew he would face him soon. Richard's feet scraped the wooden plank and thudded onto the deck limply as the shipmates practically dragged him back aboard the vessel.

The look in Jericho's eyes as he passed him gave Richard mixed emotions. He relished in the look of pain and embarrassment on Jericho's face on account of his broken nose at the hand of a boy, but the look of determination, knowing that Jericho would not let him live this down, gave Richard a dismal feeling of finality. Between the two of them, someone had to finish this, and it would end only in death.

They raped him that night, Jericho and two other shipmates. Richard wanted to die, but death would not come, and so he adjusted and lived a half-life. Yet that remembrance brought clarity to Richard now as he stood, staring, at the guffawing giant who was dancing clumsily with the woman.

He would finish this today, once and for all. He would be the Joshua that would slay this monster.

Call it fate, luck, or divine intervention, but someone forgot to check the artillery room thoroughly. Perhaps it was because they weren't expecting any stowaways on board the Marietta, or maybe the men were just too caught up in their own adventures to notice or care, but in the back corner of Richard's makeshift cell he had found one rusty pistol and a small box containing twelve bullets. He discovered them the night he was raped when the men carried him back to his room, kicked the door open, and literally threw him in. He just stayed there on the floor, crying from pain and humiliation. Hating his own body for what they had done to it, he clawed the floor in anguish. He'd considered suicide that night, contemplated jumping overboard. He had even written a note to his parents saying how sorry he was for being such a disappointment and to Captain Newton for being such a Godless man to turn a blind eye toward the evils that he knew were taking place aboard his vessel. He cursed him to hell. Richard wasn't going to give Jericho the benefit of mentioning his name or what had happened, for that would only give Jericho pleasure.

Richard had finished the letter and was looking for a place to hide it when he saw a form in the far recesses of his little room. He picked up a candlestick and held it closer to the corner where he noticed an old, oiled rag, and something metallic sticking out from under it. He bent over to pick up the rag and saw the pistol, aged and dusty but a weapon nonetheless. He used to fire his father's hunting rifle in better days and was a fairly good shot. He figured a pistol couldn't be that much different. He briefly thought he would use the gun to end his life, but then a better idea came to him. He was going to end the life of Jericho first, then whoever came next into his line of fire, but someone was going to pay with his life for the price of evil that this ship wrought.

Richard had traded his food for a small amount of cooking oil from the ship's cook, who gave it to him without so much as a question. Everyone was on rations, and the prospect of a trade for edible food was more than enough to earn one's keep. Richard oiled the gun until it shone and its parts moved fluidly. He spoke with a deckhand who was in charge of maintaining the ship's canon and learned that the barrel of the gun had to be cleaned and oiled as well to ensure a smooth shot or a bullet might stick. The deckhand then took what looked like a broomstick with a bristly end and shoved it inside the barrel of the canon to demonstrate the cleaning process. Richard had made a makeshift cleaner with a nail and a piece of rag and went about the task of cleaning his barrel. He loaded and emptied the chambers nightly and constantly tested the trigger to make sure it clicked and moved properly as best he could. He knew that until the gun was actually fired there would be no telling if it actually would work, but he was willing to die finding out.

Everyone was laughing so hard at Jericho and the woman that no one noticed Richard had disappeared. A few other shipmates had joined Jericho and were now lewdly fondling the naked women as well. Richard's heart was racing, and he was sweating like a pig; he only had a few moments of daylight to make this happen. He closed the door to his room and located the pistol, which he kept hidden under a loose plank beneath his sleeping mat. He took the box of bullets and quickly loaded the gun, placing the other bullets from the box into his pocket. He then went back to the door to make sure that the men were still occupied with the women.

Richard's next moves had been fairly well calculated. He figured if the gun didn't work the men would not shoot him but would torture and humiliate him instead. To counter that action, he decided he would take his position close to the edge of the deck where he could fall to the sharks, which would be more merciful to him than these men. Second, he knew only the captain had access to the guns on board the Marietta because it gave him more leverage in case of a mutiny—Jericho was occasionally allowed to use one of the captain's guns, but no shipmate was permitted to carry one unless instructed to and provided by the captain. The shipmates carried only knives, so if the gun did work, he'd have to keep an eye out for the captain and try to shoot him first. Finally, as he had only twelve bullets, and there were sixteen crew members, he knew each shot had to find its target directly, so he would have to locate a place where he could shoot at close range without making himself an easy mark for the crew. He picked a large wooden beam not quite ten feet above deck. From there he was close enough to hit the targets and in a position to leap off the beam into the sea, as it would take at least half a minute for a crew member to climb the beam to catch him and pull him down.

Richard crept out of the cabin and went straight to his pre-designated post. He climbed slowly and deliberately so as to not bring attention to himself. Lying prostrate on the beam, he curled his legs around it for further stability. He took aim at Jericho first. He didn't care if he missed or hit one of the poor slaves—death would be better than the life to which they were headed—but Jericho must die.

Richard closed one eye and used the metal tip at the end of the pistol's barrel as his guide. He could clearly see Jericho's neck, which was his target. Taking a breath, he held it, slipped his finger around the trigger, and squeezed. The gun exploded into life, and Jericho's neck tore open, revealing the compromised stem of his vertebrae. He dropped to the deck like a log. The shipmates were so startled they didn't even look to see from where the shot came; they just dashed for cover. Richard next took aim at one man who was running for the captain's quarters. The bullet hit the man in his side, causing him to crumble to his knees backward, his intestines blown open. It would take several hours for him to die. In the chaos that followed on the deck, many of the female slaves immediately ran and leapt overboard; others ran back toward the galleys.

Richard now looked for the captain, his aim driven by pure vengeance and hate. He had four shots remaining in his gun, but he saw no sign of the captain. He noticed the boy with the flute staring at his position and pointing a finger. Richard looked up and tried to wave the boy away. "Foolish! What makes you think that boy gives a damn about you? He's just concerned about his own hide." With that thought, Richard closed his left eye again, took aim at the young lad, and fired a shot straight through his heart. The flute twisted free from the dead boy's hand and rolled across the deck.

By now the sailors knew from where the shots were coming and were pointing in his direction. Richard was not going to waste a shot until he was sure he was going to strike his target. He glanced back at the confusion on deck where the slaves were and noticed the two women who had gained Jericho's attention were hiding with their backs to the base of the captain's quarters. They were looking at him and making signs. But what were they signaling? The sun was nearly a crescent on the ocean's horizon now, but the moon continued to provide light. Richard realized now that the women were pointing to the galleys. One pointed directly at the captain's quarter, then made her hand into the shape of a gun. Richard understood.

Richard looked up to the captain's quarters; the windows were dark, and he saw no activity, but he knew the captain was inside. This may be the one bullet that he would waste. He took careful aim and fired a shot through the window, sending glass flying everywhere. He saw movement below and glanced down quickly to see the women running toward the galleys, but a blast and flash of pain yanked his attention back toward the captain's quarters. The captain was positioned in his door with both hands clasped expertly on the butt of his gun, taking aim. He had just been waiting for a clear shot and had found his mark; the bullet took a piece of Richard's exposed calf muscle, but it was only a flesh wound. When Richard saw the captain aiming at him again, he fired two shots at the captain. The first one missed entirely and buried itself into the wooden plank of the captain's door, but the second shot hit Newton directly in his shoulder. He stumbled backward, tripped, and fell out of sight. Richard looked down again and noticed that the deck was empty. He decided to find a new position, and he needed to reload.

There were several heavy crates lining the deck. He maneuvered down the beam and, sliding down to the deck, he rolled over behind the crates with his back to the sea. Just then he saw a head peek out from behind the canon, which stood on a platform in the middle of the deck. He fired a shot right into the head and heard the body drop. Richard dug into his pocket and pulled out five bullets, quickly loading them into the chamber. He reached back in for one more and loaded it.

It was then that Richard heard a commotion coming from beneath the deck. He thought about the women. What had they done? He looked over at the galley door and saw the living cargo slowly surface. The women had set the men free. The men looked fierce, hungry, and half mad. Suddenly a series of shots rang from the captain's quarters; the captain had sent those men crashing to the deck—dead. Despite screams of horror, more slaves piled up on the deck, and more shots rang out into the night's crisp air as bodies fell with finality in rapid succession

The captain was positioned in a safe spot. Richard thought about letting him run out of ammunition. The captain would have to have more than four hundred rounds to kill all the slaves, but Richard knew the captain would try in order to scare the slaves into staying below deck. Richard made a decision to end the carnage. He crept from his hiding spot and ran toward the base of the captain's quarters. While crossing the deck, silver blades hissed through the wind as shipmates hurled their knives at him in a desperate attempt to kill him. He took cover and then slowly crept up the stairs to where he knew the captain was hiding. Shots were still being fired, so it was possible he could sneak up on the captain and put one shot in his head. He heard the shipmates hollering over the loud shots, trying to warn the captain.

Richard was now kneeling near the door to the captain's quarters. He could see from this vantage point a pile of black shiny bodies staining the deck with their blood. But, to his surprise, the slaves just kept coming out. Richard then saw three men boldly start running at him. Richard fired three shots, dropping all three men on their faces. He knew that was a mistake the moment he pulled the trigger, but his hate and anger at what this ship had done to him made him careless. He looked over the side and fired two more shots, missing his first target but hitting his second. He sat down and dug into his pockets when his stomach exploded in a ball of fire. He turned his head in time to see Captain Newton lying on his stomach with a shiny smoking pistol in his hand. The captain had crept up on him when he was shooting at the other shipmates. The captain fired again, and all went dark. Richard slumped over, a hole in his temple, his eyes, open, reflecting the red glare of the moon, yet there was a slight smile on his face—his troubles were over.

Captain John Newton rallied his remaining men and was able to contain the little rebellion. He had not seen Yemanja and Vashti valiantly try to set their fellow countrymen free, so no others were executed or punished. The captain had slain a total of twenty-three of his cargo, and fifty women had leaped overboard to their deaths. Captain Newton would have to raise the price of his slaves to compensate for the financial loss he had taken tonight. He ordered the deck scrubbed and cleaned and worked his men all through the night to throw the dead slaves overboard. He made plans for a proper sea funeral for the men he'd lost.

Yemanja and Vashti were puzzled; that night they cried themselves to sleep. Why had the gods allowed so many to die? They thought this was the moment of their deliverance. Were they not prophesied to be women of greatness? Were they not to have a great effect on the future world? How could this fiasco end in such carnage? Little did they know just how the horrible night affected the future of the captain and his crew, for this was the last slave voyage of the Marietta. The events of this night had left the captain scarred. He remained sick for the rest of the voyage and vowed never again to sell another slave. But Yemanja and Vashti did not know that this was just the beginning of their own destiny.

CHAPTER 19
INITIATION OF DESTINY

The afternoon breeze was cooler this day than most. Tiny streaks of water picked up flecks of light as they made their way down the ship's waxed, wooden floorboards. A much smaller crew and even smaller slave population littered the deck. The slaves danced languidly, but no one spoke. After Richard's disastrous one-man coup d'état, life had changed drastically aboard The Marietta. The captain stayed within his quarters most of the time. He had darkened circles under his eyes and trouble keeping weight on due to his lack of appetite. Without Jericho, there was no sailor tough enough to enforce the law the way it had been before. Right now, everyone had to work together to operate, and they saw that they could manage without the cruelty that had before dominated this vessel, but the slaves continued to be disheartened and frightened at the might of the white man and his weapons. Many had lost faith in their gods and were just empty vessels of flesh waiting to be filled with whatever cruelty life had to administer. They moved on deck like zombies, their eyes cold and glazed, staring into nothingness, their legs pumping up and down like frigid marionettes. Their lifelessness left the crew feeling as if they were on a cursed haunt. Many had made up their minds that their luck was close to running out, and once they reached New Orleans, they would never again return to the seas to parcel human life. All on board just wanted this voyage to end

The slave population had dwindled considerably. Many just quit living; they simply willed themselves to die, not realizing that the same power to die could sustain and perpetuate life—for a happy life was too distant to fathom attaining it.

Yemanja saw the land first, and the spirit within her sparked. She had managed to fight off death's advances and had been the stronghold for her friend, Vashti.

"Land ho!" She overheard a voice scream, and the crew left the slaves momentarily to look toward the approaching land, their faces reflecting joy. The crew members kept the slaves on deck and commanded them to sit while they hurried themselves about cleaning the lower hold for the oncoming inspection by dealers who gave top dollar for those slaves in the best condition. The crew hosed down the hold and spread lye to absorb the water and residual filth. Once the lye had dried into white crumbs and dusty powder, the crew shoveled the place out, tossing the waste overboard. The men then rubbed lard oil over the bodies of the slaves so that they glistened like new metal. The captain ordered the cook to prepare drafts of watered-down beer for the slaves to drink to put a little flush in their cheeks and make them a bit excited, which would mean more money because they had the false look of health.

When the Marietta docked in Port D Le Bleu in New Orleans, Louisiana, the slaves were gathered together and shackled, hand, foot, and neck, then herded to the auction block. Yemanja and Vashti had done their best to stay together, but in the hustle to get the slaves ready, the men had rudely and quickly separated slaves at random. Vashti could still see her friend's hair bouncing in the shimmering heat as she, along with the rest of the miserable lot, were herded like cattle off the ship toward the auction block.

The land looked strange and bewildering to her. The buildings were not of wood or mud, and the place had a unique smell. The people here wore garments similar to those of the men on the ship, outfits that covered their whole bodies, which had to be most uncomfortable. The streets were hard because stones had been placed tightly together to form a place for oxen, horses, and cattle to walk. A huge square loomed up in the distance whereupon a man stood wearing an elaborate outfit and tall hat. As the slaves approached, Vashti saw others like herself shackled together and others being released from chains and pushed up to the top of the square.

People were shoving each other to get a better look at the Africans. Vashti saw men holding up what looked to be wads of paper that she watched them exchange for the Africans. Some of the whites took one African male, while others took fifty men and women. These people were being sold as easily as she would barter a pomegranate for a headdress back in her homeland.

At one point, Vashti saw a group, which looked to be a family, all huddled together. There was a man with wild, bloodshot eyes looking fearfully at the whites. He was shouting at them as he held an older woman and what looked to be their three children close to him. Then a group of rough-looking men came forward and clubbed him on the head, and he dropped down but did not pass out. The men took the woman and the children to the auction block while one held the old man to the ground. The auctioneer sold them to three different bidders. The children clung to each other, crying, and the woman screamed the most bitter and heart-wrenching scream Vashti had ever heard. She realized it was indeed a family that was about to be pulled apart. Vashti felt a sudden shudder of fear, wondering if she and Yemanja would suffer the same fate. She willed it not to be so.

The slaves from aboard the Marietta were shoved and yanked past the auction block to a nearby holding cell, and once securely inside, their shackles were removed. Yemanja and Vashti immediately ran to each other and embraced, tears flowing freely from their eyes, an almost electrical connection passing between them. Yemanja kissed her best friend on the cheek, tasting the salty traces of fresh tears. She pulled back to look at her friend and give her comfort, but Vashti's grief-wrecked face was too much to bear. To cope, she focused on her tears, her eyes catching one and following its trek down the slopes of Vashti's distraught face. The light caught it, throwing a spectrum of colors in bulbous shapes within itself. Yemanja caught herself smiling, amazed at how beauty always seems to emerge out of ugliness. The prisms of light still held her gaze when her smile dashed into a look of complete astonishment. Could it be? There, in the tear, shimmering like a heat wave on a dusty road, was their old magus friend, as tiny as an ant but clear—crystal clear. She couldn't believe it. He was waving at her, and his mouth was moving, but she could not make out the words. Then the tear rolled off of Vashti's face and slowly cascaded to the earthen floor, bursting into a thousand mini-tears. Yemanja could barely close her mouth, but the sight of their old instructor forged in her a burning and palatable hope, a hope that would take much more than mere man to break.

CHAPTER 20
NEMESQU THE TRAITOR

Nemesqu sat quietly in his hut outside the Baramoore manor. His abode was simple and clean. There was no furniture except for a bedroll that lay discreetly in the corner of the mud, but Nemesqu never lit a fire; he preferred the dark. There was no hole in his roof; he never cooked his meals inside and usually ate only raw vegetables provided by his master from his own garden. On occasion, when he ate a wild squirrel or rabbit, he cooked it outside in a pit.

Nemesqu's skin was devoid of whip scars; as a matter of fact, it was actually a beautiful, smooth burnished brown; he was pure Indian. He never worked the fields and spent most of his time in his hut or in the woods gathering wild herbs for his practices. Nemesqu was a privileged slave whose services were retained long after many a slave owner gave up on keeping Indians as servants. His job was to be the eyes and ears for Master Baramoore to help in the wars against the Indians and slave insurrectionists.

Nemesqu sat starring into the copper vase filled with water that he insisted be kept clean of algae, dirt, and debris. The Negro slaves hated Nemesqu, but he enjoyed the angry stares they gave him whenever Master Baramoore ordered them to dump the vase and refill it with fresh water. He knew they resented the fact that his flesh bore no semblance of servitude and that he always had food to eat while never once lifting a finger to do any manual labor. He could feel their hate and knew that, if allowed, anyone of them would not hesitate to try to kill him. Of course, try was probably the best they could do, as Nemesqu's skills in sorcery would never allow them to harm him.

It took one incident for the slaves to become aware of his power, and after that they kept their anger bottled up, resorting to expressing it only in ocular terms. But if looks could kill, Nemesqu realized he would have been dead ten times over already.

Reaching into his pocket, he pulled out several clean chicken bones and flung them to the dirt floor. He then sprinkled crushed leaves over them and said a few words only he and the gods could understand. The water in the copper vase rippled, and Nemesqu smiled. His teeth were bone white, clean as a baby's, and his eyes burned with sagacity. The pool of water in the vase reflected a man on a horse riding hard south. Nemesqu looked harder at the image, and a word formed faintly in his mind—Freemund. "So, he finally comes." Nemesqu chuckled to himself.

Nemesqu had dreamed that a man was coming to visit soon who would change his destiny, and for days he had pondered who that could be. As far as he knew, his future was forever indebted to the Baramoore family and, to date, that was a good future to have. The image in the vase faded away, and Nemesqu began the arduous task of getting ready for his company.

He knew Freemund was coming to see him, although Freemund himself, a minister, had no idea he was being watched. Nemesqu often wondered what the world would be like if whites ever grasped how elevated life could be if they cooperated completely with their spiritual selves. He scoffed at the ministry because they spent so much time reading the Bible and talking about God and angels but never once saw an angel or tapped into the powers that were available to anyone who chose to be a student of the spiritual arts. At this juncture in his life, Nemesqu could kill his master Baramoore with a mere thought. Baramoore could have the same powers as did he, but Baramoore would never discipline himself to subjugate the physical to the spiritual. Nemesqu knew that as long as whites were unwilling to deny their physical needs, they would never experience the spiritual level of power and ecstasy that he himself felt on a daily basis. That was why his living quarters were so sparse of human comfort and gaudy elements of pleasure. He experienced in his mind such a unique level of existence, all else seemed paltry in comparison.

Nemesqu recalled the incident that had made all other slaves on the plantation fear him. A slave who was ordered to empty Nemesqu's sacred vase had refused to do so, saying one slave had no right to give orders to another. Nemesqu had looked at the slave and held him still with a gaze. The poor slave ranted and struggled viscously against invisible hands, the veins in his entire body pulsating with the life force that granted him energy and, usually, success against his foes, but, this time, all the blood and energy was for naught. He spat curses at Nemesqu, calling him a witch and a devil, all the while never stepping one foot either forward or backward, although his body writhed violently in his frozen position. Nemesqu then directed another part of his mind toward the water and focused his thoughts on raising its temperature. Immediately, steam began to fill the room, and the water's temperature rose to above boiling, causing it to splash outside of the copper vase.

Nemesqu had then exerted his mental willpower over the slave, forcing him to kneel to the floor. The slave resisted futilely with all he had, but Nemesqu watched emotionlessly as he mentally pushed the slave's face in the dirt. With the other part of his mind that had the water boiling, he tilted the copper vase over and spilled the boiling hot contents completely over the slave's exposed flesh, instantly cooking it. Boils began to rise almost immediately on the poor slave's skin as he let out a horrible yell. His black flesh shimmered with redness as blisters began to swell on his flesh. He lay trembling on the floor, still under Nemesqu's watchful control.

Nemesqu then said, in a calm and polite voice, "Would you please take this copper vase, fill it with water, and return it to my hut?" Still emotionless, Nemesqu released the slave from his mental clutches. The slave rose weakly from the floor but immediately took the vase from Nemequ's presence. He returned shortly with the bowl filled. "Thank you, sir," Nemesqu responded. "You may leave now." The slave had just enough time to tell others in the village about what happened before he died. From that point on, the slaves gave their service to Nemesqu without complaint.

As Nemesqu contemplated his imminent encounter with Freemund, his mind wandered back to when he was discovered by Baramoore, nearly fifty years ago. Nemesqu was forty-three at that time and had almost completed his education with the Iroquois tribe of priests. The training, which started at puberty, was divided into four parts, the first beginning with herbs. It took four years to master the use of every herb and how to employ each for good magic or bad. The good magic had medicinal uses and, by age fifteen, Nemesqu was known as the best healer in his village. He could restore a bird that was shot down by a poisonous arrow and on the edge of death back to full health; he could heal the wounds of warriors so effectively that there was hardly a trace of a scar. His talents made him revered in his village, and the priest thought him a most apt pupil.

The next part of the trials that would make him a priest was hunting the souls of the spirit world. Every priest had to choose an animal to hunt. This was a long and arduous process because it meant more than simply killing; hunting meant going out on long excursions that would often take weeks. The pupil would be guided by his trainer in understanding the patterns of the animals—when they slept, when they feed, when they migrated to greener pastures, and when they communed with each other. Eventually, the student would be required to dress in the skins of the animal and so imitate that creature's pattern to ensure the animals themselves would accept the human into their domain. This pattern was called domination, and the priest told of times when this type of communion was natural between man and beast, but the erosion of humanity caused the union to be disconnected, and it took much time and effort now to reestablish the link.

After dominating that animal, its spirit would guide the priest in all future hunts and battles. Nemesqu chose the wolf, the most difficult of spirits to attain. Here is where his young troubles began. None of the priests had conquered this spirit, so they usually had their pupils choose the buffalo, eagle, or bear. Each spirit was a force with which to contend. The eagle had wisdom and a lofty perspective, and it gave the person who conquered it an acute ability to see that which was usually withheld from others with a spiritual connection. Of course, the bear had strength and endurance and the ability to heal itself while sleeping. The buffalo had strength, speed, and courage. But the wolf had quickness, vision in the night, and the strength of the pack. The tribal elders spoke of only one other who had conquered the wolf and since his time, none other had been able to do so. The elders kept the writings of the priest within their sanctuary, and Nemesqu found them in secret and studied diligently.

When Nemesqu conquered the spirit of the wolf on his first attempt, it aroused the jealousy of two of the priests, who determined in their hearts not to let this young student surpass what they had worked so hard to attain. They didn't think of how his abilities could help the tribe, could save them from outside attacks, or even help them master techniques of the spiritual world. Their only thoughts were of their pride and his demise.

The third step of training was dark magic, magic that could kill, maim, or cause disease and plague at the touch of a hand. This magic was difficult to master, and usually one had to choose either good or bad in which to excel; rarely did one elect both, except Nemesqu. His dark arts matched those of the good. He could just as soon kill a rabbit as he could bring one back to full health. He could touch a man and have boils break out on his skin and just as quickly touch him again and have the boils disappear. The elders and generals used him to fight off warring tribes single-handedly, and his name began to spread across the land as Nemesqu the Great.

The fourth and final step before becoming a full-fledged priest was the art of the dead. Unfortunately for Nemesqu, the priests, who were all, save one, envious of his spiritual prowess, worked with their spiritual guides to disguise their intentions, and they tricked Nemesqu into trapping himself with his final test. According to their legend, the priest had the power to control the dead. A priest could call forth a person who recently died, before his flesh rotted away, and that person would be under his control to do his bidding. This person, for example, could go with him into war and fight battles by his side, and the priest would not have to worry about that person being killed or injured. That person would usually lead in front of the priest, taking on arrows, bullets, charges, whatever, and would fight unless completely dismembered. Few warriors had seen such feats, so it was easy for Nemesqu to be tricked. However, the legend of the dead was not true because the priests could not call forth the dead, although many had tried, but they could make a substance that, if taken by another, would render him completely under their control. That person would not be able to think for him or herself or resist any command that the priest gave. Instead of the priests telling this to Nemesqu, they told him to take a potion they said would give him the ability to conjure the dead. Nemesqu did this, trusting his teachers, and he became as one of the dead.

The priests told the village that Nemesqu had been killed in battle, and the village mourned his passing for three months, the longest time their village had ever mourned a slain warrior, while the priests kept Nemesqu shackled in the woods and tortured him daily. They would not give him food or drink for days, and when they did, it was only the most putrid of dishes. They powdered his body with pollen and then attached beehives to long poles and beat him over the head with them until the bees stung him so that his body became swollen almost beyond recognition. For more than a year he endured such tortures; all the while the crops began to falter, and the warriors were less and less successful in battle. Yet failed crops and battles against warring tribes were not the biggest problems for Nemesqu's people. What proved dastardly was the white man encroaching upon Indian territory. The priests were not able to fully defend their land. Many died, and the whites took over.

It was one of these white men, walking with his daughter out in the woods, who discovered Nemesqu, gaunt from starvation and terribly weakened. The man unchained Nemesqu and took him back to the fort where he held two surviving priests captive. The priests, believing the white man was a god, confessed what they had done and told the man— Baramoore—how to undo the spell. Baramoore, freeing Nemesqu, was amazed at how quickly the Indian healed himself and recuperated from his ordeal. Baramoore then told Nemesqu what had taken place, whereupon, in his wrath, Nemesqu quickly touched the two priests, causing worms to immediately decimate their bodies from the inside out. Frightened, Baramoore tried to shoot Nemesqu, but his bullets simply fell to the ground after hitting Nemesqu's body. Nemesqu told Baramoore he had nothing to fear of him, that only those who did him wrong would suffer, and that he owed his life to Baramoore in fair service. And thus, a relationship of violence and bloodshed began. Nemesqu no longer held any respect for Indians after his betrayal by the priests, and any who dared get in the way of Baramoore and Nemesqu suffered terribly—White, Indian, or African. Now, at ninety-three, Nemesqu had fear of no man. He was strong and healthy and didn't look a day over fifty. So, he anxiously awaited meeting the man who would change his destiny.

Nemesqu went to Baramoore's house and asked to meet with his master. His request was immediately granted, and when Baramoore came out, the two embraced. This was not a typical practice between whites and Indians, but in this case these two shared a unique history. Baramoore himself was the epitome of youth; although he was eighty-four, he looked to be only in his forties. Nemesqu had used his talent at healing to keep his master young as well. The servants brought them food and drink, though Nemesqu never accepted, and the meeting began.

Nemesqu couldn't complain about his relationship with Baramoore. If he wanted, he could have had his own plantation with the amount of wealth the two had amassed over the years. Baramoore treated him with respect, which was more than he could say of his own Indian brothers who ran the Iroquois council. He remembered reading from the Bible that a prophet was not loved in his own country, and that couldn't be truer than in his case. He only felt sorry for those he knew mourned his "supposed" death. Nemesqu never resurfaced in his community after killing the remaining council. As far as the Iroquois tribe was concerned, he was dead. He felt no remorse in helping Baramoore usurp Indians from their land; most of his life Nemesqu had lived in seclusion, and he had been severely betrayed by his own people, so he cared little about the injustices they were experiencing. He understood that life would be unfair and that one can only do but so much to avoid the travesties life had in store. Spiritual connections aided a great deal, but even the spirits at times decided one's fate without asking one's opinion on the matter.

Baramoore looked fondly at his old friend Nemesqu. He marveled as well upon how his life had changed for the better ever since he stumbled upon this man shackled to a tree in the forest, emaciated, ribs pressing harshly against his dried and disintegrating flesh. He expected to use the poor old fellow for information and then dispose of him along with the rest of his people, but instead he got a lot more than just simple information—he got the key to a fortune for a lifetime. He was always excited at meeting with this wise old sage, the man who turned his life around, because he knew their conversations would lead to adventure and wealth. Nemesqu had never let him down or ever miscalculated a vision or dream.

"Nemesqu! It has been a while since we have had a meeting. To what do I owe the honor?"

"We are going to be approached soon for support in a war against a rebellious tribe of Blacks and Indians."

"Really? And will this endeavor profit us?"

"I'm afraid not. Our involvement will cost us, and there is no way to avoid it." Nemesqu said this with no level of emotion. Baramoore didn't quite know how to make sense of it. His messages were always so positive.

"Well, that is not quite what I expected to hear. However, you seem pretty optimistic about losing money. I am not sure I understand."

"I have seen that this event will change my destiny. The concept scares me, but the gods have prophesied it. The gentleman is coming to get advice about the Maroons, the tribes of Blacks and Indians that have been causing so much trouble. He is coming to seek counsel and aid." Nemesqu paused for a second.

"So how is this going to cost us? Does this person want money? Does he think we are involved in this plot?"

"No. The problem is that we are going to have to fight against a person who has powers similar to mine. The Maroons have been successfully leading revolts in North and South Carolina, and even in Florida."

"Yes. I remember the Florida rebellion. Some say that revolt caused the largest number of lost lives among whites that has ever been recorded in history." Baramoore's ruddy complexion turned pallid at the thought of actually having competition. He had made it too far to lose his fortune, and the thought of doing so scared him. Surely, there was no one who could rival Nemesqu's spirit.

With a pause, Nemesqu continued. "This rebellion is worse than the Florida rebellion. The bodies of the whites who were found dead here in Carolina were severely mutilated. Every time the rebellion took place, there was a red moon. You may have heard rumors that a night with the red moon brings bad omens, but those are not rumors when it comes to someone of spiritual power. The Iroquois priests taught me of such powers when I was in my second year of training, but they themselves never practiced using spells on a red moon night because sometimes the evil powers turned on the spell casters. They gave me the training to use once my education was complete, but until now I've never had cause to employ it. I hesitate at the thought of doing so now. But I will wait until I have met with Reverend Freemund. He is due to arrive tomorrow."

"Reverend Freemund? How is he involved in this? Freemund has been a solid supporter of the Merchant Traders' Guild since he joined and has never once complained of rebellion or financial depravity. What is the connection?"

"The spirits have shown me that a soldier visited Freemund to tell him of his plan to usurp the Maroon tribe and of a woman who lost her entire population of slaves. Both the soldier and the women sought spiritual advice from Freemund to deal with what they believe to be demonic influences." Nemesqu took another sip of water.

"And are these spiritual forces demonic?" Baramoore queried.

"No more than the spiritual forces I have used to serve our purposes. But using the red moon can be dangerous toward the person invoking the power of the gods. Thus, that type of spiritual use has been labeled evil when in actuality it is simply a gamble, just like you making a financial decision that can have huge benefits but also risk tremendous loss. Thus far, the Blacks and Indians have experienced only success."

"So, what do we do, Nemesqu? What am I to say to Freemund?" Baramoore had learned from experience to trust his friend and confidant without question. He highly valued their relationship and made sure he exhibited appreciation through immediate action at every opportunity.

"He will ask to meet with the elders of the Merchant Traders' Guild. That is where I will meet him. Freemund needs to be humbled, or else his arrogance could cloud his and our judgment for our next move. He is unaware of your dealings with me, and once he discovers who really runs the Guild, his mental faculties will be entirely befuddled. I will also take Slave, who will sit in the head elder's chair. Freemund will balk at the idea of co-existing with Indians and Blacks, and he will resist; he will question the Guild and its leadership. There will be tremendous doubt in his mind. Yet, if he continues to pursue destroying the Maroons after his faith has been shaken, his mission will be our mission, and we will put all sources to completing it successfully."

"How soon after you meet with him will we know our next step?" Baramoore was not sure how he was going to tackle this situation, but he didn't want to seem overly eager to obtain information from Nemesqu.

"It's hard to say. I am leaving now to see if the spirits can show me more. I must admit I am not anxious to discover if what the Iroquois elders said about the burning moon is true. I am hoping that Freemund responds negatively so that we can go on with our lives." With that, Nemesqu got up from the table, as did Baramoore, and gave him a brotherly embrace. He then went back to his hut to complete the preparations.

There were many times when Baramoore wished that Nemesqu would say more. But he respected the fact that Nemesqu, like many Indians he had come to know, did not mince words with the white man. Baramoore felt honor at having such a valued friend give him an embrace. The Indians were not like the Blacks; they were civilized in a manner that was uniquely their own, and they had proven their ability to adapt. The Cherokee nation was well on its way to becoming brown white men, and Baramoore wished that all the unnecessary killing of Indians would stop. But he couldn't say the same for the Blacks. Anytime one died he considered his country a better place. If trained properly, a black slave could make a good pet, but he or she would have to be well-groomed, as were his slaves, and trained in the art of servitude. Only then could they be tolerable to live around and, at times, Baramoore wondered if it was worth all the effort. Unlike his Nemesqu, if this rebellion could be squelched, he wanted to be all in—to hell with the superstition—he had real spiritual power on his side that had never failed him. The idea of such a rebellion was beyond his comprehension. He sincerely hoped that Freemund would see life as he himself had come to see it—that cooperation with the Indians would only serve white supremacy, and that Indians deserved to be a part of the level of greatness this country was fast on its way to achieving.

In his hut, Nemesqu held his hand over a quartz stone he had found several years ago. He held the stone until it glowed a quiet purple, resonating its light throughout the hut. Slaves outside the hut saw the muted light and quietly ducked into their sleeping quarters to pray to their varied gods as a ward against the evil they all suspected Nemesqu of conjuring. For many of them, not since Africa had they seen anyone like Nemesqu, and they thought him to be possessed by demons. The purple light emanating from his hut served to substantiate their fears. Even in the master's house, where oil lamps lit every room, the purple light seeped through. Furthermore, slaves who replaced his water always marveled at how his living quarters contained so little, including no candles or oil lamps. Hell was the only other explanation for the origin of the purple light that glowed in his hut.

But Nemesqu didn't have time to concern himself with his image. He needed answers. What was he to say when Freemund went to meet with the elders tomorrow? Who was this woman who was leading the Maroons, and exactly how strong was she?

Nemesqu closed his eyes and focused his powers. He was unique in that he could exert his mental energy outside of his body in four different ways. Most priests could only do one at a time, but he always made a habit of practicing his power the night before he would really have to use it to make sure that he was still fluent in the art. During battle, these actions had to happen in a split second, and during practice, he slowed down his breathing and heart rate and calmly set his mind to work.

Nemesqu realized it was time to use the elders, the men who pledged their very lives to promoting its principles. The organization had existed before Nemesqu was born; he just found a way to turn its power to his purposes, and its members welcomed him because of the potential capital they stood to gain. Baramoore was an elder and convinced the others to allow Nemesqu to use their resources, but primarily their spirits, to achieve whatever he or they desired. They agreed, and Nemesqu used his powers to slowly take over. Nemesqu smiled to himself as he reminisced just how neatly this all had taken place.

His mind wandered back to when he was to go on his big hunting mission with his teacher. He remembered his shaman tutor, Hania, who had not only mentored Nemesqu in the sage arts, but also he had become a trusted and loyal friend. He tried to subtly warn Nemesqu of his enemies, but so cloaked in guile were their actions that Nemesqu failed to see his near demise. Hania was a great warrior, and warring nations feared and respected his prowess and ingenuity when it came to battle. Hania had a way of seeing battle strategies in his mind, and he could draw crafty war plans on parchment so that every warrior knew his role in battle. Amazingly, the results always were favorable. It was as if Hania had witnessed the battle beforehand and responded in kind to every move the enemy placed against him. It was this foreknowledge that he emphasized to Nemesqu at the end of the day.

"Nemesqu, you must learn to visualize the plans of your enemy if ever you expect to live long. Seek the spirits, and they will assist your efforts." Nemesqu was honored to have such a wise shaman offer him knowledge, and he absorbed it as pastures absorb summer rain. After a day of hunting for rare herbs, meat, and quartz stones, Nemesqu found himself too tired to sleep. He was nibbling on a small bit of the peyote he had brought along with him for their journey. It was typical for the shaman and his pupil to crouch before a fire and eat the roasted flesh of their prey, but on this particular night Nemesqu found his appetite wanting. As the fire flickered with writhing flutters of flame, Nemesqu was startled by a presence at his side. It was Hania. Nemesqu was always amazed at how nimbly the old man moved.

"It is time to move, young one." Hania whispered. And then he was off. Nemesqu's aching bones cried out as he obediently rose up to follow his great teacher. They had set up camp at the base of a mountain, and the old man was nimbly scaling the cold sides of it as if he were eighteen and not his earned age of sixty-three. Nemesqu noticed that Hania, though old, did not lose breath and barely disturbed a pebble as he climbed higher and higher, leaving his struggling pupil breathless, his aching lungs feeling as if they were full of liquid fire as he made concerted efforts to keep up. Where was his teacher going? Nemesqu did his best to discern a trail, but the movements seemed quite random. Yet, Hania moved with purpose.

The master and pupil continued this way, maneuvering with skill, greater and lesser respectively, through the darkness. Nemesqu remembered valiantly moving with effort to close the gap with the Shaman so that they could travel in single file, reaching out with his ears more than his hands to hear the soft rustle of his teacher's moccasin-covered feet to prevent losing his way. The two were surrounded by the sounds of the night, and Nemesqu remembered his waning strength began to take on newness and traveling became a little easier. Hania never let up, never looked back to see if his pupil was behind him; he just kept his movements consistent and ever-forward.

When they reached a small cleft in between two gigantic rocks, Hania stopped and held up a palm that meant halt and hush. The two had hunted long enough for Nemesqu to recognize the signal in his sleep, and he instinctively searched his mind for a spell of offense. His hands began to glow a soft blue that resembled the mist that one can see rising off a quiet lake in the early morning. Hania, sensing Nemesqu's conjure, gave him a quick glance to lower his defenses, and his hands returned to their normal hue. The master signaled his pupil to move closer to the cleft. When Nemesqu was near enough for Hania to grab him, Hania took his index and middle fingers jointly and pointed at his eyes first, then directed those fingers down into the cleft. Moving back from the aperture, Hania motioned for Nemesqu to take his position. Nemesqu peered into the darkness, unable to see or hear anything. A slight breeze alerted a sense in the back of his mind, and he realized that the full moon was obscured by clouds. The breeze stayed consistent, and slowly the large cloud that obstructed the moon's gaze cleared away, and a bright shaft of light lit the cleft. What happened next made Nemesqu's skin bristle with fear and excitement. Two orbs came into view, and a rustling sound signaled movement in the hole in the rock. The two orbs grew bright and came closer, and Nemesqu saw the furred head of a fully grown wolf emerge from the darkness, its muzzle snarled in a malicious grin that exhibited a full row of white sharp teeth. Nemesqu tried to move away, but Hania was standing directly behind him and held him steady with two firm hands.

"Calm yourself, young one, and possess his spirit. This is the final step of your training, Nemesqu." Nemesqu remembered that was the first time his teacher had referred to him by his name instead of "young one." Nemesqu, now sweating with fear, saw the beast come so close that his wet nose briefly touched Nemesqu's. There was a low rumbling in the back of the wolf's throat as it sniffed Nemesqu aggressively.

Nemesqu immediately went into his trance and closed his eyes. He visualized the wolf and the cleft and sought out the wolf's spirit. Unknown to him at the time, Hania was doing the same. If not, the wolf would have killed them both. One never could be prepared for when the vision came, but suddenly, although Nemesqu's eyes were closed, he could see the wolf again, but this time he could envision both the wolf and the wolf's spirit, which shone brightly within the wolf's chest. Nemesqu could see the wolf's organs as clearly as he saw those dangerous teeth before he closed his eyes. Nemesqu could see the wolf's nervous system, and right there, behind the heart, a glowing red light. Nemesqu pulled with his mind, blocking out all sound, all smells, and his own fear, and pulled with his spirit. He could see the spirit expanding and then closing with resistance as he exerted his efforts. Then, slowly, like a dividing cell, the wolf's spirit pulled in two, and one red glowing ball of light slowly cascaded over to Nemesqu and infused itself within him. Suddenly, he was jolted upright; he saw Hania's face being disintegrated in a flash of smoke and fire, his body falling to the ground. Below stood a white man with an evil sneer; his body jolted again, and he saw his village up in smoke and women and children running to and fro; another jolt, and a grungy forest with someone tied to a tree in anguish and pain; a jolt, and Blacks and Indians sitting in a circle repeating a mantra that he did not recognize, but he saw their spirits and they were strong. And in the middle of the circle was the most hideous woman he had ever seen. She was ancient, wearing only a ragged loincloth, but despite her advanced years, her spiritual powers glowed brighter than any of the shamans who taught Nemesqu, even Hania. He collapsed to Hania's waiting hands.

Nemesqu slowly came out of the vision of his past and steadied himself against the vase. He always felt dizzy after going into his spiritual realm. This vision had taken him back to his first real vision of the future. When he was eighteen, he had disbelieved what he saw, and the memory of that mistake always made him cringe with regret, because if he had believed perhaps Hania would still be by his side now to aid him against this formidable foe. That vision seemed ages ago; he had forgotten about it until now. Everything in his first vision had happened except the Blacks and Indians sitting in a circle. He didn't know what to make of that, and since he had no dealings with the Africans, he had never thought much about it. This was going to take a sacrifice to the gods. And Nemesqu knew from experience that the gods honored only the most heartfelt sacrifices, which meant emotional and physical pain. The question was if he was ready to inflict it, or worse, suffer it himself. He had already suffered so much at the hands of his people.

CHAPTER 21
THE PLAN

Research complete, Freemund thought carefully about his next move. At all costs the white man must be victorious; thus, every step had to be calculated. He had to meet with the Merchant Traders' Guild to discuss his plan of action. The Guild, a powerful conglomerate of traders who profited enormously from the slave trade as well as their dealings in other foreign goods, commanded their own little army of three hundred well-armed men, albeit mostly undisciplined drunkards, and they had successfully locked out all other trade competition on the Carolina coast. Their influence in neighboring plantations was seen and felt throughout the region, and many plantation owners and overseers wanted membership because of the financial profit it would grant them. The Merchant Traders' Guild was secretive, with membership so exclusive one practically had to be born in it. Any member not born into the Guild had to be voted in unanimously and go through an intense, three-month initiation.

The Guild had spiritual roots taken from papers its founder had stolen from an Ojibwa merchant from Canada after he lost a dispute over a purchase of buffalo hide and herbs to promote vegetable growth. These papers contained rituals that promised great power and, to the captain's delight, they proved to be true. After he mastered several spells of mind control and physical debilitation, he destroyed these documents. The captain taught the knowledge only to his sons, who then took control of the Guild. He lived to be one hundred ten, but when he died he didn't look a day over eighty—and a healthy eighty at that. Later, his sons decided to expand The Guild to non-blood relatives who proved their loyalty. It was through such means that Freemund became initiated into the fellowship.

Hearns, Freemund, and Elizabeth sat at breakfast, saying little. The table was set meticulously as was Rebecca's habit: eggs scrambled hard, sausages, biscuits, tea, coffee, and juice. The house slaves had been up before daylight preparing the food, and Rebecca added the finishing touches. Although she had three slaves who were under her direct charge in the kitchen, she often felt as one of them due to her husband's harsh treatment. Nevertheless, she never faltered in her "wifely" duties. In fact, she chose to stay in the kitchen under the guises of work, but what she really wanted to do was eat in peace, free from the proselytizing murmurings of her husband. Rebecca knew if she caught him stealing another glance at Elizabeth's bosom she would scream. His lack of decorum and subtlety in his pursuit of sexual pleasure upset her greatly. This time, Rebecca wanted her displeasure with his lechery to be known. Her absence from the table caused a slight tension, but Freemund broke the ice by telling the story of Captain Branagan, which also planted the seed for plans that involved one of his guests.

Freemund eyed his company casually as he dallied over his mental ruminations before beginning his delivery. Years of practice in the pulpit gave him ease. "I've discovered the root to your problem, Colonel, and yours as well, Elizabeth. It seems to me that you both are up against forces much larger than a mere slave revolt. This involves me as well, and I intend to help." Freemund's response elicited little more than a grunt between breathy gasps from Hearns as he shoveled food into his mouth. Elizabeth gazed in amazement. "This man eats like a nigger," she mused to herself. Freemund continued. "It means war, and it will be bloody." At this Hearns slammed down his eating utensils and stared at the back of his hands.

"Rev, as I told you last night, I happen to know a little about these people." Hearns paused, shifting his spoon on his plate before continuing. "I have been told several tales of devilry and mysticism that I dared not believe until yesterday." Hearns stopped again, took a spoonful of eggs into his mouth, and chewed aggressively.

"When I saw weeds growing out of that poor boy's mouth, and now hearing you confirm that we are up against otherworldly powers, my suspicions have become realities."

"Then you are willing to work with my plan to destroy these nigger infidels?" Freemund asked calmly.

Hearns looked directly at the minister. "The question is, Freemund, are you willing to work with my plan?" This unexpected response from Hearns caused Elizabeth to raise her eyebrows. Freemund was also taken aback. "What I know is the location of the infidels; what I don't know is how to deal with this spiritual element. Thus I came to you. You have what I need—the power to fight the forces of spiritual evil—while I have what you need—the power of the sword."

"Then I propose we work together, Colonel. We obviously are here for one reason: to help each other."

"How can I contribute?" Elizabeth interrupted.

"You already have, dear," Hearns replied. "You have added credence to this phenomenon by relating to us your story."

"But I want to be involved, and don't tell me that I am only a woman! I lost my daughter and my slaves, and though I cannot get my daughter back, I can restore my plantation to its rightful state!" Both Hearns and Freemund regarded Elizabeth uncomfortably, and she felt embarrassed as she realized she had nearly shouted these words, but she meant what she had said. She finished clumsily before anyone could interject, "They killed my daughter! An eye for an eye! Isn't that what the good book tells us, Reverend?"

"Indeed. Indeed, Elizabeth, it does." Freemund repressed the sneer that was itching to approach the surface of his face. Although he had been thrown slightly by Hearns's rude comment, he was pleased with how Elizabeth was setting herself up to be a sacrifice.

"Reverend, surely you wouldn't entertain—" Hearns blurted, but Freemund cut him short with a gentle raise of his hand.

"Yes, I would, and I intend to because the threat is serious. Relax, Colonel; this woman's suffering entitles her to her revenge." He gave Elizabeth a quick glance and was pleased to see that she bought into his false patronage.

"There is a story around these parts about Captain Branagan, founder of the Merchant Traders' Guild. Ever heard of it?" Freemund looked about the table, waiting for response that did not come. "Well, Branagan had quite the appetite for peyote—an Indian narcotic. He claimed it was to help him with his spells, and I suspect there was a modicum of veracity to his claims, for I know the Indians are well-versed in elements involving the supernatural. Anyway, Branagan had just completed the deal of his lifetime, and part of his secret to success was that he'd perform a ceremony that allowed him to look into the future and attempt to manipulate it. Have any of you ever tried peyote?" Elizabeth and Hearns both nodded no. "Well, I have. The effects are quite powerful, often causing one to experience physical and mental exhilaration for ten to twelve hours. There is no desire or ability to sleep. The pupils of the eyes become dilated, and salivation is increased. In this first stage, the drug allays hunger and thirst, gives courage in tense situations, and increases physical endurance. In short, there are many positive attributes of this stimulant in war and in peace. One can dance or play for hours without the slightest inclination of fatigue."

Freemund saw that he had Elizabeth's and Hearns's undivided attention. Drugs always seemed to do the trick, and he felt it a shame that the church did not condone their use. "However, such euphoria comes with a price. The high stage is followed by a second stage of depression and hallucinations in which the user may feel fear or hostility to the point of becoming dangerous or, on the contrary, experience euphoria and partial amnesia. It depends on the person's demeanor."

"Now, before he died, Captain Branagan used his powers to see into the future. Although he had not been able to fully master it, he could achieve moderate success. Besides, it was always exciting to see what was going to happen tomorrow—if he was going to get caught sleeping with his prettiest slave, or if a deal was going to work with a trader. He rarely looked farther than a week or so in the future, and he did it infrequently because it taxed his mind too much, and he always suffered profuse nosebleeds afterward. It was after a great day of trade, when his company cleared nearly one million dollars within the week, that he decided to celebrate alone with a little peyote. But that was the last time he looked into the future. His sons, who didn't like his use of peyote, said that he always told them that he had sensed that looking into the future might not be a good idea.

But Captain Branagan was feeling great, and he wanted to know how long the good feeling and fortune were going to last. He performed the ritual poorly; he couldn't focus well, but years of practice prevailed, and he was eventually successful. His sons told me that he knew he had done the job right because of the still silence that came right after the last phrase was uttered. But what he saw horrified him so much that he vowed never again to perform the ritual, and he immediately began to work on writing about what he saw to warn his future generations. He died before he finished the book, but his sons published three copies of what he had written, and they made it required reading for anyone wanting to join the Guild. I have studied the book with extreme fascination. The book talks about what we preachers refer to as Armageddon. Are you familiar with what Armageddon means?"

Both Elizabeth and Hearns returned blank glances at Freemund.

"Armageddon is the catastrophic battle between the forces of good and evil. Most of the clergy believe it will be fought near the world's end before the Christ returns to claim His children. What we at the lodge have come to learn through Branagan's vision is that this battle is to be fought on American soil between the Africans and the whites. Satan, the antichrist, and his evil minions are using the Africans to wage war against the remnant of God's people. The white man is the remnant."

"That is the most ridiculous thing I've ever heard, Reverend!" Hearns was looking at his friend with irritation. "I don't proclaim to be any sort of evangelist, but during the war I've witnessed white men commit some of the most heinous, Godless acts that you have ever seen or ever would want to. To believe that this race of people is part of a biblical war story against us is simply ludicrous. I know of Africans who are quite congenial, sir. And although spirits seem to be involved here, I have my doubts that Blacks are the sole legion of the antichrist."

"I never said sole legion, and there will be those who convert to our side, Colonel. But when we look at how the Africans were living in Africa, how they worshipped gods of stone, wood, and beast—there was no Christ to be found anywhere on their continent. Slavery is their saving grace, because it is through slavery that they have come to be exposed to the gospel. They must choose it and serve us as the Bible suggests, or they risk eternal damnation."

"Now you see why getting my slaves back is of utmost importance, Colonel." Elizabeth chimed in. "This is about more than money. It is about salvation and the end of the world as we know it."

"You're buying this sordid philosophy, Elizabeth? Don't be ridiculous. This is about money and only money. War is about wealth, never peace! So if you want to get your wealth back, that is one thing, but to argue that this is an altruistic endeavor to make saints out of sinners is simply ignorant. I won't buy it. So let's cut out the spiritual nonsense and simply deal with how to fight this battle on the physical plane. Winning is all I care about at this point. I've invested too much to lose."

Hearns was visibly upset. He ran a hand over his rugged jaw, his mouth working to say more but hesitating. He then blurted, "In addition, Reverend, with all due respect, how can you justify slavery as a means of saving lost Africans when slavers are raping them, killing them, and using them to expand the borders of the republic and our wealth without giving these men and women so much as a thought of compensation?"

What started out as a discussion was turning into an argument, and Freemund didn't want to argue. He just needed to know where Hearns stood, for him or against him, and he had his answer. He knew he had Elizabeth, but Hearns would not be as easy to convince because he didn't feel vulnerable. Hearns was a soldier, wanting to carry out his duty, and if anything, he seemed to feel sympathy for the Africans. Freemund thought carefully before responding.

"Okay, Colonel," Freemund chuckled. "I didn't mean to offend your sensibilities. I'm curious, though. You mentioned that you have invested too much to turn back now. Invested in what? Surely not time? Although I've no doubt about your commitment to the military, you are still a young man with much life to live. Your arguments against mine don't support capitalism, so I imagine your investment doesn't involve finances? So what is left?"

The focus turned from Freemund to Hearns. Both Freemund and Elizabeth stared at him inquisitively.

"Tell me, what does the military have on its agenda? You can speak openly with me, friend, I'm trained to keep the strictest of confidences."

Freemund eased his chair back with a slight creak and raised his drink to his lips with a delicate motion. Hearns had refused the beverages Rebecca brought to the table and asked for tobacco instead. Hearns now took a long drag from the pipe and held the ripe smoke deep within his lungs before slowly exhaling. Finally, he spoke.

"Sir, my hesitation is only an exhibition of my efforts to compile my thoughts to appropriately respond to your question. I trust you, friend." Although the words were spoken smoothly and quietly, Hearns's face was reddening and his brow was furrowed. As he took another drag from the pipe, wisps of white smoke slowly wafted from his nostrils. He took his time putting his response together, giving Freemund and Elizabeth a long look before speaking.

"You may judge me for what I am about to say, and I want to make clear that neither friendship nor acquaintance will stop my endeavors for the future." His serious tone captivated Elizabeth and Freemund, who said nothing in return. "I don't know you, Elizabeth, but I know you, Reverend, from when we fought against the Indians, and I respect your valor. But I am a different man now than what I was then. This is my last war, and I intend to survive. I want your help, but our philosophies differ greatly. The way I see it, we can both have what we want, so before I reveal my personal purposes, and those of the military, I must have your word that you will keep this in the strictest confidence as your training provides. You, too, Elizabeth. And I will add that I will use all my means as a soldier not to be stopped in my purpose." Hearns took another puff while he waited for a response.

"That sounds serious, if not threatening, Colonel, but as you wish. You have my vow of secrecy," Freemund replied.

"And mine as well," said Elizabeth.

"Good. I don't believe the Africans to be inherently evil because I have been in love with one for more than a year. Tanjee is my true love."

"Good Lord," gasped Elizabeth. Freemund stared in silence. They didn't realize when he spoke of her last night that this slave woman had such a strong hold on him.

"Tanjee provides me with more attention, intelligence, and personal satisfaction than my white wife ever could. All my wife is concerned with is how to get more, and quite frankly, I'm sick of it! Years of fighting Indians to take what is rightfully theirs, using slaves to do the same, and years of bloodshed and wickedness on the battlefield have made me sick of it all. I intend to get out. Once we win this battle, Tanjee and I will leave to find peace in a place that does not condemn our love while you and the rest of your cohorts fight Armageddon. But as I told you last night, I am afraid she has been discovered by their leader, and I must get to her before she is harmed. So that is my personal investment. The military was commissioned because, up to this point, no one has been able to stop the organized resistance of the Maroons. What they have done to Elizabeth they have been doing all over the south. They have two cities established, one in Florida and one here in the swamps of Carolina. My mission involves their Carolina base. I am to rout them out, kill them, and rescue my beloved Tanjee."

"Have you considered the possibility that Tanjee has betrayed you and completed her original mission?" Freemund queried.

"Not in the least bit. It took time, but she has proven herself to me and my instincts as a soldier; they tell me that she will not betray me."

"I see. Well, Hearns, you are right. Our philosophies differ, although your actions with the military do not support your personal views."

"God will be my judge in that regard, Reverend. If this battle needs to occur in order to bring an end to the violence, and get me out of it, then that is what I am willing to do. I don't believe that killing the Maroons is right; it is just giving me a chance at what I need, and that is personal peace. I'll worry about vindicating myself once this is all over. These people have the same right to be here as you and I."

"Well, then, may God bless the victor. I am certain our joint efforts will promise success. I will help you complete this quest. The rest I'll leave up to God."

"Thank you, Reverend."

"Colonel, last night you mentioned a woman leader for this cluster of slaves, the Maroons, who has been leading their revolt. What more can you tell me of her?" Hearns revealed a few of the tales that Tanjee had told him, leaving Freemund awed at this woman's power. Hearns's tale of the defeats that the military suffered at the hands of the Maroons confirmed their power, and now he had the answer for the leadership: a spiritual leader. It was apparent the Africans had an advantage that no one had assumed they would ever get. Freemund realized his task was to serve as the counterpoint to the spiritual battle that was soon to ensue.

"I must go to the lodge and make inquiries before we march, and I will hire the services of the Merchant Traders' Guild in order to get more soldiers. Hopefully, your spy will be able to complete her end of the mission."

"Thank you, Reverend." At that Hearns went to his room, leaving Freemund and Elizabeth at the table. Elizabeth was visibly upset.

"What kind of man loves a nigger woman?" She was incredulous with disbelief. "I mean, he says openly he loves her and that he intends to leave with her to start a family! That is absurd! Of all the stupid behaviors my husband has committed, that was never one of them. I mean, he has had sexual curiosities, but that is a far cry from love."

Freemund consoled Elizabeth, reminding her that her mission would indeed set right all the wrongs she had suffered.

Freemund decided to leave as soon as possible for the Guild. He was restless because he realized that the Africans not only had brought magic from their homeland, they had also been able to organize themselves efficiently to usurp an oppressive system. Traders took great pains to make sure that slaves were separated before they even left the shores of Africa to debilitate communication, and then plantation owners separated them again at the auction block, establishing a complete system of ignorance and brokenness. To overcome such oppression would take much planning and organization—a leisure slaves did not have. Slaves worked from sunup to sundown, and in their spare time they had to take care of their own children and their own needs. So the question Freemund wanted to answer was how they had gotten the time, leadership, and organization amid so squelching a system.

Freemund went to the lodge and made the necessary arrangements to hire two hundred mercenaries from the Merchant Traders' Guild to assist in the attack. The finances were not as heavy as he'd expected, because he learned that the government would also pay a handsome fee for the success of this mission, in addition to purchasing any slave who could be captured alive. While at the lodge, Freemund requested a meeting with the elders of the Guild, just as Nemesque had foreseen. This meeting was the most important and delicate of procedures before the mission began, and Freemund believed that it was only because of the paranormal events that he reported that he was granted such an immediate audience. The elders met at night in the lower level of the lodge. Only the highest-ranking officials of the

Guild could arrange a face-to-face meeting with them, and even that did not mean that the request would be honored. Freemund had never been granted an audience with the elders, but there had been no cause until now.

Freemund waited patiently in the sanctuary of the mysteriously enclosed edifice of the Guild as night fell. No one had ever seen the face of the elders, and their description was surrounded in secrecy. In fact, Freemund had only once before talked to someone who had met with the elders, and that person would not be persuaded to discuss the details of his meeting. The ever-burning lamps lit the seating area of the main vestibule, but there was no sound. The stillness heightened Freemund's sensory organs, and he could hear the resonant ebb and flow of his own blood pumping violently through his veins. Beads of perspiration littered his forehead as his chest rattled with the heavy beat of his pounding heart. He must have dozed off, for he remembered opening his eyes to a disturbance in the still air as someone, or something, quickly passed him. "Hello?" He blurted but received no response. His eyes frantically searched as he kept his head and body perfectly still. He didn't want his nervousness to be transparent.

Freemund was still a little groggy from his nap, and he realized that he was holding his breath in order to listen to the utter stillness to see if someone else was in the room with him. He heard no sound, and no matter how hard he looked, he could see no one. He could not understand why he was so nervous. These were his brothers, men with whom he had collaborated to make the white race the wealthiest in the world.

Freemund tried to comfort himself. He knew there was nothing to be afraid of. He had passed his arduous and often gruesome initiation to get into this powerful organization and, by this time, he himself had put others through the rite of passage to be a member. He reminded himself that he was safe and secure in his position. His dues were paid, and he maintained the social status quo between whites and blacks, so why was he so uneasy? Something was not right—he could feel it—but what exactly it was he found to be entirely elusive. Freemund's instincts told him he should leave; this idea of his was a stretch anyway. His leadership and Hearns's men, along with the mercenaries he hired, would be enough to stop the rebellion. But just as Freemund was getting ready to get up and make his way out of the lodge, a cold, powerful hand gripped his shoulder and gently pushed him back into the pew.

"Welcome, Brother Freemund. The elders await your presence in the lower level. Try to relax; do not look back." The voice was low, gravely, and confident, the grip, firm and consistent. Freemund knew that whoever was behind him possessed great physical power. "Do you understand, Brother?"

"I understand, sir." Freemund's voice quivered ever so slightly, and he mentally slumped at his outward display of cowardice. His emotions were a blur, and he could not decipher if he were afraid or merely excited at what could be potentially achieved. The hand relaxed its hold as the voice commanded him to rise, which he did. Then the hand gently pushed him forward toward the door behind the podium and stage where they began their descent to the lower meeting room.

As they moved through the levels, Freemund attempted to use logic to quell the irrational thoughts barraging his brain. He told himself that he was exaggerating the situation, but he would swear that he could only hear his own footsteps, and he listened between breaths to see if he could catch the inhalation of the person behind him. Freemund could detect nothing; the only sign of presence behind him was the strong hand that would goad him left, right, or forward. No more words were spoken. The two finally arrived at a well-lit room where tall candles burned brightly from their waxed perch on the floor, making this underground recess look quite surreal. The candles illuminated a path that led up a small flight of stairs. A firm but gentle nudge insinuated Freemund should mount the stairs, and he complied with the gesture.

Freemund now saw a long wooden table that had such a complete polish it reflected the shadows of the twenty men seated at it, even from a distance; the table had seating for twenty-two. Ten elders sat to the left of the table and ten to the right, while the chairs at either end of the table remained empty. The cold hand gingerly nudged Freemund to move toward the table. Every elder sitting there was cloaked in a black robe that reminded the minister of the Dominican priests of the Middle Ages, who often wore black robes with hoods that fit over their heads, leaving their faces in the shadows.

Above the table hung a dimly lit chandelier, and Freemund wondered briefly how they managed to place the device in the solid rock wall that loomed over their heads. The elders just sat at the table in complete silence, staring into the shadows of each other's faces. They were so quiet and motionless that Freemund wondered if they were real. The hand blazed cold on his shoulder, and he ached to turn around so that the hand would fall away and he would be relieved of its peculiar discomfort. Sweat ran down Freemund's back in streaks as a velvet voice abruptly broke the silence.

"We welcome you, Brother. Please sit at the table of Solomon and tell us of your wishes." Freemund no longer had to be prompted by the hand; this time he walked briskly to the chair at the end of the table that was closest to him. As he sat down, he glanced over his shoulder at the owner of the hand but saw no one there. Could he still feel the hand on his shoulder? Or had it been so cold and frightening that his brain still manifested that the hand was there? Freemund turned completely around in his seat to see where his guide went, but he saw no one.

"It does you no good to look behind you, Freemund, when such a glorious future lies ahead." The booming voice echoed through the vast chambers. "We have been following your ministry, and we are pleased. You have done great work in keeping the status quo between the races, and we will reward your request this evening in good faith if it is reasonable." Freemund could not help but loosen the buttons at the top of his shirt. During all this, the elders hadn't so much as moved but continued to stare into the shadows. Freemund nervously readjusted his collar and then spoke into the shadows, not knowing where exactly to voice his request as he responded to the invitation.

"As you are well aware, there are great forces in the universe that are referenced in the Holy Book of the Bible. I have preached of these forces, and I have evidence to believe that day is upon us now. A group of slaves, who call themselves the Maroons, have successfully led revolts against the southern plantations in Carolina and in Florida for the past four years. We cannot sit idly by and allow this to happen."

Freemund's confidence was beginning to stir as he pressed on, his voice gaining power.

"The infidels are led by a spiritual leader named Gausje, whose power—I believe—comes from a mystical tree found only in Africa. Now, part of this may sound like a fairy tale to you, but I have evidence that it is indeed true. Niggers do not possess the mental clarity to operate such successful missions against the white man's forces, and thus the only explanation is that this particular group is being helped by the devil, Lucifer, the antichrist! I request the aid of the elders in fighting this band of fallen beasts with equal spiritual force."

Freemund was feeling a little more encouraged, was breathing a little easier, but, at that moment, a pop echoed in the shadows, causing Freemund to visibly jump. The chair at the other end of the table slid away as if moved by invisible hands, but the shadows were so prominent there could possibly be someone pulling it back, it was hard to tell. Then there was another pop, followed by another, and Freemund realized it was clapping, as two dark figures began to slowly emerge from the shadows.

Freemund's mouth instantly became unhinged when he saw the first figure, a very naked, very muscular, and quite angry-looking Negro with an iron collar around his neck, take the seat opposite him. The other figure, whose hand rested on the Negro's shoulder, kept his face hidden in the shadows. When finally he spoke, it was the same voice that beckoned Freemund to address the elders.

"Your legendary gift of speech does not disappoint, Reverend Freemund. And I agree with most of what you have said, with the exception that the only explanation for the nigger's ability to usurp white power was because the devil was helping them. Have you seen the devil, Reverend Freemund? Have you tasted of his power to even make such a bold claim?" The voice paused, and silence filled the room.

Freemund had not dared stare at the elders who sat at the table, but now he glanced hard at each of them, attempting to look into the shadows surrounding their faces. What was going on here? He looked at the Negro whose eyes glared hatred across the long table. The black beast's eyes did not falter but stared right into the very soul of the preacher. The voice resumed, "I asked you a question, Reverend Freemund. Have you seen the devil or his handiwork up close?"

"I've seen the evidence of Satan's presence here on this earth. And that is enough to let me know of his existence and his capability." Freemund responded with mustered haughtiness. He was ashamed to have never seen any spiritual action up until now, and he did his best to hide it from his inquisitor.

"But how do you know it is of the devil, Reverend Freemund? Could it not be of God?" Again, a brief pause before the voice continued. "According to the Bible, who was it that caused plagues to fall on Egypt? Well, Reverend Freemund? Let me ask you another question; who was it that commanded King Saul to kill all of the Malachites, women and children included? Who struck down the elder who guarded the ark and attempted to preserve it when the Ark of the Covenant faltered and was about to fall while being carried by the priest back to the temple in Jerusalem?" The voice paused again.

"God."

"That is right. God. You do study your Bible! Excellent. Now, let me ask you another question. Have you ever seen God or witnessed His tangible power? I mean real power, like what you claim to have discovered about the power of these beasts of burden?" Freemund had to shake his head no. And again he was ashamed. He could not claim to have cast out a demon or seen a miracle. That was why he was here, because he hoped to be able to get the elders to work a miracle and resist this force. He didn't know what to say next. The voice spoke again. "So, then, how is it that you are so confident that the black slaves are in league with the devil, when both God and Satan have biblically demonstrated acts that you Christians would deem malevolent? Or, better yet, how is it you Christians claim to do so much good in the name of Christ when indeed you are doing the work of the devil—as you do with your female parishioners, Reverend Freemund?"

The velvety voice had turned icy cold, and Freemund felt, more than saw, the heads of the elders turn to stare at him. He tried to back up, but the chair wouldn't slide away, and he fell back down in his seat. His breathing was getting out of control, and he tried to force himself to be calm. He noticed that he could see his breath. Had the temperature dropped? What was happening? These couldn't be the elders of the Merchant Traders' Guild!

"Oh, but we are, Reverend Freemund. We are the truth, which far too often remains hidden due to human guile. What you know, what you've always experienced up to today, is the depth of depravity that humans can and will go to, and you have the gall to blame it on the devil. It is your own sloppy, slipshod behavior that erodes this world and its inhabitants of any good, and I find it disgusting." At that point, the figure emerged from the shadows and, to Freemund's astonishment, he saw a tall, muscular Indian with faint tattoos on both his cheeks and feathers of all different assortments standing out from his jet black hair, which gleamed in the dankness of this underground dwelling.

Before he knew what he was saying, Freemund blurted out, "I am a member of the Guild, and this is the abomination! You damn redskin!"

"That wasn't necessary, now, was it Reverend Freemund? You white people always amaze me at how you destroy that which you don't understand. My name is Nemesqu, and I will help you on your quest. I have my reasons, and they shall remain mine. But you, you need to rethink your own beliefs before gallivanting off and making claims to which you have no knowledge or merit. I have seen the ways of the devil, and, trust me when I say this, white man, his ways are cruel, but so are the ways of God, who I've also seen. One has to discipline himself to endure either path and make a choice for one side or the other. And if you decide that you do not want to choose, then the way will be chosen for you. I've just taken the time to choose my path, and I am fully aware of the consequences. I strongly suggest you do the same."

The proud Nemesqu smiled eerily at the preacher. With a wave of his free hand the very air seemed to instantly become animated, and the chandelier above began to slowly swing back and forth. The shadows that dominated the faces of the elders began to clear, allowing Freemund to see each of the members, many of whom he did not recognize. The cloaks of the elders began to blow, and the hoods of the ten on the left revealed the faces of ten Indians. They were old and their eyes had no whites. Nemesqu then turned his head to the other side of the table, and the hoods of the remaining ten elders blew back to reveal the faces of ten white men Freemund knew. They appeared strong and focused, but he slowly realized their eyes were just huge black irises. Nemesqu peered down his aquiline nose at the now totally puerile-looking minister. Freemund's mouth worked to formulate words while his head darted back and forth at the sight before him.

"This is of the devil!" I cannot! I cannot!" Freemund's eyes were filled with tears, his heart hammering violently within his chest. Nemesqu just looked at Freemund and laughed quietly.

"But you already have, Reverend Freemund. You know that in your well-educated mind, the doctrine that you have taught your congregation is a lie. Yes, you know it, and so do I." Nemesqu had been standing behind the mean-looking Negro while Freemund struggled to grasp the truth before him. Nemesqu never took his menacing eyes off Freemund as he slowly began manipulating a device on the collar of the Negro. "And it is okay, Pastor. You have done just what the spirits have wanted—"

"I have not! I have preached the word of the Lord!" Freemund spat.

"Oh, have you? Dear sir, you are deluded by your own lies, or you are lying to me. Either way, the choice is foolish. Why have you sought our help?" Nemesqu gestured to the elders, who continued to stare at an object Freemund could not see. "Why did you not pray to God to help you fight the slaves?"

Freemund still could not manage to speak. The mist of lies in his head was tripping up the emerging truth that was making efforts to get to his consciousness. He simply sat, staring at Nemesqu and the Negro, his eyes wild with fear as the metal collar slowly slipped from the man's neck. The slave nimbly moved away from his chair and stalked his way straight down the side of the table behind the elders to stand over Freemund, but Freemund could only glare at his executioner. The Negro's hands formed huge "Cs" in a gesture to grip Freemund's neck, but he paused as Nemesqu raised his hand.

"Dear sir, you know that you have ministered to your own needs and not those of the church of God. You continue to seduce the women of your congregation, and you convince yourself that you are doing what is right using scripture when your own study of scripture has shown you that you are indeed wrong!"

Freemund now sat with his head in his hands. This was the end. He knew something was amiss when he was sitting upstairs; his mind had tried to warn him, and now he was about to suffer at the hand of this Indian and his nigger slave. How ironic. The message that had been struggling to swim to the swampy surface of his mind finally broke through, and he knew that every word Nemesqu spoke was the truth. He was guilty as charged; he was a fraud. He was wealthy because he had used so many people, and now he thought he would be able to use the Guild. How wrong he had been. All of a sudden, the God he conveniently used to promote his own selfish ideals became quite real to him, and he wished He would come to save him now. But that was all about self-preservation. Freemund's nose began to run and his throat became clogged with spit. His brain began to send him another message. "You are going to die now. You are about to die!"

"I don't want to die!"

"Now, now, dear sir, who said anything about dying? I told you at the outset that I would grant your request, and that I had faith in you that it would be reasonable, and it is. The Guild will help you defeat the Maroons. I only ask that you admit to the truth, Freemund!"

"Yes—the truth. I admit I've been a cheater and a liar."

"Very good. Have you been serving God these past years or self?"

"Self—my own damn self!"

"Well done. And now that you have come to me, to seek my help, and my power—who else do you serve?" Nemesqu's eyes appeared wild and angry. He was slowly walking toward Freemund, who looked up, not sure of what Nemesqu meant.

"I don't understand," he stuttered.

"Oh, you do, sir. You do." Nemesqu then spoke in a loud voice. "Oh, open his eyes, spirits, that he may see and know the truth!"

Freemund glanced around the room, wondering to whom Nemesqu had been talking. Then he looked back at Nemesqu only to see translucent winged beings standing behind each of the elders, even behind Nemesqu. The beings stood ten feet tall, their hands held up and curved out near where the shoulders would be on a human being. What looked like golden honey with dark flecks in it was coming out of their opened mouths and pouring over the heads of the elders. Freemund looked around only to see one of them standing directly behind him, causing him to utter an audible gasp.

"Do I need to repeat the question, sir?" Nemesqu asked.

"No. I understand. I too serve the forces of darkness—just like the Maroons."

"Excellent, and that is right. Who you serve is not as important as owning up to the fact that you do serve, and you are diligent about how you do so."

With another wave Nemesqu's hand the beings disappeared, although Freemund sensed they were still there. Nemesqu opened the collar, and the servant went back to his master, who clicked the collar on and dismissed him. The black man disappeared into the darkness. "You know now, even more than before, who you serve. Do you admit it?"

"I do." Freemund's eyes peered back at his questioner, his head slightly hung down. "I do."

"Very well. Then we will ride together in victory under the same spirit and the same force. He who has the most dedicated heart shall be the victor. Now go home to your wife."

Freemund quickly retraced his steps up to the main floor. He walked slowly down the aisle to the only entrance to the lodge, pushed the heavy doors open, and listened as they closed behind him. He had no idea what time it was, only that the moon was still out and the night air was clearer than it had been inside. He took several deep breaths, but he felt no better. He realized that what had happened that night that was irreversible, and that he would pay a tremendous cost for it.

Freemund stumbled into his house, tired, depressed, and horrified. He tried to remember the jubilant feeling he had at all his successes: running into Elizabeth and Hearns, raising a mercenary group, and arranging a meeting with the elders. He had accomplished so much, yet he felt as if he had nothing. The house was dark. Freemund went to his study and got a bottle of bourbon. He didn't know when he finished it; all he knew was that despite his inebriated condition, he felt no better. He should have been happier. Armageddon had been prophesied at the lodge's conception, and this looked to be the beginning of the end. He had made sure his people were on top of the situation, yet he felt an emotion oddly like remorse. Perhaps he would feel better in the morning. Nemesqu had promised to help their cause, and Nemesqu obviously wielded much power.

The reverend tip-toed into the bedroom and gingerly closed the door before climbing into bed beside an irritated and restless Rebecca. The alcohol quickly put him to sleep, but Rebecca's cold eyes raked over her husband as he snored carelessly. Her mind spooled threads of envy and cunning into a subtle web of a plan that would reestablish balance within her teetering world. Long had she endured neglect and disdain from her husband, forced to be subservient daily because she lived in a world where white patriarchy was the standard. Her fists bunched up the covers until the backs of her hands turned white as Freemund rolled over and belched a phosphorus burp that stung her nostrils. He could be such a crude individual that she wondered why she had ever married him. Rebecca closed her eyes and thought about her web of vengeance and how gratifying it would be for her husband to be dangling in it while she pondered what to do with his corpse; with that thought, her hands relaxed and she eventually fell asleep, knowing the next day her aspirations would begin to come to fruition.

CHAPTER 22

PREMONITIONS

That night Gausje's sleep was tormented with ghoulish visions. Her spirit would not let her rest because of what her dream kept showing her. In her dream, the city was shadowed within a shroud of thick mist. She exited her tent as planned, prepared for battle, but when she stepped out to the war council, no one else was up and ready. Every weapon rack was fully stocked, and the swords and spears looked shiny in contrast to the dreary, sunless atmosphere. She ran from tent-to-tent, summoning the warriors from their slumber, only to be answered with silence and stillness. Gausje started going into tents calling for specific people, but every last tent was devoid of human life with only the remains of habitation visible: pots, blankets, smoldering small fires. Gausje did not want to go back to sleep, but she knew she must endure the dream to its completion in case the spirits were trying to send her a message. She said a little incantation that would allow her to focus her spirit while in a dream state so she could discern the meaning of this nightmare.

Gausje rested her head on the pillow again, and she fell into a deep sleep. Darkness billowed, and shades of gray and white intermingled, and once again Guasje saw herself awake in the barren Maroon camp. She went through the same actions as always, but once she returned to the gates, her body collapsed on the floor of the camp, and her eyes rolled back in her head as she fell into an involuntary trance-like state. Now Gausje was watching herself writhe on the ground as her spirit floated above body. Her spirit rose high above the clouds, where all was bright and beautiful, but soon she dipped back down under the clouds and everything was again gray and grainy. She saw a forest similar to the one in which her city was hidden, but it was prettier, with foliage of verdant green and strong-looking trees whose leaves were striated with veins thick with viscous fluids from plentiful rains.

There was a road not too far from the edge of the forest, and her spirit descended to just within the forest's edge. There she saw a white male priest, dressed in a gray cloak, leaving a building made of stone with strange inscriptions on it. The building was partially hidden in a forest. Gausje assumed it was a white man's temple. On the temple above the door was the symbol of a serpent and a language that she could not decipher. The priest's movements were stuttered and sudden instead of fluid, and at times he would jump in time five spaces ahead of himself while walking. Next, the scene dissolved to a table in his house where a pale white woman in a black dress sat in the far corner of the room while a soldier and the priest met. The woman's eyes had no pupils, and although it was hard for Gausje to focus on her because the bodies of the two men were in the way, it seemed that every time her spirit chose to align her position where she could see the woman clearly, the woman was looking directly at her. Gausje was startled to realize that the woman's entire eyeballs were as black as a scorpion's carapace.

Gausje's spirit moved her perspective towards the table so she could see on what the two men were working. It was a map of her city and a clear path to get into it. But Gausje knew that already; there was more amiss. What was the significance of the white woman in black? Her spirit floated to the back of the priest where she saw tattooed on the back of his neck the serpent. She recognized the serpent as a bad omen, its poisonous fangs dripping venom. Could it be that this man had the power of the spirits as well? Gausje was not blind to the possibilities that others possessed the skill of divination, but she had not thought that her immediate enemies would because they relied so heavily on man-made weapons.

Then, suddenly, the white woman in black levitated from her chair and floated toward Gausje, her body retaining its sitting position. Once over the table, the woman did three revolutions and then stretched out so that her body was horizontal. Gausje's vision focused on the map below the woman. It was odd that her body did not cast a shadow on the map. One man was becoming fidgety and could not focus on the details of the map or what the other was saying. Instead, he kept looking up at the woman and then back at the other man for confirmation or explanation of what he was seeing. He obviously was disturbed by this manifestation of the supernatural.

Gausje focused her energies on the details of the map and then the hands of the man who held it. Her vision caught the wrinkles in the man's skin and noticed the fine texture of the paper on which the diagram was drawn. She didn't expect the white paper's purity to be stained with the huge drop of blood that descended from the ceiling, the spot of blood widening and spreading its puce stain on the map of the city. Slowly, Gausje turned her head toward the ceiling only to see that the pale white woman was completely nude and bore a series of wounds from the base of her neck to the cleft between her buttocks. At that very moment, the silence was interrupted with a sickening sound, like the smashing of a watermelon. Gausje saw the woman's back slowly split open, her organs and entrails cascading in slow motion over the sides of her back and down onto the table. The man in charge did not appear affected, but the other man who watched had a sickened look on his face. As the entrails splattered blood onto their clothes and faces, only one man smiled, his white teeth glistening, and Gausje could see tiny red spots of blood on them. Then the priest raised his hands above his head and gestured an uplifting movement with his upraised palms toward the corpse of the woman. Several black serpents suspended themselves from the orifice of her open cavity and slithered down toward the table, devouring the entrails in huge gulps. Once every piece of flesh was devoured, all but one serpent coiled its way back into the body of the woman, but one remained, suspended between her body and the table. It opened its mouth, and the man reached into it and pulled one of its fangs. Gausje could see the poison running down the priest's hand. He then took the fang and placed it within his shirt pocket. Gausje knew the fang was a gift from his god, and that he was strong in the spiritual world.

Gausje's dream shifted, and she saw the gates of the city burst open and a huge cadre of white men race inside. Unarmed, and without guards, Gausje tried to buy herself time to invoke her magic. She ran toward the circle of spears, trying to widen the distance between her and her captors or killers. She turned her head to see how far they had advanced when her foot stepped on a soft form. She turned forward and looked down to see that she had just trampled a child. Before a scream escaped her mouth, she saw why every tent was empty—everyone lay naked and dead in the circle of spears. Everyone except Jakeel, who sat amidst the cauldron of death with tears streaming down his eyes. He pointed to the dead woman lying in his lap. There were two puncture wounds in her side, and Gausje immediately recognized them to be the marks of a snake bite. At that moment, Gausje awoke from her dream, her wrinkled body stained with perspiration. She had an ominous feeing, and she had to act before it was too late. Had she acted too harshly? Had she moved with too much haste?

"The gods must be displeased with our sacrifice," she whispered to herself. "I must rest in order to be able to conjure up the spirits for battle or else the city will be lost. Perhaps there is more to Jakeel's being here than I first believed. He wanted to stymie the bloodshed. I must listen to the spirits."

*****

Freemund sat at the breakfast table at dawn, eager to share his plan with Hearns. Anxiety woke him before the sun crested the horizon, and he sat brooding at the table, mulling over his next step. First, he'd have to convince Elizabeth and Hearns to willingly support his plan as long as he could without force but, in the end, he knew he would use whatever tactics he deemed necessary to accomplish his purpose.

CHAPTER 23

TO OBEY IS BETTER THAN TO SACRIFICE

reemund could feel its sting on the back of his neck. His hand involuntarily ran over it, fluffing the hairline that so discreetly covered its presence—this symbol, this promise of allegiance. Had he gone soft? Was his conscience now his governor? It couldn't be! He remembered quite vividly the tenacity and the vivaciousness of his efforts to be a part of the Guild, to rule this land, to subvert the niggers to fulfill his dreams and the collective desires of all the white men he knew. He remembered studying the ancient parchments that linked him and every other blood devotee as eternal brothers in life and death. And he had successfully done all of this in grand fashion. He remembered taking the blood oath, mingling it with that of his brothers; he remembered reciting his vows, so many, many years ago, to a cloaked presence who was wearing an open-hooded robe, so black that he could not see his—or its—face. He remembered his brothers and him shaving the back of their heads to receive the tattoo of the serpent, the visual symbol of their pledge. There was talk of a sacrifice, but after all these years, he had forgotten about it. He thought that night was it. He had fulfilled his obligations, but now he was coming to the realization that he had actually committed sacrifices for a long time now. He thought it was entertainment, albeit cruel. Yet, as he sat there in the shadows of his basement, he realized he had sent several lives to the greedy gods that he inadvertently served.

Freemund grimaced as his mind searched for answers that seemed to evade his mental faculties. In his heart, he knew his life had suited his desires ever since his initiation. He served the Guild through his successful ministry, sowing the seeds of prejudice, racism, and bigotry to the masses, and it was with great pride that he would glance surreptitiously at his fellow members during his sermons and catch their looks of approval at one of their brothers doing the good work. He had benefited financially, and his reputation as one of the greatest ministers in the south was unparalleled. So why did he feel guilt now at what he was about to do?

Freemund stood next to a cement table above which hung black chains that ended with sharp hooks. On the table was a surgeon's saw, which a lodge brother, a physician, had given him as a gift from England. The saw was sterling silver, and its malevolent, sharp edges glinted in the soft shaft of light that snuck between the grimy grill of one of the basement windows. Freemund marveled at how an instrument that had intimately touched so much blood, bone, and gristle could be so clean. He had personally lynched twenty niggers since his membership to the lodge, all in secret, and had dismembered eight others here in his basement. At first, the pure excitement of brutally taking a life of another made the incident an orgy of bloodlust. It had been sloppy; they didn't have the right tools, and they practically tore the life from the nigger before he had time to suffer. But by the third, they had studied their dark craft, had incorporated the use of medical doctors who had joined the Guild, and they executed death with scientific accuracy, maintaining the poor beast's life until the blood-curdling end. They killed slowly with deft precision, using surgical tools and methods imported from the Orient. How cautious they had been, how thorough! No mess, no body except parts they kept as memorabilia. All for the Guild, all part of the sacrifice to the powers that ran the lodge. But more than that, he had enjoyed it. Now he questioned whether it had all been based on a lie. The cloaked elder to whom he swore so long ago was not even white but a damn red-skinned Indian! In essence, Freemund had pledged his soul to a life form that was lower than his, and this made him feel debased. How could this be?

But the irony of it all was that he and his brothers had profited greatly from this pledge, thus there had to be truth in that, right? As his mind pondered recent events, Freemund ran his other hand against the black chains that were suspended from the sturdy ceiling. Now that he had received the truth, given him by an Indian, who had a nigger as a body guard, Freemund was faced with a decision, and he hated it because out of all the sacrifices, this was the one he intuitively knew counted the most. He was at a crossroad: should he obey his conscience or offer up the sacrifice that would give the edge necessary to defeat the Maroon tribe? He remembered a Bible phrase, "To obey is better than to sacrifice," and he felt deep within his gut that he was on the verge of making a crucial decision. This resolution would come at a high price, and he was not certain the account of his moral bank would have sufficient funds.

There was another item on the table: a rolled up parchment with a crude sketch of the architectural designs of the city that Hearns had drawn up based on his nigger woman's description—the slave woman with whom he intended to runaway. What the hell was the world coming to? Freemund had to admit that although he did not get involved with the ministry to save souls, his reading of the scriptures had an effect on his mind that he could never shake and that, he supposed, eventually made him a convenient Christian. He believed in the last days, and he had a biased view of what was right and wrong, but the co-mingling of whites and slaves, outside of slaves being offered for sacrifice or living a life of servitude, was out of the question. Furthermore, he believed such abominations were solely responsible for bringing about such spiritually dark times.

But Freemund was conflicted because he had learned he was getting his power and his money from an Indian, which meant that everything he had practiced up to this point was a damned lie. But he believed the white man was the remnant, blessed by God. What was it Hearns had said? That during war he had witnessed white men commit the most heinous, Godless acts one could ever imagine? The validity of those words now chimed in his brain, resonating truth, a reality he had submerged from his conscious mind for such a long time he no longer acknowledged it. Now he had to. How true Hearns's statement was. Evil was evil, despite race, and now that Freemund realized that Nemesqu, an Indian, was the spiritual leader of the Guild, Freemund had to accept the fact that his hands were dirty, filthy even, of committing sin while having full knowledge that it was wrong. He'd convinced himself otherwise, but his meeting with the elders brought back to the surface the truth drowned with years of bloodshed and lies.

Freemund had been so deep in thought that he carelessly pierced his palm, and the hook and chain seemed to jingle in approval. So what did this mean? It meant that what Freemund did from this point forward would be the truth. Furthermore, because knowing versus not knowing was part of judgment, he recognized that this sacrifice would have a deeper consequence despite what he chose to do. Payment would be required from the gods or the Guild. A decision must be made, and, as he pondered, a droplet of blood escaped the fangs of the hook and plummeted toward the cement table, exploding into tiny replicas of itself, making apparent to Freemund what choice he was destined to make. The sacrifice would take place in his basement as it always had. He would obey the Guild and ignore his conscience. He would offer up his sacrifice and continue to experience the success that had filled his life. And he would worry about the price later.

Freemund slowly released the hook and put the surgeon's knife back in its cuckold under the cement slab used as a table. He readied himself mentally, took a deep breath, and then went upstairs to bring about judgment.

*****

Elizabeth and Hearns entered Reverend Freemund's study cautiously, not quite knowing what to expect. Freemund had his back to them, contemplatively staring at his enormous book collection. There were dark circles under his eyes, indicating the stress of making a choice that butted against his better judgment. The body has ways of broadcasting the facts, and today those dark circles looming beneath Freemund's cold eyes told all. When he heard the two seat themselves, he put on his best smile and slowly turned around in his chair. Freemund actually thought he was smiling, but, at best, the turned up sides of his mouth only manifested a sneer.

"Well, lady and gentleman," Freemund said with his best witty demeanor, "I have good news to report. The Guild has accepted our proposal and has provided funds to support our military effort in addition to granting us two hundred mercenaries to fight." Freemund was pleased to see the look of relief on Hearns's face because he felt it was imperative that Hearns relax and trust him. "We march at first light tomorrow morning. To delay will only give our enemy more time to coordinate, and we must collectively, and in a timely fashion, shut down their evil operation." Elizabeth looked pleased.

Hearns was about to speak when Freemund held up a hand slightly and respectfully as he continued. "Hearns, my friend, I don't judge you. You are a grown man and must make grown decisions. I see you have done thus. As your friend, I wish you the best. May we both put forth our chief efforts in fulfilling this mission, and each find individual peace afterward." Hearns was taken aback by the milky conviction that filled Freemund's voice. When he looked into Freemund's eyes, he noticed that they were glassy and slightly red, though he didn't believe the irritated veins to be from alcohol but rather from emotion. Elizabeth noticed it, too, but neither realized the maniacal source of such conviction.

"Thank you, Reverend. We will experience victory, as we have always known it. You will have my best, and that of my men."

"Elizabeth, you serve a special role as made evident by my meeting with the Guild." Freemund looked at her with kind eyes, but she was unaware that those eyes had witnessed horrors her most torrid of nightmares could never have revealed. Elizabeth smiled and responded.

"I had no idea the Guild knew of me."

"The Guild is everywhere, Elizabeth, one only need ask. You have sat by many a member in my church congregation. We don't boast of our membership or our deeds; we just do our best to make the world a better place. It is our collective goodwill that provides us much of our success."

"I am impressed, Reverend, as always, with your goodwill. So what is it that I am to do? You remember what I said earlier; I don't need men protecting me. I am willing to fight for what is rightfully mine."

Elizabeth sincerely hoped these two men were taking her seriously. She realized that it was a huge leap of faith, considering that she had been in charge when her slaves abandoned her plantation; she was not a coward, and she would do anything to prove that but sit idly by and watch everyone else fight for redemption. She glanced at both men, flashing a brilliant smile, hoping to ease the silence, and was gratified when Reverend Freemund smiled back, followed by a reticent grin from Hearns.

"Elizabeth, I hope you realize what you are asking. The Guild already acknowledges your importance to this mission. I assume they must have gotten wind of the tragedy that has befallen your plantation. But I assure you that your role in this endeavor is no small one. In fact, you are crucial to this mission." Freemund looked into her eyes intently as he felt, more than saw, the gaze that came from Hearns.

"If I may be so bold, Reverend, what is it about Elizabeth that is so vital?" Hearns asked this without the slightest tone of arrogance or chauvinism.

"Well, that is why I called you both to my study today. There is a spiritual power that is facilitating the efforts of the Maroon tribe. It hails from Africa; it is quite real, as you both can attest to, especially you, Colonel, and we need a counteragent, so to speak." Before Freemund could finish, Elizabeth interjected.

"But Reverend, I am no spiritual expert. That would be you! I don't see how I can be a counteragent in this war unless I have a gun in my hand."

"Perhaps if you let me finish, Elizabeth, I might be able to shed a little light on the matter."

"Sorry, Reverend. Please continue." Elizabeth's face was beginning to redden.

"The Africans have a seed that comes from a great and powerful tree that is assumed to be in the same location as was the original Garden of Eden. Now, without going into detail, they did manage to get it here, or a manifestation of its power. Every spiritual power requires a special element that feeds it. In ancient times, God, the utmost spiritual leader, required the sacrifice of a lamb—something pure, innocent, and worthy of Him. He would not accept anything other than the best, and He spelled out what he considered to be the best. Elizabeth, I am convinced that your heart is noble, pure, and honest. I believe your story wholeheartedly. You possess that which both Hearns and I lack, and that is purity of spirit. You see, Hearns and I both shed blood in the war. Thus, in approaching such a delicate matter as spiritual warfare, our hearts are not pure enough to channel the forces of good to end this pandemic of Blacks and Indians slaughtering innocent men, women, and children who have come to this land to gain what is rightfully theirs."

"So, it's my pure heart? Sounds trivial, Reverend. I said I want to do something, not be something." Hearns was listening intently to Freemund and seemed to be agreeing with him. From Tanjee, and the incident in the cane field, he knew firsthand that the forces they were fighting against were more than simple flesh and blood. The bloodstained memories that haunted Hearns every night, except ones spent with Tanjee, were testament to how able he had been in dealing with flesh and blood. Freemund looked at Elizabeth, then at Hearns, who nodded for him to continue.

"Elizabeth, we must channel the spirits in order to attain their power. You are the one we must channel them through. Through you, we will gain the power from the spirits to challenge our foe."

"But I—"

"There can be no buts, Elizabeth!" Freemund revealed an unusual flash of impatience, but he did his best to calm himself. "This is serious, ma'am. If we don't do this right, we could all lose our livelihood, our children's future, possibly our very lives. *I know how to do this.*" Although the last phrase came out as a harsh whisper, he continued with a controlled cadence. "The Guild comes here regularly in order for me to channel the spirits. I know what I am doing and have the facilities already set up. But if you are not in this one hundred percent, Elizabeth, then say so now, before Hearns and I put our lives at risk."

Freemund looked at Elizabeth with grave eyes, his jaw muscles flexing visibly beneath the fleshy contours of his skin. He had the same pensive manner she saw when he made an appeal at church. She felt her heartbeat quicken, and now she was beginning to feel nervous. She quickly glanced at Hearns, who returned her look with raised eyebrows. She knew what he was thinking. *"Well, woman, are you going to fulfill your role, since you just have to be involved in men's work?"* Elizabeth gave her answer.

"So, how do we channel the spirits? What am I to do, exactly?"

"Before I tell you, Hearns, are you sure you are ready for this? Once we begin, there is no turning back. You don't invoke the power of the spirits and then change your mind. If you are foolish enough to do so, they will make you pay, and trust me; you don't want to make that type of payment."

"Let's get this done, Reverend. I'm in all the way. You bring the religious expertise, I'll bring the gunpowder. What is the plan?"

"Let's go to my basement." Freemund spun his chair around, and both Elizabeth and Hearns heard a click. To the right of the desk, a panel dropped three inches and then zipped back underneath the floor to reveal cables that allowed for forward and backward movement. When Elizabeth and Hearns stood up they could see a set of stairs leading down into a dimly lit room. The space was huge, and an average-size man could walk down the steps without stooping. "Follow me," Freemund said.

Their footsteps started to echo the deeper they traveled. Both Hearns and Elizabeth mentally marveled at the staircase, because neither had ever seen one so steep. When at last they reached the bottom they noticed how immaculately clean the lower chamber was. It was illuminated by four grilled windows near the ceiling at the middle of each wall. In the center of the room stood a cement table, and along the floor at each of the four corners sat two enormous candles that measured four feet in height and eight inches in circumference. The room was full of shadows, and Elizabeth took note of the subtle beauty the four shafts of light had in casting their rays strategically on the floor.

Meanwhile, Hearns absent-mindedly reached for his pistol only to discover that it was not there. He was accustomed to rubbing the handle as a nervous habit, but he suddenly remembered that he had left the weapon and his leather belt slung over the bedpost in the guest room. As they entered the underground chamber, Hearns took another glance at the candles; in the shadows he could vaguely see the nebulous shape that melted wax took on after a time of burning. He stared at the giant fixtures of wax, mesmerized, but jumped slightly when he thought he saw one of the shapes shift.

Freemund went to a cabinet that was fixed on the wall to the right of the table and took out a lantern lighter and lit its fuse. Once he carefully set fire to each of the candlewicks, the room was effused with yellow light. He took the lantern lighter and blew out its flame, returning it to its place, and removed a rolled-up parchment. Hearns heard a jingle in the room.

"What was that, Rev?" He looked around, trying to disguise his nervous behavior.

"What was what, Hearns?" Freemund responded.

"I didn't hear anything." Elizabeth countered.

"You must both swear that what you are about to witness will never leave this room. What we are about to embark on today has never been used for war, and it is strictly reserved for the purposes of the Guild. Swear to me your oath of silence!" The tone of Freemund's voice was powerful, his eyes no longer holding the compassion that Elizabeth was accustomed to seeing in church. For a fleeting moment, she wondered if she were really doing what was right. Swearing an oath seemed a little stringent.

"I swear that what I see here today will never leave my lips." Hearns stood ready.

"Elizabeth? Last chance, darlin'. You can leave now, and we won't think badly of you. Either leave or swear an oath of silence."

"I swear, Reverend. What I witness here will never leave my lips." She had done it. She was in, and it made her feel powerful. Freemund pushed forward a lever that he had stuck into the ground, causing four smooth blocks of concrete to slowly push their way out of the floor, one on each side of the cement table. Freemund gestured for Hearns and Elizabeth to sit, and they went to the table and sat down on the concrete stools.

"This house was purchased by the Guild. Its architect has built many smart contraptions in it for the purpose of our ceremonies, and no one other than you two have ever been here who were not blood-sworn brothers." Freemund rolled the parchment out on the table, revealing the design of the city to Hearns, who was amazed at the accurate detail.

"Before I met with the elders I spoke with Baramoore of the information your informant gave you. He said he had someone who is an expert in designing battle plans and could create an artist's layout of the city, along with the best strategy on how to get inside and defeat the enemy."

As Freemund spoke, Hearns noted the intricate detail of the map and became impressed by its accuracy. It was a visual of what he had only imagined after going over it with Tanjee. But what was even more amazing was the method of getting in. The positions from where troops would attack were laid out with plain delicacy, and the locations where troops would stay to kill or collect any who escaped were also marked. Also identified were the point of entry, point of retreat, barriers to surround the fortress; all had been considered. Hearns's confidence grew, although he wondered if the architect knew about the traps. Well, no matter, he did, and he would lead his troops past them and into the city. Freemund looked at Elizabeth with satisfaction as he walked slowly to her and placed a warm hand on her shoulder.

"Getting the layout and strategy was the easy part, along with securing a few hundred mercenaries to assist our plan. Now comes the hard part. I want to make it perfectly clear that when dealing with the invisible world of spirits, there is no easy way. And channeling the spirits is not an easy task, Elizabeth. I am going to need you to trust me. Everything I ask of you is absolutely necessary. It will make you uncomfortable, but it will determine our fate. Remember that, Elizabeth. What we do here determines our fate, and the fate of our way of life!"

"I understand, Reverend," Elizabeth answered in a tremulous voice filled with anxiety. Her brain began firing questions that made her feel even more uncomfortable with the ever-growing complexity of the situation. First, where was Freemund's wife? Where were the servants? How was it that in this house, a normal parade of miserable slaves, in-house servants, parishioners, and the like, none were to be found? She considered the questions, but she had no logical response. Glancing over at Hearns, she saw him fully immersed in the document that he had removed from the table and taken with him to his cement stool, placing it on the floor.

"I sense your concern, Elizabeth, which is only natural. I intend to give you a preview of the powers that we are dealing with here." He was staring so intently at her that Elizabeth felt he was looking straight through her. Freemund held out his hands, both facing palm up, and flexed his fingers jointly on both of them so that they flickered in unison toward his body. "Come here, Elizabeth. I want you to hold my hands." He spoke solemnly.

"What? You want me to hold your hands?" Freemund did not reply but continued to stare at Elizabeth. She timidly rose from her perch and walked toward the pastor, her hands far out in front of her. She remembered the nasty stares from his wife, and although she was not around, Elizabeth didn't want to involve herself with the slightest insinuation of intimacy. Her hands slowly drew closer to his and, by the time they connected, her palms were sweaty and quite cold. She remembered how cool it was in the basement when suddenly there was a quiet boom and a sudden flash, and she felt the floor falling away from her feet. Her body seized involuntarily, defensively, and her mouth formed a circular gape in an effort to make sound, but no sound came, only a severe rush of exhaled breath. Her eyes attempted to roll up in her head so that Freemund saw the lower half of her pupils fibrillating violently.

"I am here, Elizabeth. Hold on to my hands. Squeeze if you hear me." Freemund instructed. Elizabeth did as she was told, for in her mind's eye she was back home looking at herself cry as her husband pulled a pitchfork from the corpse of their daughter. What was going on? How had she left the basement so quickly to be home again? Queries once more fired in her brain, but no answers came. There was only Freemund, holding her hands.

Then the scene in Elizabeth's mind abruptly switched to a partially open field where a man was staked down to the ground with branches and leaves tumbling out of his mouth. She stared in horror and disbelief, riveted to the panorama of events passing before her eyes, trying to understand the illogical sights. What did these visions mean? What was happening to her? Her puzzled mind was in a daze when a familiar figure stepped into her path of vision. She strained to recognize the person, could tell he was military, but she could only see his back of his head. She wanted a closer look. The man pulled out his pistol and walked cautiously toward the young man staked to the ground; she saw the man with the pistol shoot the man on the ground three times in the face. When the man who did the shooting turned around, Elizabeth realized it was Hearns.

Elizabeth let out another harsh exhalation, causing Hearns to look up from the map. She was perspiring and holding Freemund's hands, her head jerked back in an odd fashion, her mouth open. Her body swayed in slight but significant jolts, and Freemund was staring at her as if she were a pariah. Though his face twisted into a grimace, his eyes never left her.

"What is happening to her, Freemund? Is she all right?" Freemund heard Hearns's question, but he dared not break the channel that he established with Elizabeth as she was falling deeper into the trance under which he had placed her. He continued to work on her, gently squeezing her palms and transmitting another signal into her hands, watching with fascination as she involuntarily responded to his powers.

Elizabeth now saw her two other daughters, her husband, and Ivan surrounded by a thick circle of fierce-looking slaves, all brandishing weapons that appeared crude but dangerous. They were chanting in a way she could not understand, their bodies covered from head to toe in white powder except for red, bleeding whelps that littered their naked backs. The scene panned upward toward the sky where stars shone amid the darkness that covered the face of the earth, the moon's face a deep red. Her vision panned back down to where her family was surrounded, but this time her daughters were naked, and a fountain of blood gushed profusely from their crotches, creating large, muddy puddles on the ground below them. As the black crowd of infidels laughed raucously and moved in for the kill, the ground began to tremble and heave itself, eventually breaking apart to reveal large, gaping crevasses. Her eyes left the sight of her family to peer down one of the cracks that looked like a black mudslide. A form moved down there, and her view was almost directly over the hole to the point where she thought she was going to fall in and be buried alive. Her legs buckled, and she fell forward onto Freemund, who never let go of her hands but simply held her steady.

"I said what the hell is going on, Rev?" Hearns raised his voice a little; he didn't like being ignored. He walked over to Elizabeth, and Hearns peered into her eyes. What he saw made him leap back. Her eyes were completely rolled up in her skull, and all he could see was their pure whites. He turned to Freemund only to find that his eyes were completely black, though they shone like dark polished lava stones. Hearns stumbled back from Freemund, his hands and mouth feeling a numbing sensation when he got within three feet of him.

Suddenly, a jangling sound diverted Hearns's attention from the macabre dance that was taking place between Freemund and Elizabeth to the area above the table. When he looked up he didn't see anything and was about to turn back toward his two companions when the basement roared with sound as thick, heavy back chains descended out of the ceiling to about five feet above the table. They had sharp, diabolical hooks on their ends, which must have been heavy because the chains shortly stopped, wavering and hanging still over the table. The pit of Hearns's stomach flushed with acid, and he swallowed instinctively as his mouth filled with spit.

Freemund's breathing became labored; he fought to resist his fatigue and put the final signal through. Elizabeth jolted again, and then she saw that the pit looked as if black mud were sliding down it. Impossibly, a large black snake uncoiled itself from the confines of the earth and rose up to the height of three fully grown men. It opened its mouth and spewed venom at the crowd, which suddenly recoiled from its poisonous attack. Elizabeth then saw herself standing in the middle of the circle, her arms outstretched; as she moved her hands to the left or the right, the snake moved accordingly, devouring the threat in smooth, sweeping motions. Her daughters looked at her with pride; her husband and Ivan, with disbelief. And then she was staring into the eyes of her pastor, realizing she was holding his hands.

Although he released his grip, she held on. "That was astonishing." She puffed, her heart pounding the insides of her rib cage with ardent fervor. "Really amazing. How did you do that?" she asked, still attempting to grasp what had happened.

"It's a gift, Elizabeth, a gift we must not waste. It is a talent that I have shared with you so that you might share in return and fulfill your role in this task."

"I understand that I have a role to play, and I would be lying if I told you I am not scared, because I am horrified. But I trust you, Reverend. What is next?"

Freemund's sorcery had begun to melt the sturdy barrier of Elizabeth's typical mistrust. Her once reticent attitude was starting to become more accepting, and Freemund led her over to the table where the chains hung, sparkling darkly under the leer of flickering candle lights, coldly but silently expressing their power, their immutability.

"Elizabeth, are you all right?" Hearns asked. "I thought the same thing that happened to that boy in the cane field was about to happen to you!"

"I saw you in the cane field, Hearns. I saw you shoot that boy. I saw horrible scenes of my life—and yours—possibly—the future."

"Then you should realize that our time is short, Elizabeth. Colonel? How are those plans looking? Do we have a military advantage?" Freemund asked, but Hearns just kept gazing at Elizabeth.

"The future? You saw me shoot the boy in the cane field?" Hearns asked.

"Yes, Hearns, I did. I also saw the shock on your face, the uncertainty, the panic, and I don't look at you as a murderer. You did what your training taught you to do."

"And now we must do what my training has taught me to do. Elizabeth, I need you to lie down on the table. You must go through this process to gain the power that you undoubtedly witnessed yourself possessing in your vision."

"But I don't see how I am to gain—"

"It is not for you to see anymore than what you have, Elizabeth! It is strictly for you to trust me. Now, please lie down on the table. Face down. Colonel, move to the opposite side of the table if you would please. I will need your assistance."

Elizabeth hesitantly did as she was told. She shuddered as the cold slab of polished concrete met her face. Freemund gently grabbed her ankles and removed her shoes, placing them gently on the floor next to the table. The sun had completely set so that the only light that now illuminated the room was cast from the flickering flames of the large candles on the floor.

"Elizabeth, I asked you to lie face down because I need to remove your clothes." Elizabeth started to clamor up from the table; Hearns just gaped at Freemund as he felt a cold chill pass by his neck, followed by a faint whisper.

"Did you hear that, Reverend?" Hearns asked.

"Reverend, I do not believe that the removal of my garments will be of any military—" A brisk slap silenced Elizabeth's sentence before she could complete it. Freemund was now fully given over to the spirits, and his patience and human charisma were completely subverted to another's control.

"You swore an oath!" Freemund forcefully spoke. "You had your chance to leave, and you forsook it! Now, you will do as you are told! Remove your undergarments and throw them on the floor. I don't want to make this any harder than it already is." Elizabeth shuddered but complied. Hearns remained at his post on the other side of the table. "Take off everything, please." Freemund's request was an implicit order. Elizabeth did as she was told, her face red with embarrassment and her body quivering against the coldness of the room and the cement. Hearns looked at Freemund to ascertain if there was any mark of lechery in his stare but found the pastor's eyes to be completely bereft of emotion. In fact, he observed only calculation.

When Elizabeth finished her task, she lay on the table but looked fearfully at Freemund. Freemund then took out what looked to be a piece of charcoal and drew eight circles on her back, placed approximately six inches from each other in length and width. He then drew four others on the back of her upper legs in likewise fashion. This he did with calm expertise. Next, he made a downward motion with his right hand. Immediately, the heavy chains uncoiled from their source, which Hearns tried to see but could not, stopping within two inches of her body.

"Elizabeth, what I am going to do next will hurt a little, but it is bearable. I am going to pinch the fatty tissue on your back and on your legs where I have drawn these circles and pierce them with these hooks. You will bleed just a little, but not much, and soon the flesh will become numb to the pain." To Hearns he said, "Hold her down tight." Elizabeth opened her mouth to protest, but Hearns hastily did as he said he would, turning her verbal commotion into a scream. Meticulously and methodically, Freemund inserted the hooks into each of the areas designated and, as promised, little blood was produced. The hooks were so sharp that it took him less than two minutes to complete the task, leaving both Elizabeth and Hearns relieved.

"Trust me, Colonel, it looks worst than it feels. I, myself, have gone through this process." Hearns looked dubious but said nothing. He just kept rubbing the place where the heel of his gun should have been.

Freemund motioned for Hearns to step back from the table, and the chains jerked Elizabeth five feet above the platform. She let out another yelp, and her breasts swung sumptuously from their weight while her stomach muscles pulled taut over her flexed skin. For the first time, Hearns had to check his own morality for he found himself enjoying seeing this woman's naked form. When he looked again at Freemund, he saw him remove a paper from his coat pocket. Freemund was whispering, but Hearns could not discern what Freemund was saying. It was sibilant, foreign, and he couldn't help stare at Freemund's pupils, which were totally black.

Hearns heard a noise in the shadows and began to look around. His instincts told him that whatever was going on here couldn't be right, but he was weaponless. His senses recognized a presence that made him feel completely powerless and vulnerable. The sound came again, this time from his right, making him jump. He patted his belt and his legs hoping that he might have inadvertently planted a blade or other weapon on his person before but, alas, he had not. Then, the impossible happened right before his eyes for the second time in one week. The chains slowly began to rattle as they began to undulate rhythmically. Elizabeth's cries became more pronounced but deadened in his ears to faint echoes of pain, for his mind was slow to comprehend what his eyes were seeing. The metallic sound that first accompanied the jangling of chains transformed into a meaty, fleshy sound, like that of a wet rope being pulled tightly into a coil. The chains had become flesh—the flesh of serpents. The scales flexed and relaxed, the hooks turned to fangs, and small slits above the fangs opened to reveal luminescent red eyes. Elizabeth's whole body was swaying now, though her cries had mellowed to low wails of—could it be pleasure?

Freemund's mouth was still moving, uttering monosyllabic tones as he recited the chant from the parchment. Elizabeth's mouth fell open, her arms hanging limply from her suspended body, and she continued to moan softly. Hearns noticed a string of saliva dripping from Elizabeth's mouth, and he watched it work its way toward the table. He noticed a glint in the fluid and recognized that something was lighting its path from below. He followed the light to its source to see patterns slowly forming on the cement table. They held a symmetry that was foreign to anything he had ever witnessed. Several concentric circles appeared on the table, their color a rustic hue of dirty yellow. Hearns's instinct told him to leave, but his conscious mind would not allow it. He knew that it was this type of power that would be necessary in winning the battle against these pests. And so he stayed, watching Elizabeth slightly sway as her body hung suspended over the table.

By now, Freemund had finished his chant and looked up, his eyes returning to normalcy. "You are now ready, Elizabeth." Elizabeth's eyes were completely rolled up in their sockets, the whites glaring blindly out. Her mouth opened and shut several times, severing the spit that languished at her lips.

"I am ready." Elizabeth moaned quietly, not quite herself and not quite her voice. Hearns looked to Freemund for an answer and received none. "What must I do?" Elizabeth asked.

"Tell us what you see, Elizabeth." Freemund's hands, extended out in front of his body, still held their rigid posture. His voice resumed its smooth yet controlling tone, but it was clear that the spell was straining his energy. Perspiration steadily formed tenuous beads on his brow, a crease twisting heavily between his eyebrows.

"I see a universe. I see a tunnel of darkness surrounded by light." Elizabeth's mouth opened and closed, her limp arms dangling lifeless.

"Look into the tunnel, Elizabeth. In your mind, ask to see the village we are to attack tomorrow, then speak your request out loud." Freemund gazed straight ahead when giving these commands, looking neither at Elizabeth nor Hearns. "Tell us what you see, Elizabeth."

"I see woods—slaves armed with bows—arrows—and much power. I see huts—gardens—Indians—a circle—spears."

"What are the slaves doing, Elizabeth? What are the Blacks and Indians doing?" Freemund anxiously requested. Elizabeth inhaled deeply as the sound of whispers entered the room. Elizabeth moaned, her voice hoarse and scratchy. Her mouth opened again, and more drool oozed out, but her lips curled up into a smile.

"They are getting ready for war. Praying—talking to the gods of their land." Elizabeth chuckled. "There is a strong light. It shines from—from the middle of the village."

"Tell us what has happened to Tanjee." Hearns spoke his request without forethought. Elizabeth's smile faded. The serpents' venom was beginning to slide down and around her sides as the serpents wriggled and hissed, their eyes emitting pure malice. Elizabeth's breathing became labored. Hearns looked up to the ceiling, again puzzling over the source of the snakes. He walked around the table to where Freemund stood, the whites of his eyes completely black, his hands still poised rigidly toward his charge. When Elizabeth opened her mouth again to respond, Hearns heard a subtle hint of humor in her tone.

"Tanjee—yes—your lover has come to a bad end."

"What do you mean, bad end, Elizabeth? What does that mean?

"It means that she no longer breathes. It means that Tanjee—is dead." The smile returned to Elizabeth's face. "The power these people possess is wonderful. Reverend, do we possess such power?"

Elizabeth's flesh rose with goose bumps; she shuddered and laughed quietly as if she wanted to stop herself but couldn't. "It would be nice to have such power, Reverend, so nice." Elizabeth's head lifted once, and a trail of anguish flashed over her face. Her eyes returned, and she glanced at Hearns with a look of abject terror. Then her head folded back down, and her eyes rolled back in her head. Hearns threw the scrolls of maps across the room, slammed his fist on the table, and screamed. Elizabeth and Freemund were unaffected, however, which angered Hearns. How could these two understand? Why would they care? They saw him as a nigger lover, and he knew at that point they had no intention of helping him. All they wanted to do was avenge themselves of the Maroons who had so effectively upset their orderly white, bigoted world. Hearns was staring coldly at Freemund, but

Freemund did not even look at him; he remained in strict concentration. This was too much for Hearns. He threw the hardest punch he could muster, aiming for Freemund's jaw, shocking himself with the meaty sound the connection produced. But Freemund stared straight ahead, his posture unmoved. Hearns punched him again.

"I want out, Reverend! I want out. I can do this on my own! Wasting time with you and your idiotic spells—for what? Tanjee is dead! Dead!" Hearns lost all composure, tears streaming down his angry face. He threw three more punches at Freemund, but he and Elizabeth seemed impervious to his tirade. Hearns began to wonder what he gotten himself into. He knew it was too late to begin asking questions, but he would be damned if he would let another person control his life. He cursed and paced and screamed, letting his emotions gain complete control of his reason. He didn't notice Freemund's head slowly turn to face him. He didn't notice the rigid hands stretched out toward him. He didn't see the steam rising from those hands or the blinding light that was emitted from them with brilliant speed. What he did remember was that a man is a fool for trusting his enemies, but a soldier is a greater fool for trusting his friends. Then darkness consumed him.

Freemund looked only briefly at the body that lay writhing on the floor before quickly turning his focus back toward Elizabeth. Her trance-like state of being would hold only for so long before the spell would wear off. At that point, Elizabeth would go into shock and might possibly die. He would deal with Hearns when this was all over. For the moment, there was more information to be had.

"Elizabeth, what will be the strategy of attack from the Maroons?" Freemund now was shaking due to the stress involved, his shirt darkly stained from perspiration, but he maintained his focus. Elizabeth paused in trance, listening to the voices inside her head while her body still swayed from the serpents' grasp.

"You will get into the city. You will capture the source of power if you escape the cloud. You will—you, you, you, you will—will—" Elizabeth's mouth rolled out the words with a sonorous growl she couldn't control. For the first time, Freemund was unnerved. "You will, will, will die—die, die, die, die—if you do not find an acceptable sacrifice. Find the sacrifice, and you will live."

"What is the acceptable sacrifice, Elizabeth? Where can I find it? I've come too far not to know the answer!" Freemund now looked fiercely at Elizabeth. Going to her body, he pulled on it, stretching the wounded flesh without mercy. She let out an agonizing gasp, and her mouth twisted open, revealing pearly white teeth. Her breathing had become labored, and the sounds of her exhalations echoed within the dankness of the underground sanctuary. Finally, she spoke.

"It must be something personal, something—no—someone—close. It must be your wife!" With that last pronouncement Elizabeth's head dropped violently, the force of it causing her teeth to clack together. The serpents wriggled and writhed until the metallic noise of chains replaced the low thud of flesh. The transformation was slow but steady, and eventually the fleshy bodies of snakes were once again the metallic solidity of chains.

After the process was complete, Freemund hit a lever, and Elizabeth's body was lowered by the chains to the table. There was little blood left on her back once the hooks were removed, but Freemund noticed that the flesh where the hooks were placed had turned a purplish green. His stiff bearing began to relax as he went to retrieve Elizabeth's clothes and a blanket to cover her nakedness. As he tossed the clothes beside the table and placed the blanket over her, he pondered the revelations that had just taken place. Why wasn't Elizabeth a suitable sacrifice? She met all the requirements of his order. Why didn't the gods accept her?

Freemund brooded quietly in the shadows of his basement as he reviewed the coded message. It was primarily positive: he would get into the city; he would capture their source of power if he survived the cloud. Now what was that? The cloud? He grabbed the plans and ran over to Hearns, who lay unconscious on the floor. Freemund bent down, and with powerful hands, hoisted Hearns's upper body up off the floor, and then lifted him on his back. He could not afford to waste any more time. He had considered everything and had the benefit of the gods. Now victory would soon belong to Freemund as the sole engineer for overthrowing the Maroons. He did not stop to think that perhaps he could be outsmarted by another, or did he see Elizabeth's eyes peeking out from underneath the blanket as he hoisted Hearns up the stairs.

Elizabeth lay on the table, feigning sleep, until she was certain that she no longer heard footsteps. All was silent, and the candle flames were beginning to dim as the wax was rising in the base of the wick. Her back ached, and her mouth tasted of cotton. She didn't know how she did it, but she had not told Freemund everything she had seen during her vision. The truth was that she had witnessed herself slain on the table, her entrails leaking out of her like a pile of bloody ropes, and Freemund would die unless he figured out that he had the sacrifice right the first time. She didn't even feel bad for Rebecca because she had seen her as well. If Elizabeth could manage to get out of this basement, she might be able to correct this matter.

A lot had been revealed to her during her vision. She didn't quite know how it happened; perhaps it was her desire to live and survive this terrible ordeal, or maybe it was what Freemund had inadvertently done to her while putting her into this state of mind. But during her vision, Elizabeth had seen Rebecca, Freemund's wife, after she had witnessed her own death on the table upon which she now sat. And when she saw her, she intuitively knew, more than felt, that she had communicated this vision from her dream to Rebecca.

Elizabeth decided to get up and get dressed. Her whole body ached, and her skin hung loosely off her back. She tried to reach back and feel the anomaly of her flesh, but she was too stiff to do so. It took her a long time to put on her clothes; she could barely raise her hands above her head, and she had to lean over to pull her blouse on. The pain she felt was intense. She was grateful that she hadn't been raped; the thought brought to mind Yemanja and Vashti. This had almost been too ironic. She had been spared, and she intended to make the best of this opportunity.

Elizabeth made her way toward the steps and painfully crept up them. It was a desperate hope to say the least, but perhaps her luck would continue and she would be able to walk right out of this predicament. When she finally reached the top, she found the door closed and locked. After fiddling with it she decided it was a lost cause. She would have to find a way to break the window and force her body through it. She descended the steps carefully, more out of pain than caution, and looked around the dark area to try to find an object she could use to shatter the window. She saw the cabinet that Freemund had gone to just hours before, and she attempted to break open the doors. She was successful, but she stood back in horror at what was revealed.

Three shelves were filled with canning jars that contained the remains of Negro body parts: fingers, penises, noses, teeth, some still attached to gums, the strings of flesh floating purposelessly in the murky substance that preserved them. When Elizabeth found herself gaping at two eyeballs that once witnessed life, now gazing out blindly into the dankness that enveloped the room, her body began to shiver.

For the first time in her life, Elizabeth briefly questioned the morality of what she and her husband and her generations before her had sanctioned as slavery. As she looked at the remnants of what once contained the soul and life of a human being, she realized that it was quite possible that she and her family were corrupting the world with doctrine and methods based in wickedness. Whites had gone far beyond using people to work for them to produce commerce and had fallen into activities far more sinister. What would be the price of robbing the very spirit of a person? What would be the purpose of keeping such horrible relics?

Her thoughts were interrupted when she heard something jump behind her; she reeled around with a scream only to see nothing was there. Darkness was slowly ebbing further into the crevices of the room as night fell, and when she turned back toward the closet the moon's glow cast a shaft of light onto an iron mallet at the cabinet's base. Without hesitation, Elizabeth picked up the heavy mallet and walked to within five feet of the window. The candles were still burning, leaving a slight haze of smoke that wafted across the ceiling of the room.

Elizabeth desperately hoisted the mallet high above her head and swung at the window. Though the mallet landed squarely, it barely caused a scratch. She backed up two steps and tried again, but to no avail. By now she had fully regained her equilibrium and desperately wanted to escape that basement.

The window was thick and solid, yet she knew it could break. She decided if she could twirl around and swing the mallet toward the window, the momentum of it would carry it through the glass. She picked up the mallet and traced her steps to a position that give her more leverage.

Elizabeth was sweating profusely now, her fatigue growing. She was amazed and thankful that she could still stand. Again, Elizabeth hefted the heavy mallet, but this time she began to swing it out and around her body as she twirled. It was on her fourth spin, when the room's floor began to shimmer and toss from dizziness, that she released the mallet toward the window. Her heart leapt for joy at the sound of broken glass, revealing her pathway to freedom.

Earlier she had noticed a small box in the corner. She went to it now to drag it under the window to serve as a step for her escape, but she was dismayed by its weight.

Nevertheless, Elizabeth started to drag the box backward with all her might. Although the box barely budged, it did slide a little forward. She put all her attention and energy toward her task. *"Come on Elizabeth! If you are going to get out of here, you've got to move this box!"* Her thoughts became frantic, and the sounds of night began to make eerie melodies. She heaved backward once more, and this time the box moved a bit. Elizabeth's thoughts were so focused on getting the box to the window that she didn't even notice the ragged hand reaching out of the box toward her straining legs. When the hand finally grabbed her, Elizabeth emitted the loudest howl her lungs could produce.

CHAPTER 24
THE SIEGE AND THE CLOUD

Hearns woke to the sound of weapons being cleaned and the constant thud of boots against solid earth. He looked around and ascertained that he was in a commander's tent. The nervous murmur of soldiers that leaders often hear in the camps of military men seemed to roar in his ears. He sat up in bed and began to orient himself to his current predicament when his eyes fell upon Freemund. Then it all came back to him in a rush; the tale of Gausje and her magic that Tanjee had reported in their bed; the vines crawling out of the mouth of the poor lad he shot; and his total shock at the chains turning to snakes biting into Elizabeth's back as this minister of darkness put her under a trance. Dark circles were present under Freemund's eyes, but his gaze did not falter from Hearns, who reached for his gun holster before anyone spoke.

"You'll find your weapons on the back of that chair, Colonel, along with the plans of entry into the Maroon village. Elizabeth was of a great help to us."

"Us? I told you I wanted no part of what you were doing! You're no better than those we are going to kill today!" Hearns was consumed with wrath. His stomach felt upset, and he spit onto the ground the bile that had crept up his throat. His eyes burned.

"Kill! Good, then you are with us, Colonel! That is my only concern. Our allegiances vary, as previously discussed. What matters most is that we work together on this plan." Freemund stood from his chair, walked over to Hearns, and extended his hand, but Hearns ignored him and got up and moved toward the entrance to the tent.

"Just show me where my men are so we can get this over with, Freemund."

"Oh, dear me. Matters have changed slightly, Colonel. The governor has placed me in charge of this raid, due to the intelligence I provided the military. I've already sent scouts out to the swamps to confirm everything that was revealed to me—to us—and, of course, the details were confirmed. No, Colonel, you are now under my command, and you will be issued fifty men to trail my party as we storm the village. I wouldn't want old-time sentiments getting in the way of completing your job." Freemund had taken out a cigar and was lighting it when Hearns spun around and started toward him with his fists balled tight, but before he had a chance to raise them, a voice interrupted.

"Freemund, all is in order, sir. Is everything fine here, sir?" Hearns stopped himself, although his heart pounded with rage. This was not going according to his plan. He realized that he lost too much of his composure with the cane field incident and put far too much trust in this villain who sat before him. Yes, originally Hearns had planned to destroy the entire village, but his ultimate goal was peace, tranquility, and a new life with Tanjee. Those three goods outweighed the murderous designs he had for the village. But now his eyes had been opened to a deeper truth of a sinister undercurrent that drove the Europeans and Americans to organize and pillage in a way that seemed malevolent and beyond human civility. All the while he had subscribed to the ideal of Negroes being lesser creatures, worthy of submissive duty, but his eyes had witnessed first-hand how the capture, trade, and persecution of the Negro slave was a dark spiritual ruse that must be stopped. It was he, Freemund, Elizabeth, whites, who were the true villains. Hearns realized that his life would no longer be the same.

At first, he selfishly knew that he would live with Tanjee and marry her in a place where they would be accepted, perhaps a remote area in Florida where the government had yet to hold a significant grasp, if any at all. He knew he would fulfill his duty to the army and eliminate the Maroons, but now his cause would be to assist them under the guise of cooperation. He would turn the tide that currently bound these poor blacks to pain and dehumanization. He resolved himself at that moment to respond to his soul the way Tanjee had taught him. And his new mindset felt right to him, damn what Freemund thought. Hearns gathered himself, slowly regaining his military poise, and directed his gaze at the petty officer who had interrupted his confrontation with Freemund.

"You soldiers don't salute superior officers in this camp, boy?" Hearns's gaze and tone were fierce. The soldier stared at him and then Freemund for a few moments before he managed to speak.

"Uh, yes sir! We salute, sir!" The boy whipped his hand to his forehead with rigidity. Hearns looked at the boy with smug satisfaction, then walked over to the chair and holstered his weapon.

"Dismissed, son. Reverend, if you'd direct me to my men, I would very much like to get on with this mission." Freemund scrutinized his colleague for a moment. He needed every man for this operation to work successfully, and he expected casualties. He now hoped one of those lost would be the man who stood in front of him. Freemund needed to make sure that Hearns would not be a nuisance.

"Your men have been garrisoned at one of my mills just a few miles from here, Colonel. They have been given full instructions and are waiting for their Colonel to lead them successfully through this mission."

"Thank you sir, I—" Freemund held up his hand, signaling Hearns to stop as he went to the door of the tent and called out.

"Hey, nigger boy. Get over here! Just what the hell ya think ya doing sitting down whittling that piece of wood!" Freemund's face looked pained, as if he had suffered the most diabolical of insults from the slave's innocuous activity. "The sun too hot for ya, nigger boy? Want some shade then?"

"No sah? I sorry, sah? It's jus dat there seems to be nothin' to do round heah, and I don't wan' tah botha nobody."

"Is that so? Well, come on inside here boy and cool off, won't ya?" The sarcasm in Freemund's voice was dripping venom, and the boy knew no good would come of it. There was no decision he could make that would free him from punishment. He cursed himself for slacking, for getting caught up in all the excitement of soldiers running around, making preparations, never looking at him, allowing him to get too comfortable. And now he had been caught whittling wood and sitting down when he should have been making certain that everyone's needs were being met. He gingerly entered the tent to see a man whose eyes were terrifyingly cold. He couldn't take his gaze off the man who looked at him with disdain.

"Reverend, seeing that you are in charge here and have situations under your control, I'd like to get my men now—with your permission, of course." Hearns did his best to keep the guile out of his tone, his throat burning as he uttered the word "permission." He looked directly at Freemund without really catching a full glimpse of the black boy who stood before him.

"Yes, Colonel, soon, soon. But first, I need assurances that you have not turned weak in your resolve. You shocked me back at my house. After what you've witnessed first-hand, I expected you to understand the situation that we are dealing with here and accept my support. You came to me for help, remember?" Hearns remained silent but attentive, nodding his assent. "When you verbally attacked me, it was a betrayal of the basest level. You! We served together, killed together, got wealthy together! Hearns, this land is our land to do with it as we please. And, yes, I use forces that have managed to shake me to the very core of my beliefs, often completely uprooting them. But I accept what I see before my eyes, Colonel, and what is within our grasp. We have an opportunity to establish a fortune that no other countryman has experienced in the brief history of this land. We possess the will, the power, and the resources to take this land and make it the greatest this world has ever seen."

Freemund turned now to the slave, who remained rooted to the same space inside the tent, and gestured at him with a graceful yet deprecating outstretched palm. "And we owe this success largely to our lesser brothers, who wouldn't know a mountain from a molehill if you laid the two directly before their wide nostrils! These beasts of burden, who are worthy only to lick the soles of our feet, who sold their own kin into slavery, who for decades live and die to make my life and yours the best this world will ever see. I know you are tired of the bloodshed and the lies. You are a man who needs to get his priorities straight, but one thing is for certain—niggers are only good when they are under control, like this one." The Negro boy smiled nervously. "But when they are threatening our very existence with violent rebellions, voodoo demi-gods, and the forces of darkness, we must stamp out this tide of evil!" Freemund's voice had surged to a booming yell. Spittle was forming at the sides of his mouth as his face flushed with anger. "I need you to convince me that you still got what it takes!"

Without hesitation, Hearns removed the gun from his holster, cocked it smoothly, and fired one round into the Negro boy's skull, disintegrating the boy's face as the bullet made its noisy exit. Bits of blood, brain, and bone littered Freemund's face and shirt. Hearns re-holstered his weapon and turned to his one-time friend.

"Is that convincing enough for you, Freemund?" Freemund's hand quivered close to his own revolver, his face a portrait of satisfaction. A thunder of boots approached their tent as soldiers hurdled toward the sound of danger. Hearns glared at Freemund coolly, his face expressionless. Freemund studied the man carefully, and then he offered a weak smile.

"That will suit just fine, Colonel." Walking over to Hearns, he patted him on the back just as several men burst into the tent, weapons drawn. The faces peered through the fog of smoke and darkness of the tent until their gaze fell on the corpse of the young Negro boy. Freemund looked at his audience, a little shaken, but managed to maintain his weak smile. "Just a little test of the reflexes for the Colonel here. He passed, by the way." Freemund chuckled and in turn received several bouts of laughter from the men, who were now holstering their weapons. Freemund pointed at two men at random and commanded them to remove the body and dispose of it.

"Well, Colonel, I guess we need to discuss the plan." Hearns's heart plodded heavily at the blatant act of murder he had just committed. Although it was only recently that he could care less for any slave other than Tanjee, the events of the past few days had done much in altering his perspective. He was developing a deeper appreciation of life than war had taught him, and he had just ended the innocent life of an unknown Negro boy. Did the boy have a wife? Children? A lover like himself? He hoped that his eyes did not betray the murmurs of his heart. He bowed toward Freemund, and then he went to Freemund's war table where lay a detailed map. They would look for the sign from Tanjee, but it really didn't matter if she gave her sign or not. With sheer numbers and inside intelligence, Freemund assured him that nothing would get in the way of their completing the mission.

Soon there was commotion in the camp, and the sound of riders entering the premises thundered through the quiet evening. Freemund looked up from their plans and smiled. "That must be my Guild brother, Baramoore, and his general. Colonel, I must say that I am certainly glad that you will be joining us on this mission. I want you to meet the further securities I have set in place. Come, I want you to meet Baramoore."

The two left the tent as the riders came swiftly into the camp. Dust floated up into the graying evening, and Hearns wished to be back inside the tent where he could breathe and think without having his body and spirit polluted by dust. What looked to be the two in charge dismounted from their horses, and several slave attendants came to take their mounts.

"Hello, brother. We are nearly set to begin this operation." Baramoore's barrel chest protruded from under his tight frock as he extended a heavy, calloused hand and shook Freemund's heartily. Freemund looked pleased.

"Reverend, I would like you to meet my general." Baramoore turned toward a thinner but taller man wearing a cloak. "Nemesqu. You've meet before at the Guild. He will be in charge of leading us into the city. Nemesqu has come by certain intelligence that suggests a power with which he alone is familiar. I am aware of your power, Freemund, but I must insist that if my men are to be involved here, my general must lead. He has never let me or the Guild down. What say you?"

Hearns glanced at Freemund and then Baramoore. There was no malice he could detect in Baramoore's proposition. The strange general stood silently behind the larger man, with his arms folded so that his hands were hidden within his cloak. Hearns strained his eyes to see the face within the cloak, and the stranger turned his head slowly to face Hearns. Hearns, after having saved face by killing an innocent man, was not about to lose it now, and he resolutely faced the cloaked figure. The figure did not move but retained his posture, the place where his face was supposed to be facing Hearns.

"That will be quite fine, brother. The Guild has never let me down, or have you. I welcome this step. If you'd step inside, we can go over the plans." With that Freemund moved inside the tent, the three soldiers following behind him. Freemund was making his way toward the table when the cloaked figure put a hand on his soldier and spoke.

"Your plans will not be necessary, Reverend. I have seen through this plot, and you most certainly were on your way to your death." Nemesqu swiped the paper, quills, and other items rudely to the floor as he produced a yellow parchment from within his robes and unfurled it on the table. Hearns thought he saw Freemund wince, but the little devil kept a solemn face and remained quiet. Baramoore looked nervously at his friend and then at Hearns. No one said a word as Nemesqu set up the new plans.

"Who is this man, Reverend? This soldier who looks at me and you with such contempt? I have not seen him in my visions. Before I go on, his loyalty must be proven."

"That will be quite unnecessary being that Colonel Hearns has proven his valor and loyalty by my side time and time again. The very fact that he is here inside my battle tent is testament to where his loyalties stand, and I consider your query highly offensive. Nemesqu, I value respect and a code of honor far more than I do spiritual powers. I suggest you be mindful of my position here before asking anymore questions." Freemund's grey temples flexed, and tiny bulbs of perspiration dotted the lines that stretched across his tense forehead. Hearns noticed that Freemund's Adam's apple kept bobbing up and down. This man was making him very nervous, despite the noble veneer he pretentiously put on.

"Your insolence is as grand as your hypocrisy for the church you represent." Nemesqu turned and swiftly reached out and gripped Freemund's neck. "The only essence I value that matters to you is my friendship with Baramoore. And it is only because of his relationship to you that I don't kill you right now, you little creature of filth! I suggest you be mindful of my position before that little hole of a mouth begins spewing more nonsense."

Nemesqu released his grip, and Freemund fell to the floor, holding his throat and coughing. Baramoore made a subtle gesture, and Nemesqu went over to him and bent down. Hearns saw the broad-chested man whisper into the darkness of the cloak. Hearns reveled at the embarrassment Freemund had just endured, and he was glad someone had put the man back in his place, yet at the same time he knew this man to be very dangerous. Freemund exhibited power in his basement that Hearns had not witnessed before, and now this stranger debased Freemund without even raising his voice above a harsh whisper. Instead of the situation looking better, it was looking worse. Hearns was used to leading, not following, and now it was Baramoore and his general who were going to be in command. This sounded more like a neighborhood brawl than organized warfare. Nemesqu turned from Baramoore and returned to the table. Freemund was pushing himself up from the floor and dusting off his clothes, his face a red mass of fury.

"Baramoore!" Freemund shouted.

"Reverend, please! I know you have questions and that you are upset, but trust me. This is the right plan of action. There is a force in that swamp that can easily destroy us all if not properly handled. My general here knows better than anyone here how to best this power. I beg you to cooperate." Hearns decided that the man was being sincere. Baramoore looked at his Guild brother with concern. "Nemesqu, kindly go on with the details."

"As I was saying, the plans you lifted from Elizabeth with your pathetic magic were in error. You almost walked into a trap, and the gods are not pleased with you. Your sacrifice walked away!" Freemund raised his hand as if he were in school. Nemesqu paused to let Freemund speak.

"The spirits told me that she was not the proper sacrifice." Freemund said, with waning dignity.

"You have been grossly misled. Elizabeth is indeed the sacrifice; you were just too engrossed in your own thoughts to recognize that she lied to you." Hearns silently breathed a prayer of relief. He had to believe that Tanjee was alive, that he would be able to rescue her from this disaster of a situation, and they would be able to live free of all the death, the duality, and destruction.

"Elizabeth is locked in my basement. She went through a very arduous ceremony and would have a tough time walking, let alone escaping, through hardened cement barriers of my basement." Freemund was beginning to regain his composure.

"I don't have time for this! I am going to explain this once, sir. Your first mistake was not realizing that your wife was secretly hiding in your basement inside a cage you normally use to house slaves before you torture them to death. Secondly, Elizabeth recovered and discovered your wife and released her from the cage, and the two of them organized their escape. Your wife knows the truth about you, and I am sure she has informed Elizabeth by now. Both of them are on Elizabeth's plantation plotting your end. I have visions also, Reverend, and unlike the infamous organizer of the Merchant Traders' Guild, I practice my talents daily and execute my charms with precision. You have many serious matters to attend to once this affair with the Maroons is finished." Nemesqu turned to his old friend and, with the utmost sincerity, said, "Master Baramoore, shall I proceed with the battle plans?"

"Yes, Nemesqu." Baramoore's eyes glanced carefully between Hearns and his old friend. He hated to see Freemund insulted so terribly, but he rested his full trust on the man who had consistently proven his worth. "We have but a small window of time." And with his master's consent, Nemesqu started the task of informing Hearns and Freemund of their new assignments.

Chapter 25

Discovery and Betrayal

Elizabeth scrambled frantically away from the box, knocking over tools and jars filled with amber fluid. The silence of the night was filled with tiny explosions of shattered glass, the clanging timber of metal tools bouncing off the cement floor. Her harsh cries resounded through the basement as she struggled desperately to get away from that hand and escape her underground prison. The floor was slick and the atmosphere pungent as she realized she had inadvertently released the aged flesh of murdered Negroes. Elizabeth lost her footing, slipped backwards, and fell. She stood up shakily and stumbled toward the broken window, grasping its ledge desperately for freedom, light, and fresh air. She jumped up but failed to gain a fair hold and sagged, defeated, to the slimy floor. Her breathing was harsh and ragged, the sound of it flooding her hearing. It wasn't until her panic had slowly begun to subside that she heard a faint whisper coming from the box. In the dim light Elizabeth could just make out the slight form of the hand that reached for her. She swallowed hard and strained to hear what was being said. At first it sounded like wind, but eventually the word was clear.

"Help." Quiet, soft, barely audible, the plea drifted its way across the macabre scene to where it rested on Elizabeth's ear. Elizabeth felt around the floor with her right hand until she found the mallet and tightly gripped its handle.

"Who—who are you?" Elizabeth shouted, her inquiry resounding in echoes in the large basement. But there was no answer, just a hand with palm outstretched.

"I am coming over. I have a mallet! Don't touch me or I will use it on you as I used it on the window!" Elizabeth got up. Her back and buttocks ached as she slowly sought out a smaller candle and lit it, hoping to gain more light. Cautiously, Elizabeth approached the box, the candle flickering madly because her arm wouldn't stop shaking.

"Thank you. Elizabeth. Please let me out." The whisper said.

"Who are you?"

"It's me—Rebecca Freemund." Elizabeth stooped down and held the candle toward the box, which she realized was more like a large dog kennel. Inside she observed the beleaguered face of Reverend Freemund's wife.

"How long have you been down here?"

"Too long. When my husband left to go to the Guild, I knew he would end up down here. I snuck away, making it seem like I was going away for a visit, but instead I came down here to spy on him. I had no idea what was in this basement, but I suspected it was the place where he'd bring his women to fornicate. I thought you were going to be one of them, but I see I was horribly mistaken. Can you please let me out? I accidentally locked myself in here."

Elizabeth took the mallet and hammered on the locking mechanism until it broke. The metal cage-like door swung open, and Rebecca crept out, her arms and legs stiff from being in a crouched position. She could barely stand up. Elizabeth set the candle down and helped Rebecca stand as tall as she could before guiding her to the broken window. Elizabeth then went back to drag the cage over to the window.

"You climb out first, and I'll come after you." Elizabeth said. Rebecca cried out weakly as her muscles resisted the pain of being pulled out of their atrophied position, but she finally managed to get above ground, and Elizabeth soon followed.

"Rebecca, I don't think it's safe here. I don't think it is safe anywhere to be truthful. But I think we'd stand a better chance if we go back to my plantation. As you may have heard, I have lost all my slaves, save one. And it is that woman who I now know can help us." Rebecca nodded her silent approval, and Elizabeth walked her over to her carriage, which was still where the attending servant had left it. She helped Rebecca in, handed her the reins, and untied the horses that were nibbling lazily on diminished piles of hay that had been thrown on the ground. Rebecca reached into a compartment below her seat and pulled out a rifle that was always kept within reach of the driver. If any slaves, Maroons, or shamans came after them, they were going to get off at least one good round. The two women looked frazzled beyond description, but their resiliency persevered as Elizabeth commanded the horses to trot, and Rebecca held on to the rumbling wagon as they rode away from Freemund's farm.

*****

Bella looked into the fire and saw her two visitors on their way. She now fully understood why the gods insisted that she stay on the place of her captivity when all others had been freed on the day of Emily's death. Her faith had struggled, but she was thankful that she had resisted the urge to defy their wants. Bella knew the benefits of staying true to the gods, as well as the penalty of disobedience. Gathering her wits, she placed her hands on the smooth stones splayed out neatly before her, but she felt nothing. She was waiting for a premonition of the next plan of action, but none came. She neatly laid the stones in a small wooden box and placed it reverently next to a leather pouch that contained her conjure bones, feathers, and snail dust. She pondered whether she should try another method of divining the spirits; there were several ways, but she sensed she should wait, and so she did. Bella stared into the fire and fell into a mild sleep.

It was then that the distinct vision of an aged woman, with skin that had the texture of bark, rushed forward in her mind's eye. The woman looked anxious yet purposeful. She reached out to Bella with ancient hands, and silvery strands of words came out of her mouth and drifted toward her. As they made contact with Bella's face, the words dissolved into her being, and Bella was then completely aware of what needed to be done.

Still entranced, a smile crept onto Bella's face and remained there until the women entered her shack. Bella welcomed them openly as friends, not hesitating to allow these two white slave owners access to her thoughts and visions. She knew they were to be keys to unlocking her years of servitude, and she talked with them now not as a slave but as a leader and seer. The women responded in kind, taking in her words as if they were manna, allowing themselves to be led by this black woman who seemed to possess knowledge beyond her natural ken. Within two hours, all three women were smiling, and the plot had been set.

*****

Jakeel sat rooted with indecisiveness in his quarters; his mind was a cadre of warring opinions and solutions concerning the near future of the Maroons and his role with the tribe. His face, contorted and furled, reflected the torment of his soul, and his blood raced through constricted veins, pummeled by a heart that increased pace with every thinking second. Although awed by the productivity and efficiency of the Maroon camp, and convinced that Gausje knew how best to lead this group of Blacks and Indians, he still could not reconcile himself to killing all whites as a solution to the racial dilemma the village faced. Despite the reality that an army of angry white soldiers was coming to kill them, Jared wondered if there were any other channel toward justice that they should take. But it was insanely difficult to discover any other possibilities when Gausje had carefully connived a way to eradicate their oppressors by using the traitor who futilely worked to undermine the success of this village. Some instinct was commanding him to resist killing, but why? Why resist when so much death was brought to the feet of suffering slaves, of friendly and helping Indians? Why spare the lives of the white man when all his life white men and women had oppressed his race so heavily? Perhaps the answer lay in how mercilessly death had taxed his life.

When he was three, he witnessed his mother's brutal murder for refusing her breast milk for her master's children. They had taken her out to the tree, striped her to the waist, and squeezed her breasts until they yielded all the milk they had, stopping only when yellow puss began to ooze from her nipples. Then, one of the field hands took an axe and hacked until he loped off both her breasts. The echo of her screams often ripped Jakeel from his sleep, ending with the ghastly image of a breastless woman who bled to death from the two gory wounds on her chest.

Then there was his childhood friend, Marcus, a white boy from a neighboring plantation who would visit to play with Mr. Tolby's children but discovered he had more fun playing with the slaves. At eight, Marcus had been teaching Jakeel to read, even though he knew that such an offense would cost him dearly. In addition, Marcus took his free time to teach Jakeel to the limit of his knowledge, and Jakeel found himself beginning to look forward to the times when Marcus would teach him all that he was learning in school. He remembered that the more he talked with Marcus, the more he was dissatisfied with his servitude. At a young age Jakeel realized that every man should be his own master, capable of forging his or her own destiny, but his enlightened euphoria was short lived when another slave caught Marcus teaching Jakeel how to count and reported the violation to their master. Jakeel was punished with seven days hard labor and confined to his slave quarters immediately after work was finished.

Jakeel had no concept of how much time had elapsed since he last saw his friend Marcus, just that when two winters had passed, he went on a trip to the plantation where Marcus lived. Jakeel was surprised that he was being allowed to go on this trip, and his heart pounded with excitement at being able to be with his friend Marcus again. He vowed to control himself, do his very best work, and when the time availed itself, to slip away for a quick visit and perhaps an exchange of thoughts, as they used to do.

This particular plantation harvested tobacco, and the fields stretched themselves out so that they seemed to go on forever. The field hand's job was to take a machete and gather the tobacco around the base of the stalk, cut the giant leaves free, wrap them in a bundle with yarn that was kept on a spool in the pocket, and then throw the bundle onto a wagon that followed him. Jakeel's job was to walk ahead of the workers and check the leaves for tobacco worms and other insects that liked to feed on the corpulent leaves, scrape the vermin off, and destroy them. He vividly remembered the sickening thud of the fat tobacco larvae, which were green and cold to the touch, exploding upon impact after being hurled to the trodden earth, leaving a greenish jelly in their wake. Jakeel worked until it was nearly dark, and he was filthy, his hands covered in a black sticky substance by day's end. The field hands were allowed a brief break to eat before they traveled home. It was while the food was being prepared that Jakeel slipped away to find Marcus. He did not have to look long, for he discovered a bewildered-looking Marcus staring at him as he walked up to a back porch where Marcus had lit several candles and was reading a book.

"Hey, Marcus! It has been a long time since you've been over to the plantation! You have grown a lot! Gotten taller, even have strong muscles." Jakeel remembered the happiness he felt at seeing his best friend again. He couldn't wait to tell him stories of events that had taken place on the Tolby plantation, and he was anxious to hear more of what Marcus learned at school. But he noticed his friend's expression had changed from bewilderment to irritation to hate. Marcus glared at Jakeel as if he were vomit.

"Marcus! What's the matter? Aren't you going to say hello?" Reality had yet to set in on Jakeel's sensibilities. "Hey, Marcus, I brought you vine, just like old times." Jakeel approached his childhood companion and held out the vine only to have his hand slapped away.

"What makes you think you are welcome on this porch, nigger?" Marcus spat out that last word with palpable venom. Jakeel could only stare with shock. "And take your little voodoo charm and put it up your ass. I don't want it. Looking at you just makes me ill to my stomach, and you stink."

"What? I don't understand Marcus; we are supposed to be friends. Why are you talking to me like this?"

"Do you know how much trouble I got into for trying to teach a nigger to read? Unbelievable amounts I tell you! At one time last year, I nearly thought I was a nigger I had to work so hard to redeem myself! So you can imagine just how unhappy I am to see your filthy hands staining my parents' back porch with your stupid sad eyes looking at me like that!" Marcus turned back to his book and turned a page.

"You don't mean that, Marcus. I know you suffered, but you knew the risks, and that is what makes you so different and better than everyone else around here. You cared ab—" A fierce stare from Marcus caused Jakeel's words to stick in his throat, and he swallowed them, forever.

"That was when I was stupid and ignorant boy, much like you still remain. I had to learn the hard way that a nigger has no business learning. I had to suffer a lashing, much like the ones you and your kind endure daily, because I had to realize that niggers will always be niggers, and it is only a disservice to you and your kind to make you think otherwise." Jakeel, hurt and angered by his former friend's comments, heard someone approaching. He hustled off the porch and crouched on his heels as a burly field hand came around the corner and smiled when he saw Jakeel.

"De cook done sent me ta luk fo' ya, Jakeel. You bes come na befo' all de viddles done gone! Ya makin' a new friend?" The man smiled at Marcus, who looked at both slaves with disdain. "Pleasant evening, little massa, we be getting on na." The man gently placed a hand on Jakeel's shoulders, but Jakeel shrugged him off and spit fiercely at Marcus. The man inhaled sharply, his eyes widening.

"You go to hell, Marcus! You think you are better than me? You the one who ain't nothing!" Jakeel's anger had risen in his soul so fiercely he barely recognized that his hands were balled into tight fists and that he was being held back. The field hand's strong grip covered his mouth. It was at that moment that the truth of Marcus's real nature struck Jakeel. The full weight of pained emotion broke through the surface of his tough exterior, and hot tears swept from his clouded eyes. The burly man who'd come to fetch him for dinner was shushing him and apologizing to Marcus. But Marcus had quickly risen to his feet and was hurling himself at Jakeel. He landed a tough blow right on Jakeel's nose, and a sprout of blood splayed out, staining the pure white cotton shirt Marcus had been wearing.

"No, nigger, I'm going to show you your place!" Marcus stood face-to-face with Jakeel, who would have fallen to the ground had not the field hand been holding him up.

"Jakeel, we bes be gone. Else youse' gointer get a def wish fo' sho!" Let's go!" With that the field hand let go of Jakeel and started to head back to the food. But Jakeel stood, shaking with anger. He couldn't understand how someone could turn so completely from a friend to an enemy. He wanted to destroy this traitor who stood before him; he wanted to silence him.

The two were alone, facing each other, muscles tense, their eyes full of fierce emotion. Marcus had an air of authority about him. In the two years apart he grown slightly taller than Jakeel, and he glowered down on Jakeel's forehead and moved close until the two were almost touching noses. Jakeel glared at him, trembling, angered by the derogatory term—nigger. Although shorter, the few years of toil had hardened Jakeel's muscles and endurance far beyond what Marcus could imagine. Without hesitation, Jakeel swung his knee up with such force that the connection completely disarmed and derailed his foe. Marcus let out a yelp and collapsed to his knees, holding his privates, his face a portrait of pain. Before Marcus could emit another sound he found Jakeel's heavy foot slamming down brutally on his neck. Jakeel heard a loud crack and watched his former friend roll to his side, shaking, thick foam bubbling out of his nostrils as he emitted one long gasp. His friend Marcus was dead.

Tears streamed down Jakeel's face, and he was consumed with anger, regret, and fear. He had killed a person he cared for while in a fit of rage, and he felt no better for it, only worse. This life was gone forever. Jakeel turned back to the camp, dispassionate, cold—ashamed of what he was becoming.

When Jakeel returned to the rest of the group, everyone was busy eating. His eyes met those of the field hand who tried to intervene, but the man said nothing. No one mentioned the blood drizzled on Jakeel's upper lip or the disturbed look on his face. Jakeel knew the silent code of minding one's own business or suffering the punishment of the one whose business you found your nose in. Jakeel went to the kettle and dipped his bowl in the broth; there seemed to be chunks of flesh floating around in it, but the sight of the meat sickened him. He made sure he just had broth, picked up a piece of bread, and sat down, despondent. The field hand came over to him and laid a gentle hand on his shoulder.

"Youse two got settled?" When Jakeel looked into the man's eyes, he saw no judgment, only compassion.

"I killed him. He's lying there on the back porch." Jakeel shuddered after whispering the truth. The shadows of light danced eerily on the older man's face, but he gazed at Jakeel with stolid austerity.

"Den we bes' git rid of de body den."

"But he's dead!" Jakeel whispered harshly. "Don't you care about that?"

"He white. Dat means you dead when his pa find out. Sides, why you care 'bout some white boy so much?"

"Because he was my friend. He was a person."

"Boy, look here. Ain't no white man yo friend! Dey ain't human like. Dey act like devils. Git it out yo head dey yo friend, boy, if youse want ya life!" The man stared at Jakeel with a glare that he would never forget.

They went back for the body and hid Marcus under the tobacco in the wagon and left that night, which was not uncommon for borrowed hands. Slaves were still expected to perform the next day's labor on their home plantation. Halfway home, the overseers rode ahead. They had been through this routine before and trusted the field hands to return home. There was a river nearby, and Jakeel and the old man were able to slip the body away because the other slaves were fast asleep on the wagon. Dark clouds wafted their way across the face of the moon, darkening the night. Jakeel remembered being thankful for the darkness to cloak the heaviness of his heart and to provide cover for their deed. He and the field hand stumbled carefully through the dark until their boots splashed in the river. They put heavy rocks in Marcus's pants and shirt, walked him to the middle of the river, and dropped him in. They stayed to watch Marcus's form settle on the river bed in the bright moonlight, and when they were satisfied, they hurried back to catch up with the wagon before they were discovered missing.

Now, Jakeel, delivered from death by the mighty hand of Gausje and the Maroon tribe, realized the truth. He resented the memory of the role death had played in his life. He had suffered loss and had been an instrument of death, and he found that neither brought him any degree of satisfaction. He would have to find another way to deal with his predicament and not offend those who had helped him.

Jakeel rose from his bed and walked out into the compound. Though the day was grey and dismal, the community still bustled with activity. He decided he would pay a visit to his trainer Keigei. He had asked to have his training revoked until after the battle, but now he was beginning to regret that decision. There was so much that he needed to learn and to comprehend about the spiritual forces that had found fertile soil in his soul. He discovered that his new-found freedom left him far more confused than when he was a slave. Life had been so simple then because he didn't need to use his brain. But now he was faced with decisions that involved his morality and his mind. Existence had become far more than life or death; it had transfigured itself to being about understanding what life meant and one's purpose within the grander scheme of living. Perhaps Keigei would be able to further expand his awareness so that Jakeel could fulfill the destiny that Gausje had been so pleased to mention.

He walked over to Keigei's tent and requested entrance. "Permission to enter. It is Jakeel." During his brief time with the tribe, Jakeel had noticed that no one just went into an elder's tent unannounced, and he had heard this greeting when others wanted to enter an elder's tent. A few moments passed before the flap of the tent door moved aside and a voice invited him in.

"Greetings, Jakeel." Keigei's black hair was tied in one strong braid and fell neatly against his back. Jakeel noticed that the cloak of deerskin Keigei usually wore was folded and hung on a chair near the back of the room, allowing Jakeel to observe the muscular build and the weird circular pattern seared into Keigei's chest. Jakeel couldn't resist the urge to glance at the two jagged lightening bolts intersecting each other inside the circle. When Keigei's eyes caught Jakeel's stare, a wan smile briefly flickered across his lips.

"Sit down, Jakeel. I sense you are troubled. You seek to be a part of the battle, you get Gausje to postpone your training with me, you disappear to your quarters after expressing your discontent with her plan, and now I find you at my doorstep. Surely you must feel the weight of our current situation, and now you seek to enlighten your mind as Gausje suggested, as opposed to running off to war. I applaud your decision. Gausje seems justified in putting her faith in you."

"You presume much." Jakeel responded, offended.

"I presume nothing. And if my statements are in error, then you can just as easily find your way out of my tent as you found your way in. I don't have time for impetuous ignorance." The words stung Jakeel, but he knew he had it coming. More and more he was realizing how difficult it was going to be to maintain control of his life. He'd learned from Bella that it took much sacrifice and even, at times, bloodshed, thus it would not be outside of his grasp to sit down, subdue his pride, and get the information for which he came.

"My apologies. Of course your wisdom has seen the truth. I have come to learn from you. May I ask you a few questions, Keigei?" The old, wise man smiled fully this time, revealing a row of glistening white teeth. He nodded his head in the affirmative.

"Ask anything you'd like, Jakeel."

"What is the significance of the mark on your chest?"

"This mark I earned after mastering the art of thunder light. My teacher burned it on my chest with his own finger as a tribal mark of accomplishment."

"Thunder light? You mean lightening?" Jakeel queried.

"Thunder light, lightening, energy—the power goes by various names. Essentially, I have the ability to conduct energy through my body and send it to a point I desire. Very few people have the physical make-up to attempt such a feat, and even less have the discipline to learn how to wield the power. I was hoping that you might be the next to bear such a mark as I." Jakeel did not look convinced.

"You speak in riddles, Keigei."

"And you speak good English, Jakeel. How has that come to be?"

"I learned from a friend a long time ago, and from my white master's wife, Mrs. Tolby. They taught me how to read, but I also learned more from a woman named Bella."

"Yes." Keigei answered. "I know of Bella. I look forward to meeting her as well. It is rumored that she will be the one to replace Gausje after she decides to move on to other tasks. I want to show you something, Jakeel." Keigei's smile persisted as he slowly raised his hand and held it out palm up, arm halfway outstretched in front of his body. "I want to show you something that might help your disbelief."

"What makes you think I don't believe you, Keigei?"

"You don't. Your faith was tested strongly once, on the day of the blood burning moon when your path was redirected from a lifetime of servitude to a life of purpose and solidarity. But in order for your faith to continue to grow, it must be tested continually." Jakeel did not respond but sat in earnest, ready to learn.

"Unlike your Christian-based teachings of faith, given to you by your master's wife, our practices allow you to witness firsthand the power we all have the potential of using. Seeing what we can do—what you can do—does much more in preparing young warriors for the arduous task that lies ahead." Keigei's hand was still outstretched. His eyes were no longer looking at Jakeel but at his own hand, and Jakeel's gaze followed that of his new teacher.

The air in the tent soon became static, and Jakeel began to notice the thin strands of hair on Keigei's arm slowly rising. "Look at my thumb and forefinger, Jakeel." Jakeel was shocked to see a bolt of electricity erupt from Keigei's thumb and shoot over to his forefinger, where it bristled brightly and powerfully, its length bending and arching mightily but never breaking. Keigei's three remaining fingers had been closed, and he now opened them until his palm was outspread, his fingers curled as if in the grips of pain, and the bolt of energy webbed its way to the rest of his fingertips, gyrating and increasing slightly in girth. The bright blue strobes of energy webbed themselves with persistence, eventually forming a white bulb of energy in the middle of his palm. Jakeel stared in amazement. Carefully, Keigei turned his hand so that his palm faced Jakeel, the powerful phenomenon still in place and controlled.

"Now, I am going to send this energy into your body, Jakeel." Jakeel kicked back away from Keigei, his eyes quickly darting toward the tent entrance. "It will not hurt you, son. This is where you must begin to exhibit your faith, having witnessed the power. Settle yourself and relax. If it had been my intent to cause you hurt, you would have experienced it the moment you walked in. My job is to help you learn. Trust is crucial, my son. Can you exhibit trust now, Jakeel?"

Jakeel again had to force his body to resist the natural reaction to defend itself from danger. He closed his eyes, remembering the training that Bella had given him on the plantation, and forced his heart to stop ramming against the ribs that protected it. He opened his eyes after a few moments, calm.

"Do it, Keigei. I am ready." But when Jakeel opened his eyes, the energy was gone, and his teacher was looking at him with mild disappointment.

"Are you, my son? Are you really prepared? Did your mental exercise help you now?"

Jakeel detected mockery in Keigei's tone and felt his irritation begin to rise. How long would it take to prove himself in this community? When would they respect him? His body had been mangled beyond description, yet here he stood! Jakeel remembered his training from Bella, and yet Keigei mocked him. Master of lightening or not, Jakeel did not have to take this insult. He was a free man and would demand respect. He immediately stood to leave.

"Did you not make a request, Jakeel?" The tone of Keigei's voice had not changed, further infuriating Jakeel.

"That was before—"

"Then I will comply, my son." A bright bulb of electrical power infused Keigei's strong palm, and he pushed his hand forward toward his unsuspecting pupil, filling the whole room with light. Webs of electricity wafted across the entirety of Jakeel's chest as his body arched backward, his toes digging deep groves into the earthen floor, his eyelids fluttering wildly as he tried to keep them focused on Keigei. His teacher's face was calm, relaxed. Jakeel detected no anger or malice. Keigei's hand was steady; the energy pouring from it was like steady rays of sunshine. Jakeel felt his vision failing; he could not keep his eyes open much longer. Was that smoke he saw wafting from his chest? He looked at Keigei again and tried to mouth the word *stop* when he saw Keigei close his palm, and the energy of light abated.

There was a pause before Jakeel fell to the ground, dazed but still conscious. Keigei got up from where he was sitting to help Jakeel sit up. Jakeel could feel the strength of the man's grip bite into his shoulder as he did so. Keigei walked back to his place and sat down.

"Well, I am reassured. Your spiritual and physical strength are pronounced. You passed what I would normally consider the third test out of five. You have the ability to conduct energy, and until the very end, you opened yourself up to receive it."

"But why not test me when I was ready?"

"Will your enemies extend you such a courtesy? No, and neither will I. Work with me, and you will be prepared for whatever obstacles the enemy throws your way. Believe, trust, and harness the power within yourself. No longer must you be afraid of the possibilities, Jakeel. Gausje brought you here to live so that others might experience similar freedoms. It is our responsibility to learn it and share it." Jakeel, shamed at his complete selfishness, nodded in assent with his teacher.

"I will learn what it is that you have to teach me. Thank you, Keigei." His teacher nodded.

"Now for the next test. Return the energy I gave you. Send it back to me. In your mind, think of the energy and reach out to me. Do whatever feels comfortable. As you can see, I conduct using my hand, fingers, and palm, but you have options. Everyone who masters this element conducts the energy through whatever mechanism feels best for them. Do it now."

Keigei sat back and looked confidently at his new pupil. Jakeel closed his eyes and focused on the energy he had just received. He immediately felt the air become static and the hairs on his forearms bristle. He sat up straighter and kept his focus. Then, as instructed, he began to reach out toward his teacher, keeping the energy forefront in his mind. He began visualizing the energy passing from his body to Keigei's. He felt his back arch and his chest extend awkwardly; his sternum grew hot and itched mildly. Then Jakeel heard it—the crackle of energy. He smelled the acrid smell of electricity and felt the strong itch slowly diminish. He opened his eyes to see a faint bolt of energy streaming from his chest to Keigei's outstretched palms. The connection lasted for only a moment before the itch went away and the bolt was disrupted.

"I can't believe I just did that!" said Jakeel.

"And that is precisely your problem. You must believe, Jakeel. Erase all doubt. What you've just accomplished is minor in comparison to what you can really do. And with what we are up against, I need you to be able to do considerably better. The first beast to conquer is your own mind."

"What do you mean? My master is not in touch with such powers. In all my years of slavery, I don't know of any white man who can do what I've seen with the tribe."

"You are correct. In this region of the world, there is no white man who I know of who is knowingly in touch with the spirits. However, the white man's greatest attribute is his ability to get others to do his bidding."

"Explain."

"How do you believe our parents, and grandparents, came to be slaves, Jakeel?"

"The white devils came over to our home and took them!" Jakeel responded indignantly.

"Without resistance? Did we fight back?"

"Of course we did! The white man had weapons new to us. They used advanced knowledge to subdue us and cunning tactics to separate us so that communication among our people would be virtually impossible."

"That is what we tell ourselves to make us feel better, Jakeel. But the truth of the matter is that there will always be Tanjees in the camp—traitors, modern-day Judases, if you will. No, Jakeel, that is only part of the story. The whole story is that the white men convinced African slave traders to cooperate with them and *sell* their own brothers and sisters into this deadly trade. Human flesh was exchanged for rum, weapons, and clothing. We cheapened ourselves and exploited an entire continent for nothing more than insignificant material gains. Selfishness, greed, and divisiveness have always been the tool of the white oppressors, and every race that has been overrun by him has been done so because they lacked the fortitude of character to rise above these foils and stand as a united front." Jakeel was disturbed by Keigei's words, but he continued to listen.

"So that is the truth of Africans. What about you and your kind who I see here with the tribe?"

"I am Indian. There are many tribes, Cherokee, Navajo, Blackfoot, the list is quite extensive. We are similar to Africans in many ways. Our nation is divided into various tribes, which the white man used against us. Both African and Indian believe in a more authentic spiritual world that revolves around us in nature, that we can see and experience daily and not be taught about only from a book, by a priest. Both cultures have suffered greatly at the hands of the white man. We facilitated him by extending our friendship and trusting his word, as humans ought to do. But we were deceived by his cunning, lured by his wealth and tools, and eventually uprooted so we have to live in swamps and barren lands as opposed to being able to roam freely the vast country that had always belonged to us. Jakeel, both Africans and

Indians have suffered from the same shortcoming—self-serving greed. Just like Tanjee. There can be no further allowance for such behavior. We must serve each other, uplift each other. There can be no room for treachery. We can accomplish much more as a unit if we honor the tribe and not allow divisiveness to consume us. We cannot behave as individuals for selfish gains; we must operate together as brothers, as family. Our individual role is only to promote the whole. Then the world will be ours again. And when it is, we must share it."

"Then we are at that place right now where it is time for us to take back what rightfully belongs to us—our independence. Looks like the hardest part is over, for we are here! I am able to continue to read and to learn about great powers and history from you. Surely, under the leadership of the elders and Gausje, there should be no problem winning the upcoming battle. No one here possesses a gun, yet you conducted my rescue without difficulty. Help me to see how I am so important to this cause. Why must I possess considerably more power than what I've demonstrated here to you today?"

"I will give you several reasons, Jakeel. First, there is Tanjee, a woman rescued, taught much as you are being taught right now, but someone who still felt a need to return to her dismal patterns of living. She ran back to her oppressor for deliverance and made the conscious decision to return our love and favor with treachery! That is one who you yourself have witnessed." Jakeel had no choice but to nod in assent. Now that he was learning more of the true past, he recognized that there could be no pardon for such a treasonous act. The entire village and future of Maroons would have been destroyed.

"The next reason will take a little more time. This tribe has been in existence for quite awhile. You should know that it was started by Indians. It was very difficult for whites to keep Indians as slaves. We know this land, and it is easy for us to hide and use the knowledge of the land to our advantage. When we discovered the guile of the white man, many tribes began to actively resist him by having all-out warfare, but the white man's ability to lure enemy tribes to fulfill his purposes made resistance difficult and set the balances against honorable tribes so that they suffered defeat at the union of traitorous tribes and whites. In exchange for loyalty, the white man gave the Indians guns and taught them how to use them. They taught them their way of war and used Indians to establish systems of defense to fend off noble tribes that wanted to get whites off their land. Jakeel, it is important to note that without this type of treachery, whites could have been pushed out of our territory long ago. A few tribes like the Huron and the Iroquois began to set up systems in hard-to-get areas in the swamps of Carolina and Florida. Of course, the enemy discovered these places but has yet to be able to usurp our hidden villages, because we are the few who have learned from our past mistakes. We trust the spirits and follow their guidance. We remain selfless and work steadily to undermine the evil establishments that whites have set up here. A few escaped slaves eventually discovered us by accident, but we welcomed them into our fold and taught them the secrets of the land and our beliefs. We learned that we had much in common and decidedly set out to help any other slave refugee who stumbled upon us. We worked together, loved together, and eventually formed the tribal system that saved you. Of course, the enemy would not stand any gap in their wicked system. They bitterly resented Indian nations for accepting slaves into their villages and were furious about our adoption system that drew no color line. Europeans demanded we return all fugitives or else, but not one Maroon tribe returned a single fugitive. The Maroons made it clear they stood ready to fight for African men and women who had become family."

Jakeel took in all his teacher told him. His brain whirled at the thought of how clever this enemy was and how vast they had spread their destruction. Two different cultures from two entirely different places had forged a common bond in oppression. He found his opinions of his role starting to sway, but he still wanted to know more. "Keigei, how is it that the white man can so easily destroy the allegiances of a people? I don't understand how one could continue to support the endeavors of the enemy after truly discovering that it will clearly destroy them."

"Young warrior, the answer to that question is both easy and complicated. With the Indians, there were many who were seduced by the promise of power. They were awed by the power and thunder of the white man's weapons. They saw just how devastating his fire sticks and canons were. Indians had never witnessed that type of power, and it is attainable by all."

"What do you mean, that type of power?" Jakeel queried.

"Prior to the arrival of our oppressors, there was still trouble among our people. Our belief systems, though similar, varied slightly from tribe to tribe, and that caused rancor at times. We also fought over land, hunting grounds, and various other matters that at the time seemed significant but, in lieu of our present plight, now seem trivial. Yet the signal element that instigated treachery was the prospect of power without working for it. You see, our shamans have always wielded great power, Jakeel, the power to heal and bring death, to stimulate harvest, or dry up crops, to win battles, predict the future, to change the weather. However, not everyone had access to these powers because they do not come easily. One must study hard, show discipline, dedicate years to learning and practice, and thus, only a select few would be called to fulfill such a role in the community. All could qualify, Jakeel, but only a few were actually willing to work for it. With the advent of the white man and his guns, that all changed. For a slight barter, anyone could possess a weapon and use it as he pleased. In addition, the enemy also traded information and aid for rum, a bitter drink that brought out the very worst in our nature. It disrupted the communion we had with the earth, and with each other, making us lazy, disloyal, and mean. We became easier to seduce and thus became bedmates with the enemy. Those of us who still respect the land, the people, and the spirits have yet to fall under the curse of the enemy. But, we had such fortitude before, and thus never fell into his trap. The eyes, mouth, and ears are entry ways to the soul, Jakeel, and must be guarded carefully. Only put in that which will elevate you to the next level of being. Be mindful of that which will disrupt your thinking. Be careful of whom you trust. We shamans use peyote and other herbs to open our minds for the spirits, but this is after years of dedicated study. Our herbs do not make us sick afterwards. Conversely, you will feel enlightened."

"That is interesting and sad. Basically, my people and your people suffered from the same sin; we both wanted quick ascension to power and in return received a lifetime of servitude."

"Yes. Power cannot and should not be received quickly. One must first learn the responsibility to wield it. Time will be given to those who dedicate themselves to learning this art. I am sixty-four years old and can beat any young warrior on these grounds in a match of wills—be they physical or otherwise. Our leader Gausje's age is unknown. She was among the first to join our group. She possessed great power and wisdom and combined her knowledge with the elders of our village. Together, we have formed a strong community. We began to use our power to actively free slaves and destroy the wicked systems that the white man set up. We burn his crops, free his beasts of burden, and send deliverance to those whose minds are open enough to realize that there has to be more to life than serving a master. Time has been granted us to learn our purpose and fulfill it. And you must recognize this, Jakeel. Do not rush into that which you do not understand. Asking to have your lessons aborted was a mistake, and I am glad that you have availed yourself to learn. It will be a good step in establishing your place with the Maroons."

Jakeel was also pleased he had made this decision. He could have acted rashly because he was reacting to that which was immediate. He had not given himself time to consider the history of their situation, or the gravity of the groundwork that had been laid, or what future task there was to be done. He would learn much from his teacher.

CHAPTER 26

SELF-DESTRUCTION

One lone puff of smoke ascended into the air from deep within the Kalehari forest. Hearns recognized the lone smoke cloud to be an ominous sign from Tanjee that matters were not in order. He had the palpable sense that death was wafting steadily toward this marshland of rebellion. He considered warning his former friend, but the harsh memory of the series of insults he'd recently experienced at his hands forbade such a courteous move. Hearns's garrison of soldiers had been diminished to fifty men, and his pride ached. Now that the sun had set, the moon loomed on the horizon, and it shown ominously red.

Nemesqu's plan of attack situated himself and Baramoore in the lead, followed by Freemund and brought up by Hearns and his men. As far as he could recollect, he still had not caught a glimpse of what the general looked like, his face always hidden behind a cloak that shielded his face. He wore a bandolier of bullets around his waist and traditional army boots, but Hearns never saw the man with a firearm.

As the army moved closer Hearns saw two more puffs of smoke sail into the dark sky, stifling his smugness at the thought of Freemund walking right into a trap. It appeared that Freemund would be on the winning side of this battle after all. Baramoore's general stepped forward and signaled for the troop to stop, then hurried a few paces ahead of the men and disappeared behind a tree. Hearns looked closely and thought he saw a flash of light blazing from behind the tree, momentarily illuminating the forest in light and shadows.

Nemesqu came out quickly, knelt down, and shielded his head; Baramoore and his men did the same, and the rest of the infantry followed. Immediately, there was a loud series of cracks that resounded in the woods, as a crisscross hail of arrows whizzed by to riddle the trees. A few soldiers who had not ducked in time were hacked down. Nemesqu heard a scream a few yards ahead of him, and when he turned his head to see from where the sound came he witnessed a body slam to the ground, two arrows sticking from the poor soul's skull. After a few moments the barrage stopped, and Nemesqu stood up and stretched his arms out in front of him, motioning that the coast was clear. Baramoore stood up, and the rest followed. The trees looked like bizarre cactuses, thick arrows protruding from their formidable trunks. Hearns shuddered to think what would have happened had not this cloaked figure set off the trap. Fifty or more men would have been cut down in that crossfire. Tanjee had been right when she had said that the traps were deadly.

Hearns wondered where the sentries were who stood guard in the trees. He distinctly remembered Tanjee warning him of their ferocity and how even tribe members were kept from knowing the identity of a sentry. Suddenly, Hearns felt an object lurch underneath his boot, so he drew out a sharp blade and stabbed at the water, but he managed to do nothing more than make loud splashes and incur the angry stares of the men surrounding him. When he stepped forward his left boot caught on something tough and recalcitrant. Hearns scrambled to free himself but only managed to become further entrapped. He could feel the silt from the swamp sifting into the now-loosened boot on his left foot. The floor of the forest was steadily becoming soggy, making it difficult to gain good traction. Tanjee had mentioned a series of underwater trails that a trained citizen of the Maroon village could easily find to avoid the traps. But he had every confidence that Baramoore's man had set off those traps, thus causing a deluge of arrows to fly to and fro. Still, having solid ground underfoot would make him feel less unnerved. He was panicky and shaken up.

Hearns needed to regain his composure. It made him uneasy that they had successfully made it this close to the village by using Nemesqu's powers. Years of fighting and nights of walking past lonely forests taught him that something was definitely not right. He pondered what it could be while cautiously watching the treetops for signs of sentries, carefully looking for other traps. And then it dawned on him. How was it that a procession of men was invading a forest and not so much as a frog's croak could be heard? No crickets, no birds, no animals of the night stirred. The only sound was the soft gurgle of soldiers wading through swamp, which was now waist deep. But Hearns thought about Tanjee, his faithful lover, and found comfort in the passion that had kept him warm for so many nights. The thought of her made him more resolute in his purpose, and he advanced to the city with renewed confidence, ignoring the ominous signs.

It took nearly an hour before they finally saw the tall walls of the city. Hearns gripped the handle of his revolver tightly in one hand while holding his blade in the other. Every man had his firearm aimed toward the city. Nemesqu signaled for the men to halt, and he went forward alone. In the dark, Hearns observed a faint greenish glow like bright morning mist coming from Nemesqu's hands. Nemesqu walked cautiously up to the door, his hands outstretched. Still waist deep in the water, Hearns saw Nemesqu leaning against the door as if listening. The men jumped, hearing a series of loud clicks and creaks and then the sound of an object on the other side of the large door unrolling as Nemesqu had used the key Tanjee provided to open the gate. Hearns's breathing had become harsh, his heart strumming a steady beat of fear. Salty perspiration slipped into his eyes, but he dared not wipe them. Baramoore gave the men the ready signal, and all repositioned their weapons, preparing themselves to move into the village for battle.

The moonlight cast reddish hues on the shadows that lurked behind two totem poles that stood guard to the left and right of the entrance. The camp looked deserted. A smoldering fire was slowly being extinguished by a gentle breeze, a lazy strand of smoke wafting peacefully upward in long ropy wisps.

Nemesqu's hands were glowing even brighter now, illuminating a tiny area in front of him. There was almost a nimbus of light around his body, and others made certain to stay clear of it, even Baramoore. There were many rows of neat tents with their door flaps open, exposing vacant holes of darkness. The gardens looked watered and weeded and the soil recently tilled. Hearns marveled at how much soil had been imported to this city, and he wondered how many trips it had taken to get enough earth so that it could be nurtured well enough to support the gardens. As the men moved closer, Freemund instructed Hearns and his men to stay back and guard the door.

Baramoore and his troops flanked left while Freemund and his men flanked right. The city was an absolute asylum of silence. Nothing groaned, moved, fluttered, or creaked. Hearns imagined that the Maroons must have been happy living here away from the slavery and the racial hate of the world he had come to loath. The question now was the location of the Maroons. The men continued to search the village, but they found nothing living about. The village looked totally deserted.

Nemesqu, Baramoore, Freemund, and Hearns met in the middle of the village to decide what their next step should be.

Freemund offered his opinion. "Torch it! Burn the whole village and draw them back here. These people have invested a lot of time and effort to build and sustain this city. We burn down the tents, destroy the crops as they have done ours, and there is bound to be retaliation." Nemesqu pondered this option for a moment before shaking his head no. At that moment, a young soldier ran up to give a report.

"The tents are empty, sir. The men searched every last one. Everything is in there—food, clothing, bedding—but that is all, sir. No people."

"Appears that they have left in fear," Freemund said piously. "The Lord is on our side this day." He swallowed hard when Nemesqu held his hand up to indicate that Freemund should be silent. Nemesqu then reached into his cloak and pulled out what looked to be a short, twisted twig.

"All is not what it appears to be. They are here. There is no sign of them leaving, no tracks, spores, or disruption to their environment. It is as if they are sitting here among us, and we are blind to see them." Another soldier, one of Hearns's men, ran up to the men with another report.

"Colonel!" He panted. "One of the men is gravely ill. He went to relieve himself in the swamp right outside the walls, and now he keeps coughing and leaning over as if he wants to vomit, but nothing comes out. He is making a tremendous commotion. What do we do, sir?" Hearns's heart paused in its rhythm before he turned to the other officers.

"I will investigate. Let's find these people and get this over with," Hearns replied. He and the soldier hurried back toward the gate while Baramoore, Freemund, and Nemesqu remained to discuss the situation.

Hearns looked through the opened gates into the shadows that lay beyond in the swamp area. He saw his troops huddled around the ill man when he watched them jump back. Hearns took five long steps, roughly shoving aside a few who were in his way, until he came upon the soldier. It was as he expected. He arrived just in time to witness the man lying on his back, his mouth open so wide the sides of it threatened to tear, a thick sputum of foam issuing forth, running down both sides of his face, followed by a bramble of thick, fleshy vines and leaves, until his entire face was covered with the living vegetation.

"Go warn the others that the Maroons are here!" Hearns said in a loud whisper. When the soldier turned to follow the command, an arrow whizzed past Hearns and struck the soldier directly between the base of his skull and spinal cord, killing him instantly. Hearns, having never holstered his weapon, turned to fire but saw absolutely nothing. The other soldiers scrambled for cover in the tents, and a shower of arrows fell from the sky, cutting them down viciously before they made it four feet. Those shooting were master archers, and there had to be at least twenty of them. Hearns, seeing the debacle of his retreating troop, ran toward the fire that was inside the giant wall of the city. Again, he looked up to find from where the arrows hailed only to see gigantic trees, many of which had branches leaning close to or over the walls of the city. "The sentries!" He looked back at his fifty men. Most of them lay still, rows of arrows sticking out of their backs and legs like cactus quills. The few remaining followed Hearns's example and ran to the wall for cover.

Outside, in the swamp, hundreds of dark heads began to rise out of the water, their faces darkened with paint, leaving the hollows of their eyes to glow in the moonlight. Slender objects protruded from their mouths, and had Hearns been able to see what was approaching slowly from the other side of the wall, he would have observed that each warrior had a hallowed stalk of corn protruding from his mouth that he used to breathe through while lying submerged in the swamp, waiting for the enemy to completely enter the city. Jakeel was among them. Armed with blades, bows, and magic, the Maroon warriors stealthily progressed into the city. The trees swayed softly in the night breeze as the sentries readied their next volley of arrows.

Hearns leaned forcefully against the wall, afraid of having his skull impaled by another lethal downpour of arrows. As he surveyed the carnage in front of him, he knew he needed to warn the others if he expected to survive, so he fired a shot into the air. He heard a commotion and then the sound of his soldiers running in his direction. It was a second before he realized how stupid that decision had been. The men were running to their death. He screamed. "Turn back! Turn back! It's a trap!" But the arrows rained down like the wrath of God. Several arrows punctured the poorly armored flesh of the soldiers so violently they exited the body and pierced the earth with a ferocity that only the devil could have conjured. Many men were struck through several times before falling to the ground.

"Help! Nemesqu! Do something! The Maroons are outside! Help!"

Hearns tried desperately to regain composure. He had fought hard to earn his title and had witnessed many days and nights of carnage, but today he simply could not manage to command the way he was accustomed. He signaled to what was left of Freemund's and Baramoore's men, the men who thought they were coming to his rescue, to move out of the line of fire by running toward it and the safety of the wall. Putting his revolver in its holster, he fell to all fours and crawled on his hands and feet, staying close to his men and the wall, before another volley of arrows started stabbing the earth just yards in front of him. He looked up to see that some of the sentries had swung from the trees and were positioning themselves on the wall. Fear stuck in his throat as he observed how muscular they were and how quickly they fired and reloaded their bows with lethal arrows. Hearns stopped and turned back, this time standing up and running full speed. An arrow found him, ripping open a flesh wound in his shoulder. He quickly returned to his defensive position back against the wall near the gates of the city.

Outside, the Maroon warriors were at the gate, and they ran into the city like black oil, pouring over the dazzled soldiers and killing them easily. One man lunged at Hearns, and he defensively swung his blade at the warrior. The men were so black, covered with leaves, mud, and silt, that it made finding killing points difficult. The warrior jumped back and pulled a blade from his side. He threw it at one of Hearns's men who was aiming a pistol in a vain attempt to defend his Colonel. The blade slammed the man's head back to the wall, and his weapon fell to the ground from lifeless hands. The soldier's body slumped, half standing, his grisly head pinned firmly in place. Hearns yelled and ran for the warrior, but Hearns was too slow. The dark warrior plunged a dagger into Hearns's belly and, though he tried to push the warrior off him, he was too weak from the wound to do so. Strangely, he could smell the swamp on his assailant. He took his blade and pushed it against the hard flesh, but to no avail. The blade just kept slipping off his attacker's body. Hearns felt his killer jabbing his weapon up under his rib cage toward his heart. He saw visions of Tanjee: her smile, her hips, and her eyes. He thought of their children, and he mustered up every bit of strength to survive as he reached for his revolver. He felt the warmth of his blood pouring around the hand of his enemy. The warrior pulled back for one final thrust when his dark eyes suddenly turned white. Hearns saw the man being pulled back and up into the air.

Hearns dropped to his knees, clutching his belly. His head slumped down, and his chin rested on his chest. He opened his mouth to speak but stayed mute, bile and blood filling his throat. He was dizzy and perspiring profusely. The sounds of battle raged but, instead of the thunder of gunfire, he only heard men screaming and the steady whiz of arrows. When he looked up he saw Nemesqu, whose hands strained and curled like raven claws, drawing Hearns's assailant away. He heard a pop, and the man's intestines leaped from his abdomen before he fell to the ground. Nemesqu ran to Hearns and knelt down beside him.

"Move your hand, Colonel." Hearns tried but could not comply. Nemesqu forced Hearns's hand away, and Hearns howled, then dry heaved violently. Nemesqu whispered as he put his glowing hands on Hearns's stomach. Immediately, Hearns began to feel the pain abate. Then Nemesqu pulled what looked to be a ball of grass from his cloak. "Chew this and swallow your spit. Tuck the ball of leaves between your teeth and gums. And get up and fight, soldier." With that Nemesqu raced back toward the center of the city. A flurry of arrows landed on the ground all around him, but nothing struck. Whenever an arrow was heading straight for him, a nimbus of green would momentarily appear, then vanish. There was an invisible force field surrounding Nemesqu.

Hearns began chewing the substance that Nemesqu had given him. He must have looked dead, because the black warriors just ran past him and continued slaughtering his men. Though white bodies lay everywhere, Hearns was feeling quite oddly rejuvenated. He hadn't felt this good in days. Hearns pulled out his revolver and checked his rounds. He replaced the one spent bullet, got up on one knee, aimed at a conglomerate of warriors, and fired all six rounds. He was pleased to see six bodies drop. The warriors looked to see from where the shots came and quickly spied him. One raised his hands, and a ribbon of bright light shot forth from them and connected with Hearns. The day had grown dark, but the bolts of energy illuminated his shadow on the wall of the city, sending fire through his veins. He had never felt anything like it before, and his belly, which started to feel better, began to ache and bleed again.

Suddenly there was a tremendous boom followed by an even brighter light behind the man who was electrocuting Hearns, and the current stopped. An explosion sent several Maroons flying back from the center of the city into a mangled pile of twisted arms and legs. Hearns doubted if anyone would make it out alive. He took the opportunity to reload his weapon and then duck low, shuffling over to the tents for cover. He passed three doors before a strong hand reached out of the darkness and pulled him into a tent. Instinctively, Hearns fired his weapon into the form of what grabbed him, and the man gasped, sagged, and opened his mouth as if to scream. Hearns knew a noise could give his position away, but he did not care. The man screamed and lunged for Hearns, and the two wrestled until Hearns kicked his knee up swiftly. His assailant loosened his grip on Hearns, giving him space to regain control of his weapon. Hearns fired a wild shot, the flare of the pistol momentarily lighting up the room. He glimpsed the man's face and saw white teeth. He took his gun and stuck it into the man's open mouth, shoving the barrel into his throat to silence him. Hearns pulled the trigger and, instead of a scream, blood blew out of the back of the man's neck. The man's eyes closed. Hearns pulled the revolver back as his victim collapsed to the ground.

Hearns stumbled out of the tent and knelt down on one knee in the darkness to catch his breath. He knew he should be dead, but Nemesqu had literally given him his life back. He slowly realized that he had been chewing the ball of leaves Nemesqu provided him during the ordeal and swallowing the bitter juice. In fact, though he should have been in pain, he was no longer hurting and found that he had tremendous energy and clarity. Although night had completely fallen on the village, the light from the moon was exceptionally bright, and his vision seemed to be even clearer. If he survived he would remember to thank Nemesqu personally for what he did for him this night, but in the meantime, he needed a place to hide and reformulate his plan of action.

Hearns decided to go back into the tent and close the flap so that he could light a match to see and gather whatever might be useful. He took a match from the box in his pants pocket and lit it. The nimbus of light the match created allowed Hearns to see the fallen Maroon, who lay in a splattered circle of blood and flesh. His eyes stared out into the darkness, his mouth frozen in a wide gape.

Hearns realized now that the tent was more spacious than the outside suggested, but the flame was quickly consuming the wood, so he searched around for an object to light so he wouldn't waste anymore match sticks. He went through three matches before he decided to light the clothes of the fallen corpse. The dead man had only a loin cloth, but his flesh was greasy, and Hearns suspected he had rubbed some substance on himself before battle, a compound that would make the flesh slippery and thus tough to grasp or stab. His guess was correct and, as he dropped the match on the fallen warrior, the loin cloth immediately started to burn. The light was bright enough for him to begin slowly inspecting his surroundings.

The tent was unlike most of the tents he had stayed in that had a cloth floor. This one instead had a cultivated floor that had gone through several treatments that made it quite even. There was a pit near the center location that he surmised was used to hold fire and to cook. He quickly searched the room but found only a sharp blade. He decided to take a look near the back of the tent and realized there was an adjoining room.

Pulling out his revolver, Hearns lifted the flap and stepped in. This room looked more like where the Maroons would sleep. There were three palates that were elevated on makeshift but sturdy beds. The sheets were white, and he noticed that there were patterns on the floor that were made with white powder. The beds to the left and right of him were empty, but on the one near the back tent wall lay a form. As he moved closer he saw the mound ran the full length of the bed and, when he got closer, he recognized that it was a body. He took his revolver and stabbed at it.

"Get up!" He commanded. But the body remained still. He tried to pull back the white sheet, but it resisted. Outside he heard screams and another explosion and knew he needed to get back into the battle, but an inner force urged him to continue to investigate. He realized that the body was wrapped tightly, and he began to pull at the sheets, slowly at first, until he smelled a familiar odor—a scent like vanilla and butter. His fingers moved more frantically, tearing away at the cloth until black flesh slowly shone from the swaddles of cloth that covered it. In the back of his mind, familiarity bled through to the forefront as the final layer of cloth was removed. A small cry escaped Hearns's tightened lips as the last piece slid serenely off the corpse, and Tanjee's dead face stared up at him. Hearns ran back to the flap that separated the contiguous rooms and tore it down, letting the light from the burning corpse shine in on the anteroom.

Hearns went back and stared at his lover's face, struck by how twisted in agony it was. Her eyes were closed but her lips were open to reveal teeth that were clinched tightly together. He looked down the length of her body and noticed gaping holes throughout her torso. The light flickered and illuminated the smooth skin on her abdomen, then her arms and hands. Tears scalded Hearns's face as he saw that the beautiful hands that once stroked him and soothed him on smoky fall evenings were bruised and badly scarred—the nails splintered and broken. He gazed down toward her thighs and privates, but he could face no more, so he turned away and fell to the hardened floor, sick with grief and disbelief.

Hearns lay convulsing with emptiness on the floor next to the woman he loved, his hopes and future dreams swallowed as the Maroons dealt death swiftly to the ill-prepared troops that had invaded their home. His belly began to ache, and warmth began to ooze from the place Nemesqu had healed. Hearns spit the ball of grass from his mouth and heaved a heavy cry into the earth. What was this all for anyway, the fighting and death; what would it achieve? The Maroons had a right to fight for their freedom, just as these white soldiers and farmers felt they had a right to defend themselves and the lives of their fellow oppressors who maimed, shot, and raped these slaves regularly. Every man had a right to support his own mind. But no man had the right to oppress the innocent, no matter how foreign the people were. At that moment, he realized that his vengeance for Tanjee's death would hold no solace for him, and that the death and destruction that he imagined would soon ensue would only further establish the white man's foothold on the land and the wealth in this country for centuries to come.

And God would judge him cruelly for his role in this racial debacle. But he was in too deep. He had no choice but to press on. He took one last look at the only woman who had been able to assuage his nightmares. All this carnage of flesh would not ease the loss he felt at the death of his love nor would it improve the plight of the white man in this particular time and place.

Hearns struggled to sit up but saw the ground waver; a burden of nausea rose on him thickly until his head fell roughly on the floor. He knew he was going to pass out but vowed as the stars began to blaze into his vision that he would start over, but then the world swooped out of his consciousness. He never saw the figure cloaked in white walk through the doorway of the tent until her feet were by his face. He did not feel the thick blade on the end of a heavy sword that she raised high above her head and plunged through his skull into the earth, spilling his brains on the ground, which drank greedily the offering Gausje delivered. She walked out of the room, remembering to step over the smoldering body of her fallen comrade, and toward her next target as calmly as the angel of death who moved meticulously through the streets of Egypt. Hearns's head was pinned to the ground, and Gausje knew if any found him, it would be a warning to think twice about trying to destroy another race just because the white man was arrogant enough to believe he was justified in doing so.

Outside the tent, the fighting continued to rage, and all manner of order was completely abandoned. Every man was for himself, with the exception of Nemesqu, Baramoore, Freemund, and a struggling troop of soldiers. Amid the clamor, they remained ignorant of Hearns's death. Nemesqu was holding off the Maroons using all the skills he had learned as a shaman with his tribe. He put up a barrier that caused the arrows to fall impotent to the ground, but the Maroon's fierce attack was relentless, and his power was weakening. Every second his strength waned more men died, but he waged on. Nemesqu had not been in a battle of this magnitude in decades, and he relished the smell of death and the opportunity to wield his power. He could care less about the mass death of the white soldiers who had thought they could take on such power, but he had to admit that he, too, had underestimated the Maroon people. Their power was great and diverse, and he marveled at the man who could manipulate lightening. He decided to focus his energy on saving himself and his friend Baramoore and live to fight another day.

The ground was now littered with more dead white men than Maroons, and Nemesqu knew he would join them if he didn't conserve his strength. The remaining soldiers were firing a steady barrage of bullets at the

Maroons, but none of the Maroons were dying or even getting wounded. Nemesqu imagined that was because the enemy was using magic as well. There was an older man with a very interesting emblem tattooed on his chest who was sitting on the ground with his legs folded underneath him, his eyes closed as if in meditation. If Nemesqu could get to him, they would most likely be able to win this battle. But he knew his limitations and learned from severe suffering not to underestimate any opponent.

Just as Nemesqu decided that he and Baramoore would flee and resume their attack later, Nemesqu heard an ominous clap of thunder and a shrill, high-pitched tone coming toward him. The sky grew dark as thick clouds covered the red moon. Everything around him faded and appeared intermittently as drafts of light flickered from the heavens. He felt his barriers weaken, then collapse, and heard, more than felt, the barrage of arrows puncture the exposed flesh of the unshielded men. Nemesqu cast one other spell for Baramoore and himself and sent out a greenish ball of fire toward the back wall of the city. He and his friend ran as quickly as they could as both watched the ball explode like greenish liquid, leaving a gaping hole in the fortified wall.

Nemesqu turned around to catch a glimpse of the person who was strong enough to debilitate his spells only to see a white robe floating his way. The clouds continued to drift and the moon shone red. Baramoore tripped over a dead body and fell to the ground and cursed, but he quickly regained his stride, his fear giving him the extra boost of energy necessary to survive. The apparition was quickly catching up with them as Nemesqu hurled backward another fireball only to have it deflected away.

The greenish light illumed his nemesis, and he saw that the apparition was not a ghost after all but an ancient woman whose face was the epitome of determination. At that, Nemesqu decided not to look back but to hastily escape the city. He and Baramoore jumped through the broken wall and heard a defiant roar as the Maroons jubilated over their clear victory.

Once outside, Nemesqu put on a charm to cloak Baramoore and himself in silhouette, and the two blended in with the forest. He thought he heard bricks and gravel rubbing together and dared not look back to see the commotion, but his sense of magic told him that the ancient woman had probably put a spell on the wall to mend it. These people were powerful indeed, and if there were ever a next time, more would be necessary to defeat them.

The two men fled the woods and only when they were clear of the forest did they slow down to a trot. They found a familiar road and began looking for a place to sleep because they would not make it back to their plantation without horses. As they were walking, they discovered a crumpled body lying on the side of the road, a man with an arrow sticking out of the back of his leg.

"I think that is your friend, Baramoore."

The two rolled the man over and saw the bloody face of Freemund. He was barely aware of their presence, but when they lifted him, he opened his eyes and saw Baramoore.

"Oh, thank God," he managed a whisper. "We are saved."

After walking for hours the men managed to reach a plantation, where they collapsed in a barn and slept until field hands alerted the owner that two white men and an Indian were trespassing on the property.

CHAPTER 27
REQUIEM FOR THE LOST

The command came. "Collect the dead and take them to the circle of spears." The tired frame of the stalwart leader of the Maroon tribe bent and swayed as the lost members of her haven were gathered delicately and taken to the central meeting place of the villagers. Her usual smile and effervescent spirit sagged, despite the tribe's overwhelming victory over the infidels who stormed into their city. Jakeel knew that Gausje was saddened with the treason and subsequent death of Tanjee, but the weight of what had just taken place seemed to tug drastically on every weathered fold of dilapidated exposed flesh more than any time before.

Yet, despite the gloom that emanated from her physical self, her robe continued to blaze bright in the black atmosphere. Her garments were completely bereft of the dark earth that soiled the faces and clothes of everyone else present at the burial. She stooped her old frame and carefully picked up fallen warriors as she would infant children and helped to carry the dead. The tally of brothers lost was miniscule in comparison to that of their enemy, but Jakeel couldn't help but feel that the deaths of these fallen comrades were much greater than the hundreds of the enemy. He sobered at the thought of all that he had learned in his short period of time in this village, and of all that he had endured, and he immediately recognized the great loss in gathering the broken shell of these great spirits, absent of life, lying on the ground.

Jakeel imagined Gausje felt as if she indeed had lost several of her own children, having cared and nurtured each and every soul in this entire village. As the night wore on, the slow, syncopated pace of moving the dead from their respective locations proved long and somber. No one said much outside of occasional commands or infrequent requests for assistance, as most of the men instinctively knew what the other needed, and they performed their task flawlessly. Fifteen warriors had been slain in contrast to the many white soldiers who had ignorantly invaded their private sanctuary. Keigei, Jakeel's mentor, ordered the men to gather all arrows that weren't damaged and place them tip down in several large baskets that were normally used to hold harvested grain, corn, and vegetables. Hundreds of arrows prickled the earth and bodies alike, and by the time the men were finished twelve baskets, each large enough to carry three men, were overflowing with the instruments of death. Keigei commanded that the arrows be returned to the sentries by floating the baskets out into the swamps. The parade of baskets looked like a small fleet, slowly vanishing into the thick mist that had arisen as the morning's dawn silently approached from the East. The fog crept around the decaying trees and wilted moss, innocuously stifling the air, making the sense of death all the more palpable. Jakeel turned away from the gate and nearly butted heads with Isiki.

"You fought bravely, brother. I'm certain Keigei is proud." In the darkness, the white of Isiki's teeth burst forth like a solar flare, revealing a most brilliant but tired smile.

"No more than you, Isiki," Jakeel replied.

"I guess you now see the necessity of using force against these people." Isiki's smile spoke venom.

"Indeed, indeed. Thank the gods we sent the women and children away. Today's battle would have been worse had they stayed behind. The white devils would have used them against us had any been captured." The two men looked at each other and silently forgave any presupposed debts the other had incurred. The recent opposition taught them one of life's greatest tools of survival and prosperity: divisiveness among one's own brothers is the swiftest path toward the genocide of all that one holds dear.

After working together to repair a few more tents, the two joined the rest of the warriors at the circle of spears. Gausje stood in the center as the bodies of the fallen were reverently wrapped and treated for burial. Gausje raised her hands and closed her eyes; Jakeel noticed that all the warriors did the same. The silence cleared the atmosphere and opened up the spirit for spiritual communion, and Jakeel felt as if an otherworldly presence had come to join them. No one spoke, but Jakeel felt compelled to close his eyes and raise his hands. After a moment, he heard, more with his soul than with his ears, a melodious sound emanate from within the aged body of Gausje, a tiny nuance that grew tremulous and powerful, somber, yet jubilant, and, as if on cue, every warrior's voice chimed in cadence with Gausje. Jakeel marveled at how smoothly this was done.

Although he was unable to join in, his spirit responded to what it heard. It informed him of the joys, pains, accomplishments, and longings of the brothers and sisters who he never had the privilege of meeting face-to-face. The cryptic longings of his heart, his spirit, came alive and slowly infused his conscience of the import of who he really was. Years of false education, brutal torture, unpaid labor, forced unions with women for American profit or licentious lust of his oppressors, all of these shackles began to fall away as the harmony of his true brothers and sisters awakened the dormant truth that lay within his bones. His mind opened itself, his frame shaking as light emboldened his senses.

Gausje began to chant in language that Jakeel's mind could not perceive but his spirit understood. He was mentally transported back to Africa, where he saw his people, dark, beautiful, and wise, erecting buildings and statues honoring the legacy of rulers and philosophers of their past. He saw fathers teaching sons and mothers teaching daughters the rites of passage that would facilitate their journeys through this life and the next. The ancient and foreign words of Gausje massaged his core, releasing more of what years of persecution and pagan propaganda had buried, and he saw the rulers of Egypt communing with gods, building temples, performing magic, and thriving as a culture. He saw other travelers visiting his continent of origin to learn from his teachers and his elders. As Jakeel's soul finally connected with the truth of his being, hot tears wet his face as realization flooded his senses. Jakeel recognized that his passive attitude and unwillingness to slay those who misinformed his world with lies was only yet another evil created by the mental poison that generations of other slaves like he had been force fed. The truth was that he and his brothers were sons of royalty. And, as such, no man should be allowed, permitted, or encouraged to defile and destroy his people as they had for the past two centuries.

When Jakeel opened his eyes, he saw that he was not alone in his experience. The face of each warrior bore evidence of being moved by the same spiritual forces that compel every man to do good or evil. Gausje led the men as they carried the dead to the swamps. Though the sun had just breached the horizon, the moon still stood poised against a beautiful pale morning sky. The men walked into the swamp until the waters rose to their waists. Gausje raised her right hand, and the procession stopped. In her left she held a torch, which she quickly touched to the corpses whose robes had been soaked in oil, and ignited them, one by one, pushing them into the depths of the marshes.

"Their souls have been set free. We will rejoice when our task is done. We will not let their deaths be in vain. We will purge this area of the cur that constantly erodes the sensibilities of humanity."

With that, Gausje turned and led everyone back to the circle of spears. Isiki, Jakeel, and Keigei were anxious for battle. Their flesh tensed at what the near future promised.

The men gathered in a tight circle around the place where Tanjee's blood had watered the palate of the gods. The shamans walked around and said a blessing for each of them. Then they rubbed the men with what looked like an oily broth on their faces, shoulders, and chests, and finally gave each of them a pinch of a grassy substance that lay in the center of the bowl.

Jakeel braced himself for his turn as a shaman neared him, looking ahead with confidence and eagerness as the shaman enunciated foreign words as he slathered his hand in the oily mixture. While holding the bowl tightly with one hand, the shaman used the other to palm the right side of Jakeel's face, wiping the messy potion from Jakeel's eye down to his neck. The shaman did the same to the left side of Jakeel's face, then his shoulders and chest. Jakeel's sense of hearing became heightened as he concentrated on respecting this ritual, even though he felt uncomfortable at its unfamiliarity. But he sensed and knew the power that ebbed and flowed from the hands of the shamans to the warriors, and he was resolute in his newfound conviction that his place was here with his brothers as a warrior. Jakeel heard the incessant slapping of flesh as every warrior went through this process without so much as emitting a sneeze. A grassy and chewy substance was forced into Jakeel's mouth, and he instinctively wanted to spit it out, as it tasted bitter and oily, but the shaman kept his fingers in Jakeel's mouth until he sucked the substance to the back of his throat. The shaman moved his hand and motioned for Jakeel to chew. Jakeel's face grew numb as a strong, warm sensation ebbed over his shoulders and chest. He felt his heart pumping furiously, and a light glaze of perspiration slipped from his pores. Chewing the bitter substance made his mouth feel light and airy. When the shaman popped Jakeel on his mouth, he involuntarily swallowed.

Jakeel looked at the others who had already been initiated and noticed that they were still chewing and swallowing. Others had stuffed the substance into the fold of their cheeks or their bottom lips and were swaying restlessly from foot to foot. Jakeel felt his hands engorge with blood and his muscles inflate as if he had been working in the fields for several hours. He sensed his own power, and it felt tremendous. He began shifting from one foot to the other, the energy sieving through his veins, hardly containable.

The sun was now up and daylight in full sway. The heat from the Carolina swamp was radiating though the circle of spears, shimmering and toying with the light in miraculous ways. Sweat poured from the glands of the men and their sweaty black and brown skin, glistening bright. From a distance the constant motion was hypnotizing. The warriors moved in a cadence that held such syncopation it appeared as if they were one body, one flesh, one mind. Their souls united in ways that surpassed their diversity; their spirits become one under the careful direction of Gausje.

Gausje gestured and two heavily muscled warriors dragged the body of a white soldier with a spear drilled through his skull into the center of the circle. Gausje joined the dance and shuffled nimbly around the dead body, singing a song foreign to all but the shamans. When Jakeel recognized the man as one of the leaders, his own rage flared. He felt hot air rush from his inflated nostrils and the taste of revenge sting his tongue. He was ready to go. He marveled at the heat and how he did not feel the fatigue that normally came with it. His stomach was on fire, but in a good way. He relished the way his body felt. Jakeel felt the ground tremble beneath his feet as they moved in cadence with that of his brothers and sisters. Gausje was still dancing around the corpses and sprinkling powder on the body while moving in rhythm with her warriors, her children. The ground shook again, the dirt billowed outward from where the corpse lay, and Gausje danced. Every man kept moving, kept sweating, and stayed in the moment. Gausje moved away from the body and called out in a shriek.

"Come forth! Receive our offering of thanks. Hear us! And receive our offering of thanks." Gausje backed up until she was nearly in the ranks of warriors who surrounded her. Then the ground rippled again and opened and Hearns's body sank down into it only to be caught by the largest, blackest, most menacing serpent Jakeel had ever observed.

The serpent caught the man in its gaping mouth, the legs and head dangling from either side of its menacing jowls. Jakeel heard a snap as the man's vertebrae gave way to the snake's power, the body doubling up so that his legs were on par with his head, and he was swallowed whole. Jakeel couldn't be sure if he was under the influence of what the shaman had given him, if he was going crazy, or if this woman had indeed conjured up a serpent to swallow the body of her enemy as a sacrifice. The process was slow, the lump of flesh and bone casually sliding down the snake's throat until it could no longer be seen. The serpent remained upright and swayed back and forth, a thick, corpulent, black tongue flickering rapidly in and out of his mouth. Gausje walked right up to the serpent. Bowing her head slightly, she held out her hands to make her proclamations.

"I trust the gods are pleased! They have accepted our sacrifice, yet this is only the start. Go forth, ye instrument of the gods, to the plantation where Jakeel was rescued. There you will find Jared Tolby. We ask that you accept him as a living sacrifice and grant us the wish of seeing a brighter future in this region, free from slavery."

With that the serpent recessed into the hole, and the earth convulsed again as the inhabitants of its depths shifted and sank into the compartments that cased their beings. The mouth of the earth closed, and what was left looked like the fresh mound of a grave. The ground shook once more and then spat forth the spear that had impaled Hearns. It shot high into the air for all the warriors to see before it cascaded down and stuck upright in the ground. Gausje went forward to retrieve her weapon and held it out in front of her sideways.

"Maroons! The time of our deliverance has come! We march!" The warriors raised their voices to the sky and cried out a roar of joy as they began to head out of the city as one.

Chapter 28
Wave of Death

Joseph Radcliff sat on his porch admiring the beauty of his neatly manicured lawn, the width and breadth of his estate, and the regimented up-and-down movement of the slaves collecting the cotton that had made him so wealthy. So immersed was he in his mint julep and admiration of his worldly accomplishments that he hardly noticed the black trail of Maroons running toward him. It was the *twang* of the arrow that violently struck the door post five feet from his hammock that alerted him that his estate was under attack. The slaves spread like black ants, wrecking havoc and destruction within minutes. Before his mind could think of how to react, Joseph saw two giant Negroes setting his fields of cotton on fire, and then a host of them lighting the tips of arrows, firing them toward his mansion and his barns. It looked as if the sky were raining hellfire.

Joseph ran into his house down the hallway, past the kitchen and the house servants, and turned right into his dining room to the fireplace where he kept a loaded shotgun high up on the mantel piece. Snatching it down, he then turned around and ran back toward the front of the house to the cabinet under the faucet. It was there that he kept his shells, and he hastily pulled the box out from under the sink and stuffed it into his pocket. He barked for his wife and children to get to a safe haven before he ran back to the front porch. As Radcliff opened his mouth to call for his taskmaster to bear arms, he felt something warm and heavy slip out of his waist. He looked down only to see his own blue-veined intestines tumbling down onto the white porch, splashing into a dark puddle of blood and flesh, and an angry black face staring up at him, and a muscular ebony arm holding a sharp blade decorated with blood. The shotgun slipped from his hands and fell toward the porch where the deft Maroon caught it. Radcliff thought of his wife, and as if in response to his cognition, he heard her scream. He pondered briefly how this could happen as his body cascaded to the floor, where his eyes met the lifeless eyes of his head taskmaster. Then darkness consumed him. Radcliff did not see his wife lose her life, his children taken captive. He did not see his entire mansion, barns, and fields succumb to the hot flames, or did he see the emancipation of his many slaves. The entirety of this ransack took all of twenty minutes.

Charlene Mendell was in the middle of putting the finishing touches on her daily exercise of discipline on Tiny Tina, so named because, although she was twenty-three, she looked as if she were still thirteen. Tiny received her name from her friends who loved her despite her shortened stature. Charlene took it upon herself to find a reason to give lashes to her niggers for any reason she deemed necessary—lateness, slothfulness, greediness, being too early, being ugly, not combing one's hair, smelling foul, anything that Charlene found offensive for the day. It didn't matter how carefully the slaves tried to walk the line she established, Charlene would find a reason to put the whip to somebody's back.

Tiny Tina could be called the model servant. Her hair was always combed; she bathed regularly because she worked in the house with Charlene. Tina completed her tasks with meticulous care, never finishing before she was scheduled or ever slacking on the job. But this particular morning, Charlene caught her son, who was fifteen, looking at Tina with eyes of lust, complimenting her on her body. Charlene accused Tina of conducting herself like a whore and told her that if it was a whore she wanted to be, then she might as well start getting into the trade. Charlene made Tina remove her clothes while Charlene's own son watched. She then had a fellow servant tie Tina's hands and ankles to the posts on Charlene's canopy bed. Charlene hated blacks, and she found perverse pleasure in torturing them.

Now she toyed with Tina, ignoring her screams of apology. Tina trembled as Charlene let her whip lightly caress the tender flesh that had yet to taste the wrath of her vile touch. Charlene's son could not hide his erection as he watched his mother tease Tina. Charlene rubbed her nails down the girl's smooth, dark spine and looked at her fifteen year-old boy, who was beginning to feel his manhood, and smiled. He would make a good master over these beasts of burden. But as she pulled the whip back to open the virgin flesh of her slave, Charlene heard a crash downstairs. She turned to investigate the commotion when four heavily muscled black men burst into the room wielding blades as long as her upper torso. Charlene screamed in disbelief as her son tried to run only to have his legs literally cut out from underneath him. He fell to the floor and slid into the wall on the exposed bone of a broken patella and femur, leaving a trail of blood and sinew behind him.

The other men quickly released Tiny from her restraints. She ran into the arms of one who quickly hoisted her up like a child and disappeared with her out of the room and down the stairs. Charlene, who still held the whip in her hand, flicked it at the exposed back of the largest one, producing a huge whelp of bare flesh, but the man did not flinch. Instead, he turned around, took one large step toward Charlene, and punched her fiercely in her nose. Charlene spat at him, but he dodged and immediately swung his blade at her face, creating a tremendous tear from her left ear to her mouth. The skin peeled open and blood sprayed out, decorating the clean sheets with pebbles of deep red. The Maroon picked up a chair sitting next to a beautifully carved dresser and swung it with vehemence against Charlene's chest. She crumpled to the bed in an agonizing scream, and the Maroon walked out of the room, leaving the bewildered mother and son gaping in horror and disbelief.

As they exited the door another Maroon tossed a flaming torch onto the bed where Charlene's crushed body still lay. Outside, on her tiny farm, cattle were released, and every slave was freed. The bodies of the field hands and taskmasters littered the ground, their bodies filled with arrows that bore the eerie black feathers of the crow. Charlene and her son burned to death wondering how these Maroons managed to overtake them so easily. Charlene's dying thought was, "It's not fair!!"

Nathan and Melissa Winthrop sat at the kitchen table of the main house on their meager plantation. They were newly married, and Nathan's father had leased him a few acres along with what he considered a small cadre of twenty-five slaves. If Nathan could prove himself business-worthy, he would soon be given charge of his father's entire estate, and that was worth a fortune. They had recently hired a taskmaster from their neighbor, Charlene Mendell, to show them the most efficient methods of how to manage slaves and keep life productive on their modest plot of land. Because it was Sunday, the taskmaster had been given the day off, and Nathan and Melissa had decided to enjoy a quiet breakfast together before they headed off to church to hear Reverend Freemund. There were two servants who worked in the house, preparing food and keeping it clean. They usually worked non-stop, whereas the field slaves were occasionally given Sunday off to keep the Sabbath. The day was quiet, but Nathan kept thinking he heard screams, though his beautiful wife assured him it was nothing. It wasn't until he went for another glass of milk and looked out his window that he saw smoke billowing from Charlene's house and, upon closer inspection, a trail of smoke on neighboring plantations.

"Melissa! Come over here, hon. I think Charlene's house is on fire. Should I go over there and see what is happening?"

"You'd like that very much, wouldn't you?" Melissa jested. "I see how you look at her every time she comes by." Melissa chuckled at the nervous look Nathan gave her and then reassured him. "Go on, Nate. I'm sure it's no more than a little kitchen fire."

"I'll be back in time for church, sweetheart." Nathaniel did not realize that was a promise he would not keep as he was cut down by a hail of arrows before he could reach Charlene's house. The Maroons ran through Nathaniel and Melissa's place with ferocity close to the wrath of God. Melissa didn't even see it coming. When she heard the chanting and commotion of slaves running away, she stepped out her front door right into the swing of a sharp axe, which cleft her jaw from the rest of her face and broke open her chest cavity. Her lungs collapsed, and the escaping air made a gurgling sound as she died.

By noon more than a dozen farms, plantations, and estates had been burned to the ground and the slaves freed. For the most part, the liberation had been clean and swift, but there were times when the darkness of hate, and the years of oppression, broke through, and the Maroons resorted to the type of bestial violence that they themselves and their generations had been subjected to for more than two centuries. This violence was atavistic, genetic, surging forth from the murky caverns inside every human soul that has been forged into existence in the cauldrons of hate and inhumanity. This high pedigree of barbarism was an inevitable outcome, and the slave holders should have been expecting it, for many of them would often lose sleep after executing torment on those innocents under their charge.

At first, Jakeel relished in the marauding and death. He felt the energies flowing through his body as he killed without remorse. He felt invincible, cocky, as he and Isiki ran through the white slave owners effortlessly. But as noon approached, and the effects of whatever the shamans had given them early that morning started to wear off, Jakeel noticed that the killing began to take on a more sadistic trait. It started after the couple. Jakeel usually took part in killing the white taskmasters, the slave owners, and any aggressive white man who tried to stop the Maroons. He never had to deal with the women, except for one who was caught in the middle of torturing a small slave girl, and he left the room before he witnessed what happened to her. But thus far, his killings had been justified in his own mind, and he did not hesitate in administering death to the oppressors of his people. The visions reigned strong in his mind, and he had wanted to root out all the evil in the land until he came upon a plantation where several white children ran out of the house firing pistols. He guessed that word might have spread of the Maroon's attacks, and people would have started to prepare themselves.

Jakeel watched with mixed emotions as women were cut down with arrows and axes, their bodies crashing to the ground with tremendous force. But his emotions became fixed when he and the others ran into the house and quickly dispatched with the men only to discover a beautiful young woman, apparently the wife, rush out of a closet to attack them. She was not a threat, but Jakeel noticed that the men wanted to do a little more than kill oppressors and free slaves. They took the woman and threw her down on the floor and fought to remove her clothes, but she resisted fiercely and kicked and spat and scraped to keep the Maroons off her. Jakeel could see that the men were getting tired of her resistance and saw one picking up his spear to end the woman's life. That was when Jakeel decided to put a stop to the senseless violence. He ran and placed himself between the woman and the Maroon, but she kicked him so he turned and hit her squarely in the jaw. She fell unconscious to the floor.

"Jakeel! What are you doing? We need to teach this woman."

"This is not the way." Jakeel responded. "She is a woman, and we are warriors. What can she do to us? Nothing. We tie her up and set her back in the closet. Warriors kill men; they do not hunt down women and children. Our training puts us above that." Jakeel glared at the woman's assailant with eyes filled with fierce confidence, and the man backed down.

"Save your blood lust for the men who rape our women and children. We must not become like them." The Maroon looked at Jakeel with intense anger, but Jakeel's words appealed to his higher conscience, and he quickly nodded, knelt down, tied the woman up, dragged her body to the closet, and moved on toward the next attack.

Jakeel sighed in relief. He did not believe that the warriors would listen to him. Perhaps this was his purpose in being brought in to the tribe. Unfortunately, this was just the first situation that made Jakeel uncomfortable, doubting the purity of his new tribe's way. He realized it was only the beginning.

At the next house the Maroons faced a small group of farmers who were armed and futilely tried to protect their property. After a fierce volley of bullets and arrows, the Maroons eventually gained the advantage and slowly began to advance upon the house. The first sets of deaths were typical. Either from heat or fatigue, a careless glance put one's head directly into the line of fire and, one by one, the white men began to go down. The remaining whites surrendered, putting out a white flag and waving it back and forth. They laid down their weapons, knelt, and put their hands up in defeat, a few of them even weeping, others with grimaces pallid with hate. The Maroons cautiously advanced, not knowing whether this was a trick or not. Their bows drawn and swords at the ready, the Maroons moved toward their prey.

Jakeel's heart was jubilant. He was getting tired of the carnage, and although these men had committed terrible injuries against the flesh of his brothers and sisters, he did not want to become like his enemy. He did not know how justice would prevail. He didn't even know what the Maroons would do with these men if held under captivity, but he thought it a start. He sheathed his weapon and darted behind the first slave owner closest to him and took a piece of string from his loin cloth that would have been used on his bow were his string to break. Jakeel wound it tightly around the man's wrists until thin lines of blood started to ebb their way to the surface, and then Jakeel pushed the man face forward to the ground. As he proceeded to go to the next he noticed not one Maroon joined him in his endeavor. Instead, all were casting mean glares at the surrendered men.

Isiki moved forward without a word and walked behind a man who knelt along with the defeated former slave owners. He stood behind the man, breathing fiercely through flaring nostrils. Jakeel looked at Isiki but said nothing. He only watched as Isiki removed a sharp blade from his loincloth and kicked the man in his back; then Isiki fell down upon the man, kneeling directly on his spine. His victim shouted for mercy, but the other Maroons drew their bows, and no one dared move. Isiki grabbed the white man's hair and pulled upward so that his eyes were slanted and nearly showing only white. Isiki took his other hand that held the blade and slowly, but firmly, drew it across the top of the man's hairline and down around his ears. He then pushed the screaming man's face back into the earth and carefully drew his blade across the back of the man's skull and then around the other side of his ear until the blade met the start of the bloody line. Isiki tugged, and Jakeel could hear the flesh tearing as the white man's scalp slowly was lifted from his head, his cries drowning out all reason. Then the arrows flew.

Jakeel watched the carnage as if it were happening in slow motion. Isiki stood up and raised the scalp and emitted a deafening yell, while arrows and swords and blades plummeted fiercely into the living flesh of the remaining whites, killing them gruesomely. Blood sprayed up onto Jakeel as the man he had tied up was bludgeoned by an axe. Every man was scalped and dismembered.

When it was done, warm blood had soaked into the soles of Jakeel's moccasins. Yet, the tribe still moved on; they had more wrongs to avenge.

Deacon Jones had just finished the morning's worship song, "What a Friend We Have in Jesus," when Brien Olsen burst through the sanctuary doors and ran down the middle aisle toward the altar. The song died out as everyone glared at him with astonishment and indignation. How dare someone defile the house of God? Two church elders quietly came forward and apprehended Brien as he screamed out, "They're coming! They are coming for you!"

Several men hurried him to the pastor's study where he was sequestered while they waited for Freemund to arrive. Of course, none of the church staff knew where their minister was; they had no idea that he had been part of the great battle with the Maroons and was now hiding on the Tolby plantation. Fred Jones, the head deacon, had welcomed his opportunity to lead the services, and he continued once Olsen was led away.

"Saints, the devil doesn't want us to worship this morning!" He smiled gently as if he had detected a secret he just couldn't wait to reveal. "But my God is mightier than that wily ole devil!" His voice was now trembling with fake enthusiasm. He took a long gander at the reverent faces in the audience and thought to himself, *"I can do this without effort. I could easily lead this flock. Lead them better than Freemund."* Deacon Jones took his hymnal and turned to a hymn he craftily thought would be appropriate for his church's recent disturbance. The morning was hot, and the bright sun cast an illuminating beam of light right down to the pulpit, lighting every mote of dust, stray hair, tear-glazed eye, and pious smile. A cooling breeze wafted slowly through the church, dissipating the stifling heat that was already starting to accumulate.

"Please turn in your hymnals to page 533, 'Will Your Anchor Hold'?" The congregation responded to Deacon Jones's clever choice of song. Brien had just brought strife into the house of God, but here they were still standing and raising their voices in triumph over the devil.

"Will your anchor hold in the storms of life,

When the clouds unfold their wings of strife

When the strong tides lift, and the cables strain,

Will your anchor drift, or firm remain?"

Their melodious voices poured from the open windows of the church as the advancing Maroons crept surreptitiously over well-worn paths. The warriors split into groups, their weapons bearing the residue of butchery.

"We have an anchor that keeps the soul

Steadfast and sure while the billows roll;

Fastened to the rock which cannot move,

Grounded firm and deep in the Savior's love!"

Keigei had informed them after they finished killing the surrendered plantation owners that their next stop would be the church that Gausje had seen in vision spreading poison to the minds of so many whites and slaves that slavery was justified and sanctified by God. This was the breeding house of lies where the word of a great prophet was maligned to fit the sordid passions of the white race, so it, too, must be a battleground. Many of the freed slaves had joined the Maroons, and now their numbers, at first impressive, had become prodigious. Jakeel was amazed at how readily and obediently the newcomers fell into order and did exactly as they were told. It had the makings of a mob but was working in perfect harmony as the men were unified and orderly in their purpose.

"Will your anchor hold in the straits of fear

When the breakers roar and the reef is near;

While the surges rave, and the wild winds blow,

Shall the angry waves then your bark o'erflow?"

The sweaty black and brown bodies encroached upon the church and spread around it in deadly silence, their cadence out of sync with the music that emanated from its apertures. Inside, the saints sang as if they had never stolen, raped, sodomized, or wrongly punished the slaves given to their charge. Their eyes looked without contrition to the mural of a slain Jesus that graced the front of the sanctuary. Their countenances never once reflected on the sexual molestation of black children or the bastards that were swarming their adulterous homes. They never genuflected in shame at the families marred for generations because of the physical, spiritual, and social torment that their systemized oppression had wrought on the Negro. And their voices exclaimed their steadfast love for their God in ignorance of the strong men who huddled right outside their church doors.

"Will your anchor hold in the floods of death,

When the waters cold chill your latest breath?

On the rising tide you can never fail,

While your anchor holds within the veil."

As Deacon Jones began the final verse, he noticed dark splotches slowly drowning out the light that glared from the open rear doors. His wide, smiling lips were quickly sent downward at the sight of half-naked men wielding great weapons of death marching down the aisle. His pride, as well as his speech, caught in his throat, and his head twisted left and right looking for the anchor that would keep his soul, only to meet the frightened eyes of the other church staff. He held up his hymnal as if it were a measure of defense as one fierce warrior reached and slapped the book from his impotent hands. Jones and other members of the church looked to the exits only to see them brimming with the sweaty bodies of angry black and brown men.

Jakeel remained outside; his past with Jared's wife prevented his committing what he felt was sacrilege. He knew what they were doing was right; he just had to take more time to heal. He would remain guard outside the church, striking down anyone who managed to escape. Inside, Keigei took the pulpit and spoke in clear, unaccented English, much to the amazement of the congregation. They could not believe a savage such as he could wield English with clarity and force. He spoke without arrogance or venom, but his sharp gaze pierced the souls of every man, woman, and child there.

"You have committed crimes against a people who are undeserving of them," Keigei exclaimed.

"Shut up, you red nigger!"

"You have killed, maimed, and destroyed our women and children."

"Like your whores deserve better!" Someone spat.

"You are a plague upon this land. Instead of developing, sharing, and building, you spoil it with your greed, you tarnish it with the shedding of innocent blood, you leech of it any value it could yield, and you do it in the name of God."

"How dare you speak His name, you damned infidel!" a woman shouted amid sobs.

"You call me an infidel, but you distort truth, you teach lies, and you come here and sing praises to God as if you have done no wrong. Don't you fear for your souls at such blatant iniquities? Don't you ever wonder when God is going to take action on you for your transgressions against your brother? Yes, I said brother, for I've seen you in other lands in visions, and you are not all vile. But in this land, your sins will not go unpunished. Today, you shall meet your maker. I wish I could say that you meet Him in peace, but in truth, I hope you meet your true master instead."

The congregation slowly realized the import of Keigei's words. Their eyes of fear met with eyes of destruction, and the faith of the "saints" gave way to the madness of the lost. Keigei ordered all the women and children to move outside. As soon as the last woman exited, the doors were closed and arrows, spears, and swords flashed, causing new colors of human fluids to mingle on the palette of the church floor. Deacon Jones was the first to be killed as Keigei buried his axe in the base of the deacon's skull. The Maroons hacked, struck, kicked, stabbed, and dismembered every man who attended church that morning, but they had spared the women and children. Perhaps, Jakeel thought, his words had started to take good effect.

The last man to die was Brien, who banged against Freemund's door, a prisoner in the pastor's study. He screamed for help, for mercy, and finally for grace. But his was a cry of desperation and not true contrition, and his soul met the same fate as the other gown adult male members of Freemund's congregation that day.

It is said that one cannot serve two masters, and Keigei and Gausje both had discerned what particular master most white slave owners served and knew that justice would indeed be delivered this day. When the bloodshed was over, bodies draped over pews, lay sprawled on the floor, or crumpled up against the wall, mutilated, filled with wounds or arrows, devoid of life. The church was then set aflame, and eventually all that remained were the ashes and debris of a house that had been dedicated to encouraging the evil rather than the good in men's souls.

The Maroons dashed off in uniformity to their last destination. The cleansing was almost complete, and Jakeel felt relieved that the onslaught had not been as insidious as it first began; he was glad they had spared the women and children. His soiled feeling and guilt for the few he felt innocent was replaced with acceptance of the blood of those who lost their lives today. He now realized that his purpose was to be the moral conscience of a group of people who had experienced tremendous suffering to the point that their retaliating would go unchecked. Now that he was here, he had earnest hope that those days were over. Jakeel, briefly, managed a feeble smile.

Chapter 29
A Woman's Scorn

The three refugees awoke to the hurried voices of men coming toward the barn. The motley crew groggily tried to assemble themselves into a respectable and calm group, but the truth was they all had a troubled sleep. The claws of fear lightly teased the surface of their dreams, scraping sharpened talons across celestial images, morphing them to ones of ghoulish proportions, making each man toss and turn restlessly as he hoped to find solace, but leaving each only in torment.

Now Freemund, Nemesqu, and Baramoore struggled to gain composure as voices drew nearer to the barn. Nemesqu was the only one to manage to get his mind straight by calming his frantic senses and delving deep into his wolf spirit to project a strong field of energy. It was fortunate that he did so, because the angry white men didn't take any time to ask questions of the trio but immediately fired shots at the unarmed Indian. To their amazement, the man they intended to kill remained poised and unharmed, while Baramoore and Freemund lay on the floor. Nemesqu, whose eyes at first were rolled up in concentration, looked upon the men and sent the protective force swiftly toward them, knocking the weapons from their hands. He stood to his feet and spoke to his would-be assailants. "We are together! We needed refuge from the Maroons. This is Baramoore, my master, and Reverend Freemund."

The men, still dazed by the reality that the Indian they tried to kill was upright and speaking perfect English to them, found it difficult to comprehend what this savage was saying. The pause was enough to let Baramoore regain his sensibilities well enough to stand and speak.

"What my servant says is correct, gentlemen," he gasped. "We have had a most terrible loss and barely escaped with our lives. We tried to attack the village of the Maroons, but our plans were foiled." Baramoore leaned over and helped Freemund to his feet. As he did so he subtly made a hand signal that only a member of the Guild would recognize, and he was relieved when one of the men gestured back in kind. He did not immediately recognize the individual but realized that if he acknowledged the sign, then they were safe. That man was the first to speak.

"So, brother, you are unaware of what has taken place today?"

"No. I—what—what is the time?"

"It's close ta three o'clock. Whole part of town been under attack! We can't tell ya how many people been kilt by them bad-blooded niggers! Dey burnt our crops, freed our slaves, spared no one! Wives, children!" his voice was ragged with emotion. "We thought maybe ya were part of dat group! When I found ya in my barn, we got our guns and came fa vengeance. I'pologize fa tryin' ta kill ya servant. I lost lots of property! I guess I'preciate' da faithful ones even more. All mah slaves have left 'cept Pluto and the old witch-woman Bella." Freemund was shaking his head in disbelief. He wondered what happened to his own slaves and his wife. What had gone so terribly wrong? How had he misread the prophecy?

"I've got to get to my wife," Freemund said.

"Why not wait. We are assembling a group of men to take arms and fight. It won't be a good idea to go alone," the stranger replied.

"Right, thank you, brother," Baramoore interjected before Freemund could attempt a response. "We could use food, if you have anything, and weapons for me and my friend Freemund. You might have already noticed that my servant doesn't need weapons. But truth be told, I don't know what difference these weapons will make. The Maroons have supernatural abilities beyond our understanding." The man who had spoken looked at Freemund with amazement.

"Reverend Freemund? The Reverend of the Church of the Laodecians?"

"The same," Freemund replied. "And might I inquire your name?"

"Jared Tolby. My wife attends ya church." Tolby was visibly shaken and less polished than his Guild brother. "I haven't seen my wife, but my plantation has suffered at the hands of these niggers. Her name is Elizabeth. Do ya know her?" Jared's eyes pleaded with Freemund's, but years of practice enabled Freemund to look at this man and tell him that while he did see Elizabeth in church, he did not really know her. Jared hung his head in defeat.

"These Maroons are vicious, Reverend. Thy murdered my daughter and stole my slaves," Jared said.

The men commiserated their lot for a moment. Nemesqu quietly played his servant role to his friend Baramoore, and they went back to the main house and were fed. In the distance, smoke clouded the horizon. Freemund learned from Jared that his church and congregation had been massacred and burned to death, and one could tell that Freemund's spirit was broken. After a little debate it was decided that the men would stay on Jared's plantation to start rebuilding their forces. Nemesqu, although curious and thirsting for revenge, was rather leery at the prospect of what they would face. A sense in the back of his mind discouraged him staying for another battle with these magical Maroons, but he decided to listen to his pride instead of his spirit. It would be a decision he would soon come to regret.

CHAPTER 30

VENGEANCE IS MINE

Ensconced in perfect darkness, Nemesqu exerted his will over Neil and Aaron. The glow of his eyes was all that remained of the patterns of cold light he stole from the bioluminescence contained in the multitudes of firefly abdomens. The intricate patterns were recognized by aged gods long since forgotten who appropriated the enzyme to pay homage to their fallen leader, whose noble position in the heavens was lost in a supernatural, political battle. Nemesqu, an apt pupil of the oldest remaining forms of mysticism, relished this moment. Though he felt the power of his foe just beyond the limits of his view, he knew he could conquer her. It was the other power—the one that nearly destroyed him at the Maroon village— of which he was most fearful and yet most intrigued.

Nemesqu drove his subjects forward to their death. Once he used them to draw out his prey he would strike. Moving carefully away from the window, he used his mind to maintain his hold on the men while finding a place where his energy could flow, unimpeded by the walls of the house, and strike down the person who was hiding in the slave quarters. Easing out the back door, he slipped discreetly behind an evergreen bush nestled tightly against the back porch. Kneeling down on one knee, he summoned the powers of the gods. His lower belly ached while his upper extremities came to life, fueled by spiritual power. The veins in his neck and biceps, fully engorged with blood, now stood boldly against his taut, tanned skin.

The red moon elongated Neil and Aaron's shadows as they neared the first hut. Nemesqu, squatting now, held both arms down toward the earth, his palms forward. A light bluish energy was softly emanating from his curled fingers like winter snowflakes that barely had time to gather density. The energy floated quietly into the earth, and his vision narrowed as he charted the direct path his power would take to blow out the insides of the person who ventured out from one of those huts. But just as he was summoning the blow that would kill his assailant, a truly unexpected event occurred.

****

When Bella saw the two men approaching with their weapons drawn, she armed herself with her hatchet. Elizabeth and Rebecca stood behind her, both equipped with rifles taken from Elizabeth's home. Bella felt the presence that was in the house; the hackles on her neck rose in alarm. Not since Africa had she felt such power, other than from Gausje. Unfortunately, she had been kidnapped before she could complete her training for combative sorcery, and intuition was telling her that she would be reminded of that tonight. What Bella did know was how to use a weapon; that training was complete and perfected.

"There are two men coming down here," Bella whispered to the two women behind her. "It's a trap to draw us out. I could kill one with my hatchet, but you would need to step out right after me and shoot the other man."

"But then our position will be given away! We will expose ourselves to other attackers. Is this the best way, Bella?" Elizabeth queried. Rebecca looked at them both nervously.

"So what do we do?"

Bella crouched low, gripping and re-gripping her weapon. It would just be moments before the two men were at her doorstep. Why weren't the gods directing her path? She was indecisive and a little frightened by all the negative possibilities. There was so much that could go wrong. Just then she noticed one of the men, the one with the pistol, stagger. In the glow of the red moon, she caught a glimpse of his face. He stopped moving, but the other one kept coming, even though his left side, the side that was closest to the man who had stopped, was lagging behind.

"Why—" She heard the man with the pistol say, a line of drool dangling from his loose lips. "Why don't—" a pause, then an impotent moan. "Why don't you get out of my head?" As he raised both hands to the sides of his head she saw one of them held a pistol. He turned his hand to his head, pulled the trigger, and black fluid spattered onto the well-worn path.

The women heard a shout near the entrance to the plantation, followed by the approach of what sounded like galloping horses. The other man was still advancing, so Bella released the hatchet, which flew with perfect precision, cleaving Neil's chin and upper lip in two, biting into the bone of his lower jaw. The rifle dropped from his hand as blood sprouted from the wound in his face. Falling to his knees, he collapsed face forward, the force of his fall twisting the hatchet free from his mouth, dislodging a few teeth.

As Bella retreated back into the safety of her hut, she just happened to see the most brilliant light out of the corner of her eye before feeling as if she were bathing in scalding hot liquid. Suddenly, she was thrown back into her doorpost, her body writhing like that of a cut snake, twisting and turning over itself. All around her was bluish white light, and she could muster only a solitary thought: she wished the pain to end. The light began to diminish, and she slowly started to regain feeling in her limbs, but she was unable to move from the doorpost. She just sat there like a wounded soldier, wanting to fight, to gain cover, but she was unable. When she looked up she saw her enemy coming forward out of the shadows, his hands ablaze with bluish white light.

Nemesqu raised his hands as the energy gathered and began to form a ball of power when Bella's dazed periphery sensed someone moving past her. A shot fired. It was Elizabeth. She had run into the middle of the path, took aim, and fired a shot that hit Nemesqu straight on. As she ran into the house to reload Rebecca ran out and fired at the man. Impossibly, hit by two shots, the man seemed stunned but not wounded. The light from the ball of energy began to dissipate, but he stood where he was. The shots had given Bella enough time to summon her spiritual forces and regain her composure. As she invoked the shield of protection, the air wavered around her like a mirage, flustering away the dwindling blue energy that had paralyzed her only moments before. Her jet black hair now was peppered with beads of gray and the man, who she could now see was an Indian, shot another bolt of bluish white energy just as she stood and leaned forward. The bright light blazed all around her but did not touch her flesh.

Elizabeth and Rebecca, both now armed after reloading their weapons, looked at Bella with their mouths agape. She was slowly walking forward, a nimbus of energy around her made prominent by the bluish white light that was cascading around the circumference of her protective shield. But the sound of galloping horses brought them back to reality, and Elizabeth motioned for Rebecca to follow as they ran to hide in an adjacent empty hut.

On the perimeter of the plantation, Baramoore, Freemund, and Jared waited while Nemesqu executed his sorcery. Baramoore had walked around and talked to the farmers and listened to their stories. They were angry at their losses and indignant at the source of their debasement at the hands of the niggers, many to the point of tears. He heard various stories of harvest, cotton, slaves, and families that were all lost because of the bad-blooded niggers. Baramoore's heart beat with its own emotion as he reflected on the losses, all at the hands of simple niggers. He had come too close to getting the economic resources of the Guild established and to obtaining his secret source of power to be defeated. The hate he felt more than heard from the soldiers and farmers made him realize just how naive he had been to believe that he could have gotten away with his forbidden partnership with Nemesqu. Yet he knew that if he had it to do all over again, he would choose Nemesqu without hesitation. Their relationship had defied the prejudices of the times, and the future depended on their survival.

The men heard the shots ring out into the night. Sensing that Nemesqu must have found his prey, Baramoore quickly roused the soldiers into attack formation. The experienced soldiers flanked the armed farmers, forming a triangle as they headed down the road that led to the big house, with Jared, Baramoore, and Freemund leading the pack. Every man—fueled by hate, greed, and lust—was intent on routing out any nigger who was on Jared's property.

******

Harsh hands had clasped Rebecca and Elizabeth's mouths as soon as they entered the hut, startling them. Even though Elizabeth suddenly felt a warm burst of urine trickle down her legs, she did her best to remain calm. This could not be happening; the future she glimpsed during her torture in her minister's basement did not place her dead in a dilapidated slave shack. Just then a voice whispered in her ear, "Do not struggle. We are on your side." At that moment the grip was released, and Elizabeth dashed forward toward the door, her breath ragged with excitement. She turned to face her captors only to discover the hardened faces of the Maroon warriors. Light flashed outside like a lightening storm as the battle raged between Bella and her assailant. One of the men stepped forward, and Elizabeth lowered her rifle in his direction.

"Your weapon could have been taken the moment you stepped through that door. We've been watching Bella lure out the one man who might have enough power to thwart all that we have accomplished. Use your weapon against the other man who approaches our way." Isiki had invoked his protective shield, despite his belief that the woman would not fire. He was not above being cautious today. Elizabeth did not move but stared at him, slowly backing her way to the door. She released the hitch and eased back outside as Rebecca followed suit. The door closed, and the two women ran farther down the path before darting between two other slave houses.

"This is too dangerous, Elizabeth! What good can possibly come of this?" Rebecca was too distraught to remain coy. The magic, the death, and the fighting were enough to drive her to regress back into her world of cheating and lies. It was a cruel world, but it was more tolerable than the one in which she was now immersed.

"Shhhhh!" Elizabeth hissed. "If I die today I don't want it because you couldn't keep your mouth shut!" Rebecca's jaws clamped tight as Elizabeth slammed her back against the wall of the hut and slid down, peeking out at the battle between the man and Bella.

Bella now was leaning forward with her full weight, her feet digging into the ground, scraping up raw earth. Her shield, although holding, seemed to be losing power, its brilliancy slowly diminishing, whereas the man's power was unrelenting. Elizabeth rolled out of her cover and lay flat on her stomach, taking aim at the Indian's face, but it was hard to gain a good angle because of the blinding light flowing from his hands. She lowered her sights to his abdomen but faced the same dilemma. She considered a shot to his groin, but then she remembered she could only get off one shot before having to reload, and the last time two shots had not taken the man down, only thrown him off. Frustrated, she rolled back over and repositioned herself against the wall. It dawned on her then that he was too engrossed in his fight with Bella to notice any distractions.

"Rebecca, I am going to shoot this man again. I need you to position yourself against this wall so that after I shoot at him, you can do likewise." Rebecca looked uncertain but haphazardly nodded her head in agreement. "The last time we shot him it didn't kill him, but his magic stopped for a second. It just might give Bella enough time to use her own magic against him."

"I will try. I just hope I don't miss." Elizabeth peeked around the corner of the house to look at the duel. Bella's force field was sputtering, the light faintly going in and out. Her weighty thighs trembled with each step she tried to take forward, but she was consistently pushed back. Elizabeth rolled away from her shelter, lay down again on her stomach, and took careful aim. She inhaled deeply, then she held her breath for two seconds before pulling the trigger. The jolt knocked the wind out of her, causing her to cough before she could see if she hit her target. Another loud blast rang out, and Elizabeth was comforted to hear that Rebecca had at last fired. Elizabeth looked up from the ground to see Bella's force field burst forward across the ground, pounding the man with intensity and wrapping around him as he fell backward.

The shots must have been enough to break his concentration and weaken his powers for a moment so that Bella could quickly retrieve her hatchet from the fallen man. She ran toward the sorcerer and tried to strike him down but, amazingly, he slid backward as if someone were pulling him and glided upright until he hovered in the air momentarily, readying himself for another attack. Wind, dirt, and flashes of electric light burst all about his hardened form. Although he was bleeding slightly from his mouth, he was grinning. Bella turned and ran back down the path toward the women when dozens of armed Blacks and Indians streamed out of the slave quarters. Elizabeth took cover again and reloaded.

It was then that the three women, Elizabeth, Rebecca, and Bella, saw her. Gausje stepped forth from the darkness of night, her black flesh camouflaged against the pressing darkness, her white robe brilliant in contrast. She was walking up the path toward the manor house, alone. Her warriors, at least one hundred of them, formed a barrier between her and Nemesqu. Her presence illuminated the night and, somehow, although they did not know how, Elizabeth and Rebecca both sensed that tonight was going to go in the favor of the Maroons. The farmers and soldiers rounded the corner next to the manor house but halted abruptly at the sight. Gausje stopped, held up one steady hand, and spoke, her voice bellowing through the once-deserted plantation so that every ear heard, without fail, her solemn command.

"Advance, warriors, we have the enemy surrounded." The sound of crackling leaves and twigs announced the Maroon's approach. The red moon's eerie glow was enhanced by the blazing torches that began to appear outside the periphery of the plantation. The motley crew of white men looked about nervously. Never before had they witnessed such unity and power among the slaves. The flickering lights continued to advance, causing some men to consider fleeing for their lives. But the warning of the hard-looking Baramoore kept them rooted to their places.

Gausje took a few steps forward before speaking again. "Leave the Indian to me." Gausje's command barreled though the silence and projected up the path until the import of her words shook Nemesqu to the very core. So this was it—his challenge, his final match. His stomach bubbled with excitement and deadly horror. The warriors advanced toward the soldiers, bows drawn, weapons gleaming, their power ready to be unleashed. Baramoore kicked his horse into a slight retreat and shouted at Nemesqu.

"Do something! Stop them!" Nemesqu did not move or turn but kept his gaze forward to face the advancing light coming from Gausje.

"I shall." Nemesqu replied. "This is the source of their strength. My talents are wasted on the others, but this one is a match indeed. You and your men handle the rest. Your weapons are of no use with this particular battle."

Nemesqu reached into a purse that he kept attached to his loin cloth and withdrew a fistful of what looked to be white dust, which he sprinkled around him in a complete circle. "Prepare your soul, my friend, should tonight's events turn calamitous. The evil spirits are hoping that you do not."

Nemesqu then whispered words only he and the gods could hear, and a slight red flame formed a circle around his feet. Red particles of light rose from the circle, seeming to absorb themselves into his body. When he stretched his arms backward so that his chest was fully displayed, his hands began to shimmer like burning coals. The circle around his feet caught fire, but the flames did not consume the grass or Nemesqu. With chest exposed, arms back, palms open, and head tilted forward, the Indian began his advance on Gausje; he no longer worried about Bella, who had admirably kept him at bay. This horrible ugly woman was his true match. Baramoore watched the spectacle as he withdrew his pistol in an attempt to fire a shot into the advancing warriors only to realize that he and his men were fully surrounded.

An arrow struck Jared in the knee, and Baramoore's stomach quivered at the popping sound. Jared squealed like a butchered calf, his tongue dangling from his mouth, but he managed to hobble for shelter before two more arrows buried themselves in the meat of his bicep and stomach. He fell to the ground, his abdomen heaving violently, blood oozing through his clothes, forming a sooty puddle. Rolling back and forth, he tried to gain a hold on the unrelenting pain, but finally he succumbed to death.

"Fire on them! Fire! Fire!" Baramoore pivoted his horse just in time to avoid a furious barrage of arrows. The Maroons were hacking into the white men with a ferocity he had seen only in combat with them. Each move was executed with well-practiced deftness.

The call for death roared above Baramoore's orders—and death responded. Bone, flesh, and spirit gave way to the pull and tug of death. Knives clanged, gunpowder flashed, and delicate internal organs exploded in a flurry of red, brown, and black, infusing the earth with the sustenance that was meant to keep men alive. Their bodies, mangled and broken, began to decorate the earth, forming a wreath of fatalities around Jared's plantation. One by one, the farmers and soldiers were killed by archers and blades of steel.

Baramoore fought the masses frantically in an effort to win the battle, but his motives were relegated to survival because the Maroons were too relentless and unified. Their violence was fueled by a hate he did not possess—a hate that oppression had systematically nurtured and suckled to full maturity. These Maroons had been hoodwinked into a lifetime of servitude, mutilated, tormented, and culturally broken by his kind. He knew he would have to retreat. Although his men despised the niggers, they lacked the conviction and anger that can only be wrought from persecution. While they had much to lose materially, the Maroons had already lost that: what they now fought for was their very own souls—and that was a battle he now knew he would never win.

Some of his men fired, allowing Baramoore to take cover behind an overturned wagon near the stables that faced the big manor house. He found two men armed and huddled tightly against the thick wooden floor of the wagon. A constant volley of arrows hammered into the wagon, and he could smell the fear radiating from the men's pores. The feathered tip of an arrow shaft protruded from one's foot, and his face had been sliced several times across his cheek.

"They are too much for us!"

"I know. We cannot expect a victory here." Baramoore said.

"We need to issue a retreat!"

"No. We make our stand here, come what may. We retreat, and they get more magic. We fight and die right here, right now!"

"We need to get Jared!"

"Jared is dead, as we will be if we don't keep our heads!" Baramoore was flustered and angry. He knew in his mind that retreat was what would be necessary, and as if to punctuate that thought, Freemund half galloped, half fell to where they were holding up.

"The damned Indian is losing! If we don't get over there to right the odds, this whole night is a loss!" Blood pumped from a large wound in his scalp, a broken arrow stuck through his calf muscle.

Baramoore briefly had time to acknowledge his pride in the old minister when two Maroons leaped over the wagon, weapons of steel flashing in the night. Baramoore's heart throbbed in his throat, and the blood froze in his veins. He fired three shots into his assailants and recoiled at the slapping sound of bullets tearing into their flesh. But their attack resumed unabated. One of the Indians pitched a dagger that pinned Freemund's already wounded leg to the ground. The Indian then retrieved another dagger from his waistband and leaped toward his fallen prey with focused concentration. Baramoore went to the aid of his comrade and slammed his body into the Indian's before the death blow was delivered. Baramoore, who was momentarily stunned by the suddenness of the attack, pivoted away from the assault as he fired a single round directly into the skull of the Indian nearest Freemund, bringing that life to a close, causing the body to flop to the ground.

Freemund had time to regain his composure and fire a well-aimed shot into the belly of the other Indian, sending him sprawling backward, eyes wide with bewilderment as he stared at his fallen brother. The other Maroon then turned and fled into the shadows. Baramoore and Freemund painfully made their way back to the slave quarters, stepping over the myriad bodies of dead white men, a few black bodies strewn in between.

The torrent of arrows never abated. Archers in the trees continually fired; the ground, prickled with feathered sticks, made the run difficult. They came across the barely recognizable Jared, his body replete with arrows grounding him to the earth. One eye was still open but cloudy, his mouth agape with an arrow running through it.

The men turned the corner to see Baramoore's friend in the deadly embrace of combat with a woman whose power emanated from her body. Although they could still feel the heat of the battle between these two wielders of spiritual power, the light effects were diminished, and it appeared that Nemesqu and Gausje were now engaged in physical combat. Yet all who observed knew it was much more than what the human eye could discern.

Nemesqu's hardened body crushed against Gausje's, their hands joined together as they both wrestled to gain a hold of submission. Nemesqu tried to swipe Gausje's feet out from under her, but she nimbly moved out of the way and sent a quick kick to his groin. Nemesqu looked visibly beaten, while the aged Gausje seemed a pillar of strength and endurance, her face the standard of total concentration. The Indian's hands started to generate particles of blue light again, and he whispered while staring into the eyes of Gausje. Their arms began to tremble, and Gausje began to moan, her eyes rolling up in her head, the whites gleaming hotly.

Baramoore felt tremors in the ground that momentarily distracted from the spectacle. As the earth rolled like the waves of a tempestuous sea, his footing was shaken. Shouts and screams penetrated the maelstrom of chaos, and Baramoore fell to the ground, succumbing to vertigo. The grating noise of earth and rock in tension made his skin crawl. When he looked again at the battle he saw that neither Gausje nor Nemesqu had lost his or her footing. A gigantic tree toppled somewhere to his left, crushing in the roof of a sturdy barn. He glanced all around him, wondering what unnatural calamity was about to take place; he then understood that there was no way of defeating these inhuman forces that used magic and sorcery. He did not want to be around for the aftermath of the horrific battle. Next to forming a bond with Nemesqu, it was the second best decision he made in his entire life.

Elizabeth was amazed at the power she felt and was witnessing. Her whole life had been based on the evidence of unseen promises and power, but tonight, with the burning moon casting its glare over the plantation and the bodies of the dead, Elizabeth was acquainted firsthand with real, visible power. And she believed and committed herself to do her best to be a part of these people whom she previously had played an integral part in denigrating. No longer did she want to oppress but rather to deliver. She did not want to appropriate from the Maroons but rather to learn and work. She had taken time to reflect on her life as a privileged white, Christian southern woman, and she recognized that her truest experiences had been predominantly negative. Her husband, who spent significant energy waging war against the flesh of his slaves with livid animosity, had also lusted after the very same flesh. His betrayal of their marriage had brought on the destruction of their family. But even before the adultery, it was his ill treatment of the slaves that decayed his ability to remain human. She shared in his transgressions, and the results had led to suffering, death, and torture. She had witnessed the misappropriation of trust, religion, and the Bible to benefit the greedy gains of slavery. Her spiritual leader, Reverend Freemund, had made her endure the second worst experience of her life, next to watching her daughter's murder, and he had beguiled her into believing that his way was right. She mentally grimaced at the lies she had attempted to inculcate into the minds of her slaves, thinking that salvation would be her reward. She regretted it all, and she prayed that her torture in Freemund's basement would be penance enough. Her vision showed her how she and the Maroons were connected. If the Maroons would have her, she would give herself wholeheartedly. And from her vision while under the spell of Freemund, she believed that they would.

Silently, she reloaded her rifle and took careful aim at Nemesqu. Some of the warriors followed suit, dipping their arrow heads in thick pouches attached to their waistbands, the tips coming out gleaming wet. The tension of the taut strings was audibly heard, every muscle in their bodies suspended in contraction. Elizabeth returned her focus to the great Indian. She noticed that he was putting all his weight on the old woman, who was, remarkably, standing her ground. She hoped that his attention would not be on anything else. The ground was shaking beneath her feet, making Nemesqu difficult to target. She heard the loud report of trees cracking under their own weight as the earth shifted, and she jumped as powerful streams of air came forth from the ground in the distance, blowing dirt and leaves into the tumultuous environment. She lowered her weapon and took a deep breath, seeking to calm her mind as she moved forward with purpose.

Out of the corner of her eye she glimpsed Bella, who had taken up a post behind one of the slave huts closer to the fight. She had several warriors behind her, tense and waiting. Elizabeth knew that the moment was upon her, and she resumed her stance, took aim, and fired a bullet directly at Nemesqu's face.

The bullet punched rather than penetrated the well-shielded warrior, but it was enough to give Gausje the chance she needed. Several arrows whizzed passed Gausje and jammed themselves into Nemesqu's flesh. As if commanded, Bella and the Maroon warriors advanced upon Nemesqu as he stumbled backward, his hands aflame with blue fire, shooting blasts of energy to his left and right, trying to defend himself. Two searing orbs of energy whipped over the ground with frantic speed, haphazardly striking two well-muscled Maroons, one in his chest, the other in his thigh. Both died instantly, singed beyond recognition, their bodies bursting apart as they landed on solid ground. Many sought cover, knowing that this man was powerful.

But Gausje took one hand that held a glowing stone and dove for Nemesqu's legs, slapping the rock against his mid thigh. Nemesqu wailed as he went down, gripping his leg in agonizing pain. The rock fell to the ground and the tremors, which had been constantly rumbling, increased. Gausje retreated from the fallen sorcerer as three more arrows gored his chest, his spiritual mantle of protection ineffectual. Nemesqu coughed once, reached for the arrows, and pulled one free. Bending on one knee, he used his left hand to support his body. A jet of blood sprayed forth, decorating the hem of Gausje's white coat. Nemesqu fell backward as he worked on freeing the two other arrows from his chest, leaving the ones in his thighs and left arm.

As he coughed again a mist of blood flew from his mouth. He enchanted a curse that he had stolen from his elders as a youth, and the hardened arrow quivered and turned into a black snake that hissed. A stream of black venom squirted from taut fangs at Gausje, covering her hands and cloak with putrid stains. Gausje clutched her left hand and leaped backward before another jet could poison her. She gritted her teeth in pain and stared at her hand as it withered and crackled, all sinew and subcutaneous tissue dying from the attack, until the bones of her left hand were embalmed in dried skin like the ancient pharaohs. As dark as her skin was, she could still see the streaks of death making their way up her arm. She placed her good hand around her wrist and intoned a healing chant. White light emanated from her palms and stopped the onslaught. She turned back to Nemesqu, who was still struggling with the other arrows. He noticed and defensively rolled on his back and whispered more indistinguishable charms. The ground coiled up under his body, then relaxed before the trembling earth opened and swallowed him in what looked to be a giant pit. Several more arrows followed him down, but he managed to nimbly swat them away.

Baramoore shouted in resistance, leaving his hiding place, but he was immediately struck down by an arrow to his throat, killing him.

The Maroons advanced to look in the hole where Nemesqu had fallen but quickly retreated, making signs with theirs hands in an effort to ward off bad spirits. Nemesqu had fallen in a pit that seemed to be moving. Gausje alone had the strength to look in undaunted. In the bottom of the pit swirled thousands of writhing black snakes, their corpulent bodies moving steadily against one another. Nemesqu had managed to take the other two arrows from his chest and was howling and laughing simultaneously in a juxtaposition of pain and incredulous mirth. These arrows he also transformed into two snakes. The snakes then buried their heads inside the arrow wounds and seemed to be feeding off them, but after a few seconds they slid off his body, revealing scars but no wounds. The snakes healed him and were under his command. He looked up at Gausje and spoke, "You were worthy, but this is not the end for your race." He paused, gasping for air. "You gained a victory today, but I—I have seen the future—and it will not be as you have planned. It won't be as you hope for your people."

Gausje held forth her right hand, and a blinding white light flashed down on Nemesqu. His body arched in pain, but he shook his head in defiance and smiled, staring at the old woman. The magic intensified the frenzy of the snakes, but much to Gausje's dismay, they were not harming Nemesqu but rather shielding his flesh from her magic. Indeed, this Indian displayed the only sorcery she had ever witnessed that was nearly as powerful as her own. He gazed at her, laughing, and folded his arms around his chest. One of the serpents crawled into his hand and straightened its form, turning into a black staff. Nemesqu's face held such peace that Gausje was momentarily at a loss. She pondered on this while still sending a barrage of energy down into the pit before she knew what she must do.

Rebecca witnessed this and more; she saw her husband peek his head out from where Baramoore had last stood. Her rifle was loaded, and she quietly crept up on his hiding place, with a few warriors following behind. Reverend Freemund was huddled on his knees, hiding, when he felt the cold barrel of her gun against the nape of his neck.

"Please! Lord—not this way!" His body shivered, his hands clasped tightly in folds of abeyance. Rebecca roughly nudged the gun and told him to get up. He did so without resistance. "You are alive, my love." Before he could finish, Rebecca forced the barrel of the gun roughly against his mouth. "Move, coward!" Rebecca ordered. Tears ran down her face, but her eyes were cold. The Maroons near her looked on in keen interest. "Move!" Her head motioned toward the pit.

"Rebecca? Are you crazy? Wife—what has gotten in—" The bullet Rebecca fired into his shoulder sent the minister screaming to the ground. She put the barrel of the rifle to the ground and quickly reloaded, albeit with shaky hands. "The next one goes in your head, Reverend!" Rebecca shouted. "Now move to the pit!"

With great effort Freemund got up and staggered toward the pit. Gausje was still standing there, focused on extinguishing Nemesqu's life, the powerful light radiating brilliantly in the night sky. Rebecca did not lose focus of this but continued shoving her husband closer to the edge of the pit. He was now panting heavily, sweat streaming down the sides of his face, tiny drops dangling from his disheveled hair. Freemund's eyes were frantic, looking everywhere for help that he knew would be unavailable. Clumps of loose earth began to fall into the pit as his feet shuffled backward against Rebecca's force.

"Rebecca, stop! I accept my fate—my reward. But please don't make me go into that pit." Freemund turned around quickly and cast a sorrowful look at his wife. Her face remained stone. "I was unfaithful to you, to my God." He gulped a mouthful of air before continuing. "I brought this upon our house because I was unfaithful." He shook his head in agony, blinking away the salty sweat and tears from his eyes. Rebecca's impenetrable shell of revenge momentarily faltered. "I must be punished, but I do not deserve to die in that pit with him! God forgives all sinners, Rebecca!" he shouted. "All! No matter what they've done! The Lord says vengeance belongs to Him, my wife!" His voice became softer at the sound of her name. "Let God decide my fate. And I will accept it willingly—with humility."

With that statement Freemund closed his quivering lips and knelt down before his wife as if in a position of marriage proposal, one hand lifted up, open and unassuming, to grasp hers, all the while the other hand, still at his side, loosening a small blade he had hidden near his wrist. He would make this woman pay for ever pointing a gun at him.

But Freemund's face disintegrated before he had time to finish his thought. Smoke drifted from Rebecca's gun. All watched the white cluster of his Adam's apple bob down once before his body fell back and downward into the pit of serpents. His silent corpse slowly dissolved to a black moving lump as the serpents relished his flesh. The snakes swarmed over him, burying him while Nemesqu lay on top of them, still alive. Gausje raised her hands and turned toward the sky.

"You have it now! You have your sacrifice! We shall be free!" Guasje gathered her blood-stained cloak about her and outstretched both her hands, then slowly began to close them together. The earth, in response to this gesture, did the same, and the pit closed, finally shutting off Nemesqu's haunting laughter. At this sight the warriors let out a great roar that could be heard for miles around. But they did not pause to celebrate here in this evil place. Instead, they gathered their dead and wounded, collected the arrows and placed them in great baskets, and trudged home toward their city. Bella was finally to live among her people, to be free from the curse of the Tolby plantation.

Elizabeth petitioned Gausje to become one of the Maroons, and her wish was granted, but Rebecca's request was just as quickly rejected. While Gausje appreciated all Rebecca had done during the battle, she could not forgive her the years before when she had lived and embraced the hurtful treatment of Blacks and Native Americans. Elizabeth, unlike Rebecca, had suffered at the hands of her own people. She had offered her body as a living sacrifice to amend the wounds she bore from the death suffered by her daughter. Her willingness and suffering had purged her of her sins, and Gausje felt confident that Elizabeth's admittance to the tribe could only enhance their village. Elizabeth had proven that her spirit could be tested, and Gausje felt the contriteness of Elizabeth's heart. Rebecca, however, was only a survivalist.

Elizabeth wrote a letter to her two remaining daughters revealing her decision. She willed the plantation to them to govern as they saw fit, but her children chose to remain with their aunt, far from the home that had brought them so much tragedy. They felt the Tolby legacy had been soiled, and they no longer wished to be affiliated with the Tolby name. The letter was rife with hurtful judgments of Elizabeth's association with niggers and of their father's incompetence that led to the total fragmentation of their family. Elizabeth was deeply hurt, but Gausje comforted her and took her to the water vase where she could view the future of her daughters. Elizabeth witnessed them marry and start new lives before she broke away, satisfied. Gausje was impressed with Elizabeth's balance of maternal instincts and her wise decision to align her loyalties with the tribe. Elizabeth and Jakeel established a civil relationship, at first tenuously, as trust had to be reestablished. Jakeel's Maroon instructor now became her teacher, educating her in the arts of mysticism and body control as he had Jakeel when he first entered the camp. Over time, a soulful connection developed, defying the prescribed bigotry and short-sightedness of the times.

Rebecca was left alone on Jared's plantation, but she eventually wandered back to the home she had shared with Freemund. She was there only three weeks before two poor white farmers, drunk and brute, stumbled upon her as she was kneeling in the garden, wrestling with several weeds. The farmers took turns raping her before they got into a fight over who should get her last, and one of them strangled the other. Rebecca was able to escape during the fight, but the incident shook Rebecca to the core, and she learned that her value as a Southern white woman was really not much higher than that of the black slave. This knowledge, combined with her witnessing the power and dignity of the Maroons, led Rebecca to become a prominent abolitionist. Eventually, she moved to the North, where she championed the cause of many a Negro who was determined to gain freedom in Canada. For her efforts she was stabbed one cool November morning by a fugitive slave hunter, who had discovered that Rebecca was now working to free those whom she had once enslaved.

Within ten years of the rebellion, the former Tolby plantation was again teeming with slaves. Jared's daughters had sold the property to Mr. Coltan, the neighbor who had fielded the vicious beast that killed Buck. The rebellion had tempered Mr. Coltan in his dealings with slaves, so though he reduced the cruelty of the treatment of his chattel, they nonetheless suffered from their inability to live as free men and women. And the tree, on occasion, still drank of their blood.

At first the Maroons attempted to rescue the new breed of slaves; however, this time they found great resistance, though not in the way they had before. Slave owners, having learned from their unexpected and devastating loss to the Maroons, decidedly changed tactics. They no longer waged war against the Maroons, leaving them to settle their lands. Overseers were instructed to lessen the cruelty typically administered to slaves and, conversely, were encouraged to give slaves more comforts: food, liquor, leisure time, Sabbaths used for worship and rest from labor, and gifts of clothes and used toys for children. They sated the Negroes into complacence so that rescued slaves, instead of appreciating the promise of personal and financial growth that could only be gained through freedom, instead yearned for the easy yolk of bondage that required little of them but their labor. They stayed on their plantation homes, shunning the hard labor of owning their own property for these easy comforts.

Eventually, the efforts of the Maroons to rescue slaves abated. Instead, they lived peaceably for several generations, planting and harvesting much from the land. Their warriors continued to train, and Gausje remained the source of their teaching and nurturing. They never returned to Africa, but as their tribes grew, some moved to Florida and others to small islands off the coast of Carolina. Eventually it was decided that a complete withdrawal from the mainland would be best to preserve the sanctity of the tribe, as so many had shunned deliverance that the mere mention of it was disheartening. Tales were told of a few miraculous escapes and new leaders who decided that a life of servitude was akin to death, but they did so without the help of the gods. It was a long time before the meaning of Nemesqu's words came to fruition. But that came with another time, and another age, when the descendants of the Maroons lost sight of their heritage.

EPILOGUE

Months after the battle, Bella did return to the plantation. She found her old quarters and slipped inside unnoticed. She ignited a coal that she took from her pouch, and the glow illuminated the dirt floor where she had practiced her craft for years. Then she removed her hatchet from her waistband and began to dutifully set about her purpose. Bella chopped into the floor, softening the earth, scooping out the soil by the handfuls. She continued to dig until the hole in the center of the slave quarter was eight inches deep. Then she carefully placed a seed into the hole and covered it. It was the seed of Jubal, the seed she had been meant to find while slaving in the white man's field all those months ago, and its fruit would one day serve as deliverance for her people, should they accept it. Neither she nor Gausje had given up on the misguided slaves, but they knew deliverance would take much longer than they had originally hoped. Bella packed the earth tightly and placed a spell of concealment to make it appear as if the ground had never been disturbed. Then she quietly left, returning to her fulfilling life of peace and prosperity. As she disappeared into the forest, tiny roots immediately began to flutter and issue forth—a small sign of hope for her kind.

Gilbert Cooper II is an eleventh grade English teacher in Maryland. He enjoys teaching American literature at the high school level, and he has recently written an approved curriculum for African American literature. He coaches both Boys' and Girls' Varsity Tennis and plays the game himself whenever possible. This is his first novel.

Made in the USA
Lexington, KY
06 November 2013